An author of more than nin... adults with more than seve... **Janice Kay Johnson** writes about love and family and pens books of gripping romantic suspense. A *USA Today* bestselling author and an eight-time finalist for the Romance Writers of America *RITA®* Award, she won a *RITA®* Award in 2008. A former librarian, Janice raised two daughters in a small town north of Seattle, Washington.

Kacy Cross writes romance novels starring swoonworthy heroes and smart heroines. She lives in Texas, where she's seen bobcats and beavers near her house but sadly not one cowboy. She's raising two mini-ninjas alongside the love of her life, who cooks while she writes, which is her definition of a true hero. Come for the romance, stay for the happily-ever-after. She promises her books 'will make you laugh, cry and swoon—cross my heart.'

BLACK WIDOW

JANICE KAY JOHNSON

COLTON'S SECRET PAST

KACY CROSS

MILLS & BOON

First Published in Great Britain 2024
by Mills & Boon, an imprint of HarperCollins*Publishers* Ltd
1 London Bridge Street, London, SE1 9GF

www.harpercollins.co.uk

HarperCollins*Publishers*
Macken House, 39/40 Mayor Street Upper,
Dublin 1, D01 C9W8, Ireland

Black Widow © 2024 Janice Kay Johnson
Colton's Secret Past © 2024 Harlequin Enterprises ULC

Special thanks and acknowledgment are given to Kacy Cross for her contribution to *The Coltons of Owl Creek* series.

ISBN: 978-0-263-32251-4

1024

This book contains FSC™ certified paper and other controlled sources to ensure responsible forest management.

For more information visit: www.harpercollins.co.uk/green

Printed and Bound in the UK using 100% Renewable Electricity at CPI Group (UK) Ltd, Croydon, CR0 4YY

BLACK WIDOW

JANICE KAY JOHNSON

Prologue

The front door slammed. She straightened, the muscles between her shoulders knotting as her husband stomped toward the kitchen with a heavy tread that roused fear she hadn't felt in a while. They'd been doing so well! He'd been especially unhappy at work recently, though, and if his supervisor so much as mentioned he'd been impolite to a customer, it would have festered all day. If he'd been fired…

The pie! After grabbing pot holders, she hastily took it from the oven, shoving the door shut with one foot. He'd be happy that she'd baked it for him, wouldn't he?

A solidly built man who towered a foot over her average height, his hands were already tightened into fists when he came in sight and a dark scowl made his face ugly. "What's that?"

"It's…it's a raspberry pie." Hating herself for feeling timid, she held it out even though it was too hot for him to take into his hands. "Raspberries are just coming ripe. When I saw them, I thought about you—"

He advanced on her, menace in his body language. "Where did you see them?"

She retreated until her back came up against the kitchen table. "I…had lunch with Mom. We stopped at the farmers' market after."

"Who were you meeting?" snarled the man she had once believed she loved and had been trying to convince herself she could love again.

"What?" Her tongue tangled. "I don't know what you're talking about!"

"Then why didn't you tell me you were seeing your mother today?"

He was so close now, she felt his spittle on her cheeks. Her hands shook. If she didn't set this pie down... "She called this morning—I didn't think—"

"You thought wrong!" he bellowed, fist already swinging. Connecting with her right cheekbone.

Crying out, she staggered and dropped the pie. The ceramic dish shattered at her feet, splattering its hot contents on her legs and his. As she cowered, she couldn't tell if her blurred vision was from the blow or from tears.

"You promised!" she cried. He'd *sobbed* when he apologized and swore he'd never hurt her again.

"You know the rules." His next blow struck her shoulder as she turned away to protect herself. "You tell me if you have to leave the house *before* you leave it."

She fell to her knees and then hands, which slid in the berry filling. Blood. It looked like blood.

He kicked her in the belly before she could curl into a ball to protect herself.

"No!" she cried. "I was trying to do something nice for you!"

"You think I'm a fool?" The blows kept coming.

After the time when she thought she might die, almost six months ago, she'd sworn that she wouldn't submit to this again. Now, fear awakened anger. She wouldn't be his punching bag because something had gone wrong today.

Even knowing it to be useless, she thrashed, kicking her feet out at him.

His booted foot slammed into her, over and over, as if her ineffectual struggles only enraged him more. Terrified, she looked up to see his gun in his hand. He always carried it somewhere on him. Nobody was going to tell him he couldn't. Not even his boss.

Now, it was aimed right at her, and she saw death in his eyes.

He was supposed to love her. And now…was it too late to stop him?

No. Somehow, she calculated distance and angle. Sliding to her back, she slammed both feet up as hard as she could, with such effort her butt left the kitchen floor. Those feet struck him right where it hurt him most.

On a guttural cry, he clutched himself, letting the gun slip out of his hand. It fell into the mess from the dropped pie. This was her only chance.

She flung herself forward and got her hand on that gun. He bragged about having one of those cop pieces with no safety, so she didn't have to think whether it was locked or not and take a chance of getting it wrong.

"You bitch!" he screamed, and followed that up with a string of the worst obscenities she'd ever heard. "I'm going to kill you. I swear I am."

Despite his pain, he kicked her head. Ears ringing, she slid a few feet, but still managed to lift the gun and point it at him. Trying to scrabble away gained her mere inches. Pain splintered through her head.

Through chattering teeth, she cried, "Leave me alone— Let me go, or I swear…"

He threw his big muscular body at her.

She pulled the trigger. Once, twice…and he crashed down on her. Her head hit the floor, and the whole world went black.

Chapter One

Jordan Hendrick stared up at the night sky, rapt, as impossibly golden fireworks melted while drifting in twinkling sparks toward the ground before vanishing. Her butt was sore, because she was sitting on a blanket spread over a rock-hard mowed soccer field, but that was a small price to pay for the fun of joining the townspeople to watch a really spectacular fireworks show. And she hadn't come with a casual group of friends this time, either; no, she was on a real date.

The music playing from giant speakers reached a crescendo, and a dozen fireworks at a time exploded into the sky in the grand finale. Everyone oohed and aahed, including her. The wonder on the face of a young girl sitting near Jordan was almost as entrancing as the fireworks. Jordan's heart melted just a little, but for some reason the sight of such open, uncomplicated joy also triggered a pang of sadness. When had she last let herself feel anything like that?

Unfortunately, she knew. She hadn't been that much older than the girl when she'd last been able to trust life to be full of possibilities.

As the display ended, she shook herself. All around her, people started gathering themselves and their possessions. The man she'd been sharing the blanket with did the same, and she stood to help him shake it out and fold it. A minute later, he held out his hand for hers so they could join the crowd clumped and waiting turns to mill through one of the handful of gates in the chain-link fence surrounding the field.

Being on a date at all felt surreal to Jordan, even though this was actually the second time she'd gone out with Elliott Keefe. He was a real estate agent at a Walla Walla Windermere office, where she dropped off mail daily. Pleasant chats had become a mild flirtation, and she'd astounded herself by agreeing to dinner last weekend at a highly rated restaurant that specialized in the local wines this area in eastern Washington was known for. Then came the picnic and fireworks for the Fourth of July this week. Nice as it was—he smiled at her just then and squeezed her hand—Jordan already knew this wouldn't go anywhere. For her, though, this was a venture into the strange new world of pretending she had something in common with her peers.

She was twenty-eight years old, and this was only the second guy she'd gone out with in the past eight years.

A whisper in her left ear that she couldn't quite make out had her turning, off guard when a moment later, a shoulder bumped her, hard. She stumbled and would have gone down if Elliott hadn't caught her. He glared, but from the way his head turned it was apparent he couldn't tell who'd been so determined to get ahead. By the time they reached the gate, she'd been jostled a couple more times, but the lighting wasn't good and anyone who bumped her could just as well have been pushed from behind themselves.

Or so she told herself. This past week, she'd felt uneasy, off and on, as if someone was watching her. The past couple of years, she'd had three distinct periods with the same creepy feeling that lingered for a few days, but nothing had come of it. Something was different this time, though:

Wednesday she'd have sworn someone had been in her half of a duplex, and *that* was new.

Except…it was all in her mind. It had to be. She hadn't actually *seen* anyone staring at her or following her, and just because her butcher knife lay out on her clean kitchen counter where she'd never have left it wasn't enough to call 911…and tell them what to investigate?

Ignoring that twinge she sometimes got between her shoulder blades, the one that whispered, *look around*, she gripped Elliott's hand and focused on keeping to her feet as they hustled in front of cars inching toward the exits from the lot. The headlights were too blinding for her to make out faces around her, anyway.

"I had a good time," Elliott said just then.

"Me, too." Jordan didn't protest when he wrapped an arm around her shoulders and steered her toward her car. She liked the warmth of his embrace as long as he kept it loose like this, but was also a tiny bit glad she'd insisted on driving herself.

"I wish I'd been able to pick you up," he grumbled mildly, "but it's not as if I won't see you sometime this week."

"Unless you're out showing houses when I drop by," she teased. "Which you should hope you will be."

"I do have some great listings right now."

Her diversion had worked, and his enthusiasm sparked. He kept talking, stopping only when they reached her car, and she unlocked it.

This kiss was more serious than the one last weekend, but not a lot. More…warm and pleasant. A coworker of hers who liked to talk about the constantly changing roster of men in her life would have said, *meh*. Jordan knew that in this case, it was likely because of her, not anything wrong with him. Given her history, letting herself relax enough to enjoy any kind of intimacy with a man might never be possible.

They said their good-nights, and once behind the wheel of her car, she worked her way into the slow traffic dissipating onto the city streets.

At least she'd found the courage to *try* to start something with a man again. Even baby steps were something to celebrate, Jordan decided twenty minutes later, as she let herself in her front door.

JORDAN DIDN'T HAPPEN to see Elliott the next day when she dashed into Windermere with a pile of mail bundled with a rubber band. Some days she left it in their box at the street, but today the batch had been too bulky. The cheerful woman at the front desk looked up with a smile. "I haven't seen Elliott yet today."

Jordan flipped a friendly hand at her just before the glass door closed behind her and she trotted toward her postal vehicle. It was out of character for her to have ever taken the time to talk to the good-looking guy who'd shown an interest in her. Truthfully, she hustled all day.

Mail delivery looked a lot easier than it was. Her first day on the job, her grumpy supervisor had had to wait for her, the last person by over an hour to make it back into the office. But now that she was on her fourth year, she'd long since learned the tricks to allow her to move fast.

Even now, though, she hadn't gotten over being exhausted by the time she carried her empty trays into the back of the post office at the end of the day, sorted what mail had appeared in the interim to give herself a jump start in the morning, and clocked out.

Maybe she'd settle for a salad tonight. Or something out of the freezer. She was happier in her solitude than a young woman her age should be, but she had several episodes of a show she was streaming to watch and was eager to get back to it.

She hadn't gotten further than studying the contents of her freezer before her doorbell rang. Jordan jumped at the sound. Who on earth…?

She of all people didn't like surprises. She hadn't forgotten that the last guy she'd dated had been killed several years ago after surprising burglars in his house—or so the police believed. Violent crime happened everywhere, even in a nice town like Walla Walla, built around a high-end liberal arts college. Since there was no peephole in the door, she cracked the blinds to see a large, dark sedan in her driveway. It bristled with antennae, and the bumper didn't look like the one on *her* car.

Wary, she opened the door without removing the chain. A man and a woman stood on her small front porch. Both wore badges and holstered guns on their belts. Jordan had seen stern looks like that before.

"Ms. Hendrick?" the man said politely, but with no give in his voice. "I'm Detective Shannon and this is Detective Dutton. May we come in?"

Her fingers clenched on the door and her heart pounded in her ears. "May I ask what this is about?"

"It has to do with an attempted murder that took place last night. I believe you know the victim."

"Victim…" Her forehead creased. A coworker or— "Oh, God, not Elliott Keefe?"

"I'm afraid so." The words might sound sympathetic, but the expression on his face remained watchful.

No. How could that be?

She closed the door as her fingers fumbled with the chain to let the cops in. Not just cops—detectives. They had to be, didn't they, since they were plainclothes?

She evaluated them automatically. The man was bulky in the way of a former high school or college athlete, his hair graying at the temples. His wedding ring caught her eye.

The woman had to be midthirties, lean like a runner. Her glance took in Jordan's small living room thoroughly before she met Jordan's eyes with a look that hadn't softened at all.

"Please, sit down." Jordan gestured at the sofa before her legs dropped her into the wooden rocking chair. "Can you tell me what happened? Is he badly injured?"

The man took the lead. "Mr. Keefe was found unconscious midday by a coworker who went to check on him. Apparently, he had appointments set up, but didn't come into work."

"He was…excited about some new listings." She almost continued, but of course they knew how real estate sales happened.

"A different coworker mentioned that the two of you were seeing each other. She said you're employed as a mail carrier."

With her hands twined together on her lap, Jordan's fingers tightened painfully. "Yes. Although seeing each other is putting it strongly. We've gone out twice, that's all. He's nice, but…"

Those implacable stares silenced her.

"When did you see him last?" the woman asked.

Jordan had no doubt that they already knew the answer to that question. Elliott had probably talked about his plans at work.

"Yesterday. Because it was the Fourth—" as if they didn't know about the national holiday "—he brought a picnic dinner, and we ate it at the soccer field before the fireworks started."

"And afterward?" Detective Dutton again.

"He walked me to my car, and we said good-night."

"Said good-night?"

Her cheeks heated. "He kissed me. It was brief because there were people all around."

"You had driven separately." The male cop—Jordan couldn't remember his name—picked up where his partner had left off.

"That's right. Even though it was a holiday, earlier in the day Elliott showed several houses to a couple who had trouble finding time. He offered to pick me up anyway, but…" She looked away for a moment, then made herself face them. "I preferred driving myself. I'm not in a hurry to take a casual relationship anywhere. It's easier if he doesn't see me to my doorstep at the end of the evening."

Something shifted on the woman's face that suggested she understood and had made the same choice in the past.

Jordan looked from one to the other. "You haven't said how he is now."

"I'm afraid he's in a coma." The woman cop spoke with surprising gentleness, given their attitude to that point. "We believe his assailant thought Mr. Keefe was dead. In fact, he's still in critical condition."

"Oh God." Jordan bent forward as if she had to protect herself. How could this be?

"Your name came up," the man said.

Of course it had. She waited with dread.

"Having to do with another man you were *seeing* at the time." The emphasis on *seeing* was unmistakable. "A Pete Shroder."

"He was killed during some kind of home invasion." Did she sound shrill? She took a slow breath to calm herself. "Or at least, that's what I heard. That his house had been cleaned out, and he surprised them just before they left."

"That's true, but it's interesting that the physical assault on Mr. Keefe looks a good deal like the one on Mr. Shroder. A gunshot—two in Mr. Shroder's case—that probably brought each man down, followed by a brutal beating."

She had to face her peril straight on, even if she felt so

nauseated she wanted to run for the bathroom. "And you think *I* could have had something to do with those attacks."

"I didn't say that," the man corrected her. "We're interested because of the fact that you had a relationship with both of them."

Mouth dry, she said, "Pete died three years ago. He and I went out only a couple of times, and I doubt either of us would have bothered to continue seeing each other. I hadn't seen him in several days before he was murdered." Jordan glared at them. "I don't see how you can have failed to find and arrest his killer by now."

Wooden expressions suggested she'd hit them where it hurt.

"Unfortunately, neither the bullet nor the trace evidence led us anywhere, suggesting the killer had not formerly been in trouble with the law."

Both raised their brows as they continued to look at *her.*

"You're wasting your time with me. I don't, and have never, owned a gun." She'd only fired one once in her life, and the memory so horrified her she shied away from it. "I'm law-abiding, polite and verging on timid. I rarely even date. I can't imagine any way these two attacks could have anything to do with me." She rose to her feet. "If you feel the need to come back with more implied accusations, I'll need to hire an attorney before I speak to you again."

A twitch in his face might have been a suppressed grimace. Both produced cards and handed them over.

"Thank you. Now, unless there's some other way I can help…?"

"Can you think of any other connection between these two men?"

"Only the obvious, which I trust you already know. Pete worked in property management, and very possibly crossed paths with Elliott." She swallowed. "Am I permitted to visit Elliott at the hospital?"

Detective Dutton—Beverly, according to the card—shook her head. "He's in the ICU. Only family is permitted in to see him, and even they're limited."

Jordan nodded, a sort of numbness creeping over her. Shock, of course.

Detective Shannon opened the door and held it for his partner, then turned back to Jordan. "I encourage you not to leave town."

She was still speechless when he closed the door behind him. A minute later, she heard the car out front drive away.

THE NEXT FEW days were agonizing. She couldn't stop thinking about Elliott—she called the hospital each evening to hear how he was doing, despite the fact that she was given only nonanswers.

The first time she had to take the mail into the real estate office, she said, "I heard about Elliott. It's so awful! You must all be shaken up."

Of course they were. At least no one looked at her as if it had occurred to them that she might have started knocking off men after she'd gone out with them a time or two.

She searched reviews online for a criminal attorney in the event she needed to hire one. The experience was new to her, even though she'd had one before. That time, her mother had decided who to hire while Jordan was still in the hospital.

However, she didn't hear a word from either detective in this case. The *Walla Walla Union-Bulletin* reported that police were investigating but had given no indication they were closing in on a suspect or suspects.

Friday when she handed over the mail at the Windermere office, the woman behind the counter beamed at her. "You probably already know Elliott has regained consciousness!

It'll still be a few weeks before he can make it back to work, but that's such good news!"

A huge weight lifted off Jordan's shoulders. "Yes, it is."

"He's going to be mad that two of his listings have sold while he was in the hospital. He was so determined to be the selling *and* the listing agent on both of them."

"He talked about that." She hesitated. "I was told he couldn't have flowers in Intensive Care, but maybe I'll order some now."

"We're planning the same," she was assured.

Jordan felt wobbly with relief when she returned to her vehicle. For once, she didn't jog and leap in. Once behind the wheel, she just sat there for a minute. Nothing about the attack had been her fault, but still… Thank God. He was going to be all right.

A few days later, she received a stiff note thanking her for the bouquet—from Elliott's mother. Maybe he wasn't up to writing notes yet—but Jordan wondered. If one of the detectives had shared the *interesting* coincidence of her having dated two men who had almost immediately thereafter suffered similar attacks, wouldn't Elliott tell himself he'd be smart to stay away from her?

The continuing silence confirmed her guess. It stung, even though he could just have sensed how tepid her interest in him was. He might well not have asked her out again no matter. She did her best to wedge mail into the Windermere box that she once would have carried in.

Jordan kept expecting to hear from the detectives again—they would surely have researched her background more thoroughly by now—but the call that came in just as she left the post office at the end of her shift, two weeks to the day after Elliott was attacked, didn't come from the local area code. She knew this one, though; she'd grown up in Storm Lake, Idaho. Only…she didn't recognize the number.

It wasn't her mother's or one belonging to any of the few other people she'd stayed in touch with.

"Hello?" she said cautiously.

A woman said, "Is this Jordan Hendrick?"

"Yes, it is."

"I'm calling from Cavanaugh Memorial Hospital in Storm Lake," she said kindly. "I'm sorry to have to tell you that your mother has had a stroke."

Chapter Two

Mom is alive. Jordan had at least that much to cling to. Some of the rest of what the hospital representative had said wasn't as encouraging. The ER doctor had done everything he could for her, but Mom hadn't been found as quickly as would have been ideal, so there were noticeable and disturbing effects that, she was assured, would improve with physical therapy.

Jordan had no idea who had found Mom. Was it like Elliott, that she hadn't shown up at her job in the city auditor's office? Maybe. Probably. Although Mom had more friends than Jordan did. Any of them could have been concerned if Mom didn't call when she'd promised, or missed a garden club meeting.

Oh, she hated thinking of her mother collapsed on the floor, unable to grasp her phone or, if she had succeeded, make herself understood. Had she tried to crawl?

Jordan shuddered.

She didn't remember the drive back to the duplex, only flying in her front door. All she could think was to pack as fast as she could. Most of the furniture had come with the place; the rest, she'd abandon. Mom would need her for a long time. She couldn't let herself think that Mom wouldn't because... No!

Jordan didn't have enough boxes to contain her books, so

she carried piles of them out and set them loose in the trunk of her car. Clothes and shoes, first in her suitcases, then in white plastic trash bags.

Coat closet. Couldn't forget that.

The doorbell rang and she jumped six inches. What now?

Mostly uncaring, she flung open her door. Of course it had to be the pair of detectives on her porch again, expressions unchanged from the last visit. She knew why they were back, but right now she didn't *care*.

Both of their gazes went past her and fixed on the suitcases sitting by the front door. That couldn't be a surprise, since they had parked at the curb this time, and walked past her car with the trunk and one door standing open, many of her possessions already loaded.

Detective Shannon raised an eyebrow. "Going somewhere?"

"Yes." She backed up. "You can come in, but whatever you plan to say, you have to make it quick."

The detective stepped inside, followed by his partner. "Hoping to get out of town before we came back to talk to you?" he asked sardonically. "Or did you forget I asked you to stay available?"

"I would have called." Her eyes burned from the tears she'd refused to shed. "My mother had a stroke. I'm going home."

"That would be Storm Lake in Idaho."

"Yes. Mom's in the hospital. It was a serious stroke. If—*when*—she makes it home, I need to be there to take care of her."

"Interesting timing."

Interesting had become one of her least favorite words.

"It's horrible timing. I've been sick about Elliott, and now this."

"Please sit down," he suggested. "You have a long drive ahead of you. I guess you're not planning to fly."

Jordan shook her head. "That would be so complicated, it would take longer than driving." And she'd have to leave way more behind, or figure out how to ship it, or…

"Well, then, ten or fifteen minutes isn't going to make any difference."

Of course it could! But she was law-abiding, and she understood why they had more questions. So she sat, even as she quivered with the need to leap up and keep packing, to get on the road.

"We found your fingerprints on file in Idaho."

"If you'd asked, I'd have told you they are. I know what you discovered, but there was never any suggestion that I was at fault for what happened. It was clearly self-defense. I was in the hospital for days after the…incident." Oh, why be squeamish? But she couldn't make herself be blunt.

"You're right," he conceded.

His partner hadn't said a word, but she was listening. Her gaze was trained on Jordan's face, too, reading the range of emotions that must be crowding each other.

"That said, it's hard to believe it's chance that you would have been involved in another man's death. That you fired the shot that killed him."

She shuddered and resented the vulnerability he'd exposed. "He would have killed me if I hadn't pulled that trigger."

"That seems to be the consensus," he agreed.

She bounced to her feet. "Please. I need to go. You didn't find my fingerprints or anything else pointing to me at either Pete Shroder's house or Elliott's because I'd never been to either one. There's nothing more I can tell you. You can call me anytime. I'll answer unless I'm in the hospital."

Detective Dutton touched her partner's arm. Only a brief

contact, but he gave her a surprised glance. Then his mouth tightened, and he grudgingly stood.

"Very well. At this point, I can't compel you to stay in Walla Walla. Please get in touch with us if you think of anything that might be helpful. We'd appreciate it."

He'd think she was making up stories if she told him about feeling watched, about the whisper in her ear that she hadn't made out just before someone buffeted her, about the knife left out on her kitchen counter. A knife she hadn't used in days.

But even if they didn't doubt her credibility, none of that had anything to do with an attempt to kill Elliott. Jordan didn't see how it possibly could.

So she nodded, thanked them when they carried her suitcases and a couple of bags out to her car, and got a tiny bit teary when stern Detective Shannon paused after opening the driver's side door of the unmarked car, looked at her over the roof, and said, "Drive carefully, Ms. Hendrick. You're shaken right now. You need to focus on the road." He sounded positively human.

She smiled shakily at him. "I'll do that. I've driven this route plenty of times."

He dipped his head and climbed in. A moment later, the unmarked police car drove away.

Kitchen. She couldn't leave food to spoil. Jordan hurried back into the duplex, making lists in her head of all the people she had to call, and everything that remained for her to do before she left.

Given the difficulty of her mother's recovery, Jordan knew she'd be committed in Storm Lake too long to ever take up her job again or move back into this duplex.

THE FIRST THING San Francisco PD Homicide Detective Tom Moore knew was pain. The second was recognition of one of his least favorite locations: the hospital. He didn't even have to open his eyes to know where he was. The beeps of life-sustaining machines and the smells were all he needed.

Those beeps sounded close, as if it might be *his* life the machines were sustaining. Given the extremity of his pain, that seemed possible.

A firm voice spoke in his ear, and he flinched. He immediately regretted even that tiny motion.

"Detective Moore. Are you back with us?"

Where else would he have been?

He grunted.

"We're preparing to take you into surgery. I don't know if you recall what happened to you…"

He hadn't gotten that far yet, but now he did. Approaching a house with his partner to speak to a witness to a murder who was possibly a suspect. Reaching for his sidearm when the front door was thrust open unexpectedly. Max yelling a warning Tom hadn't needed even before gunfire erupted. Reeling as the first bullet struck him, losing some touch with reality as he felt as if a horde of yellow jackets were stinging him. Falling, falling, his nerveless hand losing touch with the grip of his Sig Sauer. That hand flopping on top of a dandelion. Strange that was the last thing he saw.

"Max," he mumbled.

"What?"

"Max." His mouth felt like sandpaper. "Partner."

"Oh." The pause stretched painfully long. "I'm sorry. Detective Cortez didn't make it."

Tom hadn't realized he'd opened his eyes until they fell shut. He couldn't have said what the woman looked like, except she wore one of those starched white uniforms.

"My fault," he managed to say.

Her hand touched his forehead like a benediction. "I very much doubt that," she murmured.

A bright light hung overhead. Somebody else started talking to him as they lifted his arm. Must be time… Yeah.

MACHINES BEEPED, although Mom was breathing on her own.

Jordan had stayed at her mother's bedside as much as hospital personnel allowed. The chair was comfortable enough that, with the addition of a pillow and a blanket, she could nap for stretches. She found her way at intervals to the cafeteria drawn by the smell of coffee, her feet knowing the way. Life had a surreal quality. Most of her breaks happened when one or the other of her mother's friends came by to check on her, or even asked for a turn to sit with her.

Mom's face was twisted enough to make her appear almost a stranger. Jordan wondered whether her mother's friends found that as disturbing as she did. The hand Jordan held so often was a claw; with the IV on Mom's other side, the chair had been placed so that visitors didn't get in the way of nurses and doctors coming and going.

Worst of all was when Mom tried to speak, and all that came out was a garbled mockery of her voice. She couldn't speak a coherent word.

Jordan swore Mom recognized her. Her eyes—one only partially open—stayed fixed on Jordan's face whenever she was in the room and Mom wasn't sleeping.

"I think she looks better," Bonnie Feller insisted as they met in the waiting room. A plump, attractive woman who was allowing a streak of gray to appear in her dark hair, she'd arrived for today's visit shortly after Jordan was banned from the room while Mom underwent physical therapy. Jordan couldn't imagine what that consisted of.

"You really think so?" she asked doubtfully.

"I do," Bonnie assured her. "She couldn't lie on her back at first, only curled on her side in this almost—"

Fetal position. That's what she'd been about to say.

Jordan nodded. It was true.

Hurrying to change the subject, Bonnie patted her on the hand. "Guy was so glad to hear that you're home again. I'm sure he'll call you one of these days."

Uh-huh. Sure he would. Personally, Jordan would rather hear from Detective Shannon.

Bonnie and Mom had been friends since Jordan's family moved to Storm Lake when she'd been a toddler. Bonnie's son Guy was a year older than Jordan. Apparently the two of them had happily been playmates into the early years of elementary school, when he'd dug in his heels one day and said, "She's a *girl*!" He'd been forced to attend one more of her birthday parties, but had been so appalled that he was the only boy, his mother gave up thereafter. By high school, they were casually friendly, but never having even a hint of romantic feelings. Back then, Jordan would have said they regarded each other almost as siblings.

Guy had been away at the University of Idaho during the years of Jordan's marriage. After a summer home, he'd left for Washington State University for a graduate degree in veterinary science. Jordan saw him a couple of times that summer, and wished she hadn't.

Mom, who kept her updated on everyone she'd known, had reported that a couple of years ago he'd bought into the only small animal practice right here in town. That knowledge would be enough to keep her from adopting a dog or cat. For all the years she and Guy had known each other, he'd been one of the many people who'd had doubt, and more, in their eyes when they'd looked at her that summer.

Did you really have *to kill your husband?*

How could Guy not have known her better than that? But then, he'd played on the football team with Steve Dunn, taken classes with him, gone to the same keggers. For all that Guy was in an accelerated academic program, he mostly hung out with his jock friends. Jordan had been to those same parties as Steve's girlfriend, awed by his swagger and charisma even as she hovered unobtrusively to one side, sipping at a single beer as long as she could make it last. Astonished at her luck, wondering what the homecoming king and star football player with Steve's looks had possibly seen in *her.*

Well, she soon learned. He'd seen a vulnerability she didn't know lurked deep inside her. Having her father walk out and never bother with her again did damage that she hadn't really understood. Steve? He'd seen that he could dominate and terrorize her, and thought she'd never fight back.

He'd almost been right.

She could ignore people like Guy Feller. Mom had always been there for her when Jordan would allow it, and she had every intention of doing anything and everything she could to get her mother back on her feet, able to deadhead the roses in her garden, have lunch with friends like Bonnie and flirt with Mr. Enyart, who owned the plant nursery. Most of her contemporaries in this town could go to hell, though, as far as she was concerned.

The nurse appeared and beamed at Jordan. "You're welcome to come back again!"

Jordan smiled at her mother's friend. "Why don't you go first?" Only one person was permitted at a time. "I might wander out in the courtyard and see if there's still a sun in the sky."

Bonnie laughed and rose to her feet, clutching her handbag. "You take your time, dear. You know your mother wouldn't want you to exhaust yourself the way you have been."

"Thank you, Bonnie."

Watching her hurry away behind the nurse, Jordan

slouched deeper in the waiting room chair. The sun would feel nice—but another cup of coffee might do her more good.

TWO DAYS LATER, more tired than ever, Jordan parked in the driveway—Mom's car occupied the single-vehicle detached garage—detoured to grab the mail from the box out at the street, and was flipping through it as she trudged back to the house. Not much today, thank goodness—mostly advertising flyers and a couple of what appeared to be get-well cards from people whose names Jordan recognized. Not until she glanced up as she put her foot on the first step did she see a bobbing movement right in front of her. She started, then realized a helium balloon was tied to the doorknob.

Several white gravestones featuring skulls-and-crossbones stood out on the black balloon. Standard Halloween fare, she thought, in the distant way one did at a moment like this. It was the bloodred words scrawled below the stones that chilled her.

Large letters spelled out *Welcome Home,* while smaller letters beneath added, *Where You Belong.*

Was someone watching, enjoying her reaction?

She spun on her heels but saw no one. Which didn't mean someone wasn't out there.

If she hadn't been so tired, the message might not have hit her so hard. As it was, hurt warred with rage. Rage won. Let whoever had done this *see* what she felt!

She already had her keys in her hand. She leaped up the steps and used the car key to stab the damn balloon. She wanted to keep stabbing, but it deflated fast with a hiss. All she could do was tear the ribbon from the doorknob and take the thing into the kitchen.

There, feeling vengeful, she cut it into shreds with scissors, wishing she could send them to whatever creep had been so determined to remind her of those shattering moments when she had to choose her own life or Steve's. Then she buried them—unfortunate pun—under some messy vegetable trimmings in the trash can.

Finally, she sat at the kitchen table, hands shaking, teeth chattering, and asked herself, *Why?* And, *Was this a threat, or only a needle jab to remind her what a terrible person she must be?*

Only belatedly did she wish she'd photographed the balloon before she destroyed it.

TOM ALMOST DIDN'T recognize the woman who stepped into his room at the rehab center, where he'd been moved after a ten-day stay at the hospital. Emilia Cortez looked as if she'd lost more weight than should be possible so quickly, her eyes were red-rimmed, and her skin no longer had that usual glow. Max had worshipped his pretty wife and been thrilled when she gave birth to the world's cutest baby girl six months ago. It would never have occurred to him that he'd be killed on the job. For all the drama injected in thrillers, movies and TV shows, detectives were far less at risk than front-line patrol officers.

She shuffled like an old woman to his bedside. "Oh, Tom." Her failing attempt at a smile told him how bad he looked.

Damn it, he was going to cry now. "Emilia, I'm so sorry. I should have guessed we were walking into a disaster. Max was depending on me."

She perched on the edge of the bed, tiny enough to barely depress the mattress. "No, you two worked together. Don't lie to me. He had no more idea than you did."

That was true, but—

"He shot that monster, you know." Actually, *monster* wasn't her choice of word; she used a deeply angry word in Spanish that Tom hadn't known until he paired with Maximo Cortez and expanded his own vocabulary. None of which he'd have expected to hear from this sweet woman. "At least he's dead."

"Yeah." He reached out for her hand. "Max saved my life." Another bullet or two hitting him, or even just a delay in getting him to the hospital, and he wouldn't be here now. "I wish it was the other way around." His throat felt clogged and his eyes burned.

"He would be glad. That's what I came to say. You were Max's best friend, not just his partner. If he'd had to choose—" This time, her voice broke.

"He should have chosen himself," he said harshly. "He had you and Lidia to think of. I don't have a wife or children. I wouldn't be missed the same way."

She tilted her head and studied him for longer than felt comfortable. "You've been given a chance to have all that. That's what I came to say. Live gladly, Tom."

His throat all but closed up.

"For now, Lidia and I are going to stay with Max's mama. She needs us, and it will be good for Lidia to have her *abuela*, too."

"Yes." He tightened his fingers on hers. "If you ever need me—"

She kissed his cheek lightly. "I'll always know you would come if I called, but… I have family."

He didn't, something he rarely regretted, but this was one of those moments. He had friends, sure, but they had lives and families of their own. He couldn't exactly go knocking and say, "Hey, can I move in for a few months? Just until I can walk and maybe grip a gun and even squeeze a trigger?"

No.

But lucky him. Barely ten minutes after Emilia had left him to a grim mood, a light rap on the door presaged the upbeat voice he'd come to dread: his physical therapist.

Tom had never backed off from a challenge before, though,

and wasn't about to start this time. Whatever it took to regain strength in his damaged body, he'd do. So far, he tried to avoid facing the truth that returning to the peak physical conditioning required for his job with the police department in a major urban city was a long way off, if possible at all.

They had already let him know he could go on desk duty, which held zero appeal. Maybe he'd find a...transitional job. Yeah, that was it. Probably not for a couple of months yet, if not longer, but he'd bet there were smaller towns out there who'd hire him because of his experience, understanding he might not be prepared to run down a suspect and tackle him the first day of his new employment.

And maybe he'd be investigating the theft of equipment from a rental business, minor embezzling, a holdup at the tavern. Considering his goal had always been to work homicide, that didn't stir a lot of excitement, but it would beat shuffling paper and answering phones. When he was ready, he had no doubt SFPD would reinstate him after his time away to heal.

Growling under his breath as he laboriously transferred himself to the wheelchair, he thought, *Make it a small town on flat ground.*

Chapter Three

"You…gave…up…" Mom swallowed hard before she was able to continue working to shape her mouth and control her tongue to make her speech legible. "So…much."

Having no trouble understanding her anymore, Jordan smiled and gave her a side hug. "Don't be silly. I'm taking a long vacation because I don't have to pay any rent. My job wasn't very exciting, you know. I'd made friends, but none close enough for me to be likely to stay in touch. I've missed you so much. You gave me the excuse I needed to come home. I just wish it wasn't such a traumatic one for you."

They sat in the sun in the backyard of Jordan's childhood home, a white-painted clapboard house built in the 1940s and distinguished by the graceful porch that stretched the width of the front facing the street. One of the tasks she'd taken over as the weeks dragged on was maintaining her mother's extensive garden that wrapped from the sidewalk out front to the back of the property, gorgeous enough to have starred on several garden tours. It frustrated Mom to be able to do no more than watch her and occasionally try to give her a tutorial in such topics as dividing perennials and mixing the proper strength of fertilizer for hanging baskets, but she'd come so far in only a few months, Jordan had begun to regain an almost lost belief that her mother *would* rebound from the stroke.

After all, she was home, no longer confined to the rehab center, although therapists of various kinds and home health care workers still came daily. So far, Jordan wasn't thinking about looking for work; housecleaning and yard work, plus helping her mother as needed evenings and during the night, was all she could handle. When she said she was happy to be home and to be able to help, she was being completely honest.

She had *not* told her mother about the attack on Elliott or the phone calls from one of the Walla Walla PD detectives.

In fact, her phone vibrated right now and when she glanced down at it, she immediately recognized the number.

"You okay if I leave you for a minute to take this call?" she asked.

"Yah." Her mother's eyes held a speculative expression that she couldn't convey in any other way.

Jordan would rather Mom be suspicious that her daughter had left behind a boyfriend than realize the truth: that she couldn't shake two police detectives who really wanted her to be a viable suspect in an attempted murder.

She let the screen door slam behind her and went deeper into the house to be out of earshot before she answered. "This is Jordan."

The woman's voice told her the caller was Detective Dutton even before she identified herself and then asked, "How's your mom?"

Both detectives had softened up some, Jordan reflected.

"She's doing really well, considering. She needs help to walk and is just learning to shape intelligible words, but considering the severity of her stroke, it's amazing that she's sitting out in her garden right now and we were having a conversation."

"It sounds like this isn't a good time," the detective said stiffly.

"No, it's okay. She can enjoy the sun without struggling so hard to make herself understood. I think it must be frustrating beyond belief." Of all people to confide in.

But she wasn't as surprised as she should have been when Dutton agreed. "My grandmother had a stroke. She…didn't recover, but I remember worrying about whether her brain was working as well as ever while she'd lost the ability to express herself. What if you had an awful itch, or hated the food they were shoveling in your mouth? And I shouldn't have said that."

"No, I've been thinking the same. Fortunately, Mom *is* starting to be able to communicate some of her needs and thoughts. And no, you don't have to tell me that she's at high risk of having a follow-up stroke."

"I've seen people completely recover," the detective said.

If that was a lie, Jordan appreciated it. "This isn't why you called."

"That's…not entirely true. We're not heartless, you know."

Jordan stared blindly at the drawn drapes on her mother's front window. "I do know. I might not be taking your calls if I thought you were."

"Have you heard from Mr. Keefe?"

Her mouth twisted. "No." His silence said it all.

If only he'd heard or seen anything! Police were unsure whether he really hadn't, or whether he could have suffered from some traumatic memory loss. Supposedly, all he did remember was walking into the kitchen from the attached garage and dropping his keys on the counter just before the *bang* of what must have been the gunshot that sent him crashing to the floor. Something slamming into his head was his only other memory until he awakened in the hospital.

If he remembered going into the kitchen, that meant he hadn't forgotten the Fourth of July celebration, or her.

"You're an unlikely suspect," the detective surprised her by saying. "We'd have moved on if it weren't for your, er, history."

"I understand." A familiar, bitter taste filled her mouth. "It will haunt me forever. There's a reason I moved away from Storm Lake, you know. I could see people speculating, even old friends. If people locally hear about what happened to Elliott, wondering will become certainty. My husband—" Oh, how she hated saying that much. His name would be even worse. "He had a bigger personality than I did. He was a star on the football team, had half the girls in high school trailing him through the halls, was comical enough he could get even the teachers to laugh and let him off the hook when he was caught breaking rules."

Soon after their marriage, she'd started noticing his humor had a nasty edge. Or maybe it had changed when he'd begun to resent his first boss, then the one after that, until it became a pattern. He thought *he* should be the supervisor, even though she suspected he slacked off like he had in classes. She didn't dare to so much as hint that anything could be his fault.

She'd be embarrassed that she hadn't seen through him in the first months of her marriage, but she had. It was more that she'd convinced herself things would change, that she had to show her faith in him by sticking through the hard times. She understood that this life wasn't what he'd been so sure he would have. Even after he hit her a few times, then exploded once and came so close to killing her, she desperately convinced herself a family was supposed to stay complete.

Now she suspected that mostly she didn't want anyone to know her judgment had been so bad. She'd almost died because she had been too embarrassed to ignore her pride and say, *You were right, Mom. Help.*

Her mother had been appalled when Jordan announced

after high school graduation that instead of going to college, she was marrying Steve Dunn. Once she discovered what a horrible mistake she'd made, Jordan had pretended everything was fine. Eventually, after the traumatic end to her not-quite-twenty-month marriage, she'd figured out that she'd gotten herself in that spot and stayed in it for a lot of complicated reasons she hadn't seen clearly at the time. What she hadn't guessed was how much her pretense would hurt her mother once the truth came out. The result was that Mom blamed herself for Jordan's mistakes.

I was so young, she thought sadly.

"There was nothing out of the ordinary in the weeks before Mr. Keefe was attacked," the detective said. Or was that a question?

"Shouldn't it have been him who noticed anything weird?" Jordan asked.

"He claims the only thing new was that he'd started to date you."

Thank you, Elliott. "He'd gotten a couple of listings that were an especially big deal for him," Jordan said. "He was excited, because he thought he'd taken a step toward being a top seller. He was seeing dollar signs. Somebody could have resented his success."

"We've considered the possibility," the detective said neutrally, "but haven't come up with any, say, sour grapes."

She was talking to Jordan, which was new. Jordan still didn't believe anything that had happened to her could have led to Elliott being nearly killed, but after a hesitation, she said, "There were a couple of things. Nothing I could prove, and…it just doesn't make sense!"

"A couple of things?"

"I kept feeling like someone was watching me. You know? Just a prickling at the nape of your neck, but when you turn around, no one is there. And then a few days before the Fourth, I thought someone had gotten into my apartment."

"It was unlocked, or a window left open?"

"No. Or, at least, I'm pretty sure I unlocked the front door when I got home from work, but I can't swear to it. You know what it's like when you're juggling stuff you're carrying, including groceries, and you think you turned your key in the lock. The only sign someone had been there was that my butcher knife lay out on the counter." The memory still gave her the creeps. "I'd left the kitchen clean that morning. I swear I did. And I hadn't done any serious cooking, certainly not cutting up meat, for, oh, at least the previous week if not longer. But if I'd called 911, I knew a patrol officer would have stared at the knife and then said, 'Is that yours, ma'am?' I'd admit it was, and he or she would say, 'You don't think you could have been reaching in the drawer where you kept it for something else and maybe just set it aside without thinking?' Could I one hundred percent claim I hadn't? No, but the knives were in one of those wood blocks with slits in them to one side of a deep drawer where I kept linens. I wouldn't have *had* to take one out to reach anything else!"

She still thought it had been a threat, but everything she'd just said would sound so logical to Detective Dutton, Jordan didn't even bother to say that.

"That's it?"

"Somebody bumped me really hard when we were leaving the field after the fireworks display, and I thought whoever it was whispered something in my ear, but I couldn't make it out. And…there was a lot of jostling. You know what a crowd like that is like, even if everyone has had a good time."

There. She'd told them. It probably didn't look good that she hadn't earlier, except they'd have thought then that she had a wild imagination—or that she was trying to divert attention from herself. *Somebody was following her;* he *must have attacked Elliott.*

Sure.

"Well," the detective said with more tact than Jordan might have expected, "we can't check any of that out now. And it is a little hard to see why someone interested in you would go after a man you've gone out with twice. Now, if you had a possessive ex-husband or—boyfriend?"

"My ex-husband was very possessive," Jordan said flatly, "but he's dead. And no, there hasn't been anyone since who gave even an indication of that kind of behavior. Like I told you, I've hardly dated."

There'd been the other stuff over the years: the wedding— and funeral—anniversary cards, and, even worse a couple of times, bouquets that always looked as if they should be set beside a casket at a funeral, or perhaps left on a grave as an annual remembrance. Those would have been expensive, which didn't fit with any of Steve's friends. The handwriting on the cards wasn't always the same, either. The problem was, she could think of several people offhand who had outright accused her of murdering Steve, and then there were the uneasy or even narrow-eyed looks. Steve's brother and mother surely hated her. Maybe his sister; Jordan didn't know. He'd had a big circle of friends, the ones he continued to meet at the tavern evenings after their marriage, when he left her home. People probably thought they were being clever, tormenting her for taking away a man who had been bigger than life, much too good to be the abuser they refused to believe he'd been.

Jordan had given up even bothering to wonder who sent any particular card. She had tried to find out from florists who had ordered the bouquets, but the businesses were determined to honor their customers' privacy, so she gave up asking.

She trashed the flowers and cards alike, refusing to acknowledge how much it hurt to know that so many people in her hometown would rather detest her than believe what was in the police report. Steve had been Somebody, with a capital *S*. Her shyness and the self-doubt that took deep root the day her father had left and never bothered with her again had combined to turn her into a nonentity in most people's eyes. She even understood that; it had taken her years to discover who she really was.

Detective Dutton didn't comment on Jordan's teenage marriage that had ended so catastrophically after twenty months. She'd likely seen enough on her job to be able to read between the lines on that report. Unfortunately, she and her partner could have convinced themselves that, after being battered, Jordan might have nursed underlying rage and developed a taste for offing men who'd maybe said or done the wrong thing.

That was her, she thought: the angel of death.

The detective didn't try to extend today's conversation.

Jordan forgot all about it after she hurried out the back door to find her mother tipped so far in the chair, she was inches from tumbling to the brick pavers.

After gently helping Mom into the closest to a sitting position she could achieve, Jordan caught her breath and vowed not to take her eyes off her mother for more than a minute unless she was safely tucked into bed with a bolster of pillows that kept her from rolling off the mattress.

So much for confiding in a supposedly sympathetic police detective.

AS WAS PROBABLY INEVITABLE, Shelly Hendrick's recovery slowed. Jordan was aware of very little that lay outside her childhood home, her mother's garden, the physical therapists, the city swimming pool where she took part in a water aerobics class aimed to help physically challenged people. The pharmacy—Jordan was on good terms with both the pharmacist and an assistant she'd known in school who seemed happy to see her and genuinely regretful about her mother's stroke. The grocery store, the several home care workers who came and went. Oh, and the couple of different doctors Mom saw on a regular basis.

The local hospital served as a regional center for specialists. Her mother had been lucky in that respect. A neurologist had taken over from the trauma team quickly. Mom's family doctor stayed in the loop, along with a cardiologist, a rehab nurse, physical and occupational therapist, a speech pathologist and a case manager. Jordan had been assured that a psychologist or even psychiatrist might be a big help once her mother's speech improved enough.

Jordan was grateful for every one of them, although she couldn't help being appalled by the bills. The many tests, from an MRI to a cerebral angiogram, did not come cheap. So far, Mom's insurance was paying the bulk of the bills, but taking care of what was left could still end up totally depleting her funds.

Her mother was currently undergoing an echocardiogram for the second time, as the doctors had never been entirely satisfied that they had identified the source of the clot or clots that had traveled to the brain and caused the stroke. Jordan sat in the waiting room, scrolling through news on her phone without getting very engaged when she heard a voice.

"Jordan Hendrick!"

She looked up and recognized one of the ER doctors who'd checked in several times while Mom was still hospitalized to see how she was doing. She'd wondered at the time whether big-city docs ever did anything like that.

Now she smiled. "Dr. Parnell. How nice to see you. Mom's

having another echocardiogram, thus me sitting here twiddling my thumbs."

"Make it Colin," he said, lowering himself to the seat right beside her. "I'm not your mother's doctor anymore."

She blinked. Was that a glint of interest in his brown eyes?

"Colin," she agreed. "Did you just happen to wander this way?"

He laughed, making her realize that he was an attractive man. When she'd briefly met him before, all she'd seen was the white coat and stethoscope. The physicians all blended together at that point.

"No, I heard your mother would be here and thought I'd say hello to you. Find out how you're holding up."

"I'm not the one struggling. That's Mom. People keep telling me she's progressing well, but...oh, she is. It's just so slow."

He laid a warm hand atop hers on the armrest of the chair. "I know. But it hasn't even been three months, and she's home. From what I've been told, she really is bouncing back faster than we originally expected. She was young to have a massive stroke."

"I know, especially when she didn't have any obvious risk factors."

His eyebrows rose. "She'd been ignoring her higher-than-ideal blood pressure and what we now know was atrial fibrillation."

Jordan made a face. "She was sure her symptoms had to do with the amount of coffee she drank."

"She's not the first person and won't be the last I've heard that from."

His hand remained atop hers. She didn't quite know how to react.

"I'd suggest we go get a cup of coffee, but I don't suppose you have time," he said.

Was that a tiny thrill of anticipation, or dread? "I'm afraid not," Jordan said. "She should be out pretty soon."

"Are you able to get away long enough to meet for coffee another time, or even to go out for dinner?" he asked.

"I...maybe?"

He laughed. "A solid answer."

How could she not laugh, too? Impulse seized her. "Sure. Why don't we start with coffee so I don't have to leave my mother for too long?" Good excuse.

"Tomorrow?" he said immediately, taking out his phone and pulling up the calendar. "Say, three o'clock?"

She did the same. "I can do that. Mom's physical therapist will be there, and then an aide takes over to help her shower."

"Great." He was especially handsome when he grinned at her and squeezed her hand before rising to his feet. "Clearwater Café?"

A trendy—by Storm Lake standards—establishment, the café was only a few blocks from the hospital and had both good food and coffee, so she said, "That sounds great. Thanks for suggesting it."

His name was called over the PA system just then. He shook his head in mock dismay and left at a brisk pace.

Not until he was gone did she wonder whether this was smart, given her recent history. She wondered whether anybody had told him she was at the heart of one of Storm Lake's most shocking tragedies, one that nobody seemed to have forgotten.

I should cancel, she thought—but the two of them weren't planning to go out on the town. It would be the merest chance if anyone who held a grudge against her happened to see her sipping coffee and chatting with a doctor she obviously knew from the hospital. And what was she supposed to do? Quit trying to have a semi-normal life because of the assault on Elliott Keefer? The one Jordan couldn't believe was connected to her?

No, that was ridiculous. She'd been home for months. Wasn't she entitled to start *some* kind of social life?

Still, she circled back to thinking maybe going out with anyone right now wasn't a good idea, then feeling mad because there wasn't any good reason she shouldn't...until a nurse pushing her mother in a wheelchair came through the double doors.

"She's all set to go home!" the nurse declared. "Dr. Taylor says she'll give you a call to talk about what she saw. Why don't you go get your car, and we'll meet you at the portico?"

"I'll do that." Jordan bent to kiss her mother's cheek, then hurried toward the main entrance so Mom wouldn't have to wait long.

Chapter Four

It was one date. No need to panic.

Still, Jordan sat stiffly in the passenger seat beside Dr. Colin Parnell and thought, *I shouldn't be doing this.*

She also wished she could drop the "doctor" part in her mind. She would *not* let herself feel the inadequacy that had haunted her as a teenager. She was working toward a BA. It was just taking time.

What if he didn't see her as an equal and was thinking about nothing but getting her into bed?

He'd be in for a big disappointment. She'd worked hard on herself to accept that, while she'd made one massively bad choice, she'd also proved her strength by surviving. Heck, she bet her personal life had been more colorful than Colin Parnell's.

"What are you thinking?" he asked just then.

"I'm giving myself a pep talk," she admitted. "This will be the longest I've left Mom since she had the stroke." Nice excuse.

"You said you found an aide to stay with her."

"Yes, and Mom's doing really well. She kept telling me she didn't need anyone, but even with the cane she walks so unsteadily I keep being afraid she'll fall." Jordan sighed. "Enough about Mom, already."

He laughed. "I can agree with that, although if you need to talk about her, I'm available."

"Nope. I'm ready to expand my horizons." Just…not too far.

He'd asked her if she liked Italian food, and minutes later they walked into a small restaurant in a space that had been a dry-cleaning business in her day. The smell was amazing, and her first quick scan of diners didn't identify anyone she knew. She let herself relax.

After shedding their coats, they were seated at a table in the corner. The fat candle added to a romantic ambiance created in part by dim lighting. After they ordered and their waiter poured a red wine Colin had chosen, he lifted his glass and said, "To getting to know you."

She lifted hers as well and smiled. "To getting to know *you*."

They'd covered some ground over coffee last week. Jordan knew he had grown up in Idaho Falls and had always intended to come back to the area to practice medicine. What she didn't know was whether anybody had whispered to him about the scandal that had shaped her life.

"Do you plan to stay in town once your mother is more solidly on her feet?" he asked now, dipping a slice of bread in the spiced olive oil. His mouth quirked.

She frowned a little at his question. "I actually haven't even thought about future plans. I was so focused on being here for Mom, and then the slow pace of her recovery makes it obvious that at best I can't leave her anytime in the foreseeable future. So… I don't know." Her frown deepened. Strange she hadn't let herself think about this. Being home in Storm Lake stirred up a lot of complicated stuff, much of it bad, but she was rediscovering how much she loved, too, starting with the wooded, mountainous setting on a beautiful lake. It really did feel like home. "Some of the issues

I didn't like here have probably changed," she said slowly. "Right now, I can't see myself moving out of the area and leaving Mom behind. I mean, realistically..."

He obviously knew what she was thinking.

She got him talking about why he'd chosen trauma as a medical specialty and found he could be really funny when confessing to his youthful exploration of adrenaline-inducing activities, from jumping onto a backyard trampoline from a second-story window in his parents' house to amateur bungee jumping.

She was laughing when the restaurant door opened and a couple entered. She froze mid-breath. Guy Feller, with a woman who was probably his wife.

Maybe because she was staring, he saw her right away and met her eyes.

Surely he'd be civil, if he spoke to her at all. Crossing her fingers out of sight, she wanted to believe that.

In fact, once he and the woman had been shown to a table, he murmured something to her and steered her toward Jordan.

Tall and lean, he'd matured well, she thought. She could see the boy she'd known best only because they'd gone all the way through school together.

"Guy," she said pleasantly. "How nice to see you. Your mother talks about you."

Colin stood and the two men shook hands, introducing themselves as well as Guy's wife, Autumn.

"I know I've told you about Jordan," he said to her as she smiled politely.

Determined to keep it light, Jordan asked, "Did you tell her about the birthday party when I turned—what was it? Eight? Nine?—and you stayed with your back to a wall staring at your feet for something like two hours?"

His laugh appeared genuine. "Yeah, I was paralyzed. All those *girls*."

Jordan grinned.

"In fairness, I did bring a present—"

"Which your mother undoubtedly chose and wrapped."

"And I ate cake and ice cream."

"Hunched over it while you pretended no one else was there."

"C'mon." He appealed to Colin. "How would you have felt about being the only boy at a birthday party with a gaggle of girls all dressed in pink and giggling nonstop?"

"I'd have been out of there," admitted the man who'd just told her how much he enjoyed risking his life.

Jordan rolled her eyes.

"Pleasure to meet you," Guy told Colin, then looked steadily at Jordan. "I wasn't as good a friend to you as I should have been. I…regret that."

Stunned, she bobbed her head.

He didn't give his wife or Colin a chance to ask what he meant, and even though she saw questions in Colin's eyes, he didn't pry.

Instead, they returned to the "getting to know each other" conversation that Jordan tried hard to keep superficial.

Still, she was surprised to realize what a good time she was having with the doctor and didn't feel too nervous about him delivering her to her doorstep. Dr. Colin Parnell wasn't a man to be pushy, she felt sure. To the contrary, she suspected he wielded patience, that charming smile and his innate kindness to achieve his aim when it came to women.

He did kiss her on her front porch, but gently. "I have this feeling you've been burned," he said quietly, confirming her belief when he raised his head. "I had a good time tonight."

"I did, too," she was able to say honestly.

He pressed his lips to her forehead, said, "I'll call," and strolled back to his car.

She waved before she let herself into the house. The evening had left her with way too much to think about—but that would have to wait until she'd seen the aide out and reported to Mom.

JORDAN SLEPT BETTER than she had in a while. Getting out, laughing, forgetting for a couple of hours the main preoccupation of her life, was better than a sleeping pill. Mom must have made it through the night, too.

Wait. What if she'd decided to get up to go to the bathroom on her own? She was definitely starting to rebel against the "don't move without someone standing beside you" rule. In one way, that was good news, but in another...

Jordan leaped up, feeling some relief because she didn't find Mom lying in the hall or the bathroom. Mom's bedroom door was always partially open, and...there she was, awake and reaching for the bell that sat on her bedside stand.

Jordan stepped into the room. "Good morning! Do you need a hand?"

"No." Her ever-stubborn mother slowly pushed herself into a sitting position, albeit twisted to accommodate her weak side, then swung her feet onto the floor. Her walker waited to give her support standing. Once she was upright, she said, "Hah! Told you."

"Yeah, you did." Jordan grabbed her robe and draped it over the walker as Mom shuffled toward the bathroom. Thank goodness this was mostly a one-story house, the attic reserved for storage. Stairs would have been impossible for Mom to navigate now.

Ear cocked for any worrisome thuds or crashes behind her, Jordan went on to the kitchen, letting her mother follow. Loss of independence was a big trigger for depression in stroke victims. She didn't want to contribute.

They both had coffee. Jordan sliced the banana that went on top of each of their bowls of cereal, since her mother's right hand was still both weak and frozen into an unfortunately clawlike position. It had improved noticeably, though, after a whole lot of PT. Life would be easier for Mom if the stroke had crippled her left side instead of her more dominant right.

"How…was…your date?"

"Good," she said. "Do you remember Dr. Parnell?"

"Yah." Mom's tongue still refused to form the *S* sound. Mostly, Jordan's brain simply filled it in. "Nice."

She chatted about dinner, how good the food was—Mom had lunch with friends regularly but had never been to the restaurant—and mentioned seeing Guy Feller. The two of them laughed again at the memory of the birthday party that had severed the friendship. Jordan still remembered the doll his mother had picked out to give her, and the beet-red color that crept over Guy's cheeks while she was opening it.

An hour later, the doorbell rang and Jordan let in the aide who helped Mom take a shower. Later today, Mom's hairdresser was going to drop by, too, which she was excited about.

Jordan took advantage of the time to work outside, starting by raking leaves. After checking to find an occupational therapist with Mom, she continued her ongoing task of cutting back brown stems of perennials and annuals and then mulching flower beds—sort of like piling on the comforters—in preparation for the really cold weather to come. Late October teetered between the heat of summer and the bitter cold of winter in mountainous Idaho. The electric bill was climbing by the day, she reflected, but at least the water bill had plummeted now that she was no longer laying out soaker hoses for the forty-something roses in Mom's garden. In fact, the hoses were now curled up neatly in the garage; if left out, they'd crack over the winter.

Jordan had grown up rolling her eyes at Mom's over-the-top enthusiasm for gardening. Since she'd gotten home, she'd taken on the work so that when Mom made it home from the hospital, her garden would be brilliant with bloom and welcoming. Now…maybe it was odd, but Jordan had become invested.

Lunch was sandwiches, applesauce and chips—so imaginative—and Jordan had put the pillow bolster into place once her mother had lain down for a nap when the doorbell rang again.

Who on earth? Jordan had bought a whiteboard calendar to keep track of her mother's many appointments. Had she forgotten to note one?

She didn't even think of looking to see who was here before she opened the door. All-too-familiar shock struck her at the sight of two uniformed police officers on the doorstep. And, dear God, wasn't one of them Cody Bussert, better known in high school as Buzz? Jordan had had no idea that one of Steve's good buddies had become a cop.

Apprehension had her clutching the door. "I…how can I help you? My mother is—"

Cody interrupted without apparent compunction. "It's you we need to talk to, *Ms*. Hendrick."

The other officer glanced at his partner in what appeared to be surprise and possibly warning. Had to be the sneer in *Buzz's* voice.

It made her mad enough that she was able to say coolly, "And why would that be?"

The second cop said, "I'm Officer Wilson. This is—"

"She knows me," Buzz snapped.

"May we come in?"

Jordan glanced over her shoulder. "Can we talk on the porch? My mother had a stroke recently and is napping."

"I'm sorry," Officer Wilson said. "That's tough. Yes, we can sit out here."

Thank goodness the day was cool but not bitingly cold so she didn't have to ask them in. Buzz leaned a hip against the porch railing while his partner perched on an Adirondack chair, obviously not wanting to slide far enough back as to impede his being able to leap up to…? Tackle her? Pull his weapon?

Pulse racing, she sat on the swing hanging from chains. "What is it? I haven't been back in town long—"

"And another man is already dead," Buzz said with a razor-sharp edge in his voice.

Her fingernails bit into her palms. "What?"

Officer Wilson looked reprovingly at Bussert, but said, "We're speaking with people who knew Dr. Colin Parnell well."

Knew. Past tense. It couldn't be.

"You mean, he's… Something happened to him?" That sounded mealy-mouthed, but she couldn't even let herself picture—

"I'm afraid he was murdered last night, Ms. Hendrick."

"Oh my God." This couldn't be. She heard herself whimpering, "Oh…my God."

"I believe you and he went out together yesterday evening."

Panic clogged her throat. She couldn't let them see anything but the grief, not now, not until she had time to think about what this meant. "Yes. We…had dinner. He dropped me here afterward."

Why hadn't she said no? Why, *why*?

"Do you know what time?"

"About eight thirty." The pressure behind her sternum

hurt. "I'd hired an aide to stay with Mom and promised not to be out late."

"Someone was here when you arrived."

"Yes. She...was in the living room. She saw Colin and smiled and waved. He wished her good-night, too. I guess their paths have crossed before."

A small spiral notebook had materialized in Officer Wilson's hand. *Small town, low tech.* "Her name?" he asked.

"Uh... Patty Younger. She's one of Mom's and my favorites."

The questions went on and on. How had she met Colin? Hospital. How long ago? Three months. Had they been dating that entire time? No. She explained about the most recent encounter with him at the hospital while she waited for her mother who was undergoing a test, about the casual invitation to coffee, then dinner. Yes, she'd seen someone she knew at the restaurant. Buzz obviously recognized Guy's name.

Colin had kissed her lightly on her doorstep. Yes, that was the first time. No, except for the two occasions, she'd never seen him outside the hospital. She had no idea where he lived.

They didn't tell her. But how hard was it these days to find someone's address online?

Only at the end did they allow her to ask, "Was he killed at home? Or...or did he stop somewhere else?" Had a bullet from a high-powered rifle struck him as he was driving? As horrible as all this was, she prayed his death didn't resemble the attacks on Pete and Elliott. Because if it did...

She would have to tell these cops before they found out on their own.

"He was attacked in his own home," Officer Wilson said stiffly.

"You mean...someone was waiting for him?"

"It appears he'd been home long enough to make a cup of coffee and settle down in a home office to work on his laptop."

Had his assailant already been in the house? Hidden, so as to muddy Jordan's alibi? Oh, that made sense.

She could see the attack with painful clarity. Had he been shot first, or had a blow to his head that came from behind taken him down? Weirdly, that was the moment when grief struck like a lightning bolt. She saw him, kind eyes, handsome face, the dimple that formed in one cheek when he laughed, which she thought he did often. His stories, a quality she could only think of as joy in life.

Had he really been killed because of *her*? How was she supposed to live with that?

"The caliber of bullet that killed Dr. Parnell was the same as the bullet that killed your husband," Buzz said, and the expression in his eyes spoke for him. "What happened to that gun after his death?"

Even though she was afraid hot tears were dripping down her cheeks, Jordan held her head high and spoke with as much steel in her voice as she could summon. "I have no idea. I never wanted to see it again. That's something you should be able to look up. What's more, as a police officer, you have access to reports about Steve's death. Not a single person, from responding officers to the doctors, believed I shot him for any reason but self-defense. He had been abusive in different ways almost from the beginning of our marriage. And yes, I should have left him before it came to that, but you have no right to hear the reasons I didn't. The man you knew was not the man I had to live with."

His glare didn't soften.

She transferred her gaze to the other officer. "Was Dr. Parnell...beaten, too?"

Wilson's expression sharpened. "Yes."

If they threw her in jail, what would Mom do? But she had to tell them. They'd inevitably find out anyway.

"I told you I don't know where Colin lives." *Lived.* "Except to save my life, I have never committed a violent act in my life. But…" She took a deep breath. "I think his murder may have to do with me."

Chapter Five

The interrogation that followed was a nightmare. It made her realize how incredibly lucky she'd been with the detectives in Walla Walla. They, at least, started as impartial. Once Detectives Shannon and Dutton heard from the Storm Lake PD, though, their opinions about her would probably do a one-eighty.

Thinking of them, Jordan asked, "Shouldn't I be talking to a detective?"

The two men exchanged a glance. Wilson answered, "In a small department like this, we all step into major investigations. I'm…expecting a promotion to detective anytime, so I'm sure the chief will leave me on this anyway."

It wasn't him she wanted to get rid of. It was Buzz, who made no pretense of hiding his opinion of her.

She had her chance when he asked an especially offensive question. Rising to her feet and completely ignoring him, she looked at Wilson.

"As you may have gathered, your partner holds a grudge against me because he was friends in high school with my husband. Apparently—" now she allowed herself a scathing glance at the jerk "—he still believes because Steve was a football star, the life of the party and a popular man on campus, he couldn't have had a darker side. I will not speak with Officer Bussert again."

Buzz said nastily, "What makes you think you have any choice?"

She raised a hand, her gaze once again on Officer Wilson, who stood, too. "I won't talk to anyone again without having a lawyer present. I did not commit these crimes. As I told you, I believe I've been stalked on and off all these years by someone who blames me for my husband's death. Someone—" she made this stare incinerating "—who has a lot in common with Officer Bussert."

Officer Wilson winced.

"Yet you kept no evidence of that stalking," Buzz sneered.

"Now, you'll have to excuse me—"

"Wait! You said you'd give me the names of the investigators in Walla Walla and their phone numbers. I'm sure I could track them down, but…"

"Give me a minute." She hustled into the house, careful not to let the screen door slam, grabbed her phone, and pulled up the names and numbers by the time she was back out on the porch.

Wilson scrawled the info on his pad. "Thank you. I'll be in touch."

At least he'd said *I* rather than *we*. She kept her mouth shut, just watched as they retreated to their patrol unit and drove away. Then she waved a weak hand at a neighbor who was out raking—but mostly watching the excitement—and retreated back into the house.

No, a sob was building in her chest. She'd wake her mother. She hurried out the back door, a hand clapped over her face. Only after she dropped into a bench as far from the house as possible did she let the wail erupt.

"I'M NOT REAL happy about this," said the Storm Lake police chief, Tom's new boss. His call had come in while Tom was packing his last possessions to vacate his condo, which he'd let out for the next year. "Even though we're past the tourist season, we need you fully on board, but this case is a strange one."

Hip and thigh aching, Tom pulled up a barstool that he was leaving for the young couple moving in. "Tell me about it," he said.

Chief Guthrie had decided it was ideal that Tom would be moving into town now, knowing no one. "Place this size, we couldn't usually pull off any kind of undercover operation. But the house almost across the street from the suspect is up for rent. Decent place, too—you might want to stay in it."

Tom had done a couple of undercover stints in his career and hated both of them, so his first feeling wasn't positive. That said, this might give him a little longer before he had to participate in any hard physical operation—say, a search and rescue.

So he made an inquiring noise.

The facts Guthrie presented about a woman who seemed to leave dead men behind everywhere she went created a strange picture in Tom's mind. The chief wasn't kidding. Jordan Hendrick, age twenty-eight, had married right out of high school. The husband had allegedly been abusive. She'd shot and killed him to save her own life. In fact, she'd spent days in the hospital recovering from the damage he'd done to her in that struggle.

"At the time, I believed her story," Guthrie admitted, before continuing.

She moved away, first to Great Falls, Montana, then to Walla Walla, a smallish city in eastern Washington, staying off the radar until roughly three years ago. At that point, a man she'd just started dating was killed in an apparent home invasion. Five months ago, she started seeing another lucky guy, who after the second date was attacked and nearly killed in his own home. The investigators there couldn't pin anything on her but were uneasy. Her mother had a stroke, and this Hendrick woman rushed home to take care of her. Unlikely she'd had time for any social life at first, the chief said, but just recently, she'd gone out with a doctor from the hospital. A week later, they had dinner—and he was attacked and killed in his own home later that same evening.

"We have no witnesses, no trace evidence leading to her, but I'm not a real big fan of coincidence," Chief Guthrie said. "We don't have a ballistics report back yet, so we don't know if the same gun was used here and in Walla Walla. The detective I spoke to there said different guns were used in the murder of the one man and the attempted murder of the other."

Coincidence didn't sit well with Tom, either. Still, a woman in her twenties made an unlikely serial killer. Unlike the classic black widow, she apparently hadn't gained a thing from any of these deaths. She claimed a stalker but had zero proof. Somehow, she'd never been disturbed enough by the strange messages left on her doorstep and in her mailbox over the years to bother calling 911 to report any of them.

The two men threw around the possibility she'd left behind other victims who hadn't been linked to her. There were some big gaps in time to be accounted for.

"It was hiring you that gave me the idea," Guthrie said. "You'd be in a good position to watch her. Not saying you should push it too far, but with a little luck, you might make friends with her. I can't think of any other way to be proactive."

What he meant was, at thirty-four, Tom was close enough in age to their target to potentially appeal to her. In the end, Tom agreed. It sounded like a soft assignment, but intriguing. After ending the call, to give himself something to go on, he looked up Jordan Hendrick's Washington State driver's license, since she didn't appear to have gotten one in Idaho yet, but the photo didn't tell him much. Blond hair—although he squinted and wasn't so sure that was quite right, brown eyes, five feet five, 120 pounds. Weight on a driver's license was almost always about as accurate as a carnival psychic's predictions. She was a pretty woman, he thought, but given the quality of DMV photos, he couldn't even be sure about that.

He had a feeling Chief Guthrie was hoping for more than a casual friendship sparking between his new detective and this black widow. If he could persuade her into a date or two, a trap would be a logical tactic.

Then he'd only have to worry about surviving a relationship with Jordan Hendrick.

JORDAN IDLY NOTICED a moving truck in the driveway of a house on the other side of the street that had been vacant and for sale since she'd come home. Men unloaded, but she didn't catch sight of anyone who was an obvious new homeowner. No children were running around, anyway. She didn't see a woman.

She wouldn't have paid any attention at all if not for her mother, who could hardly wait to find out all. Mom knew everyone on the block, and despite Jordan's new notoriety, most of them stopped by to chat when Mom was out front or dropped by with offerings of baked goods on a pretty regular basis. Mrs. Chung, a tiny woman in her eighties who was almost as ardent a gardener as Jordan's mother, had been the first to visit her in the hospital.

They'd all carefully stayed neutral where Jordan was concerned, for which she was grateful. Despite rampant gossip, in the days following the murder, they continued to stop by for her mother's sake. They smiled even at Jordan, commented on the weather or asked in low voices how her mother was really doing before spending time with Mom. But Jordan knew *they* knew she was being investigated by the police, and neither they nor she could ever forget that.

The facade of normalcy was almost unbearable.

The Storm Lake police had made it clear they expected her to stay put and available. Not like she'd flee anyway; she couldn't leave her mother. What she knew was that her life had taken another hard left turn. Steve's death, she'd come to terms with. But what happened to Pete Schroder, Elliott, Colin was a horror that weighed on her every waking minute.

Whenever she had an idle moment, she tried to remember everyone who might possibly be responsible for trying to set her up as a murderess, but how could she separate the burning stares that might have held hate from the snubs that might have grown into more if she'd stayed around? Then there were the doubtful glances, the avid ones, the… She shuddered every time she circled through her memories of those expressions, those faces.

She would never dare again have even a friendship with a man. Unless and until the police identified and arrested the killer—and how likely was that when they focused on her?—the future she'd still sometimes imagined, in which she had a husband and children, had faded from sight like an oasis in the desert that never had been real.

Desperate for occupation, she began to wish there was more to do in the garden, but she'd already divided perennials. With it now November, in the next few weeks she could plant more bulbs, but that was about it. The next big job wasn't until March when she'd be pruning roses for the first time in her life. If she wasn't in jail by then.

She'd started running again but could only do that when someone was here with Mom. Today was relatively balmy for the season, so she'd put on a parka but didn't bother to zip it, and sat on the porch with a book on her lap. With fragmented concentration, she was easily distracted by the sight of a man emerging from the house recently visited by the moving truck. He gave her something new to think about.

He walked down the driveway, his head turned as he seemed to ponder where he wanted to go, and then he ambled along the sidewalk toward his next-door neighbor, going up to knock on the door. He disappeared inside for long enough to suggest he'd sat down for a cup of coffee. When he reappeared, he progressed to the next house on his side of the street.

Jordan rolled her eyes at her nosiness, but what else did she have to do? Once Mom was up from her nap, she'd want every detail Jordan could glean about this new neighbor.

On a block occupied mostly by senior citizens who'd been in these houses as long as her mother had, this guy stood out by his youth alone. Youth being relative. Jordan guessed him to be in his early to midthirties. He was also tall, broad-shouldered and...not quite handsome, at least from this distance, but something. Quintessentially male, she decided—and, after all, she had plenty of time on her hands to watch him. She'd have guessed him to be athletic except that his walk was noticeably stiff even though he didn't let whatever bothered him shorten his long strides.

After sitting on the porch with Mrs. Chung for an interval, he apparently caught sight of Jordan, because he strode across the street directly toward her, his gaze intent on her.

She didn't move, just waited until he reached the foot of the porch steps. Short, unruly brown hair and piercing blue eyes added to her impression of a man who didn't have to be model-handsome to catch any woman's eyes.

She wouldn't let *any* man catch her eye.

"Hi," he said. "I just moved in across the street."

There was no reason not to be polite. "The moving truck

made you the talk of the neighborhood. People were starting to wonder if the house would ever sell."

"It didn't. I guess the owners gave up. I'm renting, although if I like my new job and the town, I have the option to buy." He paused, looking up at her. "I'm Tom Moore."

"Jordan Hendrick. This is actually my mother's house. You may not see much of her, because she's recovering from a stroke and still doesn't get around very well. I'm in town to take care of her."

He smiled, planted a foot on the bottom step and leaned a hip against the railing. "She's lucky you could drop everything and come home."

He had a deep, resonant voice that Jordan did not want to find appealing.

"Mom's always been there for me," she said simply.

He nodded as if he understood.

The pause became a little awkward. Obviously, he was in no hurry to move on. It appeared he didn't yet know he was speaking to a murder suspect. She'd have to thank Mrs. Chung and Mr. Griffin later for not giving him a heads-up.

"What's your new job?" she asked.

"I'm with the county parks. I moved here from San Francisco, a city I enjoyed, and which has fantastic parks, but like your mother I'm recuperating, although in my case from an injury. The hills in San Francisco, not to mention the beaches, challenged my physical capability. I thought this would be a change of pace, and I could look forward to some hiking and climbing down the line. Maybe take up cross-country skiing."

She didn't feel like she should ask *how* he'd gotten hurt. He could volunteer that if he wanted her to know.

When she didn't comment, he finally withdrew his booted foot from the step.

"I'll let you get back to your book. Just wanted to introduce myself. If I can give you a hand anytime, I'm close by."

"Thank you, but we have a constant stream of health aides
and therapists of one kind or another coming and going."

"You an only child?"

Her mouth tightened, but she saw no reason not to say,
"Yes."

She was being rude not to take him up on his conversational gambits, she knew she was, but Jordan wasn't trying
to make new friends, and particularly with a man. *Any* man.

A flicker in his eyes told her he knew she was just waiting for him to go away, and he bent his head. "I may see
you around."

"I'm sure you will," she said, sounding stilted.

He studied her for another few seconds, smiled faintly
and turned to walk away.

Message sent and received.

WELL, HIS FRIENDLY introduction had pancaked. Ms. Hendrick was not receptive to a new neighbor who wanted to become buddies. Tom would like to think she'd been as aware
of him as a man as he'd been of her as a woman, but he was
honest enough with himself to admit he had no idea. The
whole conversation had been forced.

She was probably wondering why a guy his age was trying
to get chummy with all his neighbors. Which was actually a
good question. He'd never done more than nod with most of
his neighbors in the tall brick warehouse in San Francisco
that had been converted to condominiums. A guy his age
met people at work, bars or the health club.

He had to assume she was watching, which meant he went
on to talk with an old guy next door who either needed hearing aids desperately or didn't bother wearing them when he
didn't expect a caller. After tearing himself away and bel-

lowing, "Nice to meet you!" Tom crossed the street and let himself into his own new home.

He'd brought most of his furniture, but that familiarity didn't make the house feel homey. Furniture wasn't in the right place. Neither were light switches, or the dishwasher, which was strangely placed an irritating distance from the kitchen sink.

He liked the era of the house—1940s, at a guess, along with the others on this block. There was a solidity to it. If he were really to buy it, he'd want to do some serious remodeling, though, starting with the bathrooms. It might be worth spending the money, at the very least, to get a plumber out here to replace the showerhead so he could have a satisfying shower.

Tom sighed and walked far enough into the living room to allow him to stand mostly hidden by the drapes but be able to look across the street and down one house. He thought his target hadn't moved.

Frowning, he mulled over his impressions of the woman. *Stricken* was the first word that came to mind. As he'd approached, he had the impression she wasn't really reading. She looked like someone emotionally paralyzed. That could be true whether she was guilty of these crimes or not. Being under scrutiny by law enforcement wasn't a lot of fun. There were plenty of times he'd done his best to lay on the pressure, waiting for his suspect to crack.

Tom winced. Wasn't that what he and Max had done with that last investigation? Jared Smith had cracked, all right, and come out firing.

Tom thought what he'd seen in her eyes was pain, but he couldn't put any weight behind what might be a trick of the light. Preliminary impressions were just that.

Fortunately or unfortunately, he wasn't sure which, he could say with certainty that she was more than pretty. The delicacy of her features hadn't been shown to best advantage in that DMV photo. Her slender wrists and graceful neck made him think she was fine-boned overall. He'd been right about her hair, thick and shiny, sort of a streaky dishwater blond that she wore bundled in a knot on the back of her head. Curves, undetermined. Her brown eyes were more caramel than dark chocolate. He felt sure she hadn't worn any makeup at all, and in his opinion didn't need it.

He didn't like the complication of having his body stir just because he was picturing her. On the other hand, he wasn't good at faking attraction, and he couldn't expect a reciprocal response without laying it out there.

Frowning at where she sat, still unmoving, he tried to decide a next step. Asking her out…yeah, no. As a renter, he was expected to keep up the yard, but it was pretty bare. Casual encounters would be tough. He had no flower beds, like the ones that wrapped her house, and several of the others on the block, too. He definitely needed to rake the leaves blanketing the lawn out front, which would make him visible from her house, but he'd save that for tomorrow. Actually, a couple of old fruit trees in the fenced backyard had dropped most of their leaves, too, but he'd be out of sight working there.

He had to keep active, Tom reminded himself. He'd brought weights and a treadmill, and was thinking of buying a rowing machine, too. If there were any indication Ms. Hendrick belonged to a gym, he'd have taken that route, but Chief Guthrie said no. Maybe she'd turn out to be a runner, and he could casually meet up with her.

His main intent was to stay alert so he could be sure she wasn't slipping out once her mother slept come evening. He doubted that would happen, given the police scrutiny, but he bet she hated feeling watched.

His number one priority was making sure she didn't notice that she had a new watcher—right across the street.

And he needed to be patient. There was no big hurry here, not unless she got involved with another man.

Chapter Six

Didn't it figure that Mom decided she had to meet the new neighbor?

"We should do something to welcome him," she declared—or at least that's how Jordan translated her speech. "Bake cookies."

Bake cookies. Okay, she couldn't misunderstand that.

"Mom, I'm sure it's not necessary."

Her mother firmly disagreed. Taking a casserole or cookies to a newcomer was part and parcel of belonging in this neighborhood.

In fairness, Jordan had seen others on the block knocking on Tom Moore's doorstep and handing him something.

All she could do was make a face behind Mom's back before pulling out a cookbook with familiar tattered pages.

Snickerdoodles, she decided, after determining she had all the ingredients.

The baking part actually turned out to be fun. She let her mother do everything she could while seated, even if that took way longer. A double batch meant they could enjoy home-baked goodies. Uh, not that they'd been short of them thanks to Mom's friends and neighbors, but still.

Once the cookies had cooled and Jordan had climbed on a step stool to unearth some round tins with lids to hold them,

Mom also announced that she wanted to walk over to deliver the "welcome to the neighborhood" cookies.

"Mom! That's farther than it looks."

Her mother's facial muscles had recovered enough to let her almost raise an eyebrow. And it was true that the therapists were encouraging her to walk. Jordan checked to see that Tom Moore's big black SUV was parked in his driveway. Probably his single garage was too small for a monster vehicle like that.

Today was chilly enough, Jordan bundled her mother up as if she were a toddler, threw on her own parka and led the way. The first obstacle was crossing the threshold with the walker. That the recently built ramp was at the back of the house meant it took them a good ten minutes to reach the front walkway.

Down the driveway, onto the street. The pace slowed. Taking mini-steps, Jordan looked from one direction to the other and hoped no teenager would rocket down their block right now.

"Doing okay, Mom?"

"'Course."

Okey doke.

The new neighbor must have glanced out a window because he appeared on his porch, grabbed a rocking chair and carried it down to the walkway. Evidently sharing her concern, he turned his head sharply at the sound of a car engine not too far away, but no vehicle appeared.

He called, "I hope this means you're coming to see me, Mrs. Hendrick." Smiling eyes met Jordan's. "And you, Jordan."

"We are. Mom, this is Tom Moore, who I told you about." She touched her mother's back. "Let's get out of the road, why don't we."

Mom shuffled forward. Jordan noticed how, without making a big deal out of it, Tom moved in close on her mother's other side, probably as ready to grab her as he was. That was...nice, she couldn't help thinking.

Mom sat with obvious relief and a little help in the chair he'd provided.

"I can get something for us to sit on—" he began, but Jordan shook her head.

"Ground's fine for me." She did hand over the tin of cookies. "Snickerdoodles. I hope you like them." She sat cross-legged on the cold but fortunately dry grass.

"I love them." He sat, too, but stretched out his long legs. He grinned. "Friendly neighborhood. I may have to let out my belt if people keep bringing food."

He asked her mother how long she'd lived here, and at least pretended to understand her answer. Jordan stayed, watchful, to one side. Mom struggled to ask something, and he told her he'd never been to Idaho until a week ago; he'd grown up in northern California—McKinleyville in Humboldt County, which Jordan recalled had once been famous for illegal marijuana farms—then gone to college in San Francisco and worked there ever since.

He opened the tin of cookies and offered them each one. Mom took one with apparent pleasure. She tended to dribble crumbs when she ate, but Tom gave no sign of noticing. Fortunately, Jordan had a tissue in her pocket.

She broke up the party so they could be home by the time an occupational therapist arrived. Tom looked quite seriously at her mother and said, "I'd be glad to drive you."

"Supposed to walk," Mom told him—minus the first syllable.

Again, he clearly understood and said, "Then let me walk you two home. You have quite a garden, Mrs. Hendrick. I wish I'd seen it when all those roses were in bloom."

Somehow, he managed to continue gently chattering as

Jordan's mother labored along at a snail's pace. He admired the ramp, and suggested they add an arch over it by spring. "With a climbing rose, it'd look like it's been here forever."

They parted at the back door on a cordial note, Jordan relieved when he left with that long, confident and yet slightly stiff stride. Could he possibly be as nice a guy as he seemed?

Jordan was disconcerted by her suspicion. Of course there were decent men out there. That didn't mean she wanted anything to do with one who showed up on her doorstep.

Now all she had to do was listen to Mom talk about what a gentleman he was, and how perhaps they ought to have him over so he and Jordan could get to know each other.

Not a chance. The very fact that she found Tom Moore to be attractive—never mind his *niceness*—punctuated the importance of keeping her distance. Really, that shouldn't be a problem now, with him apparently having started work. He'd soon find friends.

What she should do was quit sitting out on the front porch.

TWICE IN THE next week Tom saw Jordan heading out for a run. The second time he was able to change to sweats and athletic shoes in time to trail some distance behind, waiting until she'd circled to head back to finally catch up with her maybe half a mile from their homes. He didn't mind the hanging back part, given that he had plenty of time to appreciate how good she looked in stretchy women's running pants and top. He'd been right about her build—long, slender legs could give him plenty of fantasies, and he liked the curvaceous hips just as much, although they wouldn't serve a dedicated runner.

They were fine by him.

Once he stepped it up, she heard his approaching footsteps, looked over her shoulder and half tripped before catching her balance. She appeared startled to see him, and not really pleased, but slowed down when he did and asked civilly, "Don't you have to work?" Her face gleamed with sweat, but she wasn't gasping for breath which meant she was in decent condition.

"I'm doing some work remotely." He was intensely relieved to slow from a jog to a walk. He pushed through pain every day but didn't enjoy it. "I'm...not so much the guy you'll see mowing the grass at the park or cleaning the public restrooms." He grinned. "Can't say I mind that. I'm mostly in administration, which means endless reports. The county is like any form of government—they're fond of rules and regulations. I'm acquainting myself with all of them and issues the parks department has had in the past as well as ideas for expansion." He paused, glancing out of the corner of his eye at her. "I'll be called out for any public disturbances or crimes, too. If you see me carrying a weapon, that's why."

"Oh." She didn't look at him. Had she just slotted him into place with the cops who were making her life miserable?

Officer Wilson and Deputy Chief Bowen, recognizable to Tom from photos, had stopped by together twice this week, keeping the pressure on but learning nothing new. Tom had no idea how much Jordan's mother knew. He hoped not much.

"If my truck is in the driveway and you want company on a run, give me call," he suggested. "In fact, how about I give you my phone number in case you need a hand with your mother?"

Her glance struck him as suspicious, but she took out her phone and entered his number. She had to know that if her mother took a fall in the middle of the night, say, he could get there quicker than anyone else.

They parted ways, Tom smiling, Jordan merely nodding. He'd believed he'd made some inroads the other day, when she and her mother visited, but Jordan must have been faking it for her mother's sake.

This was his investigation now, but the department was pretending he didn't exist. He was working remotely, all right, reading every scrap of information he could find about her.

Yesterday, he'd killed hours researching violent crimes that occurred in Great Falls, Montana, during the couple of years she'd lived there. A city of over 60,000 people, Great Falls was impacted by a lot more tourism than he'd have suspected given the distance from Yellowstone to the south and Glacier National Park to the northwest. The police department and county sheriff's department stayed plenty busy, he determined, but he also hadn't hit on any murder or violent assault that jumped out at him. He might circle back later, but had decided to take a look at the couple of years she'd stayed here in Storm Lake before moving away, and her first year in Walla Walla and then the two-year gap between the deaths of the two men so far linked to her. He assumed the Walla Walla investigators were doing the same, but he preferred to do his own research. In fact, he felt some uneasiness about the competence of his new department.

Call him credulous, but he was having trouble envisioning her as a killer. He kept seeing patience and tenderness with her mother. The small touches that spoke louder than words. He'd felt some tightening in his chest that was unfamiliar.

He was also perplexed as to how to build trust between himself and Jordan. She was conspicuously *not* hanging out on the front porch anymore. Four days after the cookie delivery, he succeeded in setting out on a run only minutes behind her, but when he caught up, she came right out and said, "If you don't mind, I like running alone." After a pause, she did make an effort to soften the rejection. "It's the one time my mind can free float."

"I understand that." That might even be true, but he suspected that wasn't why she'd slapped him down. "See you," he added, and turned on the afterburners to leave her behind.

When he passed a small neighborhood park, he turned to round the block it occupied and saw Jordan continue on ahead. Probably running to the lakeshore and maybe a distance beyond it. The minute she was out of sight, he slowed to a walk and bent over with his hands on his hips.

Damn, damn, *damn.* He felt as if his left femur had snapped—again.

Walk it off, he told himself, and did. He chose a route that wouldn't intersect with Jordan's and finally was able to ease into a jog again. Yeah, he definitely wasn't ready to run a perp down, unless it was a six-year-old who'd just lifted a candy bar from a convenience store.

The chagrin he felt for the slowness of his physical recovery might be the cake, but Jordan Hendrick had supplied the icing. His ego insisted her attitude had nothing to do with *him*, and everything to do with her predicament. Unfortunately, he couldn't be sure.

He'd gotten home and showered before he saw her walk into sight and head up to the front door. A minute later, a smiling fellow came out, lifted a hand and left in a sedan parked in the driveway. He looked familiar and was presumably one of the aides or therapists that came and went.

Tom brooded. Maybe this wasn't going to work. So far as he could see, the pressure the cops were applying wasn't working, either. She was a strong woman. So strong, he'd like to know what had happened in her brief marriage.

He'd read the reports from first responders, including the eventual interviews with her, and he'd seen the photographs. The one of her brutally battered face sickened him. He reminded himself that she had only been nineteen and in the marriage for a year and a half. Teenagers weren't famous for common sense. Hadn't she felt she could turn to her mother?

He didn't think it'd go well if he dropped by and asked, "Hey, can we talk about your marriage? Didn't end so well, did it?"

To cap an unsuccessful week, he was out in front raking up what he hoped were the last leaves from that enormous maple when a police car pulled into her driveway. The front door of the house opened, and Jordan stepped out. She looked straight at him, and for a long moment that look held. He couldn't be sure from this distance but thought her cheeks reddened. She turned to Officer Wilson and didn't let herself so much as glance at Tom again.

Damn. Now she knew he knew if he hadn't already. Unless he pretended to worry and knocked on her door later to ask what was up, and imply he'd be glad to listen?

That little fantasy lasted about five seconds. She'd hold her chin high and say, "This doesn't concern you," followed by, "No, thanks."

What he'd do was keep investigating without talking to her. He'd spoken once with a Walla Walla detective. Since then, he had thought of additional questions. Surely it had occurred to those investigators that, if she were a killer, there might be other victims?

So far, he hadn't dared talk to anyone here in town, in case his name got back to Jordan. He was itching, though, to get a better idea why she didn't seem to have friends who welcomed her back to town. There might have been red flags about her personality all along that had been ignored. And what about her dead husband's friends and family? He bet they could give him an earful. As it was, the only relatives he knew about for sure were the mother, sister and brother. Small town like this, there might be others.

For now, he'd keep his cover here in Storm Lake. With

time, Jordan might soften. Given the apparent lack of friends, if she were innocent, wouldn't she be desperate for someone to listen, to maybe believe in her?

Here he was, ready and waiting to be that guy.

WHAT DIFFERENCE DID it make that Tom Moore must now know what police suspected about her? She hated the humiliation that washed over her when he saw the cops arrive and his eyes widened. It wasn't as if he was anything more to her than a new neighbor who disturbed her for reasons she refused to analyze. So what if he immediately concluded he'd associated with one of the rare female serial killers?

The police were leaning hard, but it hadn't occurred to Chief Guthrie that including the deputy chief would just get her back up. Wilson was too young to have been around then, but knowing Bowen could have been in a position to see her unconscious and battered made her skin crawl now. Plus, Steve had really liked the man, who had stepped in some once Steve's dad died. They'd gone hunting together but took their trophies to Steve's mother instead of Jordan, who couldn't have dealt with a dead deer or a wild turkey complete with feathers. Of course, that was a small town for you. She knew several other of the officers from school, or because she'd gone to school with their kids.

In the next week, she tried harder not to notice Tom when he set out for a run or washed that big black SUV in his driveway even though it already looked shiny to her. She should probably do the same to her mother's car, and hers, but that would leave her exposed out front, where anyone could see her and wander over for a friendly conversation.

Better not.

Mom had become more time-consuming, not less, as she became more active, her natural determination and stubbornness surfacing. She became testy when Jordan hovered. She had enough of that from the therapists and the aide who still didn't think she should shower by herself. She could handle enough tasks now, she thought she ought to be unsupervised while she did so. Jordan could only be grateful that November had brought plunging temperatures. If it had been high summer, Mom would have insisted on working in the garden, and just try to stop her! As it was, she watched like a hawk while Jordan planted bulbs, handing out a few at a time because only *she* knew what she wanted where.

Mom's garden, she reminded herself. *Not mine.*

Mom didn't like the row of pillows that kept her from rolling out of bed, either.

"I feel like I'm in a crib," she complained.

Increasingly, Jordan found she'd kicked a couple of them onto the floor by morning. Mom was getting stronger by the day now, but slowly, not by great leaps. Jordan understood her frustration. She'd started demanding to see the bills, too, and didn't appreciate having them withheld. *If anything was likely to give her another stroke*, Jordan thought, but really, Mom's insurance had covered a surprising amount.

Even so, Jordan was starting to think it might be a good idea for her to find a job. Mom wouldn't be going back to work anytime soon, and one of them should bring in some income. Oh, no—at what point would Mom lose her health insurance?

Thank God she owned the house outright.

Jordan had barely fallen asleep one night after her usual hour-plus of worrying when she snapped awake again. What…?

She frowned at the darkness. Mom hadn't cried out. No, she'd heard a thud. Something hitting the side of the house, or someone falling.

Pulse accelerating, she leaped from bed, stumbled over the rug and regained her balance before she reached the hall.

If it was Mom, she hadn't turned on a light. Jordan switched on the light in the hall. She immediately saw her mother's bare feet and legs lying on the floor just inside the bathroom.

"Mom! Oh my God, what happened?" She rushed forward to see her mother lying on her side, absolutely still on the bathroom floor. Blood ran over her face and darkened her newly washed and styled hair.

It was all Jordan could do to straddle her mother's body—no, no, to straddle her *mother*—and to search for a pulse. For a frightening minute, she couldn't find one, but then did. It seemed…steady, but her mother was unconscious.

Had she had another stroke? Or overestimated her strength and fallen? It appeared she'd bashed her head against the toilet going down.

911.

Jordan scrambled backward and raced into her room, snatching up her phone and dialing with a shaking hand. The woman she spoke to projected calm.

"If you'd like to stay on the line…"

"No." Tom. He'd come. However resistant she'd been to him, she knew he'd come.

He answered on the third ring, voice muzzy.

"My mother fell… Or… I'm not sure. This is Jordan," she remembered to explain. "Across the street. I…actually don't know why I'm calling you."

"Have you called 911?" Was that clothing rustling in the background?

"Yes." Tears seeped from her eyes. "I'm sorry. I shouldn't have—"

Any vestige of sleep had left his deep voice. "I'm on my way."

He ended the call. Jordan hurried to stand by her mother's feet, then realized she'd have to let the medics in anyway, so she raced to the front door and flipped the dead bolt just as a knock hammered on the door. She flung it open, and Tom stepped in.

The next instant, his arms were around her and he gave her a hard hug that was immensely reassuring for no reason she could determine.

Because someone else is here, she decided. *I'm not alone.*

"Down the hall?" he asked, and she nodded.

Without another word, he moved fast. Jordan left the front door wide open despite the cold air rushing in and followed. She found him crouched in the bathroom, obviously taking Mom's pulse with his fingertips. He abandoned that to gently probe her head. He must have some medical training. Maybe that was a requirement for people working in parks.

Seeing Jordan, he said, "She's definitely developing a bump. Until she wakes up, there's no way to determine whether she just got too ambitious and fell, or whether she had an attack of dizziness, or—"

"Another stroke," she said dully.

She'd been hearing a siren, she realized, which grew in volume. Within minutes someone rapped on the open door. "Hello?"

"Back here," Tom called, and feet sounded on the steps.

Jordan retreated out of the way. When the pair of EMTs or paramedics or whatever they were came in sight carrying packs of equipment and a backboard, she stepped into a bedroom.

"It's my mom. She's been recovering from a stroke. I don't know what happened. She's supposed to ring a bell if she needs to get up in the middle of the night."

"All right."

Tom stepped out of their way and went right to Jordan's side. She didn't resist when he wrapped an arm securely around her again, or when after a few minutes he said,

"We'll want to follow them to the hospital. Why don't you get dressed?"

She looked down at herself wearing a sacky T-shirt and faded flannel pajama pants. At any other time, she'd have been embarrassed. As it was, she snuffled and backed away. "Yes. Of course. Thank you."

The medics took her mother out with stunning speed. Jordan had barely donned jeans and a sweatshirt when they passed in the hall. Mom looked so frail Jordan's fear ratcheted up.

She heard Tom saying something about them being right behind the ambulance. She pulled on socks and thrust her feet into a pair of boots she could zip, then rushed to the living room.

The siren still wailed when she reached the front porch where Tom waited. Lights on the rear of the ambulance receded. Neighbors had come out on their porches, but she couldn't acknowledge them.

"Wait," she said. "I have to get Mom's wallet with her insurance card." Her own bag with her keys, too.

She found both quickly. Still on her porch, Tom displayed no sign of impatience. "Let me drive," he said. "You shouldn't when you're so rattled."

Oh, heavens—he sounded like Detective Shannon. He was right, though. In retrospect, she didn't know how she'd made it so many miles home with her thoughts racing and only a couple of phone updates to let her know that her mother was still alive.

Now...she tried to calm herself. "I can make it on my own," she said. "I'm...okay. But... I'm really glad you came. Thank you."

Those blue eyes never left her face. "You're welcome. I'm not letting you do this alone, either."

"You hardly know us," she argued, even as he watched while she locked the door, then hustled her across the street.

He simply bundled her into the passenger side of his massive vehicle without bothering to argue. The engine roared to life, and she huddled there, grateful. So grateful.

Chapter Seven

In the excruciating hours that followed, Tom barely left her side. His presence felt…surreal. Who was he? Why was he here? He couldn't possibly *want* to be. Could he?

And yet, at some point, she realized he was a sturdy bulwark she'd never had before. Not once did she see so much as a flicker of discomfort in his eyes. For a stranger, he had a remarkable ability to figure out what she needed before she did.

Most of the time, they sat side by side on chairs in the waiting room. His feet stayed square on the floor. He didn't fidget the way she did. When he moved, it was to get her a cup of coffee, or to lay a strong arm around her shoulders when he guessed she was close to shattering.

A doctor or nurse appeared a few times to pull down a mask and give them an update.

"We don't believe she had another stroke," was the first and most heartening.

"Our worry is that she could have broken a hip."

Oh God; something else to terrify her. Recovering from a broken hip could take months that would set Mom's recovery back immeasurably.

"No broken bones," was the next report, "but she hasn't

regained consciousness. We'll do an MRI as soon as the staff get in."

Regional hospital or not, it wasn't huge. They probably didn't need MRIs run in the middle of the night very often.

Nodding her understanding, Jordan felt herself sag. This time, when Tom wrapped her in a reassuring embrace, she let herself lean into him and shed a few tears against his sturdy shoulder. What would she have done without him?

Called one of Mom's friends, she supposed. Bonnie would have come in a heartbeat, for example, but she'd have needed to talk and talk…and a hug from her wouldn't have been the same.

Maybe, Jordan thought, she'd isolated herself from old friends more than she needed to. The thing was, their lives had moved on, and she'd been conscious of how little they had in common with her on those occasions she'd encountered one or the other at the grocery store or post office.

She could just hear herself say, *You haven't been interviewed by a police detective? Why, you haven't lived until that happens!*

Plus, she bet the few female friends who weren't married could go out with a guy they'd met as many times as they wanted without condemning him to death.

Speaking of police…she wondered why Tom hadn't asked about the cops he'd seen on her doorstep. Or did he already know from neighbors or people at work?

More people filtered into the waiting room when morning arrived. Jordan kept a wary eye out for anyone who looked familiar. What if Steve's mother had some health blip and Kevin brought her to the ER? Oh, Lord—she'd been lucky not to see either of them so far. Of course, that would be because she left the house only to accomplish essential errands, and to drive Mom for checkups and tests here at the hospital.

And to run. But why would Kevin Dunn be in her neighborhood by happenstance to see her go by? One thing she had done when she first came home was look him up to be sure he didn't live nearby.

Unless he knew she was home and was keeping an eye on her? Creepy thought. He and his mother and plenty of Steve's friends had made it known that they believed Jordan had murdered her husband, who would never have attacked her. Not the sainted Steve Dunn.

She sighed, made herself straighten, and went back to staring at the closed double doors she had yet to be allowed to go through.

TOM HAD FORGOTTEN he was a cop, far less a detective investigating this woman, from the minute her call had pulled him from sleep. He had hated hearing how frantic she was. Given that he had medical training to deal with many emergencies, he'd shot out of bed and across the street. Seeing fear in those warm brown eyes that had to be genuine, he wouldn't have left Jordan's side even if their acquaintance was as casual as she believed it to be. She needed someone, and he found he didn't at all mind being that person.

She smelled good. Shampoo, maybe, but he liked the sweetness. He'd come close to burying his face in her hair several times during the night. He liked her slender bone structure, the generous breasts he was careful not to inadvertently glance at, and the strength that ensured every time a medical professional appeared, she sat or stood straight up on her own.

He wondered if she questioned her decision to trust him this far.

They'd sat together in near silence for a lot of hours when she turned those troubled eyes on him and asked, "Are your parents alive?"

He hesitated long enough for her to say, "It's none of my business. You don't have to—"

He interrupted. "I don't know."

Her eyes widened. "How can you not know?"

"I grew up in the foster care system. There are plenty of us in this country who did."

"But…weren't you told about, I don't know, your mother at least?"

"They guessed she was a teenager who couldn't keep me. I was dropped at a fire station. Since I was obviously premature, I had to stay in the hospital for a couple of months. There were concerns that I'd have ongoing health issues, which kept me from appealing to adoptive parents who wanted a baby."

Her mouth fell open. "That stinks!"

She wasn't thinking of her mother now. Maybe that's why he forced himself to go on, talk about something he usually kept to himself.

His mouth twitched in a half smile at her vehemence. "You're right. It does. I also understand. When people have a child with problems, they usually deal. Taking on one that isn't yours is different."

Jordan snorted.

He laughed. "It wasn't that bad. After a few short placements, I ended up in a really solid foster home for years until my foster dad had an early heart attack. One of those things where he just dropped dead on an outdoor basketball court where he was playing a pickup game. There was a flaw in his heart, and it kicked in."

Her gaze hadn't once left his since he started talking. "How old were you?"

Had she even blinked?

"Twelve."

"Oh." She seemed to wrench her gaze away at last. The

pause drew on long enough, Tom began to think it was up to him to fill it, but then she said, "That's how old I was when my parents got divorced."

"Tough age."

"Is any age good to lose your father?" Anger and something else infused her voice.

The background info he was given hadn't mentioned her father. Now he wondered whether that gap didn't hold critical insights into her psychology.

She shook herself. "Oh, I don't know why I started this conversation."

"Hey, what else do we have to do?" He managed a wry smile. "It's...natural to think about your parents when one of them is in the hospital." The way his foster father died, he'd only attended the funeral. "Did you keep seeing your father?"

"No. I never saw him again, and he didn't even really say goodbye." She was back to staring at the doors into the ER, but probably wasn't actually seeing them. "I...grieved for a long time. I built him up into something he never was. It took me forever to admit that he hadn't been that great a parent." She shrugged. "He became a long-haul truck driver, which meant he was gone a lot. That would have been okay if he'd been more *present* when he was home, but he tended to drink a lot of beer and watch sports. Maybe it was different when I was younger, but... I don't remember. I'm pretty sure he wasn't much of a husband, either. I guess one day he just announced he could find a better berth between hauls and walked out."

She did turn her head then, and the pain in her eyes was very apparent. "Mom never faltered, and I always knew it was for *me*. I know how lucky I was. Because...because she tried so hard, I felt protective of her, too. You know?"

Tom didn't say anything—platitudes wouldn't help—but

he took her hand and held on. That was one question answered. She could well have felt she had to hide the problems in her marriage from her mother.

"I can't lose her." Her eyes swam with tears for only the
second time of the night. "I can't."

"Hey." He bent far enough to kiss the top of her head.
"Here's the doctor again."

"Oh, God." Jordan swiped frantically at the tears and
straightened. "Dr. Pratt?"

This time, the middle-aged woman was smiling. Jordan
shot to her feet, but the doctor came to them and sank down
in a chair.

"I'm glad to say, your mother has regained consciousness. Aside from the concussion itself, she has a headache
and some bruises, but that's all. We want to keep her for at
least another twenty-four hours, but you can come back and
see her now if you'd like."

"Please." Jordan quivered like a deer in that second before it sprang away.

Weariness on her face, the doctor laughed. "Only you,"
she warned, and Tom nodded his understanding.

Jordan whirled to face him. "I should have thought of this.
If you want to go home, I can—"

"No, Jordan." He took her hand again and squeezed. "I
don't mind waiting. Take your time."

The shimmer of tears in her beautiful eyes gave him a
kick in his chest. Damn, he had to watch this. If she found
out—no, *when* she found out—there'd be no forgiveness,
even though tonight hadn't been about his job at all.

Uh-huh. He hadn't volunteered information on his own
background just so she'd open up about her own? That wasn't
about the job?

Weirdly, he wasn't sure it had been, but she wouldn't believe that, would she?

He felt a little sick as he watched her walk away and disappear through those doors.

JORDAN WALKED ALONG when her mother was moved upstairs to a room. She'd gotten used to the physical damage from the stroke, but now her awareness of Mom's fragility shook her.

She tried to hide that. When her mother grabbed her hand—the one Tom had held for so much of the night—and said in that slurred voice, "I was so silly! All I did was make more trouble. I'm so sorry!"

"You have no reason to be sorry," Jordan said sternly. "I don't want to hear it. You're a smart woman who thought she could do something as simple as go to the bathroom by herself. You just haven't adjusted to your muscle loss. And with the help of all those evil therapists working you so hard, you'll regain your strength before you know it."

"If I just hadn't worn my slippers. One of them got tangled up, and…"

Jordan vaguely recalled seeing a slipper lying in the hall. The other must be in the bathroom. "How about we buy you a new pair that aren't so floppy?"

A sound startlingly like a giggle came out of her mother. "*I'm* floppy!"

A laugh burst out, and the two of them kept laughing long enough to let go of some of the awful tension.

Mom settled down after that and was asleep within minutes. Jordan sat there for another twenty minutes, but she felt guilty about leaving Tom waiting, and anyway… She was exhausted.

She slipped out in the hall and told the nurse who'd settled her mother that she was going home for a nap but would be back this afternoon.

Then she went back downstairs and found Tom in the same chair, seemingly engrossed reading something on his phone. When he heard her footsteps, though, he looked up with a smile.

"Everything okay?"

"Yes!" Then she made a face. "Except I need a nap."

"You and me both." His grin presumably wasn't intended to be sexy, but she couldn't help noticing the way it deepened a crease in one cheek and flashed even white teeth. Foster kid or not, he'd obviously had excellent dental and orthodontic care.

Or had been born with perfect teeth.

She had to be giddy.

The daylight startled her when they got outside. He rested a hand on her back as they walked out to where he'd left his truck in the parking lot. She noticed the contact, but it felt normal after the last twelve hours when he'd been touching her much of the time.

His hand *almost* touched her butt when he boosted her up into the passenger seat before slamming the door.

When he got in, she said, "Why do you drive something so humungous?"

His sidelong grin was even sexier, if that was possible. "Because I like big trucks?"

She blew a raspberry.

He laughed. "I bought it new after I accepted the job here. It seemed sensible for hard winters. Looks like a fair amount of snowfall is the norm."

He was right. She should upgrade her tires.

Warm air barely had time to start blowing before they pulled up to the curb in front of her house. He turned off the engine as she reached for the door handle but turned to face him.

"I don't know how to begin to thank you."

He shook his head. "I'll walk you to your door."

"You don't need—"

He hopped out before she could finish her sentence and circled around to meet her. "Feeling better?"

"Yes!" She was going to crash anytime, she knew she was, but right now she buzzed with giddy energy. "I want to dance!" A tune came to her, and she started to hum "I Could Have Danced All Night," from *My Fair Lady*. She didn't remember the rest of the lyrics, but she held out her arms as if she had a partner and began to twirl across the driveway.

To her astonishment, Tom bowed formally and held out a hand. "May I have this dance?"

Laughing, she laid her hand in his, and they began to waltz, albeit in a very confined space. Only for a few minutes, but her heart had swelled by the time they slowed, and he smiled down ather.

"You can waltz."

"Took ballroom dance in college." This smile was more wry. "To impress a girl, of course. Haven't done it since."

"Most people our age don't." Wow. She had to blink to bring the world into focus. "Thank you again. I think I need to lie down."

He ushered her to her front door, kissed her forehead and gently pushed her inside.

She was crossing the kitchen when it occurred to her the front door hadn't been locked. No wonder, in the frenzy of getting out of here. She did lock it behind her, thinking only about her bed...until she saw it. She froze in the doorway, staring. The covers were pulled invitingly back...and a butcher knife lay on the pillow.

She rushed to search the house, including her old bedroom upstairs. Once sure she was alone, she fell to her knees in front of the toilet and surrendered to the nausea.

Afterward, she considered photographing the scene, but what was the point? She could so easily have set this up herself, who would believe her? So she returned the knife to its place in a drawer in the kitchen, changed the sheets, dragged a chair from the dining room to brace her room door, and fell into bed. She'd think about this later.

Along with the fact that anyone at all could have seen her dancing on the driveway with her handsome neighbor. How could she have been so careless?

TOM MANAGED TO sleep for a few hours, but was awake to watch from his front window when, midafternoon, Jordan drove away, presumably to the hospital. A part of him wished he was going with her, but of course that was ridiculous. Unwise, too. He'd felt more for her since that middle-of-the-night call than he could afford. It wasn't like him to feel these stirrings.

Black widow, remember? Lures men into her web, then kills them.

He believed that was true even less than he had before. That said, he couldn't forget that plenty of general scumbags—*and* killers—also loved someone. Jordan obviously didn't blame her mother in any way for what happened with the husband, so her loyalty remained solid.

Last night, the cop in him had briefly wondered whether she might have gotten tired of taking care of her mother. The scene hadn't supported anything like that. Mom's only injury, as it turned out, was the blow to the head, which had clearly been from contact with the toilet. Not a very sure way to knock anyone off, and the risk was there that her mother would wake up exclaiming that she'd been pushed. Jordan had to know eyes would turn her way.

Plus, Jordan had called him and let him see her fear.

She couldn't be that good an actor, could she?

Damn, Tom hated knowing how she'd feel if she learned he had even briefly suspected something like that.

Circling back to the marriage, Tom might have doubted

that the husband—Steve Dunn—was abusive, except that about six months before the blowup when she shot the guy, he'd taken her to an emergency room. Not here in town; he'd driven her a ridiculous distance to a hospital across the state line into Washington, presumably not wanting anyone who knew either of them to see her. The injuries were classic: spiral fracture of both lower arm bones on the left side—typically caused by violently twisting the forearm—along with a broken collarbone on the right side of her body as well as bruises and a burst eardrum. There had to have been bruises. It would have taken quite a blow to burst the eardrum.

Even if Jordan had lied to protect her husband, how had nobody asked serious questions and red-flagged the visit? As a patrol officer and detective, Tom had dealt with enough domestic violence to recognize the particular injuries.

Thinking about the complex, damaged woman he was getting to know, he had a feeling that any man who tried to lay his hands on her that way now would be deeply sorry. He was also beginning to understand why she'd been susceptible to abuse at such a young age.

Father walked when she was on the cusp of womanhood, probably leaving her lacking some confidence. Handsome, popular guy wants *her*—of course she'd be dazzled. Then the slow progression to turn her into an abused wife—a slap, a blow, apologies and even gifts, a teenage Jordan dazed enough to wonder if it all wasn't her fault.

What she'd said tonight had given him a clue about why she hadn't left the guy early on and gone home to mommy. Pride, first. Who wanted to make their first big decision as an adult and have to admit within months that it had been a whopping mistake? But worse, in her case: she wanted to protect her mother from upsetting news. She'd likely been afraid her mother would blame herself because of her own failed marriage and the impact it had had on her child. No,

Jordan had told herself she could deal with it—and maybe she'd even believed that, if good ol' Steve was still apologizing and doing his best to convince her that theirs was a love match, he'd just been under a lot of stress, it wouldn't happen again.

By the book.

Unless, Tom thought, *I'm fooling myself because I like the woman.*

Entirely too much.

Yeah, her marriage had been a disaster, but it sounded as if she'd given the man she'd initially loved every chance. Tom's reaction to that was complicated, given that he'd spent a lifetime wondering why his biological mother hadn't made even the smallest effort to keep him.

He was usually good at detachment, necessary for a homicide detective and coming naturally to a kid who'd been tossed around in the foster care system. If he'd ever needed it, it was now.

He had to reserve judgment. Investigate, instead of trusting what information he'd been given. Try to draw Jordan in, sure, but only because he was undercover for that express purpose. Any kind of relationship would not end well, no matter how his investigation turned out, but he couldn't worry about that. Instead, he'd take ruthless advantage of the opening her mother's fall had given him.

He'd start with a call this evening, a simple *How's she doing?* Couldn't go wrong with that.

He shook off the memory of sweeping Jordan around in a briefly magical dance and paced off some of his restlessness. Time for some PT, he decided, including weights. A dose of pain and suffering might get his head in the right place, too.

Chapter Eight

Jordan had never fallen into friendship so fast. She wouldn't even let herself *think* that it might be more. Unless and until the police, here or in Walla Walla, arrested a killer, she could never *have* more. She wasn't even sure she was capable of more.

Yet Tom was just *there* when she wanted to talk. After Mom's doctors decided to keep her a second night, he insisted on coming with Jordan to pick her up the next morning—although they took her car, given the height disadvantage of his SUV.

Jordan hovered closer to home for a few days, but once the awful bruise on her mother's face began to fade and she insisted the headache was gone, running seemed like a good option to de-stress and get out of the house. She hesitated the first time, but it would be rude not to call Tom and find out if he wanted to come, wouldn't it? Honestly, she was surprised he was home—he seemed to work remotely most of the time—but, after all, an increasing number of Americans did work remotely these days.

She'd actually looked up the parks and recreation department to find there were a whole lot more parks than she'd realized, including trails, picnic grounds and ball fields. The rangers apparently had the power to issue anything from a

ticket to taking someone in custody for a misdemeanor of-
fense. Who knew? She didn't see his name listed, but the
site probably hadn't been updated recently.

The air was crisp and cold when the two of them set out.
Their breaths puffed out in clouds. It seemed to her he was
moving with less stiffness, although she could tell he hurt
by the time they got back to their block. Whether it was true
or not, Tom insisted doctors and physical therapists assured
him that running was a good exercise unless he pushed it to
the point of excessive pain.

"Oh, I've had plenty of PT," he said ruefully. "Your mom
and I have more in common than she knows."

After all he'd done, it seemed only decent to invite him
to dinner.

As they trotted to a stop mid-street between their houses,
he gave her a surprised glance.

"You sure? I don't want to make more work for you."

"I cook every night. I won't guarantee fine dining."

His devastating grin came close to buckling her knees
given their already weakened state. "I'm not a fancy guy."

"But you know how to waltz," Jordan teased.

He laughed as he walked away.

She'd never tell him that she'd put more effort into the
meal than she did on an average day. Mom ate like a bird,
so cooking for her benefit wasn't very satisfying.

Jordan felt uneasy when she watched Tom approach from
across the street and come up to the front porch even though
there was no reason anyone would think he was here for her.
Whoever hated her so much couldn't be watching *all* the
time, and neighbors had always come by this house even
before Mom's stroke.

Unless they'd also seen him running with her.

We're not dating, she told herself firmly, and let him in
before he even had time to ring the doorbell.

She felt as if she were in a lull—maybe the eye of the hurricane would be a better analogy. Every time she opened the mailbox, she expected to find a rattlesnake coiled and ready to strike, but nothing threatening came. Until the knife, the helium balloon was the last suggestion someone was watching her, and that had been months ago. If she hadn't so carelessly left the front door unlocked, she wanted to think the knife thing wouldn't have happened. Was her enemy mostly satisfied because, once again, the police suspected her of a murder? But so far, the investigation seemed to have stalled, probably because there was no physical evidence to connect her to the crime, just as there'd been none back in Walla Walla.

What would happen if this murder dwindled into a cold case? Would some guy she'd chatted to briefly at the grocery store be killed?

Or—oh, God, the nice guy who lived across the street from her? The one she'd spent more time with than she had any of the men she'd dated before their deaths?

But she wasn't dating Tom Moore, and she wouldn't. She convinced herself that's what mattered. What relationship she had with him didn't fit the pattern.

Over the course of the week, they ran again together. He showed up unannounced once, tools in hand, to work on the railing framing the front porch steps. He'd noticed one side wasn't quite solid.

"I know your mother goes out the back," he said, "but that'll change." When he was finished, he left without saying anything.

Jordan invited him to dinner again. He was all but offering to let her and Mom, too, lean on him. She owed him. Plus, he had devoured that first meal, making her suspect he might normally subsist on microwavable meals from the frozen food case at the store.

That evening, Jordan served a spicy vegetarian chili that she and her mother both liked and added corn bread and defrosted home-baked oatmeal and raisin cookies that had come from Mrs. Welsh in the house on the corner.

As they ate, Tom asked Mom about her physical therapy. What she didn't mind doing, what she dreaded.

"Like exercising to make me stronger," her mother said after a moment. Her speech had noticeably become clearer, but so slowly Jordan was surprised in that moment at how easy she was to understand.

Certainly Tom understood her, because he nodded. "I felt that way, too, even if it hurts sometimes."

"What…happened to you?" Mom asked.

Would he answer?

His hesitation was noticeable, but finally he said, "I was shot. Multiple times." Seeing their expressions, he grimaced. "Yes, it happens to park rangers occasionally, too, especially in a big city. I approached a guy we'd been keeping an eye on. He didn't want to talk. He opened fire instead." His voice thickened. "A friend was killed, too."

Another ranger, presumably.

Her mother lifted a shaky hand and reached out farther than Jordan had known she could with her weak arm. She laid the hand on Tom's arm. He looked down, up quickly at Jordan, letting her see how moved he was, then pressed his own hand over her mother's.

"Thank you," he said quietly, that deep resonance in his voice giving Jordan goose bumps.

Once everyone had time to take a couple more bites, he smiled at her mother. "We got sidetracked. Which PT do you like least?"

This answer required Jordan to translate, although she tried not to make it obvious that's what she was doing. "Occupational and sometimes speech? I didn't know that, Mom."

Her mother's frustration trying to explain distressed Jordan and, she thought, Tom, but the gist became clear. Therapists often assumed she didn't know *how* to do something, when in fact she did. She just *couldn't* do it because of limited physical ability. "I'm not a child."

When Jordan walked Tom to the front door, she said, "I know I keep thanking you, but I have to do it again. I never thought to ask whether she felt all her PT was useful. I'm glad you got her talking."

"There may still be reasons why her doctor will insist they keep on," he warned.

"But at least I know to talk to them." She lifted a hand and realized in horror she wanted to lay it on his chest. Curling her fingers, she snatched the hand back.

His eyebrows rose, and there was a peculiar pause, the kind where oxygen seemed to be lacking. It must be the way he was looking at her, his blue eyes so intent she had to fight the desire to sway toward him.

No, no, no! She couldn't afford a complication like this. They were becoming friends, that's all.

Suddenly, he shuttered his expression. "Good night, Jordan," he said in a low rumble, and let himself out.

She hustled to the window and watched him cross the street in reverse, his passage obvious thanks to the light at the corner.

For a second time in a matter of minutes, the very air seemed to be stolen from her. What if somebody had let themselves into his house and was waiting?

Her rib cage tightened. She should back off. Make it coolly apparent she and Mom didn't need him.

Only, she hadn't felt alone this past week the way she had for so many years. She'd never tell him that; it would be completely normal for him to make friends through work, start seeing a woman, and as Mom regained her normal capabilities, do little more than wave at her or Jordan when he saw them coming or going.

Would it be so bad to soak in his strength and calm good nature while he offered it?

CHIEF GUTHRIE WAS of the opinion that the recent lack of the kind of threats Jordan had claimed she'd gotten previously made it pretty plain she'd made them up...or was responsible for them herself. Otherwise, why nothing since the helium balloon, which she'd destroyed and thrown away without giving a single thought to saving it to show police?

"If she has a stalker, he or she could be satisfied by the intense scrutiny Ms. Hendrick has been under after the latest murder," Tom suggested in their latest face-to-face. He'd have preferred not to chance ever being seen with the police chief, but Guthrie liked a more concrete connection.

Now pulling out his wallet to pay for the lunch they had shared at a hole-in-the-wall café, the chief grunted his dissatisfaction at Tom's point. "Just don't get soft on her."

Tom raised his eyebrows. "You seem to have made up your mind about her, which is just as dangerous."

Guthrie nodded genially at a constituent as they walked out. Only when they paused before parting in the parking lot did he half complain, "Doesn't seem like you're getting anywhere with this."

"Being undercover has advantages, but also a lot of disadvantages. I can't do any investigation into people from her past who might be targeting her. I've compiled a list from social media and started researching backgrounds, but that's the best I can do. Even if she is the black widow you want to think her, these deaths have occurred several years apart. No, the latest was, what, six months after the killing in Walla Walla? Still a break. What makes you think she's going to change that? It wouldn't be smart, not when she knows you're suspicious. In fact, it might be a good tactic if your investigators appear to be backing off. If we're looking at someone besides Ms. Hendrick, he might be angry that she's not being punished the way he thinks she should be."

Guthrie scowled. "My guys won't like it, though. Everyone hereabouts has an opinion about her. But yeah, fine. They're not learning a damn thing, anyway."

Maybe because there was nothing *to* learn from Jordan? Tom carefully didn't say that. He did question whether anyone had looked into the doctor's background, as would be standard. His murder could be completely unrelated to the assault on Elliott Keefe.

The chief snapped, "Of course we did. You concentrate on the Hendrick woman. Push her a little. Dating a man is the trigger, for her or for someone else. You're ideally situated, just the way we planned."

"And she's wary."

"Tempt her then!" Guthrie walked away.

Irritated, Tom watched him go before going to his own vehicle. *Tempt her.* Damn it, *he* was dangerously tempted by *her.* The identification of the killer aside, the idea of setting himself up to be shot again had a cooling effect every time he thought about doing something as foolish as kissing the woman. What's more, that felt like crossing an ethical line that repelled him.

Growling under his breath, he headed over to his office at the parks department. The one he'd been assigned to maintain his cover, just as everyone who worked there knew to take messages for Head Ranger Moore.

So far, there'd been not one. Even the local newspaper remained unaware of a new hire who didn't actually do anything except spend time on the internet in that otherwise pristine office.

He brooded for a while about the pushback he was getting

from the chief. *Everyone hereabouts has an opinion about her.* What did that mean? Had Guthrie included himself? Tom sure wasn't satisfied with what details from the investigation he'd been fed. Or maybe it was more what *hadn't* been done or had been left out of reports. Whatever Guthrie claimed, this department hadn't seriously considered the possibility that Jordan was a secondary victim. Because that meant the killer was a local? One of those people who had "an opinion about her"?

He didn't see Jordan or her mother that evening, although he kept an eye on the lights in their house. When he'd first moved in here, he hadn't thought there was a chance in hell that Shelly Hendrick had any chance of truly recovering from what had clearly been a devastating stroke. Now, he was impressed by her. Inspired, too; he knew how hard she had to be working, how discouragement must feel like a high wall in front of her, one she had to knock down brick by brick. She was a gutsy woman, he'd concluded—as was her daughter.

He was always an early riser no matter what time he'd gone to bed. Tom made a habit of starting his mornings with coffee—and, these days, a look out the window at the Hendricks' house. He didn't know what he expected to see—A moving truck backed into the driveway? An ambulance? Fire bursting from every window?—but he had a growing sense of disquiet where his investigation was concerned.

Did he just *want* to believe she was the victim, not the killer? Max had always accused him of being too soft on women. Was it true? Tom would have given a lot to be able to toss around ideas about this investigation with Max.

Growling under his breath, Tom carried his first cup of coffee and strolled into the living room where he had the best view of the houses across the street.

The kitchen was at the back of the Hendrick house, so if

the light was on, he couldn't tell. Jordan typically seemed to get up mornings as early as he did. Otherwise... He frowned.

There was...something on the front window. And the garage door?

He set down the mug on a side table, let himself out of his house and trotted at a slant toward Jordan's. He didn't like not carrying, but his cover wouldn't last long if he always wore a shoulder or ankle holster. The back of his neck prickling, he wasn't halfway when he made out the addition to the garage door: spray-painted in bloodred, all in capital letters, the single word *KILLER*.

Swearing, he switched his gaze to the glass of the front window. Smaller of necessity, *KILLER* was spray-painted there, too.

And then he saw the same word sprayed on the driver's-side window of Jordan's car.

He took the steps two at a time, pausing only long enough to touch the paint and determine that it wasn't going to wipe off easily, before he knocked lightly on the door. He hoped Jordan's mother was still asleep. Quiet footsteps approached, there was a pause while Jordan likely checked on who the visitor was through the peephole, and she opened the door.

"Tom?"

He ignored the momentary hit the first sight of her often gave him. He especially liked seeing her first thing in the morning, when she looked less closed up, softer, as if she hadn't donned her armor.

"You need to come out here," he said grimly.

Those caramel-brown eyes widened. "What...?" But she didn't finish the question, instead stepping over the threshold. Her gaze followed the direction of his outstretched hand and she saw the lettering.

"Oh God. Oh God!" She sounded frantic. "I have to clean it off! If people *see* it—"

With her horror so convincing, he hated to say this, but did. "It's on your garage door, too. And your car."

Shoulder brushing him, she ran down the stairs, almost falling on the last two. She was still barefoot, he saw, following her as she ran far enough down the walkway to be able to see both her car and the detached garage.

"Oh God," she said again. "Everybody will see. This will never end!"

"You need to call 911. I don't know what's going on here—" the hell he didn't "—but this is a threat."

Her shoulders sagged as she stared at the two-foot-tall lettering. "Yes. I'll do that." She almost laughed, but without any humor whatsoever. "For what good it'll do."

"You need to get some shoes on, too. It's cold this morning."

Jordan looked down at her feet as if she wasn't sure what he was talking about, then nodded numbly. "I'll have plenty of time before an officer responds."

He could get a faster response for her, but that wouldn't be a good idea. Instead, he walked her back to the porch and said, "I'll circle the house. Make sure the vandal didn't bother with any other surfaces."

A pained sound escaped her as she opened the door. "Thank you."

"Jordan?"

She went still, her back to him.

"You going to explain this to me?"

It was a long moment before her shoulders stiffened again, and she said, "Yes, but…not now."

He made sure he spoke gently. "Okay."

His last glance back saw her on the front porch, phone in hand.

SOMETHING ABOUT THE paint job on her car disturbed her most. The other lettering was sloppy, but this was more de-

liberately done; one leg of the *K* almost looked like an arrow
pointing downward. She was sure she'd locked the car door,
she always did, but when she tried it, it opened. Probably
she shouldn't be touching the car, but—

Was that her driver's license lying facedown on the floor
in front of the gas pedal? How could it be? She bent and
picked it up, gave a stifled cry and dropped it. That wasn't
her license—it was Colin Parnell's. Her teeth chattered. That
it was in her car was meant to implicate her further in the
murder. And, oh God, it now had her fingerprints on it.

Tom would reappear any minute. *Pocket the license...?
No. Push it out of sight under the seat. Lock the door. Close
it.*

She had barely done so when she saw the first police unit
coming down the street. At least there were no sirens. Jordan had to be grateful for that. She'd asked, but sometimes
thought cops all loved drawing as much attention as possible.

Otherwise, Tom determined there was no paint in her garage to cover the writing, so he volunteered to go pick some
up, as well as any products he could find that would clean
the paint off glass.

While he was gone, it seemed as if every member of the
Storm Lake Police Department, from the newest rookie—
who'd been the first responder—to Chief Allen Guthrie
showed up to take a look. She watched, stiff as a porch upright, scared to death.

Detective Wilson—yes, he'd evidently received his promotion—and Deputy Chief Ronald Bowen finished studying—or were they admiring?—the spray-painting and
interrogated her. As always, Wilson sounded almost pleasant, but with a hint of "don't think you're going to fool me"
thrown in. The deputy chief balanced him by the contempt
overlaid by a veneer of civility. Other people might not notice, but his attitude wasn't much better than Buzz's. She

could just imagine the result if she demanded a replacement for him, too.

Jordan responded to questions by rote. No, neither she nor her mother had heard a sound all night. No, she didn't own any cans of spray paint—or cans of any kind of paint, for that matter, unless there were some old ones in the back of the garage. If they found the can of red spray paint, it wouldn't have her fingerprints on it because it wasn't hers.

Detective Wilson asked what she thought the point of the vandalism was. Beside him in the living room, Deputy Chief Bowen raised his eyebrows in challenge.

"Whoever is doing this must be frustrated," she said wearily. "You haven't arrested me. It's a nasty accusation for me, but it's also aimed at you. He clearly thinks he's set me up so well, you're incompetent because you haven't arrested me."

She could tell they didn't like that assessment. If she hadn't hidden the driver's license and locked the car door before they got here, she was chilled to know they'd have had reason to arrest her.

Tom walked into the living room as she finished.

"Mom's in the kitchen," she told him. "The occupational therapist is staying until, well, we're done."

He nodded at her, then at both cops, and went straight through the house toward the kitchen. Thank goodness— Mom was so upset by the events, she was gabbling more than actually speaking, and mad because her tongue wouldn't keep up.

Looking back at the two cops, she said, "I can't tell you anything else. Please let me go to work cleaning and painting."

They glanced at each other. Bowen grunted and heaved his weight to his feet. "I believe we have adequate photographs. Unfortunately, because your driveway and walkway are both paved and the past few days have been dry, there are no visible footprints. We haven't found the spray can, either, which isn't surprising."

She could see in his eyes what he was thinking: because they didn't have a warrant to search the house top to bottom, there were plenty of places she could have hidden an object that size until she saw an opportunity to dispose of it.

Standing to let them out, she felt exhaustion settle down on her as a crushing weight. She even swayed slightly. How much more of this unrelenting suspicion could she bear? It wouldn't stop. Whoever hated her this much wasn't done.

She stood out on the front porch for a moment, watching as the couple of remaining official vehicles drove away. After she soothed Mom again, she'd do her best to obliterate those messages. Too late, of course. She had no doubt everyone on the block and plenty of passersby, drawn by the police presence, had already seen the accusation everyone knew was aimed at *her*: KILLER.

A hand came to rest on her shoulder. She hadn't heard Tom approaching, but she felt his warmth at her back. He was being supportive…so far.

"I'll take care of the garage if you want to tackle the window," he said.

Even though, when she turned, she saw questions in his eyes, she said, "Thank you for staying."

He only nodded and loped toward the back of his SUV, now parked in her driveway.

Swallowing the lump in her throat, Jordan wondered how much he'd hang around once he heard her story…and got to wondering which parts of it were true.

Chapter Nine

It ranked right up there with the other longest mornings of her life. And gee whiz, they were all ones when police officers had shown up at her door.

When lunchtime rolled around, she found another cause for intense gratitude. Instead of ordering out—Tom must have guessed Mom would have had trouble with pizza—he took the time to make egg salad sandwiches on soft bread in their kitchen and sliced a blueberry cheesecake Mrs. Chung brought over when she came knocking to be sure Mom was okay.

"I don't understand any of this," Mom fretted at the table, although she'd calmed down some. "How could anyone think…?"

Jordan patted her mother's hand. "The police will figure it out, Mom. It's just…a nasty trick."

It occurred to her that *she* was now treating her mother like a child—maybe had been in some ways ever since she came home—but at the moment, she didn't have the energy to do anything else.

She coaxed Mom into lying down for her nap, and sneaked several peeks into the bedroom until she was sure she was asleep. Then Jordan returned to the kitchen, where Tom had efficiently cleaned up and put the remaining cheesecake in the refrigerator.

Hearing her, he turned and met her eyes. "You look like you could use a nap, too."

Her attempt at a smile had to be pitiful. "Except I'd never fall asleep." She wondered if she'd ever again be able to relax into sleep without a care. Who knew what would happen while she was oblivious?

"Why don't we sit in the living room?" he suggested.

She desperately wanted to put this off, but knew she couldn't. Imagine how he'd wonder if she sent him home, then hustled out with a hand vac and dustcloths to frantically clean the *interior* of her car, like that was the most urgent thing she could do. No, no. The police were gone, satisfied for now. Getting the driver's license out of the car and hidden could wait.

She just wished she could forget for a second the knowledge it was sitting there, a trap with sharp teeth.

She took some deep breaths for calm before focusing on the conversation she had to have with Tom. Outside would have been better, but on the front porch they could be seen, and really, it was too cold today to sit and chat outside. So she nodded.

He sank down at one end of the sofa, and after a hesitation, she chose the other end, curling one leg up. The wing chair wasn't all that comfortable, and Mom's upholstered glider...no, it was *hers*.

Tom shifted to better face her. "This isn't really my business."

"You deserve to hear about it. Anyway, you must have heard some of the background."

Gaze steady, he said, "Not enough to put the pieces together."

"*I* don't understand it. It's... I think someone is determined to ruin my life. Only, that person has to be beyond obsessive." She couldn't keep meeting Tom's sharp blue eyes.

She looked down at her hands instead. "It has to go back to my marriage. I married right out of high school, even though Mom tried to talk me out of it." Her laugh sounded broken. "Because why wouldn't that be a good idea?"

She skated over the abuse, because she didn't want this man to see her as someone who'd put up with it. Jordan did tell him, briefly, about the disastrous scene where she'd truly believed he would kill her if she didn't kill him first. When she pulled that trigger.

"I was in a coma for twenty-four hours, in the hospital for days. Eventually I learned he'd been fired from his job that day. He...seemed to be in trouble at work a lot. He didn't like to be told what to do, and he had a hair-trigger temper." This laugh wasn't any better. "How could I not know this about him? But I didn't. The thing was, at school, he didn't care much about grades and shrugged off the bad ones, and the football and baseball coaches worshipped at his feet. He really was a talented athlete, but he didn't get recruited by any top colleges. I wonder if they could tell by his grades that he didn't have the discipline they would expect? I don't know. *He* wasn't going to play for some second-tier program that might be willing to take him, so he went to work in construction right out of high school. I don't think he expected the comedown from being admired, girls flirting, guys wanting to hang out with him." She gave a short laugh. "This is a small town. Everyone came to games. I vaguely remember seeing the mayor and most of the members of the police department in the stands, or slapping Steve on the back in congratulations after a game. Everyone wanting to blame *me* for what happened isn't a surprise."

Tom didn't comment, just listened.

She shrugged awkwardly. "Our marriage started great— I thought so, anyway—then went downhill. There was one big blowup, and I was prepared to leave him, but he cried and begged me not to. I had no idea that's the way it goes with men like him. I believed he had it in him to change if I forgave him and stood beside him."

"Did you talk to your mother?"

She blinked away the water in her eyes. "Not the way I should have. In fact…most of it, I didn't tell her. Anyway, not everybody in town was convinced that I had to shoot and kill Steve, even though none of the responding police had any doubt. I was…hurt really badly. But afterward, I'd see these looks. Later, a few people came right out and said hateful things. I tried to avoid running into anyone in Steve's family, or any of his teammates and best buddies. Even with friends, I could see doubt. That's why I finally moved away."

She told him about the couple of years in Montana, getting most of an AA degree but scraping by financially, deciding to try somewhere else and moving to Washington State. "I finished the AA, started taking a few classes with a goal to eventually get a bachelor's degree, and was lucky enough to get on with the post office. The pay let me have a decent place and be able to tell Mom honestly that I was okay and didn't need financial help."

He nodded. She waited for him to ask what she'd majored in, tell her what *he'd* majored in—he had to have a degree for his level of work, didn't he?—but he didn't offer anything.

For an instant, Jordan wondered why she was being so open with him. Chances were good he'd pretend to believe her side but pull away. Why wouldn't he? Everyone else had.

But what was she supposed to do? Say, *See, three men I got involved with were attacked, two are dead, and the police think I did it.*

"I didn't date for years after…you know."

"You didn't trust men?"

"Or myself." She shrugged awkwardly. "Maybe mostly

myself. How could I? I married a man who, when he was in a bad mood, thought of me as his punching bag."

Tom's mouth tightened.

"After I moved to Walla Walla—I guess that was the first time I stayed put and didn't apartment hop—I started having some weird stuff happening. Bouquets delivered on the day Steve died. Some creepy cards. I figured Steve's brother or one of his closest friends—maybe even his mother—was holding on to enough anger to need to lash out. It wasn't like they needed to remind me. How could I ever forget that day?"

She waited a little anxiously for his nod of understanding, which comforted her more than it should.

Then she continued, "But a little over three years ago, a nice guy asked me out. I wasn't really attracted to him, but, see, that made him safer. We had two very casual dates. I doubt he'd have suggested we go out again. It was kind of a mutual shrug. Except, three or four days after we had dinner, he apparently walked into his house when some men were stripping it. He was beaten, shot and killed. A detective talked to me a few days later, but briefly. It seemed pretty obvious what happened, although there's never been an arrest."

"So they didn't associate the attack with you."

"There wasn't any reason to. I think there'd been some other similar home robberies. The homeowners just didn't walk into the middle of it. As far as the police were concerned, I was just someone who knew Pete." She sighed. "Maybe a year later, the creep campaign stepped up. Every so often I'd have this feeling someone was watching me. There'd be raps on my windows. The letters and bouquets, of course. My car got keyed. Just enough to keep me on edge."

"I didn't try dating again for three years. Elliott was a Realtor. He started flirting with me when I dropped off mail, and when he asked me out, I thought, why not?" She met

Tom's eyes even though he probably saw her desperation. "I'm ashamed to say I wasn't so much interested in him as I wanted to feel *normal*. I was a twenty-eight-year-old woman with hardly any social life."

When the man who'd gone from neighbor to, maybe, best friend so quickly reached out and took her hand in his, she gathered strength from the contact.

"We had dinner once. The next week we took a picnic to the city fireworks display. I'd driven myself, so we parted ways in the parking lot. Next thing I knew, two detectives are on my doorstep. Elliott had gone home and been attacked. Maybe shot first, they're not sure, then beaten. Police think he was left for dead. He was in a coma for days, but he did survive and recover. Unfortunately, he doesn't remember anything that happened. But my name popped up associated with the victim whose attack was similar."

Tom frowned. "Except for the burglary."

"Right." *Get this over with*, she told herself. "The detectives in Walla Walla pushed pretty hard, but they couldn't place me at the scene because I didn't even know where he lived, and we hadn't dated long beside that. They didn't let up, though, because they had no leads at all. In the middle of all that, Mom had her stroke and I came home. Those two detectives called a couple of times after I came home, but... they were mostly decent."

He nodded.

"Then, just recently an ER doctor who'd treated Mom when she was first taken to the hospital asked me out. I knew I shouldn't say yes. I *knew* it." She was probably crushing Tom's hand. "But I was still deluding myself. I kept telling myself the attack on Elliott didn't have anything to do with me. How *could* it?"

Emotions, or maybe thoughts, flickered over Tom's face. "Anything else going on back when this Elliott was attacked?"

"Yes, but I was big in denial about that, too. It was one of those weeks when I felt like a spider was crawling up the back of my neck. I kept whirling around, but there was never anyone there." Then she told him the rest of the weird stuff.

"I'm sure it goes without saying that the detectives there weren't interested in any of that."

"And here in Storm Lake? Have you noticed anything like that?"

"I get the creepy-crawlies sometimes, but people are always staring at me. Steve's death was like the biggest tragedy and scandal in Storm Lake history. There was plenty of controversy—he'd had so many friends, or really fans—that everyone thought they knew him. Football star, champion baseball pitcher? Prom king, knocking a woman around? Steve Dunn? Everyone thought I had to be lying. So I've been slinking around avoiding people I knew in high school or while I was married." And doing her best to avoid looking anyone in the eyes. "And remember, for the first month or two, I pretty much lived at the hospital. I ate three-quarters of my meals in the cafeteria. I wasn't on public display until Mom improved enough to come home and I actually started heading out on a regular basis to the grocery store, the pharmacy, the plant nursery, and working in plain sight in Mom's garden."

"I take it that brings us to the murder of the doctor. Colin Parnell?"

"Yeah. We had coffee, then a week later, dinner. He was killed that night after he got home."

Tom's gaze sharpened in a way that made her uneasy. "Someone was waiting for him?"

"They don't know, except whoever it was got into his house somehow. After arriving home—they also haven't figured out whether he went straight home or not—he apparently had time to make himself comfortable. He got a cup of coffee and was on his laptop in his home office. So it could have been half an hour after he got home, or two hours." She frowned. "Maybe the medical examiner nailed down the time closer than that. Like they'd tell me. All *I* know is that, bang, I'm the central suspect. One of the two cops who showed up the first time was a teammate and buddy of Steve's. He made his feelings about me crystal clear."

"I hope you pointed out that he was seriously biased."

"I did." She grimaced. "Not that Deputy Chief Bowen is much of an improvement. No, he is. He isn't rude, at least. I was going to lawyer up, but I haven't. What's the point? I didn't do it. I had no idea where Colin lived. I didn't know him that well. Except...he was funny and *nice*. He didn't deserve that. No one does. I can't keep my head in the sand anymore. I have to accept that he died because of *me*. Pete, I don't know. And thank God Elliott survived. But of all people to be killed, Colin was a compassionate doctor who followed how Mom was doing long after he was responsible for her. Why him?" She shook her head. "I have to believe now it was because I went out with him. He barely pecked me on the lips when he walked me to the door that night. There was no big romantic or passionate scene to make someone mad. It just doesn't make any sense!"

No, IT DIDN'T. Seeing her emotional fragility, Tom wanted to tug Jordan across the cushion that separated them and wrap her in his arms. Instead, he had to keep that distance. She'd expect him to maintain some doubt and might even be suspicious if he announced he was completely on her side and ready to fight the world for her. He had to hold back for his own sake, too. Because he had a job to do.

He had to *prove* this woman hadn't attacked any of those men. And that wasn't easy to do, mainly because they hadn't found the forensic evidence they needed either to clear her or point to other suspects. That was unusual in and of itself.

These attacks had to be meticulously planned after Jordan showed interest in a man. They were damned cold-blooded, and also clean. The killer knew how to avoid shedding trace evidence—although thanks to the plethora of cop shows and thrillers out there, everybody had some idea what not to do. Still, Tom didn't like the idea that one of Steve's best buddies was a cop who'd have learned on the job everything he needed to know to accomplish the perfect murder.

"Back to Elliott—?"

"Keefe."

"He doesn't remember whether his assailant appeared as soon as he walked in the door?" Shouldn't have used the word *assailant*, he thought, but she didn't seem to notice.

"No. He remembers parking in the garage, then going into the kitchen. After that, nothing. The head injury was bad enough, it could have wiped out hours from his memory. He wasn't discovered until the next day when he didn't come into work for some appointments." Jordan's forehead creased. "Why do you ask?"

"Just struck me you'd have had to drive like a bat out of hell to beat him home and be waiting for him."

"If only a neighbor had *seen* something. Maybe Colin would have survived, too, if he'd been found right away."

Given what Tom had seen in the autopsy report, there'd been no possibility of that. He only made a sympathetic sound.

He asked more questions, delving into the creep campaign, as she described it.

Her mouth twisted. "As things turned out, you don't know how much I wish I'd called the police. But…can you imagine what kind of response I'd have gotten? An anniversary card that you take as subtly threatening given the date you received it? Mightn't you have an admirer sending the bouquets, ma'am? Or could someone be expressing sympathy? One of your own knives left out on your counter? How can you be positive you weren't thinking about something else and took it out for some reason, then got distracted?" She made a soft, pained sound. "Even if I'd kept those notes, what are the odds they'd have any fingerprints on them except for the mail carrier's and mine? From the attitude I'm getting from police officers, they'd be sure I sent them to myself so I'd look innocent." She disentangled her hand from his and sat up, putting both feet on the floor. "The police want to blame me. They might as well be wearing blinders. Plainly, I can't trust that they'll really investigate without bias. In fact, I can't trust anyone wearing a badge. No matter what happens, I may never be able to again."

She might as well have punched him. It was all he could do not to reel at the blow. She didn't know she'd taken aim against him, but she'd hit her target all the same. Tom couldn't even blame her. He had the impression from his couple of conversations with the detectives in Walla Walla that they really were looking for other possibilities. Chief Guthrie wasn't. He'd hired Tom to go undercover because he was so damn sure she was a killer. Tom wished he'd understood sooner how biased the police chief was. He might not have taken the job, or at least not agreed to go undercover.

Now…he wouldn't go back for a redo. Jordan too badly needed someone on her side—or at least impartial.

He turned his thoughts back to the latest event. Whoever had painted that word on Jordan's house and car last night was getting impatient. But was that because he believed passionately that she was guilty? Or was the killer trying to influence the local police department because she deserved to be punished for what he saw as a crime she'd gotten away with?

The obvious was the death of her husband. But even with family, it was hard to imagine anyone fixated enough on his or her grievance to be willing to murder several people in hopes of sending Jordan to prison. Steve Dunn had died almost nine years ago. Long time to hold on to this level of rage.

Tom still believed that was exactly what was happening, but had to circle back to the hard reality that nailing down her innocence to everyone's satisfaction wouldn't be easy. It was one of those conundrums: proving someone had done something was a snap compared to proving they *didn't*. That was the very reason the US justice system insisted on the concept of without a doubt.

If he succeeded, he could be Jordan's hero—until he confessed to lying to her from the beginning.

She was withdrawing before his eyes. In fact, she rose to her feet and said, "You've wasted a lot of time on us. I appreciate it, but I won't keep you anymore."

His stomach coiled. *"Wasted?"*

"Thank you for being here again today, but I think you should go home. You do have a life."

No, actually he didn't. As things stood, *she* was his life, but he could hardly say that. What he did say was, "Don't hesitate to call," and left because that's what she wanted.

IF MOM'S ROOTS weren't thirty years deep in this town Jordan positively hated at the moment, she would have seriously considered packing Mom up and moving with her. Selling the house, finding a community where not a soul knew them.

Peering through the blinds at a car that slowed down in front of the house before abruptly speeding up, she thought, *Uh-huh*. Because starting over had gone so well for Jordan before. If someone hated her enough to kill men he didn't even know, probably hadn't met, he could find her anywhere.

Anyway, she had a number of blessings to count. Number one on her list would be Mom's many friends who kept rallying around, whatever they thought about Jordan. The hospital and care workers had been amazing, too.

Tom Moore was on that list as well. Higher than he probably should be given what a short time she'd known him—and how much about him she didn't know—but from the night Mom took that fall, he hadn't failed her. How could that not scare her?

Thank heavens, the next morning she saw him back out of his driveway and his big SUV disappear. Jordan wasn't sure how much longer she could have waited.

She told her mother what she was up to—minus her actual motivation—then assembled what she needed to detail the interior of her old car, unlocked all the doors and the trunk, and set to work. She searched the trunk first, in case another little surprise had been left for her, then vacuumed the thin carpet that covered the wheel well.

Classic avoidance: she started with the back seat, ashamed of the trash she'd ignored, then took out the floor mats, and vacuumed thoroughly.

Front seat, passenger side next. Ditto. More vacuuming, and she used a spray bottle and clean cloth to clean the door and dashboard.

She'd just wiped the glove compartment when she thought, *can't skip that.* Fortunately, there wasn't a lot in it except for the official papers, a flashlight and a few receipts.

By this time, her heart was hammering. Around to the driver's side. What if the license was *gone*? No, that would negate the whole purpose.

She took out the floor mats, shook them and vacuumed them, then groped under this seat, too. The first thing her hand touched on was Colin Parnell's Idaho State driver's license. For an instant, she let herself look at his face. He was one of those rare people who looked good in a DMV photo. Along with his warm smile, a hint of humor showed in his eyes.

Jordan shuddered and whisked it into her jeans pocket.

Just to be thorough, she kept searching. There was less trash here; she supposed she too often tossed receipts, paper napkins, whatever, on the passenger seat. But then she touched something stiff that might have kept the seat from sliding on its track if she ever had reason to move it.

She knew, even before she pulled it out. Another driver's license, this one from Washington State. Elliott looked straight at her from the photo.

Chapter Ten

Had this license been left on the seat, too, right after Elliott was attacked, but she'd hopped in with her arms laden and unknowingly brushed it off? Thank God there hadn't been any evidence that would have allowed those detectives to get a warrant. Why hadn't anyone ever said that each man's driver's license was missing? Maybe Elliott hadn't noticed until way later and hadn't associated it with the assault, but *someone* should have seen that Colin's was missing from his wallet.

She pushed this license into her other pocket, hurriedly finished her cleaning job, and dashed inside.

Who would believe her if she admitted finding these? But she shook her head instantly. Nobody.

The next question was, where best to hide them?

Because it had momentarily crossed her mind that Tom was the one person she might be able to talk to, she set about avoiding him. She waited until she saw him leave in his huge SUV before she set out to run, and once she pretended not to hear the doorbell when she knew it was him standing on the welcome mat. It wasn't right to keep depending on him when there was so much wrong with her life. Face it: she'd become a Jonah. Bad luck followed her. No, be honest: *deadly* luck followed her.

A few days after the vandalism, a photo of Mom's garage made the Storm Lake weekly newspaper. Thank goodness Jordan had carried the paper into the house along with that day's mail before she opened it to see the front page. In black and white, the words didn't have quite the same impact, but it was bad enough. The caption read, *Vigilantism in our town?*

At least it didn't say, *A killer in our town?*

The editor wouldn't have dared. That would have been inviting a lawsuit.

The article was brief, every word carefully chosen. The writer did remind any reader who'd forgotten that Jordan Hendrick, a graduate of Storm Lake High School, had killed her husband in self-defense eight and a half years ago. They didn't say, in *possible* self-defense, but the reminder alone whispered, *A killer does live in that house.*

Jordan slumped in her chair, aware of the murmur of voices from the kitchen where a speech therapist worked with Mom, but focused on her own whirling thoughts. There was no hope of hiding the paper from her mother. Poring over every page including the classifieds was part of her routine. She'd demand Jordan go buy another copy if this week's had apparently failed to be delivered. Anyway, someone would have a big mouth.

Not like Mom hadn't shuffled out onto the porch to see "KILLER" painted on her front window anyway.

Feeling sick, Jordan bent forward and rested her forehead on the table. Would this ever end?

The doorbell pealed, and she jerked. Maybe she'd be lucky and this would be a neighbor instead of cops back for round six or eight. She'd lost track.

It was Tom on the doorstep, and he looked mad. "Did you see your newspaper?"

She smiled wryly. "How could I miss it?"

"I'm sorry," he said simply, and stunned her by pulling her into his arms.

For a moment, she stood there stiffly...but then she collapsed against him. Not to cry, just because she *needed* his strength and solid body. She flung her arms around his waist and held on for dear life. That had to be his cheek resting on her head. His chest rumbled with words she didn't even try to make out. This felt like more than reassurance.

Jordan kept clinging even as awareness of him as a man, not a friend, stirred in her. His powerful thighs pressed hers, and her breasts were flattened on his broad, muscular chest.

She couldn't let him see what she was feeling. She didn't dare *feel* any of this. But when she finally summoned the will to step away, that involved lifting her head and looking at him.

His gaze flickered down to her mouth, and she knew: he was thinking about kissing her.

And right this second, there was nothing in the world she wanted more than that.

TOM DIPPED HIS HEAD, as he'd wanted to do almost from the first moment he set eyes on Jordan. He wouldn't have been surprised if she'd yanked away, or at least pretended she didn't know what was about to happen, but instead she parted her lips and—damn, was she rising slightly on tiptoe? Yes!

Her lips were soft and sweet, the hum in her throat exciting him. He pressed and nibbled, and waited while she did the same back. And then, God help him, he slid his tongue into her mouth, rubbing sensuously against hers. He didn't sense any resistance, but she met the kiss awkwardly, as if she didn't quite know what she was doing. Had it really been so long—?

She had to know how aroused he was. His hands had been

moving without conscious thought on his part. One cupped her butt and lifted her. The other had slid up to her nape. He plunged his fingers in hair as silky as he'd imagined and held the back of her head so he could improve the angle for deep, long kisses that grew in urgency.

Jordan whimpered, and he thought he might have groaned. He needed to think this through...but right now, he wasn't capable of that kind of reason.

He ground his erection against her softer body and nipped her lip. She tried to climb him. Fine by him. He could help with that—

Background voices seemed to be gaining in volume.

"You're doing so well, Mrs. Hendrick! I don't think you're going to need me for much longer."

Tom tried to process that. He knew who *he* needed, but that didn't make sense. Then, suddenly, it did. Oh, hell! He and Jordan weren't alone.

He lifted his head, made himself lift Jordan away. "Sweetheart. Your mother is coming."

Her lashes fluttered. "What?" Then an expression of horror crossed her face and she backed into the doorframe with a bump. "Oh, no! What are we *doing*?"

Stung, he said, "We kissed. That's all."

"We can't let anybody *see* us," she cried...and his brain kicked back in gear.

She was right—and not only was the therapist coming, but also judging from the tap of the cane so was her mother. Worse yet, he and Jordan still stood on the threshold. Front door wide open, *any*one could have seen them.

"No, no!" Jordan keep retreating, expression panicked, cheeks flushed...her eyes holding both shock and the remnants of passion. He hadn't been alone in that firestorm.

"Oh, Jordan," her mother called. "Is somebody here?"

Tom said, "Just me, Mrs. Hendrick. Wanted to check on

you two." Remembering suddenly what he had come over for, he looked down, disconcerted, to see that he'd dropped the damn newspaper. In fact, he'd crumpled it beneath the sole of his boot.

"Did anybody drive by?" Jordan whispered urgently. "Or…or…"

Walk by? How would he know? He'd been that unconscious of their surroundings, something that hadn't happened to him in years. Cops couldn't *let* themselves be oblivious.

A lump in his throat, he said, "I don't know. But I'm taller and wider than you are. I doubt anyone could see past me."

"It wouldn't have been hard to tell what you were doing. And you wouldn't have been—"

Kissing her mother? Yeah, no stretch for an observer to guess his partner in that steamy embrace.

In a low voice, he said, "I'm not as vulnerable as the men who'd been attacked. You know I carry a gun." Would it make a difference if he'd introduced himself as a cop from the beginning?

Sure it would have—she wouldn't have given him the time of day.

After one wild look at him, she stepped to the side, giving a less than convincing smile to the middle-aged woman waiting for them to quit blocking the doorway. "Nora, thanks for coming."

Nora beamed, said goodbye to her patient, and trotted down the porch steps and to her car in the driveway as if she hadn't noticed anything.

Jordan's mother had been behind her, and probably hadn't, either. No, she was fussing because he was trampling on the newspaper, crumpling pages.

"This is my paper," he assured her mother. "I guess I dropped it."

Jordan took a deep breath. "Mom. There's a photo of the

house on the front page. You know, with the spray-painting on it. That's why Tom came over. He wanted to be sure I'd seen it."

Mrs. Hendrick stared at them in bewilderment. "Why would they put something awful like that in the paper?"

Tom glanced at Jordan, who seemed speechless, and said gently, "I guess they think it's news. There was quite a fuss here, you know. I can't remember the last time I've seen so many official vehicles in one place."

Actually, in his world, that kind of gathering was common, but usually provoked by a shooting with fatalities. He could only imagine what the scene had looked like after he and Max had been gunned down. Funny, he'd never thought to ask who had called it in. As if it mattered…except that if there had been any greater delay, he probably wouldn't have survived.

"Why don't you sit down, Mom? Our copy of the paper is on the table."

Jordan wasn't meeting his gaze, or, really, looking at him at all. Shyness? Or something else?

"Tom," she added, "thanks for telling us. It's too late for us to do anything about it, but everyone in town is already talking about me anyway." Resignation dulled her voice. She was trapped and enduring. Her only way out would be to abandon her mother, and his gut said she'd never do that. That absolute loyalty tapped something vulnerable deep in him. He'd had friends, but never anyone he knew with complete certainty would never abandon him.

He had to clear his throat. "Give me a call if you want to take a run in the morning," he said, backed the rest of the way onto the porch, gathered up the torn pages of his newspaper and left.

As he ambled across the street, pretending nothing was out of the ordinary, he scanned sidewalks, lawns, the depths of front porches. If any of the neighbors were out front, he didn't see them. That didn't mean some hadn't seen the show, then scuttled out of sight to call everyone they knew.

There wasn't a lot of traffic on this street, especially at this time of day, but casual passersby weren't what worried him. What he had to wonder was how much time her stalker was able to give to spying on her, and where he hid. At this moment, utterly exposed, Tom knew exactly what Jordan meant when she described this feeling: as if a spider was crawling up his neck.

Even more disturbing was his realization that he couldn't have staged that kiss any better if he had plotted it. Chief Guthrie would be slapping him on the back in congratulations.

After the last guy she'd dated had been murdered so recently, Tom doubted she would be willing to be seen in public with any man, even if she felt something strong for him. In fact, the more she liked him, the *less* likely she'd be to agree to a date.

Unless, of course, she was the killer. Little though he believed that, his job required him to add the usual addendum.

Either way, Tom had just accomplished much the same purpose as a date at whatever restaurant in town was most popular...assuming that embrace had been witnessed by the right—or wrong—person. Or that gossip reached that person.

There was a certain relief at letting himself into his rental house and locking the door behind him, even though somebody could be in the house already, waiting. That was improbable, but still he stooped and pulled his backup weapon. He listened to the silence before clearing the house, room by room.

He did feel just a little paranoid now. He'd already been

sleeping with his gun close at hand, but he thought it might be smart to take other precautions.

Speaking of traps, he hadn't set this one…but he was very willing to take advantage of it.

TOM WAS ABOUT to set out to spend a couple of hours in his fake office before picking up groceries when his phone rang. Jordan.

"Hey," he said, going for relaxed, "you up for a run?"

He hadn't seen her leave that morning, but he'd sure as hell seen her coming back, tearing down the street as if a pack of vicious wolves was snapping at her heels.

There was a short silence. Then, "I've already been. It was weird. I thought… Oh, never mind." She drew a shuddery breath. "I'm seeing shadows, that's all."

"Why didn't you ask me to run with you?" he asked gently.

"You know why. I can't be seen with you."

He felt a wrench in the vicinity of his heart. He didn't mind being needed; he'd protect her in any way he could. He wished he believed she trusted him—even though she shouldn't.

"I'd rather you did ask me," he assured her, marveling at his calm voice.

Damn, this had him as dizzy as if he were staggering off the kind of carnival ride that was fun when you were a kid but that he wouldn't be caught dead on anymore. Up, down, all around.

He cared about Jordan Hendrick more than he wanted to admit, even—maybe especially—to himself. He could fall for her. But always, the cynical side of him that he'd learned as an unwanted kid and honed as a cop murmured, *There's no way to prove she was followed. Did she just want to throw that out there?*

"This one of those times you felt that spider crawling up your back?"

"Something like that." She chuckled, although he didn't buy it, said, "Maybe we can run Wednesday," and pretended she needed to help her mother with something unnamed.

Tom closed his eyes. He shouldn't have agreed to this. Originally, it had seemed straightforward, as undercover work went. Keep an eye on the woman living across the street from him. Befriend her if he could. Prevent anyone from attacking her even as he tried to trick her into going after *him*.

Don't feel too much.

And lucky him, his plan for the day was to spend a couple of hours in his fake office, then break for lunch with Chief Guthrie, who insisted again on a face-to-face. Fortunately, one woman without much of a social network was unlikely to hear that he was hanging out with the police chief.

JORDAN WOULD HAVE been happier not to leave the house again today, but Mom started fretting about one of her medications due for a refill.

"I forgot to ask you to call it in yesterday. I'm sorry."

"It's fine. Are you completely out?"

"No, not until tomorrow, but…" Mom would worry until she had a nice, full bottle safely tucked in her medicine cabinet.

"I'll call and then go pick it up." Jordan smiled. "Won't hurt me at all." She could go while the caregiver who helped Mom bathe was here.

An hour later, she went out to her car. She didn't see any hint of movement up or down the street. Tom's big vehicle wasn't in his driveway. She should quit noticing if it was there or not, except…she couldn't help feeling reassured when she knew he was close and would come running if she called.

The pharmacy was downtown, and she had to park a block away. Once inside, she fidgeted as she waited in line while pharmacy techs searched, seemingly in slow motion, for the prescriptions people ahead of her had come in for.

Once her turn had come and she'd paid, she glanced at her watch and realized that hadn't taken as long as she'd thought. Being on edge all the time—swiveling her head constantly to see who came in the door, who was in each aisle—seemed to stretch the minutes torturously.

Maybe she'd treat herself to a latte. Betty's Café had served nothing but plain coffee when Jordan lived here before, but was apparently doing a booming business once an espresso bar was added.

She could treat herself, even if the caffeine wasn't ideal given her state of mind. But, heck, she wouldn't get the jitters until she was safely home again.

The booths and tables were mostly occupied, she saw at a glance, not surprising at around one o'clock. She walked briskly past several tables to the bar, careful not to look at anyone.

She'd given her order and was waiting when a deep but low voice coming from a nearby booth penetrated. Was that Tom? Why wouldn't it be? By this time, he must have made other friends.

Unable to resist looking, she saw only the back of his head. But across the table from him...that was Storm Lake Police Chief Guthrie. Uniform, badge and all. An empty plate pushed away, he appeared intent on his conversation with Tom.

For some reason, her heart thudded in a heavy beat. They might know each other because Tom was responsible for law enforcement in the county parks. They might—

"I think I've set myself up." Tom's voice filled a lull in the overall chatter. "She'll never be willing to go out with me—she's afraid even to run with me in case we're seen together too often, but we did have a…moment on her front porch. If anyone was watching…"

The chief leaned forward. "A moment."

Frozen, she waited. Tom wouldn't say. He wouldn't—

"A kiss."

She didn't analyze what she heard in his voice. It didn't matter.

"This is our chance," he said.

Behind her, the barista called, "Jordan!"

As if everything around her had gone into slow motion, Jordan saw Chief Guthrie's gaze pass Tom to lock on her. Tom turned to look over his shoulder and met her eyes. His expression was appalled.

Jordan backed away. One step, another. She bumped into a diner seated at a table, then whirled and ran.

Chapter Eleven

"Well, damn. There's a good plan down the tubes." Guthrie sounded annoyed.

Every muscle locked into battle mode, Tom just looked at him. He'd never in his life wanted more to say *I told you so*, but he did currently work for this man.

Sliding out of the booth, he stood, said, "I'll see what I can do to patch things up," took the tall cup labeled with Jordan's name from the barista and walked out.

Yeah, who was he kidding? Everyone knew that no glue ever made could patch trust, once broken.

Convince her we're on her side. Spying on her to protect her.

Stomach roiling, Tom wished he hadn't eaten that burger and greasy fries.

He drove home on autopilot. He'd try to talk to her, but then what? Start wearing his badge and gun openly, maybe walk into the police station and introduce himself as the new lieutenant heading investigations? Or would Jordan let him continue passing under the radar as far as the rest of the world was concerned?

Talk to her first.

Turning the corner, he saw her car in the driveway. He parked in his own, sat unmoving for too long, then grabbed her drink and got out. Somehow, he knew she'd hear the slam of his door. His knock wouldn't be a surprise.

That she answered the knock *was* a surprise. Her face was cold and set as she stepped out on the porch and shut the door behind her.

"Your mother is napping?"

She didn't bother responding to that. She did take the cup from his hand and set it on the broad railing. Then she crossed her arms.

"This is the last time I'll open that door for you or speak to you. I'll ask you not to try to bypass me and go to my mother for any reason whatsoever." Pure ice.

"Jordan, will you listen? Give me a chance to explain?"

"That you were hired to wriggle your way into my life and find evidence that I'm the killer the police want me to be?" She made a harsh sound. "Given their tunnel vision, I should have suspected. Are you a PI or a cop yourself?"

Voice rough, he said, "Cop. I'm a detective."

"Of course you are. Well, you can tell Chief Guthrie that I'm through speaking to you or his detectives without an attorney being present. I was a fool."

The flash of pain in her eyes had him stepping forward. "Will you listen?"

She studied him with contempt. "You've lied to me from the beginning. Every word. Why would I believe anything you say? Isn't what you're saying now a lie, too? Just a new, expedient story." She shook her head. "Please leave, and don't step foot on this property again. Do you hear me?"

"I can help you. Keep you safe." Damn, was he begging? "I don't believe you ever hurt anyone."

"But I did, didn't I?" The one sentence was both scathing and filled with pain.

"I mean it," he said to her back.

She grabbed her to-go cup and opened the door.

Before she could shut him out once and for all, he said, "Don't tell anyone I'm a cop."

Jordan went still.

"Help me keep my cover so I can catch the scum who murdered the doctor."

She hesitated before giving an abrupt nod and disappearing inside. Tom heard the dead bolt slide shut with steely finality.

FORTUNATELY, MOM APPARENTLY hadn't heard the knock.

When she appeared after her nap, she used a cane instead of the walker, demonstrating her increased steadiness. She must have brushed her hair on the way, too.

Jordan was struck again by how much she'd improved. In the absence of another feared stroke, Mom might not truly need her for that much longer.

Dishing up leftover potato salad, she wondered if it was too late to apply to the University of Idaho or other schools for fall semester to finish her BA. If she stayed in Idaho, she could claim in-state tuition and be close to her mother, too. She wanted so much to believe she had a future.

Except, moving on was a fantasy until the killer trying to set *her* up was arrested, tried and convicted.

I can help you. Help me keep my cover so I can catch the scum who murdered the doctor.

Could he? Would he?

Anger seared her. *Sure. You betcha. Mr.—no, Detective Trustworthy.*

The one who'd kissed her as if he meant it, then bragged about it to his boss because really, he'd positioned her where anybody might see and done it because a date wasn't happening, and he was getting desperate. Not desperate for *her*, but for a triumphant closure for his case.

Thank God she hadn't told him about those driver's licenses.

Her eyes and even sinuses burned, but if tears were responsible, she wasn't about to let them fall. She joined her mother at the table and helped herself to servings of potato and fruit salads she didn't want.

For the second time in her life, she'd let herself fall for a man. Jordan had to marvel at her own judgment. *Fool me once*, she thought, but she hadn't learned anything. Look how spectacularly she'd been fooled the second time.

Never again.

She went through the motions of a normal afternoon and evening. She vacuumed, scrubbed the downstairs bathroom, made and pretended to eat dinner, watched a streaming show Mom liked without hearing a word herself, showered, and helped Mom with bedtime tasks. This was why she'd come home. For now, she was needed, and always loved as long as her mother lived.

But no matter what she did, no matter how firm her vow, her thoughts spun.

How could Tom Moore live with himself? Or was that even his real name? He'd pretended ignorance about her, then listened to her story with compassion and intelligence. Fake compassion, probably real intelligence. Too late, it was easy to imagine Tom weighing her every word, slotting pieces into place and seeing the gaps. His kindness the night her mother fell. Was that real, or had he been on the clock the entire time, gloating at the chance to build trust with her?

Was he a runner at all? Had everything he'd told her about the parks been gleaned from the city and county websites and maybe a few career articles: So You Want to Be a Park Ranger. San Francisco? For all she knew, he'd visited the city once or twice.

Of everything he'd said, Jordan was most inclined to believe he'd been shot. His stiffness and grimaces of pain looked too genuine. She'd bet cops were shot a whole lot more often than park rangers.

His strength when he held her, his tact and kindness with Mom, those hurt to remember. The part she'd never forgive him for was the heat in his eyes when he looked at her. Either he had somehow faked it, which she doubted given his erection—or he'd have been happy to take her to bed because, hey, she was a woman, he was bored, why not? She'd be mad at him when she found out the truth anyway, so what was one more betrayal?

Jordan pulled down the covers and sat on the edge of her bed, exhausted but knowing what would happen when she lay down and closed her eyes. She'd keep picturing Tom's every expression, the way amusement crinkled the skin beside his eyes, the deeper groove in his left cheek when he laughed or gave her a wickedly sexy grin. His impatience with the unruly waves in his hair, his funny stories, the warm clasp of his hand.

Him.

Two nights later, she was still going through the motions. Sleep remained elusive, her dreams disturbing. About to get into bed, she heard her mother call, "Jordan?"

She found Mom dumping out the contents of the drawer from her bedside stand on her bed.

"Mom? What are you doing?"

"You know I have asthma. I suddenly couldn't remember—"

Oh God—was she struggling for breath? She was definitely breathing hard.

"Isn't it usually brought on by allergies, or when you get a cold?"

"Yes, but—I'm going to have an attack! I know I am, and I can't find my inhaler."

Jordan felt almost certain that her mother was getting

worked up only because she'd suddenly thought about the asthma that hadn't once reared its head since Jordan came home, and then got to thinking about where she left her inhaler.

Almost was the key word. What if...?

Jordan joined the hunt, finding and searching her mother's purse, the bathroom, the kitchen junk drawer, between cushions anywhere Mom might have sat in the living room. Under the bed. She delved into the pockets of her mother's coats and bathrobe, checked an old purse. By the time she had to concede defeat, Mom was panting for breath.

"I'll call your doctor."

"It's the middle of the night!"

"He's part of a clinic. I bet they have someone on call. If not, we'll go to the ER."

There was indeed a doctor on call, who agreed to phone in a prescription to the hospital pharmacy. Jordan just had to go get it.

Her mother had calmed, and Jordan became even surer that this was all unnecessary, but it was also true that Mom had lost control of so much of her life. She'd definitely become fixated on her medications, as if they were the armor that kept her from disaster. Who could blame her?

"I'll call Jennifer Pierce," Jordan decided. The Pierces lived three houses down. Jennifer wasn't as close to Mom as several other neighbors, but she was considerably younger. Getting up in the middle of the night and making it over here wouldn't be as big a deal for her as it would for Mrs. Chung, for example. "I won't be gone long."

Jennifer's husband answered the phone, and Jennifer immediately agreed to come over. He came with her and said he'd stay, too. Of course he did. After all, this was the house where an accused killer lived.

Jordan thanked them and said, "I think she's okay now, but if breathing really becomes difficult, call 911."

While waiting, she'd already scrambled into her clothes, and she hustled out now. Something moved in the darkness between the house and garage, so she threw herself into her car and locked the doors. As she stared in a vain attempt to see a person or dog or cat that might have jumped onto a garbage can, she turned on the car to warm it up.

Shivering, she knew she'd been imagining things. She did that a lot these days. She was not being watched 24/7, no matter how it felt.

Annoyed at herself, she drove the all-too-familiar route to the hospital. Fifteen minutes, she'd be home, Mom could take a couple of puffs on the inhaler, and they'd all get some sleep.

RESTLESS, TOM TRIED to stay too busy to brood. He sat at the kitchen table working on his laptop. Maybe he *should* break cover. That would allow him to seriously investigate everyone close enough to Jordan's deceased husband to hold a grudge. Given that he hadn't been able to interview anyone, what information he'd gathered from databases had been more sparse than he liked.

The best he'd been able to do today was peruse the high school's yearbooks, which were online. He'd already seen DMV and news photos of Steve Dunn, but studied these of the guy who was, as Jordan had said, obviously a star in the eyes of his classmates. In the senior yearbook, he was in at least a dozen photographs aside from his class photo. Football and baseball teams, live action photos during games, being crowned homecoming king—no sign of Jordan there, Tom noted—even student council. Chosen most likely to become famous.

Really?

The kid was good-looking in an unfinished way, buff

but probably not big enough for major colleges looking for
linemen, and he had a grin that would have impressed Tom
more if he didn't know what a piece of you-know-what he'd
turned out to be.

Of course, Tom looked up Jordan in the several yearbooks. She was just as pretty as he thought she was now,
but noticeably shy, or maybe just reserved. Didn't wear a
lot of makeup, didn't look polished the way more confident
girls did.

Tom searched out Steve's sister and brother, too. The sister, Carolyn, was a year older than Steve. She had some of
the reserve, even watchfulness, that Jordan did, making Tom
wonder what her home life had been like.

Kevin Dunn was two years younger than his brother and
had some of the same shine but not quite at the same level.
He played football, too, running back because he wasn't as
big as his brother. Not as many photos in the yearbooks. No
prom crowns. Question was, did he resent his big brother,
or idolize him? Or both?

Tom wondered if other people would know. Man, he
wanted to talk to the guy.

He noted the names of boys on the sports teams, under-
lining the ones who seemed especially buddy-buddy with
Steve in candid photos. Bussert—or Buzz, according to a
caption—fell into that hanger-on category.

The list he made of girls who posed with Steve, or appeared to be part of his crowd, was shorter. Tom didn't see a
single picture of the great and glorious Steve Dunn with the
girl he'd married months after their high school graduation.

He started by searching for information on those people
in the intervening decade plus. A few popped up with criminal records, including Kevin Dunn. He'd had a couple of
DUIs and been tagged for bar fights, although he hadn't actually done time. So—a short temper, like his brother. He'd

worked for four different roofing companies since he graduated from high school two years behind Steve and Jordan. Maybe moved around for a better salary or because of layoffs, maybe not. He'd married a couple of years after high school, and his wife had been active on Facebook but seemed to have gone quiet, without a post in the past eight months.

Sister Carolyn was married, waited tables at a restaurant Tom hadn't yet been in, and had two children, according to her Facebook page, which was only sporadically updated.

Buzz had a sealed juvenile record, which interested Tom a good deal given his speculation about the pristine crime scenes. He'd ask Guthrie about it.

Tom starred names that jumped out at him for one reason or another. Eventually, his eyes began to cross and a headache defied the painkillers he took. He still had some of the heavy-duty stuff, which he rarely used anymore because it knocked him on his butt. Right now, he particularly had to be on his guard. If the kiss had worked as bait...

He flinched, ashamed of himself. Okay, yeah, purely by accident that kiss had presented an opportunity in this investigation. But there were things a man kept his mouth shut about, and this was one of them. Jordan had plenty of reasons to be furious, even if she didn't care enough about him to be hurt—and he thought she had been.

Damn it, he'd *known* it would come to this, one way or another, but hadn't expected that he'd feel as if he lay bleeding on the ground again. How could he have failed so spectacularly in letting himself forget that nothing between them was real? That was especially ironic, considering how stunned he'd been by a kiss that felt so damn perfect. For a fleeting instant, he'd felt as if he had held everything he could ever want in his arms.

He was afraid he knew where that had come from.

You have been given a chance to have all that. He'd

known exactly what Emilia was talking about: a wife, kids, happiness. With her words in the back of his mind, had he wanted to see something with Jordan that wasn't real? The unexpected byway his life had taken might be responsible for that hollow inside that wanted to be filled.

Or had he just blown the chance he'd never expected to have?

With a groan he closed his laptop, slid it into a sleeve and then in a cupboard with pans and lids where it wasn't obvious.

He turned off the light above the stove, reached for the switch for the overhead light but frowned at seeing the only other light he'd left on was in the bathroom. He'd cleared the house, but the window locks in particular were inadequate and the one on the back door less secure than he liked.

Note to self: even if this was a rental, add a dead bolt to the back door tomorrow.

Frowning, he flicked off the light and started down the short hall to the bedrooms and single bathroom. He wondered if he'd be able to sleep at all—or whether he dared.

The air behind him stirred. If he hadn't already been in a heightened state of awareness, he wouldn't have moved fast enough. As it was, he jumped sideways and a club— no, a metal bar—slammed into his shoulder instead of his head. He started to spin while falling into the open door to an unused bedroom.

Pop.

Shot fired!

Tom dived for the floor and pulled out his backup piece, rolling to face the dark doorway. He had to see his assailant. The dark shape gave him no answer.

"Drop it!" he yelled.

Pop, pop. Suppressor.

He pulled the trigger of his own weapon. Once, twice. Running footsteps told him he'd delayed too long.

He shoved himself to his knees, intent on pursuing when he heard the back door hitting the house, but his left arm hung uselessly at his side and he staggered into a wall once he reached his feet.

He couldn't decide if the iron bar had dealt the worst blow, or the bullet. Or, hell, had there been two?

Tom carefully lowered himself to his knees again, propping his good shoulder against the wall to keep himself from going all the way down, and pulled his phone from his pocket.

Chapter Twelve

Two blocks from home, Jordan saw flashing lights. Mom! Oh, no. Had she really had a major asthma attack, after Jordan hadn't believed her? Or had worse happened since Jordan called Jennifer from the hospital?

Terrified, she strained to see. There was a police car with flashing lights in her driveway, but the ambulance was in Tom's, another police unit at the curb in front of his rental. For an instant, she didn't understand, but then a cold trickle entered her veins.

He'd been assaulted, just like the men she'd dated. What if he was dead?

Given how he'd betrayed her, she didn't expect the anguish. She braked hard at the curb in front of her house. She'd barely jumped out and reached the sidewalk when a police officer planted himself in front of her, gun held with his arms outstretched, and yelled, "Freeze! Hands in the air! Drop whatever you're holding!"

The cold turned to ice. The small paper bag holding the inhaler fell to the concrete. Shaking, she said, "I live here. This...this is my house."

"Turn around!" he snapped.

Turning let her see Tom's house where medics were carrying an unmoving patient out to the ambulance. The anguish heightened, as did her fear.

"I don't understand." But, oh, she did. The police here had made up their minds about her long since. Her mind flickered back to what she'd thought was motion, and now she knew she'd been right. *Someone* had seen her leaving the house, oh, so conveniently.

The memory was wiped out when, next thing she knew, the cop had grabbed her left hand and wrenched it down. A metal cuff snapped closed on her wrist. She struggled instinctively as he forced her other hand down and cuffed it, too. He grabbed her by the scruff of her neck and shoved her forward. She stepped off the curb without seeing it and fell hard onto the street, trying to take her weight onto her shoulder but ending up with her face skidding on the gritty pavement. She was momentarily dazed.

"What's going on?" another voice called. This one she knew—Deputy Chief Bowen, who had a conscious or unconscious swagger to impress onlookers with his authority even when he didn't wear a uniform, like tonight. He'd probably been getting ready for bed, she realized, or even *in* bed when the call came.

"Ms. Hendrick just arrived home. Real convenient timing."

He loomed over her, staring down with typical contempt. "What's she doing on the ground?"

"Fell after I cuffed her."

"Okay. Hoist her up. We need to take her in."

"Why?" she cried. "What happened?" Her view of him was distorted, just a tall figure rearing over her.

"Oh, I think you know exactly what happened. Once you get her loaded, search her car," he ordered.

Scared as she was, anger sizzled, too. "Do you have a warrant?"

"I have probable cause." And oh, how smug he sounded.

"I can prove where I was. But I'm not saying another word until I'm given the opportunity to call an attorney to be with me. And if you search my car without a warrant, count on a lawsuit."

The silence didn't tell her whether she'd intimidated them in the slightest or whether they were only pausing to watch the ambulance back out of the driveway and accelerate in the same direction she'd come from.

Despite herself, she pictured Tom smiling at her, and prayed, *Don't die. Please don't let him be too badly hurt.*

Another of the SUVs the Storm Lake PD liked rolled up to the curb, the lights blinding her. Jordan turned her head away to rest her other cheek on the road surface. When she did, salty blood trickled into her mouth.

A door slammed. "You arrested Ms. Hendrick?" the police chief asked.

"Ah...not officially. Just made sure she couldn't go for a gun."

"Does she have one on her?"

"Doesn't look like it." The original officer sounded nervous. "I haven't patted her down."

"Well, help the woman up!" the chief growled. "Then do it."

They essentially had to pick her up and set her on her feet. She closed her eyes and held herself rigid as a strange woman officer's hands groped her.

"Nothing, sir. I was going to look in her car, but she said she'll sue if we do."

Chief Guthrie snorted, but said, "We'd best have a talk with her first. What's that on the sidewalk?"

"I don't know. I made her drop it."

One of the men walked over and picked up the small sack. Paper rustled. "Uh, I think it's an asthma inhaler."

"What?"

She refused to look at them, but from the sound of it they were passing the sack around and peering inside.

Mad as it made her to ask for anything, she finally said, "Would one of you please take that to the house? My mother was short of breath. It's for her."

That elicited some discussion, but after a minute, one of them moved away.

"Well, let's take Ms. Hendrick to the station—"

"No," she said.

"Don't think this is your decision," the chief remarked.

"I called a neighbor to sit with my mother. She and her husband can tell you when I left. The receipt in that bag will tell you when I paid for the inhaler at the hospital. I drove straight home. I didn't have time to do whatever you think I did." Should she have even said that much? "Now, I want to call an attorney."

"Plenty of time for that," Bowen declared. "You can use the phone once you're at the station."

Bowen and the officer she didn't recognize muscled her into the back of one of the vehicles. The chief had apparently walked away, maybe to talk to another officer across the street at Tom's house.

With her arms wrenched behind her, Jordan's shoulders ached, the pain sharper in the right one she'd fallen onto. Her head hurt, too. It must have bounced when she went down. No wonder her brain felt rattled.

She stared at the back of the officer's head while he drove her the ten minutes to the city police station. He wasn't any gentler pulling her out, even though she didn't fight him.

She was aware of some stares as she was hustled to a windowless room and propelled into a wooden chair. There she sat for what felt like an hour, but probably was more like fifteen minutes. It was Chief Guthrie and Deputy Chief Bowen who walked into the room then.

She turned to look at them, hoping her stare incinerated them.

"You have *no* evidence connecting me to these crimes. After the way I was treated tonight, I'm going to bankrupt this city. I swear I will. Now, uncuff me and give me a phone."

They remained solid instead of crumbling into the hot cinders of her fantasy. The muscles in Chief Guthrie's jaw did flex before he circled behind her. A moment later, her hands fell to her sides. She stifled the groan.

A phone and the skinny local phone directory appeared on the table in front of her.

"Leave me alone." They'd be able to listen from outside the room, she felt sure, but right now she wanted the illusion of privacy.

The selection of local attorneys was skimpy, but one name leaped out at her. Susan Throndsen was an ardent gardener and longtime friend of Jordan's mother. She also happened to be a criminal attorney who'd moved here, if Jordan remembered right, after her partner died, and she'd practiced for ten years or more in Portland, Oregon.

Given the time of night, she was surprised when a woman picked up on the third ring. Jordan fumbled an explanation.

"This is Susan Throndsen," she said. "I remember you, Jordan. Where are you?"

"At the police station."

"I have to throw on some clothes, but I'll be there in twenty minutes or so. Don't say another word to anyone until I get there."

Jordan struggled with a lump in her throat. "Thank you."

TOM WAS AWAKE through the ordeal in the ER, unlike last time. They sedated him while a surgeon dug out the bullet, but he felt clearheaded surprisingly fast. They must have used a local instead of full anesthesia.

Suddenly a doctor stood above him, surgical mask pulled down to reveal the face of a man in his forties, at a guess. "Mr. Moore, we've removed a bullet from your shoulder, and cleaned and bandaged a slice on your thigh that must have been a bullet graze. I believe you suffered a head injury, too, although any concussion doesn't appear serious. We'll be keeping you for the night, though." He hesitated. "Either you make a practice of living dangerously, or you were struck by a barrage of bullets at some point."

"Barrage," Tom managed to say through a dry mouth. Was he still supposed to be undercover? Clearly no one had told the surgeon that he was a cop.

The surgeon's eyebrows climbed, but he said only, "You'll be doing some rehab for that shoulder. I doubt that's a surprise to you."

"No."

The man patted his good shoulder, said, "Glad it wasn't worse," and departed.

A nurse took his place a minute later and slipped some ice chips into Tom's mouth. He was moved from what looked like recovery to a curtained space in the ICU. He desperately wanted to talk to Guthrie, to know what happened after he went down, but the man didn't show up.

Tom would have given a lot to be able to say, convincingly, *It wasn't Jordan*, but unfortunately he couldn't. From what little he'd seen, his assailant was shorter than him, and could conceivably be a man or woman. Man, he thought, from the breadth of shoulders, but it had all happened so fast.

God, he hoped they hadn't jumped to the conclusion that it was Jordan who'd attacked him and come down hard on her. Either way, she hadn't rushed to his side.

And why would she do that?

He let his eyelids sink closed and realized how much he wished she *was* here, firmly holding his hand. Her scent was distinctive enough he'd be comforted even when he couldn't keep his eyes open. Last time, his lieutenant had been the first person he saw after regaining consciousness, and Yates had assumed Tom didn't need anyone sitting at his side. Nothing in Tom's background explained why this time he ached for someone—not just someone, Jordan—to care enough to come right away and stay with him.

Instead, he saw her face when she understood that he had betrayed her.

SHE AND SUE sat in that claustrophobic room for some time while a police officer drove to Jordan's house to retrieve the receipt from her purchase at the hospital pharmacy. For all she knew, Jennifer had dropped it in the wastebasket, but at least she had been able to locate it.

Chief Guthrie sat across the table from Jordan and her attorney and said woodenly, "Mrs. Pierce had the time of your call on her phone, and took a guess at how long it took her and her husband to get dressed and get to your house. She said you talked for a couple of minutes about what to do if your mother had a crisis."

Jordan didn't speak. All she wanted was to go home, take a hot shower and crawl into bed, after reassuring her mother. The only positive she could think of right now was that, while Tom had been shot, the chief said his recovery was likely to be swift.

"Mrs. Pierce also mentioned that you called later to check on your mother, saying that you were sitting in the parking lot at the hospital." His eyes narrowed. "You could just as well have called while you were driving. That opens the possibility you had a few minutes more than the timing you're claiming, but I'll admit that gap isn't a large one."

"It's ludicrously small, and you know it!" the attorney snapped. "Have you yet interviewed Detective Moore?"

He clearly didn't like that Jordan had given away the true identity of the wounded man, but had no right to complain.

"Deputy Chief Bowen spoke to him briefly. He didn't see his assailant well enough to give a description."

"What was this assailant wearing?" Sue asked drily. "Did it bear any resemblance to what my client is wearing? Or is she supposed to have managed a quick change in that infinitesimal *gap*, too?"

Guthrie transferred his gaze briefly to Jordan, who wore a Seattle Seahawks sweatshirt over leggings. Her bright blue parka had been torn in several places when she slid on the pavement.

"Ah…it was dark."

Sue drilled him with her gaze. "I'm placing you on notice that I will be pursuing remedies for the treatment doled out to Ms. Hendrick for no defensible reason by your officers. She would have willingly answered questions and did not in any way resist, yet she was held at gunpoint, cuffed, manhandled and injured although no arrest was made. I will be taking her to the hospital on the way home for a shoulder X-ray and to get her face and hands cleaned up." She stood, an athletic woman who might be fifty. Her graying dark hair was disheveled enough to suggest she hadn't stopped to brush it on the way out the door. As she helped Jordan stand up, she said quietly, "I thought better of you, Allen."

Jordan shuffled out the door ahead of her attorney, wishing she'd taken the time earlier—an eon ago—to put on socks as well as the wool felt clogs she wore as slippers. Although being cold for a few minutes going out to the car, into the hospital and out again was nothing compared to everything else about this evening.

During the drive, wishing the car heater would hurry to warm up, Jordan said, "I threatened to sue them."

"Their treatment of you was abominable. I think we need to follow through on that threat just on principle."

Thinking about Dr. Parnell, Jordan winced at having to walk into the ER. Did people working here know her name, and that she was a suspect in his murder? But Sue stayed at her side, insisted on an X-ray even though the physician felt sure Jordan's shoulder had only been wrenched, and watched as her face, hands and, yes, ankle, were cleaned, bits of gravel picked out, ointment applied and then bandaged.

Jordan almost opened her mouth and asked about Tom, who must have come through the ER, but restrained herself. He didn't *deserve* for her to care about him or worry about his injuries. She couldn't imagine he'd welcome a visit from her anyway. For all he knew, she'd been the one to shoot him. Although you'd think the police would have spent more time wondering what gun she'd used, and what she had done with it. Couldn't they have done that gunpowder residue test she'd read about in mysteries? Too late now, she thought, looking down at her hands, swathed in what seemed like an unnecessary amount of gauze.

Once Sue started the car again, Jordan said, "I don't think the Storm Lake department has a clue how to investigate a murder. Or an attempted murder. Assuming Detective Moore has the experience they need, they were dumb enough to put him in a position where he couldn't do anything but cozy up to me."

"Will you tell me more about that?" the attorney asked.

Jordan hesitated, then did, but kept her account abbreviated. Guthrie hadn't mentioned that passionate kiss in front of Sue, and Jordan would just as soon keep that to herself. The humiliation dealt to her tonight was bad enough, but admitting she'd fallen that far for his act was another story.

Sue walked her in at home, waiting while she fervently thanked the Pierces, who had stuck with Mom despite what they must be thinking about Jordan, and saw them out.

At last, Sue left, too, and Jordan thankfully locked the door, checked every window and the back door, and finally peeked in Mom's room to find her mother sound asleep.

And, no, according to Jennifer Pierce, Mom hadn't needed the inhaler. None of this needed to happen, not tonight, anyway. Once she knew Jordan had left to pick one up, she'd calmed down.

She had heard the to-do outside, meaning Jordan had a lot to tiptoe around come morning, but right now…the shower sounded blissful.

DISCHARGED, TOM ENDURED the ride in a wheelchair out of the hospital, then got stiffly into the back of a taxi. One of only two in town, he'd heard. Lyft and the like hadn't made it to a town this size. Guthrie had sounded a little embarrassed during his call that morning when he suggested that Tom make his own way home so as not to undermine his cover.

"Assuming it stays intact," he added. "We'll reimburse you for the cost of a taxi if you don't have anyone else who can pick you up."

Big of him, Tom couldn't help thinking.

"I don't want it to stay intact," he said. "It's time I investigate the way I should have from the beginning." He ended the call, not letting the chief argue. He didn't think there was anything else the subterfuge could accomplish.

The taxi driver offered to help him into his house, but Tom declined and limped up to the front door. Guthrie had thought to grab Tom's car keys and wallet last night, so Tom was able to let himself in. His backup piece had been taken into evidence in case he'd succeeded in wounding his assailant and the bullet turned up. Hard to imagine anyone lying in wait for him now, after the night's drama, but he still moved as quietly and cautiously as he could through the house, peering behind doors, making sure he was alone. Then he took his Sig Sauer 9-mm from the gun safe. He'd keep it close for comfort.

Back in the living room, he separated the blinds enough to peer out. The facade of the Hendrick house told him nothing. Worry sat like an indigestible meal in his belly. Guthrie had admitted in this morning's conversation that they'd hauled Jordan in last night to interrogate her, but that they'd ended up having to release her for lack of evidence. He'd been reluctant to say more.

Something in the chief's voice made Tom wonder. Had Jordan answered the door in her pajamas, hair sleep-mussed, maybe a pillow crease on her cheek? If so, how had they justified taking her in? Had they searched the house for a weapon and failed to find one? How far had they gone in their determination to nail her?

Did she finally hire a lawyer?

He found himself hoping so. She'd been naive in believing she could continue to answer questions so that the police would eventually rule her out and pursue other possibilities. Tom wished he'd looked deeper before he took this job. Yes, the murders clearly had some connection to Jordan, but Guthrie had jumped right on her as the only possible suspect. Tom hadn't let himself question that the way he should have. The job was convenient for him, the timing good for him to do this undercover gig.

He just hadn't understood what he'd be doing to a woman who might be innocent...and terrified.

Or that he'd be pathetically grateful if she'd just walk across the street, knock on his door and say, "I'm still mad at you, but I hope you'll be okay." If she'd give even a hint that she felt for him a fraction of what he felt for her.

The blinds in the front windows of *her* house didn't even twitch. And, damn, he needed to lie down, where he'd cuddle up to his handgun and, he felt sure, dream about another stint of agonizing physical therapy.

Chapter Thirteen

The squeak of a grocery store cart right behind her was enough to tighten the muscles in the back of Jordan's neck. Ridiculous, when she'd almost become used to unexpectedly coming face-to-face with people she'd hoped never to set eyes on again. That's the price you paid for a homecoming.

Annoyed at herself for cowardice, she glanced over her shoulder fully expecting to see someone she'd never met in her life grabbing a box of macaroni and cheese off the shelf. But no such luck.

Steve's mother stared at her, eyes blazing with hatred. The knuckles of her hands gripping the handles of the cart showed white. She'd aged drastically.

"You!" she spat, faced flushed red.

Jordan held her head high. "Hello—" Not "Mom" as she'd called this woman so briefly. "Nancy," she settled on.

"How dare you come back to this town and strut around as if you belong! I was glad—*glad*—to see that picture in the paper and to know someone had the guts to remind everyone that you *are* a killer. You should be serving a term in the state penitentiary, not going on with your life when Steve is dead because of you!"

Rustles from behind gave Jordan a bad feeling they had an audience now. Although what difference did it make?

"I know you loved your son," she said, as gently as she could. "I did, too. I tried—"

Last time they'd met face-to-face, Steve's mother had blamed Jordan for the fact that he hadn't had a chance to go on to play college ball and ultimately end up in the NFL. In her version, Jordan had demanded he marry her and give all that up.

Jordan had no idea where the woman had come up with that fantasy version of her son's life.

Now, of course, she all but shouted, "You shot him!"

Jordan continued as if she hadn't heard. "I tried to keep loving him even when he hurt me. You had to know what an ugly temper Steve had. I always wondered if he got it from his father. Whether you had to cower when he was alive, hide your bruises, pretend everything was fine when you watched him raising his boys to be just like him."

The nearly gaunt face drained of color.

Guilt flayed Jordan. From things Steve had said, she was almost certain about what this woman had endured. But, no matter what, she'd loved her child. How could she let herself believe he was as bad or worse than her husband? Steve had been her golden boy and always would be in her memory.

Did I think I could puncture her illusions? Jordan wondered.

Face now bone-white and lips thinned to reveal the unhappy lines that had worsened since Jordan knew her, Nancy Dunn's eyes flicked to whoever was eavesdropping behind Jordan.

"You're the monster," she whispered, voice shaking. "You've fooled everyone. Even now you killed another man, a good, respected man. I don't know how you keep getting away with it, but sooner or later, they'll see through you, and you'll be cuffed and behind bars. For Steve's sake, I can't wait."

She wheeled her cart around and rushed away down the aisle.

Jordan gritted her teeth and turned to see who had been avidly listening.

Three other shoppers averted their eyes and grabbed, probably at random, for items on the shelves. One was a woman who looked familiar, probably from high school. The others Jordan didn't offhand recognize, but clearly they all knew who *she* was.

Heat seared her cheeks, and she wanted to abandon her own half-full cart and flee, but pride and practicality wouldn't let her. She and Mom were low on groceries, and she didn't want to have to do this all over again. Maybe next week she'd drive to the next town that had a decent size store instead of shopping here in town.

Ashamed that she'd let herself become embroiled in a scene, she moved fast, barely glancing at her list. She didn't see anyone else she knew except one of the checkers. She chose a checker she didn't recognize, paid and left the store. Just outside the doors, she paused and looked carefully around before she dared venture into the parking lot.

What a way to live.

"I've known Bussert since he was a kid," Chief Guthrie said. He already sounded cautious. Possibly offended, too. "What are you suggesting?"

Phone to his ear, Tom lay back on the workout bench that had been one of his few additions to the furnished rental. "I'm saying he may have been one of Steve Dunn's best friends in high school. When he and Wilson knocked on Ms. Hendrick's door after the doctor's shooting, Bussert didn't even try to hide his hostility for her. When I started looking into the backgrounds of Dunn's close friends, the fact that one of your police officers has a sealed juvenile file leaped right out at me. You must have known it would."

It was difficult to interpret a silence. Was the chief trying to figure out how to finesse his way out of answering the question?

But instead of a curt response, Guthrie sounded chagrined. "To tell you the truth, I'd forgotten he and Dunn were friends. Got into trouble together a few times," he admitted. "Nothing big—just pranks."

Uh-huh.

"Kid had a temper. No surprise, his family was a mess. There were half a dozen domestic violence calls to that address, but Cody's mother was never willing to speak out against her husband. Sad woman. Cody attacked his own father in defense of his mother. I suspect it was justified, but he spent some time in detention and then a group home. By the time he earned his AA degree, I believed he'd turned himself around, and nothing's ever happened to make me doubt that judgment."

"He pretty clearly harbors anger at Ms. Hendrick."

"You taking her word on that?"

"You made sure he didn't go back to talk to her again," Tom said mildly.

"You've got me there. Wilson suggested he sit this one out."

"Normally, I'd want to interview Officer Bussert," Tom said. "But as things stand, I'll step back and let you do it."

"You're seriously considering him for this?" the chief asked incredulously.

"You have to know he's a possible. I want to know if anyone else in the department had a close relationship to the Dunn family as well."

"What the hell?"

Another call was coming in, and Tom recognized the number.

"I need to take a call," he said. Without compunction, he cut off Guthrie and answered. "Lieutenant Moore."

A woman's voice said, "Lieutenant, this is Detective Dutton from Walla Walla. Thought I'd update you and find out if anything has happened on your end."

The detective and her partner knew Tom had been working undercover, hoping to attract the attention of this perpetrator. He told her about the assault, and his regret that he'd neither gotten a good look at his assailant, nor taken him down.

"You still suspect Ms. Hendrick?" she asked.

"I don't, but the chief does. Just between us, I think he's reluctant to believe anyone in town he might have known for years could be this obsessive."

"Ms. Hendrick is a local, too," Detective Dutton pointed out.

"But hasn't lived here in some years. When she did, she stayed in the background." She'd apparently excelled at that. "I doubt Chief Guthrie ever met her."

"Ah."

"You said you have an update?"

He'd be glad for any new tidbit he could chew on—or that might lead to the real killer.

"You know Ms. Hendrick caught our attention because a man she'd dated briefly was murdered only days after she'd last seen him."

"Pete Shroder." That was the guy who had seemingly interrupted a burglar, or a team of them, in the act of cleaning out his house.

"Right. Well, a couple of days ago, a fingerprint we ran from the scene finally popped." She sounded quietly satisfied. "Belongs to a man named Bill Bannan." She spelled the last name. "He and a partner were just arrested in the act of carrying a fancy big-screen TV out of a house in Eugene, Oregon. Real nice house, apparently. They'd pretty well emptied it, and once local police had addresses, they found both the men's garages filled with stolen items. We're hoping they'll find something that came from Shroder's house, although after all these years, that would be a stroke of unexpected luck. Nonetheless, I think we can assume they—or at least Bannan—were responsible for Pete Shroder's death."

"So only the assault on Elliott Keefe can be linked to Jordan—Ms. Hendrick," he corrected himself.

"That's correct. We'd probably have done no more than interview her once if it hadn't been for Shroder's unsolved murder."

"Was her name mentioned publicly in connection with that investigation?" Tom asked.

"I'll have to check, but yes, a reporter from the *Walla Walla U-B* got her name somehow." She offered to email the article to him.

They parted on that promise, and his reciprocal one: he'd let her know when or if they got a big break here in Storm Lake.

Detective Dutton didn't dawdle. Within fifteen minutes, Tom had his laptop open and was reading the relevant article about what was apparently a rare, mysterious murder for the college town. And yes, there was the name, Jordan Hendrick.

He sat staring at it, highlighted in his imagination. What-ifs could be pure fantasy, but this time, he thought he was onto something.

What if the real killer had happened on this article, maybe because he'd hated Jordan all along and done regular Google searches for her name? What if the murder gave him an idea? The police had spoken to her because she'd so recently dated a man who was then murdered. What if it happened again? And maybe again? What if the police could be convinced to arrest her? She hadn't been held accountable for Steve Dunn's death, but wouldn't the next best thing be setting her up to serve a long, long sentence in prison for murdering another man?

If so, the idea obviously took a while to firm up. Might have initially been no more than a kind of revenge fantasy. Only then, because his rage grew for some reason, that fantasy became a real possibility to him.

As a scheme, it was diabolical and in some ways impractical...but Jordan had been a hairbreadth away from being arrested for Dr. Parnell's murder. If Tom had died—

She'd never been in his house. Her fingerprints wouldn't have been found. But sooner or later, this killer might come up with a way to be sure her fingerprints or even something that belonged to her *was* found at a crime scene. Or the other way around; suppose cops found something from one of the men's homes, as if she kept trophies. Planting an item wouldn't be difficult. He thought uneasily about her car, sitting unguarded in the driveway.

Then he thought, hell, had she handled anything *he'd* taken home? The newspaper that had fallen to their feet came to mind, but he was sure she hadn't touched that. Anyone could root in the garbage or recycling cans, though.

If it wasn't too late, Tom would have searched his own house to be sure that hadn't already happened. He'd have heard by now if anything connected to Jordan had been found, though.

Thank God, he thought. Time to have a talk with Chief Guthrie. Turned out there was good reason for him to hide his real job here in Storm Lake after all.

He wanted some cooperation in checking the work schedules and vacation time of anyone in the department who'd had a connection with Dunn. Even while he was following that thread, assuming Guthrie didn't balk, they could goad the killer with a newspaper article that discussed the doctor's murder and the attempted murder of park ranger Tom

Moore, but had no mention of Jordan's name at all. The police spokesperson—who might well be Guthrie himself—could imply that initial leads had fizzled and they were left with a real puzzler, but felt confident that sooner or later they'd solve the case. They could even hint that they were pursuing a new possibility.

Wouldn't *that* enrage someone trying to pin these crimes on Jordan?

The danger was that this would push this nutcase to give up on the idea of making Jordan's life hell by getting her sent to prison and fall back on a more certain alternative—sending her to her grave instead.

TO BE PROACTIVE, Jordan took a different route each time she went out for her run and found with the bitter cold and sometimes icy or snow-covered streets that she had to abbreviate her runs. Midmorning, she'd scarcely see a soul out and about. No matter which direction she went, though, she always upped her wariness quotient when she approached her house.

Today the streets were still slushy despite having been plowed. From a couple of blocks away, she recognized Tom walking toward her. Not running—he probably wasn't up to that yet. The stiffness she remembered in his gait was back.

Turn at the corner and circle around to approach the house from the other direction? No, she decided. She'd just ignore him.

Sure, because being snubbed by *her* would deeply wound him. She grimaced, then forgot Tom at the uneasy realization that a vehicle was coming up behind her. A glance over her shoulder told it was a pickup truck she didn't recognize.

She wasn't half a block away from Tom when the truck came even with her, then swerved and braked in her way. She scrambled a couple of steps back. The driver's-side window rolled down, and she saw Steve's brother for the first time since he confronted her after she got out of the hospital.

His expression was as ugly as she would have expected. "Well, well. Mom was right. Here you are."

He had a friend with him—Ryan Carpenter, teammate of Steve's and, later, one of the buddies he frequently met at taverns several nights a week. Leaving her, of course, behind. At first, she'd been hurt, later grateful for the time to herself.

Ryan glared at her, and for a moment she gave herself the luxury of glaring right back.

Not wanting to give them the satisfaction of any other reaction, she spun to circle behind the truck.

Kevin slammed it into Reverse, and it skidded back. Jordan had to dodge, slipping as she did and barely staying on her feet.

She pulled her phone from her pocket. "I'll call 911."

"'Cuz the cops are your best friends," he sneered. "Just what did you do for them when they hauled you in? Has to be some reason they can't see what's in front of their faces."

She would not engage with him. She turned again, this time toward the sidewalk. The truck rolled forward again to cut her off.

Another man called sharply, "What's going on?"

Relief swelled in her. Tom. She'd forgotten he was so close and coming this way. Stepping off the sidewalk, he flicked a glance at her. "Called 911 yet?"

She lied, "Yes."

Kevin looked angry. "We're just having a little talk. This is my sister-in-law. None of your business."

"I'm making it my business," Tom said with an assuredness they lacked. "What I saw is harassment edging toward assault. If she'd fallen when you backed this truck toward her—"

"Took you a while to get here, didn't it? What's the matter?" Kevin's gaze raked him as he mocked, "Did someone *hurt* you?"

Tom gazed calmly back but didn't sound as stunned as she felt. "Interesting you know that's exactly what happened. You wouldn't have had anything to do with it, would you?"

Ryan muttered, "We should get out of here."

"This guy deserves to be taken down a notch." Kevin started to push the driver's-side door open.

Tom stepped forward and with a slap of his hand slammed the door, then reached through the open window and grabbed a fistful of Kevin's coat and shirt right at his throat. "I'm faster and smarter than you are, and don't forget it." He still sounded unnaturally calm. "Now, I think your friend has the right idea."

The hate on Kevin's face eclipsed even the way his mother had looked at Jordan. She stepped back involuntarily.

The next second, Kevin jerked the gearshift into Drive and stepped on the gas. The truck shot forward, rocked and slithered as he swerved to avoid a parked car, and spat dirty slush back at Tom and Jordan.

Tom looked at her, his eyes not at all calm. "I don't hear a siren."

"I didn't finish the call. After you arrived, I figured you could deal with him. You're a cop, after all."

The muscles in his jaw bunched. "Good thing for you, too."

"Is it?" She started to turn away, but he grabbed her arm. "Wait. I need to talk to you."

"I've talked to almost everyone in your department." Her

expression was as devastated as any he'd seen on her face. "I'm done."

"I'm trying to keep you safe," he said to her back.

He might as well have ignited an explosion.

Chapter Fourteen

"Safe?" Blazing angry now, she swung back to face him. "Is that what you call being handcuffed, knocked down, shoved into a police car? That's the least safe I've ever felt!"

"What?" His eyes darkened as he focused on her cheek and jaw. The scrapes were mostly healed, but the bruising lingered like a yellow stain. "How did that happen?"

She wanted to stay mad, but his obvious outrage made that hard. "Did I mention 'knocked down'?"

"Who did that?"

"An officer who never introduced himself. I was more focused on the gun he was pointing at me than seeing his name tag."

Tom growled an obscenity, thrust his fingers into his hair and yanked. "What were they *thinking*?"

"Same thing you think." A harsh reminder. Still…she owed him for what he'd just done. "Thank you for…intervening. I mean, with Kevin. But I need to get home."

"I'll walk with you."

She had to cool down anyway after standing here so long. "Fine."

Despite obvious pain, Tom stretched his legs to match her speed.

"They said you were shot," she said after a moment.

"Shoulder." He touched his fingers to what must be his wound beneath the parka. "Less serious wound to my thigh."

"I'm sorry."

Those turbulent eyes met hers. "Not your fault."

"But it is!" she cried. "Some way, somehow, it has to be."

"You need to know that you're no longer considered a suspect for Pete Shroder's murder."

She stopped.

"I talked to one of the detectives in Walla Walla." He told her about the fingerprint, such a small thing, that identified one of the burglars.

Not sure what she felt about news that would have been earthshaking if not for the other attacks, Jordan resumed walking.

"Who was the other guy in the truck?" Tom asked.

Switching gears took her a minute. "A friend of Steve's. One of his closest friends. Ryan Carpenter."

"Huh. Not quite the hothead Kevin is."

She fixed her eyes on her mother's house, half a block ahead. Almost there, thank goodness.

"Kevin implied that he'd just heard from his mother that I'm back in town. She and I met in the grocery store. But he couldn't have missed hearing about the vandalism."

Tom frowned. "No."

"What did you want to talk to me about?"

"I had an idea I just discussed with Guthrie. There's a big downside to it, though."

Jordan stopped where she was on the sidewalk, free of snow because several men on the block regularly came out with their shovels the minute a few flakes fell. "What?" she asked apprehensively. How could her life get *worse*?

He told her, and she immediately saw what he meant by downside. *She* would become the target if the murderer was made to believe that, after his attacks on three men associated with her, the cops *still* refused to believe she might be guilty.

Feeling lightheaded, she realized she'd quit breathing and made herself start up again. "But... Mom. She's so vulnerable."

"Jordan," Tom said quietly, "I mean it when I say your safety *and* your mother's is my number one priority."

Why was she even listening to this? She squared her shoulders. "I told you I wouldn't believe a word you said again, didn't I? I'll buy a gun. Keep myself *and* Mom safe." She walked away, not hearing the crunch of his footsteps behind her.

Then she had a thought. Would a gun shop sell one to her after she'd shot and killed her husband, even if the police labeled the act justified?

She quaked, glad Tom wouldn't be able to tell from behind. She was the one to lie to him now; she never, *never* wanted to touch a gun again.

NOT UNEXPECTEDLY, Guthrie didn't entirely buy into Tom's theory, but he did concede that eliminating Jordan from Shroder's murder introduced some doubt.

With Tom having nixed any more meetings, this conversation was taking place on the phone. He stayed silent, letting Guthrie think.

"Okay," he said finally. "It's worth a try. As often as reporters get in our way, it'll be good to manipulate them for a change."

"You'll handle it?" Tom asked.

"They're used to me giving the press conferences, so yes."

Tom had watched clips of a couple of those press conferences before he accepted the job here. They were pretty standard for small towns or rural counties: the sheriff behind the mic, a couple of other uniformed officers at his back to emphasize his authority.

The two men talked for another ten minutes, pinning down exactly what they wanted to see in print and on the news.

"We'll do our best to get TV here as well as print reporters. We catch the interest of stations out of Coeur d'Alene, Moscow, even Missoula or Spokane on a rare occasion. A follow-up on the shocking, unsolved murder of a respected ER doc who worked at a regional hospital might do it."

"I want to look at vacation and leave times for last summer for everyone in the department." Guthrie had dodged Tom's previous demand. "Unexplained absences."

"Why would you be arrowing in on other cops?" The chief sounded genuinely puzzled—or he was a hell of an actor.

Tom explained why. "Some of the obvious suspects don't strike me as patient or organized enough to plan, wait for the perfect moment and leave such clean crime scenes." He'd said this before, but the chief didn't want to hear it. "There may have been friends of Steve's or the family who got taken on at other departments. We can pursue that. But first, this is a small town. You could well be unaware of officers in your department who have a connection to the Dunn family. I'd like to be sure Bussert wasn't out of town the week leading up to the Fourth of July, for example."

This silence told him the answer before the chief said reluctantly, "He was on vacation. A couple other members of the department were, too. For people with families, it's natural to want time off around the holiday."

A couple other members.

"Who else?" Tom hoped he sounded as grim as he felt.

Guthrie named two young officers whose names hadn't caught Tom's attention before. "Bowen, too," he threw out with more reluctance.

"He has a wife and kids?"

"Ah, no. Lost his wife a little over a year ago. Freak thing. They'd never had kids. Wasn't himself for a while. Thought he needed some time."

Tom had already felt uneasy about Ronald Bowen without quite being sure why. Maybe he just hadn't liked what he'd seen and heard about the guy's attitude toward Jordan. That could be his usual style—intimidate anyone he interviewed—but there could be something personal, too.

Bussert's feelings for Jordan were definitely personal.

By evening, Tom was second-guessing himself. Had he just painted a target on Jordan?

Wasn't that the point?

Keeping her safe was his number one priority. How was he supposed to do that? Did he start patrolling around Jordan's house from dusk until dawn? Doable, except the intermittent snowfall was a problem, given that footsteps in it would be all too obvious. Also…reluctant as he was to admit it, that was an arduous schedule and activity for a man now recuperating from two separate shootings. Would Guthrie lend him someone? Could he trust that someone?

What Tom wanted was to be inside the Hendrick house. If he could achieve that, he'd have a lot more confidence in his ability to protect Jordan and her mother. Maybe once she saw the newspaper or the press conference on some local TV station, she'd give in.

He grimaced. Pride was a powerful force. He'd betrayed her trust, and he didn't see her forgiving that.

Once he'd checked all his locks and set his handgun on the bedside table, Tom lay back against his pillows, feeling residual pain in every single one of the places on his body that had taken bullets. Worse was the sick fear that he'd screwed up. He should have made a protection detail for

Jordan a requirement for this plan, but he'd been too cocky. *He* could keep her safe.

What if he couldn't?

AFTER A LOUSY night's sleep, he called Jordan. Repeatedly. She didn't answer.

He talked to Guthrie again. Clearly he wasn't the chief's favorite person anymore. That man eventually growled, "I'll see what I can come up with. You know what a small department I have. Adding you to the payroll when you're not contributing day to day is straining my budget already."

Tom wouldn't have been surprised if one of his molars cracked.

Nonetheless, the chief pulled off the press conference, although attendance wasn't what he'd hoped to see. Tom didn't give a damn; this killer didn't live in Spokane or even Coeur d'Alene. He or she lived right here in Storm Lake. Tom would bet on it.

He watched the sheriff giving his statement online. He appeared deeply concerned and sincere. When the reporter from the local paper asked about the suspect he understood had been taken into the station for questioning—he was careful not to name her, Tom noted—the sheriff managed to look earnest and regretful.

"That was someone we had to look at, but there was a solid alibi. I can't say more than that."

A couple more questions followed, mostly interested in future steps in the investigation. Might the chief request assistance from the Idaho State Police Investigations?

Guthrie dismissed the question with a curt, "We're not at that point yet."

Tom tried to picture the people on his suspect list—almost all men—watching the nightly local news. He also wondered how much the chief had confided in his second-in-command.

He took a late-afternoon-into-evening nap, then spent the night sitting by his front window, staying alert. His instinct said this was too soon for the killer to make a move, but his gut roiled at the same time with the fear that he was wrong along with the knowledge that someone could slip into the back of the Hendrick house entirely unseen.

The article appeared the next day on the front page above the fold in the skimpy daily newspaper. The headline: No Suspect in Doctor's Murder. Tom winced, but read on. The body of the article might have been written using his script as an outline. He was both satisfied and unnerved. The implication was clear: police no longer suspected Jordan Hendrick...even though that wasn't actually true.

It seemed to Tom that the killer had a couple of best options.

One: murder someone else linked to Jordan, and this time make sure there'd be evidence of her presence at the scene. The problem there was she'd been careful to keep to herself since the doctor was killed—with the exception of Tom. Knowing now that Tom was armed, would the perpetrator try for him again? Was there any chance the perpetrator knew he was a cop? Guthrie had sworn to keep quiet, but who knew?

Two: go for Jordan. Tom liked that option the least, even though he had set it up himself.

Was Jordan really so stubborn she'd go it alone? Even risk her mother's safety? He hoped not, since he had a plan to ensure Mrs. Hendrick was safeguarded.

Maybe he should buy a down sleeping bag and start camping out on her front porch nights. Wouldn't help if someone broke into the back of the house...except he'd be close enough to hear wood or glass breaking.

"JORDAN? IS THAT YOU?"

Uh-oh. Jordan had been trying to be so quiet. Mom had

read the article in Wednesday's *Storm Lake Tribune* and had been relieved that "those police officers" had finally come to their senses. How could they have thought for a minute that Jordan was capable of such awful things? Jordan had managed to smile, pat her mother's hand and say, "I just hope they figure out who killed Dr. Parnell soon. He was a really nice man who dedicated his life to saving other people."

Mom agreed and had seemingly put the whole thing out of her mind. She'd started browsing gardening magazines and catalogs that showed up in the mailbox, planning orders for new hybrids. Mom found the local nursery to be disappointing since it carried only the usual standbys. Her optimism in planning for spring lifted Jordan's spirits, too, especially since Mom had made such significant strides to full recovery.

Her own worries about the effect stress might have on Mom seemed like a good excuse to keep her intense anxiety to herself. That she spent half her nights creeping through the house, listening for any sound that didn't belong, wasn't something she wanted to share with her mother.

But apparently the floorboard had creaked.

"It's just me, Mom," she said. "I'm sorry if I woke you."

Her mother's voice carried from the bedroom. "What *are* you doing?"

"Oh, I—" Cell phone, that was it. "I think I left my phone in the kitchen, and I need to charge it."

"You've been sneaking around for the last half hour," Mom said tartly.

The few times Jordan had tried to sneak out of the house as a teenager, her mother had caught her. Why had she assumed a stroke diminished Mom's excellent hearing? She sighed.

It was weird talking in the darkness. "I'm having insomnia, and I keep thinking of things to fuss about, that's all."

"You think someone's going to do something else like the vandalism, don't you?"

"I guess that scares me a little," she admitted. A lot, actually, since it wasn't anything as innocuous as spray paint that worried her.

"I wish you would talk to Tom. He was so kind and helpful. I don't understand why you've cut him off."

Mouth open as she tried to come up with a believable excuse, she was suddenly hit by the realization that she'd underestimated her mother's acuity. Clearly, Mom had a lot better idea of what was going on than Jordan had wanted to believe. A stroke could cause cognitive damage, but there'd been no indication it had in Mom's case. The difficulty with forming words wasn't the same thing.

"I'm turning the hall light on," Jordan said. She followed the rectangle of light into the bedroom and sat at the edge of her mother's bed. Mom reached out and took her hand in a surprisingly firm grip.

"I...thought he was becoming a friend," Jordan said. "Maybe—"

"Even more?"

"Yeah. Then I overheard him talking to the police chief and learned that he'd been pretending all that time so he could get close to me. They did think I could have committed murder." She swallowed. "Tom is a cop, Mom. A police detective. He was hired to cozy up to me and catch me red-handed." That implied bloodstained hands, didn't it? She shivered.

"Are you sure?" her mother whispered, her fingers tightening on Jordan's.

"He admitted it."

Mom stayed quiet for a minute, then said, "Does he still believe you could have killed someone?"

"He claims he doesn't, but how can I believe him? He lied about everything."

"I saw the way he looked at you. Is it possible he started by doing his job, but also came to care about you?"

"How am I supposed to know?" Jordan asked simply.

"Maybe…you have to go with your instinct."

Like you did with Dad? Jordan wanted to ask, but that would have been cruel. They never talked about her father.

"I've always worried," Mom said softly, scarcely any slur in her voice. "After your father left, you changed. I think you've never been able to trust."

"I trusted Steve."

"Did you really? Or were you trying desperately to make a family, because that was something you wanted so much?"

Shocked, Jordan stared at her mother's face. "I…you knew?"

"Of course I knew, but you were so set on marrying him. Nothing I could have said would have stopped you. I just prayed he'd turn into a better man than I feared he was."

"But you were right about him."

"I didn't want to be."

Were those tears trickling down her mother's face? Jordan leaned over and rested her head on her mother's shoulder, accepting comfort she'd denied herself for so long.

"I didn't want to admit that I never let myself see who he really was," she whispered. "I kept thinking if I pretended—"

"It doesn't work that way," her mother said sadly. "I… tried that, too. Eventually I realized that for all the grief I suffered after your father left, he'd given me more joy. You."

Jordan lifted her head slightly so she could see Mom's smile.

Jordan cried, and knew as her mother cradled her, she was doing the same.

She sat there a long time, until she was sure Mom slept. Then she got up, turned off the hall light, waited until her eyes adjusted to the darkness, and crept to the living room so she could peer out the front.

Nothing was moving. No light shone in Tom's house. Was he awake, too? Watching? Afraid for her?

What did her instinct say about him?

Chapter Fifteen

Two days after the press conference, Tom accepted how much he hated his current role, and decided the time had come to shed it.

He started by crossing the street and ringing Jordan's doorbell. A car he recognized was parked at the curb, which told him a therapist of some kind or other was here keeping Jordan's mother occupied. He couldn't be positive that Jordan hadn't slipped out the back for one of her risky solitary runs, but—

Wearing skinny jeans, clogs and a sweater that hung to mid-thigh, her hair in a high ponytail, Jordan opened the door. She'd never looked more beautiful to him even though he saw no welcome on her face. Instead, she gazed at him in astonishment. "Really? You can't take a hint, or ten?"

"Please," he said, sticking out a booted foot so she couldn't slam the door. "I need to talk to you."

Tiny furrows formed on her usually smooth forehead. He still couldn't tell what she was thinking, but some emotion had momentarily darkened her eyes. Whatever it was, she chose to step back so he could enter, although she sounded distinctly sardonic when she said, "Disturbed that your plan hasn't worked?"

His plan. To goad a cold-blooded killer to go after *her*.

"Yes and no," he said. "I've been watching. I'm the one getting impatient even though I didn't expect immediate action."

"Why?" She waved him to the couch and sat down in an easy chair.

"Because he follows his rules. You have to go out with a man—normally twice—before he acts."

She gazed at him expressionlessly. "Except for you."

"It may have become apparent to him—I say *him* for convenience's sake—that you were unlikely to date a man anytime in the next decade or two. *Especially* while you were in Storm Lake."

"I didn't date you at all."

"We spent quite a bit of time together. Running, at the hospital…and kissing."

"We kissed once." Each word froze into an icicle.

"We did. In plain sight."

Her eyes narrowed to slits. "Like you planned."

"No—"

She went on as if he hadn't opened his mouth. "So this guy was eager to go for it, but when that was a flop, he decided to be…patient?" Her eyebrows had a quirk to them.

The muscles in his jaw flexed. "I've decided I need to investigate, not keep sitting around waiting for another attack on me, or one on you."

Jordan just waited.

He pulled his phone out of his pocket, called up his list of suspects, and said, "I want you to talk to me about these people. Whatever comes to you."

She closed her eyes momentarily, then said, "All right."

He started with the women: Steve Dunn's mother and sister, and a former girlfriend who'd gotten the boot when he became interested in Jordan.

"Kendra Gruener? I can't imagine. I mean, they were only

sophomores when they dated for a few months. She should be grateful she *didn't* stay with him."

"She should, but that doesn't mean she is."

Jordan sat thinking about it for a minute. "I don't think it can be Kendra. She was shy. I heard her dad was an alcoholic and her family life was a mess."

"Making her vulnerable," Tom said slowly.

"Right." She opened her mouth, then closed it. Had she been about to admit the monster she'd married had chosen her, if only subconsciously, for the same reason? Too bad Dunn couldn't see the gutsy woman she'd become, the one who'd had no problem holding off the cop who'd lied to her.

"Any suggestion he had an affair?"

Jordan shook her head decisively. "I can't swear one of those nights he was out at the tavern he didn't take a woman in back, but I don't think so." She focused again on his list. "Steve's mother... She hates me. She, um, thinks it's my fault he didn't go to college and continue his glorious football career, because she can't blame *him* for anything. I ran into her at the grocery store not long ago. Did I tell you? I pointed out that she had to know what Steve was, that I was willing to bet he'd learned from his father and that *she* knew what being married to an abusive man was like. I'm pretty sure from her expression I was right. I felt hateful for reminding her."

In retrospect, the sister reminded her a little of herself, too. "She almost seemed...skittish around Steve. Trying to please him, you know?"

"Kevin?"

Jordan frowned. "They weren't the kind of family that held Sunday dinners. And with him the youngest... I didn't see them together that often."

When prodded, she gave impressions of Steve Dunn's friends. Most, she thought, hung around him for the reflected glory. He had her study the list again to trigger memories. She knocked some names off his list. One guy had gotten a full ride to college with a baseball scholarship; another had moved away and died in a motorcycle accident. One lived in town, but was working with his dad in an auto repair business and doing some custom paint jobs on the side. Married, too, according to Mom, with at least one kid.

Cody Bussert, she'd disliked intensely. "After Colin— Dr. Parnell—was found dead and Cody came to the house, I could see he *wanted* to blame me."

"Or to make sure you were blamed?"

Jordan bit her lip. "Maybe. His level of anger didn't make sense after all these years. I mean, Steve and he were friends, but…"

"Unless Steve had done something extraordinary for him. I hear Cody's family was seriously troubled, too."

"Yes, I vaguely remember that he went to juvie for a while, but what could Steve have done to earn loyalty so strong, Cody would kill innocent people to get revenge on me?"

That was the problem, wasn't it? The motivation was so damned twisted, Tom had trouble assigning it to anyone, even the brother, who had earned a spot at the top of his list after the way he looked at Jordan the day he confronted her.

"Kevin," she said, reverting to the brother. "He desperately wanted to *be* like Steve. I used to wonder if Steve had stood up to his dad for his little brother. Maybe took some blows for Kevin's sake." Her eyes met Tom's with sudden alarm. "I don't know anything like that. I'm not even sure their father was abusive. I…guessed. That's all."

"What happened to the father?" Now, if *he'd* still been alive…

"Killed himself and another motorist when he was driving drunk. I saw him at games, and around, but he died when

Steve and I were seniors, so I never met him." She wrapped her arms around herself.

Comforting herself? Tom wondered.

"Steve blew up because his father was being blamed. He insisted the other driver must have flashed her brights at him or something like that. Couldn't have been the booze. Didn't matter how much he had to drink, he was a good driver."

"Lot of denial in that family," Tom commented.

Jordan's crooked smile was sad enough to perturb him. "I guess it was contagious."

Or her own SOB of a father had damaged her as much as an abusive drunkard had his family.

There were a couple of other names they discussed that Jordan seemed more uncertain about. Tom mentally shifted them to his B list.

He tried to sound offhanded when he asked about Deputy Chief Bowen. "Sounds like he's given you a hard time."

"He shouldn't have been allowed to be part of the investigation," she said, instantly angry. "But I suppose the department is too small to rule out two officers."

Tom stiffened. "Why shouldn't he have?"

"He was around back then. Steve called him Uncle Ronnie. I'm not sure whether there's really a blood relationship, or whether he and Steve's dad were friends. Steve and he talked pretty often, and they went hunting and camping together a few times while we were married. I'd see him out by his truck when he picked Steve up, but he never came to the door and we never had anything I'd call a conversation."

Tom had some incredulous and profane thoughts. *Knowing* the guy had that kind of relationship with Jordan's dead husband, Guthrie had still thought it was fine and dandy to let him be involved in an investigation into her possible complicity in two murders?

That said, the guy had been a cop for a lot of years. His

promotion to second-in-command suggested that he hadn't had uncontrollable anger management issues. How likely was it that he'd go off the deep end now?

Still, Tom couldn't believe the chief had been shielding an officer and maybe old friend. Maybe going so far as to steer the investigation to Jordan to be sure no one looked at his deputy chief?

If all of this been conscious on Guthrie's part, he needed to be fired—probably along with Bussert and Bowen. If that happened, Tom wouldn't be real popular in this department. Right now, he had one reason why he'd consider sticking to the Storm Lake PD after this was over: Jordan.

He didn't say any of that to her, but he moved Bowen up to his A list. Kevin Dunn was still up there, but their one encounter had introduced some real doubt into his mind. Was the guy capable of being coolheaded enough to pull off these murders? Bussert was still an unknown. Bowen, though, had experience and an ego on display. He was capable of the planning and execution of these crimes. Didn't mean he'd done it; even if he'd had a warm relationship with a real or surrogate nephew, why would he harbor so much rage over the course of years?

Still, a scenario was already playing out in Tom's head. What if Steve's mother told Bowen to butt out? Hadn't she implied that? Carolyn married and started her own family. Maybe Kevin was too angry to turn to his uncle. But there was Steve, the golden boy, the son Ronnie hadn't had.

And what if there was some guilt because Ronnie hadn't stepped in soon enough to keep Steve from sharing his father's anger and brutality? Hard to accept your own failing, Tom thought. But there was Jordan, who'd killed Steve. Blame *her*.

It made sense, even if Tom had just made the whole thing up.

Finally, he said, "I'm going to track everyone down. Find out where they are now, where they were when the doctor was killed, and where they were on the Fourth of July. Were any of them footloose enough to be able to go to Walla Walla for a few days or a week without anyone noticing?" He didn't mention that he already knew two of the people they'd discussed had in fact been free and unaccounted for that weekend.

"Kevin's married."

"Appears his wife left him. Don't know exactly when yet, but last summer. He lost his job about the same time—bad attitude, not his work ethic—and that could have triggered him to want to blame you for all his woes." Would have left him free for a side trip to Walla Walla, too.

For a moment, they just looked at each other. "Thank you," he said. "For talking to me."

"I should have done it sooner."

He tucked away his phone and rose to his feet, gazing down at her. "Do you know how much I hate nights? Knowing by the time I hear or see something, I could be too late?"

She gave him a wild look, then bowed her head for a moment, letting him see the fragile vertebrae on her nape. "I... didn't try to buy a gun."

He didn't know whether to be glad or sorry. The idea of her having to kill somebody, with all the horror that would stir up, disturbed him almost as much as knowing she and her mother were defenseless every night.

"I know you're angry with me." He sounded hoarse. "I don't blame you. But I'd give a lot to spend nights over here. I could bunk down on the couch. You'd barely know I'm here."

"I can't remember the last time I really slept." She gripped one hand with the other, white-knuckling it. "I keep thinking, pride goeth before a fall."

When Jordan paused, he quit breathing.

With the faintest tremor in her voice, she said, "I don't want to fall. And especially…"

She was afraid of anything happening to her mother.

Exultation ripped through him. She hadn't forgiven him… but she'd taken the first step.

Plus, once he introduced his plan to get her mother out of the house, Jordan embraced it. Mom was going to have a fake crisis and be transported to the hospital, after which she'd be shifted to the rehab facility where she'd been before. She could continue to get therapy there. He'd made calls today to arrange all this—subject to Jordan and her mother's agreement. Tom was careful not to let her guess how much fast-talking he'd had to do to set this up. It might have been impossible if he hadn't encountered such fondness for Shelly Hendrick and her daughter. Plus, he'd been able to use Dr. Parnell's name.

It was hard to keep his hands to himself when he saw the relief on her face. "I'll persuade her." She met his eyes. "Thank you."

LATE AFTERNOON, Tom called. After she said hello, there was a long pause. "You answered," he said finally.

"I let you in the house," she pointed out.

"Not necessarily the same thing. Ah…be ready for the ambulance. Probably another hour or two. I'll make sure I'm not around. Better if you look scared and on your own."

Jordan agreed.

The whole operation went incredibly smoothly. Mom obligingly helped the two medics settle her onto a gurney. Jordan ran outside holding Mom's hand and watched as she was loaded into the back of the ambulance. The male medic winked at Jordan, who tried to sound frantic. "I'll follow you to the hospital."

Mom barely paused in the ER, where a clearly complicit

doctor immediately admitted her. Had Tom gained so much cooperation because hospital personnel were angry and grieving about Colin Parnell's death? Did the administration know what was happening?

After sitting with Mom, she left to be home in time for dinner and to take half a dozen calls from friends of her mother and neighbors who had heard about the new crisis. She assured them that Mom was doing fine; it had just been a scare, but the doctor wanted her to spend a few days in rehab again where she could be watched closely. Nobody asked her to detail exactly what symptoms had led to the supposed 911 call.

Tom had let her know that he planned to slink through a few backyards well after dark and get to her house without openly crossing the street. Hearing no sounds out of the ordinary, Jordan waited at the kitchen table for his knock on the back door. She couldn't concentrate enough to browse news online or read. It was the first time she'd let herself fully realize that all of this had been designed to leave her ostensibly alone.

No, *really* alone for a good part of the day.

She thought about getting out a blanket and comforter and a pillow and piling them on the sofa to make it obvious where she expected him to sleep, except then it occurred to her that maybe he'd want Mom's bed so someone breaking in didn't see him right away. She plopped back down at the table.

He didn't rap lightly until almost nine o'clock. When she let him in, he asked how the transfer to the hospital had gone today.

"Like clockwork," she admitted. "I don't know how you talked so many people into cooperating. I mean, she's taking up a hospital bed tonight that somebody else might need!"

Tom smiled. "No, they have plenty of room right now. Everybody there knows your mother. They'd do anything for her."

That made Jordan's eyes sting. This was all so elaborate, it was hard to see how it could be a ploy to catch her in the act. Yet whatever her instincts insisted, she hadn't a hundred percent settled into believing he had faith in her innocence and really was here for her.

"I'm so grateful. I guess you figured out that right now, Mom's my weakness. If somebody hurt her…"

"Hey. Let's go sit in the living room."

She nodded. Tom checked the blinds to be sure they were all closed before he sat down with a sigh, stretched out his legs and patted the sofa cushion beside him.

Too close to him. She perched in the wing chair.

He watched her thoughtfully, except that wasn't entirely it. Her fingernails bit into her palms. Okay, thoughtful might be right, except she'd never had anybody focus on her so relentlessly. And *what* he was thinking so hard about was open to question.

She scrambled for something to say. "Did you learn anything today?"

"I talked to Kevin's ex-wife. She left him a few weeks before the Fourth, and says he got canned from his latest roofing job right before that. She said she'd had enough. She agreed he hates you but says he doesn't use a computer much. She can't picture him following you online long-term."

She blinked. "I guess that's what happened."

"Given that you lived in a different state, nobody from back home just stumbled on an article about Shroder's murder and your association with him."

"I didn't have—"

"You had enough to merit a visit from a detective," he

said grimly. "And potentially to provide a model for future killings."

Jordan found herself curling forward. "But three years later?"

He leaned toward her, any suggestion that he was relaxed gone. "Here's what I think happened. I think the killer *was* following you online. Could have been only occasional. Maybe he just hoped to find out you'd been killed in a car accident, or murdered a second husband and were in jail. He wasn't really motivated to take action until some bad stuff happened in the late spring or early summer. Whatever it was, that was the trigger. He couldn't fix his marriage or bring his wife back to life or time travel so he wasn't fired, but *you* gave him a focus for all his rage and grief."

He'd explained this before, without mentioning the trigger part. Shivering, she almost wished he hadn't been so graphic. "Bad stuff," she murmured.

"I have some doubts about Kevin, but he fits the pattern in a lot of ways. Job loss, wife leaves him, he's feeling humiliated, powerless, and his big brother isn't around anymore to shore up his ego."

"If Steve ever did," she mumbled. "I heard him be really sharp with his mother, but Kevin…maybe that was different. They were close."

"Did Kevin go hunting with Uncle Ronnie, too?"

"I don't know."

His jaw set before he added, "Carolyn says Bowen really was Steve's uncle, her mother's brother. She remembers him being nice when she was little, but he and the dad clashed. She thinks he might not have been that welcome."

"Clashed. Like two bulls?"

Tom grinned. "Ronnie didn't have his own herd, so maybe he was getting a little too possessive with another man's."

"But what does that have to do with *me*?" Except she knew. She did. She'd killed Steve, the shining boy.

Back to that watchful thing, Tom said, "Bowen took his own hit not that long before the Fourth of July. His wife died. Guthrie called it a freak accident. She fell down a flight of steps into the basement of their home. What if she was pushed?"

"You mean, he was abusive, too." Her stomach had tied itself into knots. If she'd known more about Steve's family, would she have married him however excited she'd been by his attention?

"No domestic violence calls, so I can't say. Either way, with Steve gone, too, he was suddenly left alone."

"Does Bowen know you're a cop?"

"If he didn't, he does now. Everyone will be talking. Whether Guthrie opened his mouth sooner... I don't know." He sighed and, as if he'd said all he intended to, he lifted his arms above his head and stretched. Winced, too, as if he'd forgotten his newly wounded shoulder wasn't going to cooperate and he wasn't as limber as he thought he was.

"I'll get you some bedding. Unless you want Mom's room?"

"No, the couch is fine."

It didn't take her a minute to produce a pillow and a couple of blankets. Then, hovering, she said, "I should think about bed, too. Do you plan to slip out early tomorrow?"

"Yeah."

"Okay." Jordan let herself look at him, really look, and said shakily, "I'm glad you're here. Thank you."

She was ready to flee when he rose to his feet and said abruptly, "You may never believe me, but... I didn't kiss you as part of the act."

Chapter Sixteen

He hadn't meant to open his mouth.

Jordan looked as stunned as he felt. "You bragged to him. I heard you."

"I know. I can't even explain. I was ashamed the minute the words left my mouth. Kissing you for the first time… it should have stayed private. You have to know I've been drawn to you since our first meeting. Not until after it happened did I realize it was a good setup if the right person had seen us."

"I wish I *could* believe you," she whispered.

"You can," he said hoarsely. "About this. I swear." What he wanted was to reach for her, but instead he didn't dare move.

She pressed her lips together, hesitating while he held his breath. This was like being back in junior high when you thought your life would end if she said, *Get lost.*

Only…she didn't. She took the smallest of steps forward and said in that same, soft voice, "It just happened for me, too. I should never have let myself even think about a man like that, only there you were."

"Will you let me kiss you again? Nobody can see us." Had he ever begged a woman in his life? He was pretty sure not, but that's what he was doing now. What he was asking for was a level of trust, and they both knew it.

Jordan gave a tiny nod and stepped forward. With a groan, he engulfed her in his arms and kissed her with ravaging hunger and very little tenderness. She whimpered, threw her arms around his neck and kissed him back as if she was as hungry for this as he was. As if she'd lain awake nights aching because she couldn't quit thinking about him.

He broke off long enough for them both to suck in air, then nipped her earlobe. "God, Jordan. I've been so afraid..."

The kisses got deeper, more passionate. Somehow he'd sprawled back on the sofa with Jordan straddling his lap. He pushed his hands up inside her shirt and under her bra, groaning at the feel of firm, ripe flesh topped by hard nipples.

"I have to see you." He was in the act of ripping her shirt over her head when he felt her stiffen.

"Wait!"

Wait? He was dying here.

"This is...awfully fast." She sounded as agonized as he felt, but she went on, "Hearing what you said to the chief... That *hurt*."

Because she'd been falling for him, the way he was for her.

But there was another reason she was right. This wasn't a good idea. He had a disquieting memory of that other kiss, when he'd been utterly—and, as it turned out, almost fatally—unaware of what was happening around them.

Easing his hands from beneath her bra, sliding them down her slim belly, he tugged her down to rest her forehead on his. "Once I get my hands on you, I get distracted. I'm supposed to stay alert."

Tom knew he shouldn't make love with this woman now that their trap had been set, not the way he wanted to. "God, I don't want to let you go."

"I know." She kissed his neck, then climbed off him as

he pried his fingers from her butt and nape. Her lips were puffy, one cheek red from the stubble on his jaw, but a hint of her wariness had returned.

She'd been right to put on the brakes. If they made love, it might kill him to see that expression in her eyes again.

But what did he do but blurt, "I've never felt anything like this before." Yeah, that was it; roll over and expose his bare belly.

Her face softened, but what she said was, "I...haven't either. But... I swore I'd never let myself be that vulnerable to a man again. You reinforced my vow when you lied to me."

"You're saying you can't get over that."

"No." She apparently tried to smile, but it didn't fly. "Just...asking you to be patient."

He took some deep breaths. There was only one answer. "I can do that. Whatever you need. However long you need."

Her lips trembled, her eyes shimmered, and she said, "Thank you," before backing away. It was all he could do not to stop her.

Tom could hardly wait for his night on the too-short sofa while living with the knowledge that she was only a couple of rooms away.

A DETECTIVE'S TOOL kit included the ability to stay calm and outwardly nonjudgmental. Tom didn't remember ever struggling the way he was while he listened to that jackass Kevin Dunn explain why he hated Jordan Hendrick.

"Isn't 'obeying' part of the wedding vow? Steve let her get by with not taking his name, and what's that say about her? What kind of marriage is it when she's defying her husband before the ring's on her finger?"

"Your wife seems to have gone back to her maiden name," he observed mildly.

Kevin sneered. "She knows she won't get a second chance with me!"

The two men stood on the porch of the shabby house Kevin rented. Both kept their hands in their pockets and thanks to the cold were puffing white clouds as if they were sucking on cigarettes between every breath. Kevin hadn't issued an invite for Tom to step into his place. Tom preferred to stay in the open.

He pointed out that every cop and medic who saw the scene after Jordan shot Steve felt sure she'd made a life-or-death decision.

Kevin's response was to spit onto the porch boards, just missing Tom's foot. "*Every* cop didn't think that. Probably not every medic, either. Else there wouldn't have been so much talk after."

Tom raised his brows. "Do you know a cop who disagreed?"

"Sure! My uncle Ronnie. He was one of the first guys there."

Actually, he hadn't been a first responder. Interesting that the deputy chief had let Kevin believe he was.

"Looked like a fight to him," Kevin claimed, "maybe both of 'em beating on each other, 'til that woman went for Steve's gun."

Tom had to remind himself that Kevin may have heard what he wanted to hear from Bowen. Nothing in the police reports indicated any such opinion.

Kevin continued to spew his vitriol, insisting, "A guy's got a right to know what his wife is up to. Don't seem like too much to ask."

Tom's jaw had begun to ache with the effort of holding back. Even now, he stuck with conversational, not necessarily disagreeing with this SOB. "I understand he lost his job that day. Went home steaming."

The sneer was imprinting itself on Kevin's face, the lines deep. There'd come a day when he wouldn't be able to erase the expression. "Who's to say *she* wasn't the one got mad because they might have to tighten their belts a little? He didn't like that job anyway. He'd have done better, but I guess she didn't believe that."

After another five or ten minutes, Tom worked his way around to asking whether Kevin had ever wondered where she was or what she was doing after she recovered and made the decision to leave town.

He shrugged. "Didn't have to."

"Because?"

For the first time, he displayed some caution. "I know people who don't do nothing but follow social media time wasters."

"Anybody in particular keep you updated?"

"Not one person especially. And I'm done talking to you now. Uncle Ronnie got to arrest her. He can tell you stuff."

Tom didn't bother to mention that "Ronnie" hadn't actually arrested Jordan, because he'd had no legal justification. It was unlikely Bowen had ever actually told Kevin any such thing. Tom nodded politely enough, and felt sure Kevin watched as he walked back to his vehicle and drove away.

His cover was definitely blown now. He was still driving his own SUV, but he'd shown a badge to Kevin, whose shock had been apparent. Tom had no doubt Kevin was on the phone with Uncle Ronnie right this minute.

How did Bowen feel about the subterfuge, assuming he hadn't known about it all along? Hell. Tom had never exchanged a word with the man.

Deciding to tackle Bowen next, he went by the police station, getting lucky when he saw the man walking across the parking lot. He didn't see any resemblance to Steve; Bowen had to have been shorter than both his nephews and his sister's husband, but was bulked up enough to suggest he did some weight lifting.

When Tom approached him, Bowen's eyebrows rose. "Well, aren't you the surprise. I hear Guthrie's letting you call the shots these days."

Tom held out a hand. "He hired me to initially focus on the one investigation."

They shook, Bowen not looking happy but not hostile, either.

"Yeah," he agreed, "Steve Dunn was my nephew. Far as I saw, he was always a good kid. I thought of him as a son."

"What about Kevin?"

"I offered to give him time, but he tried my patience." The deputy chief shook his head. "I thought I could get my sister to leave that SOB she'd married, but she wouldn't break up her family. Better for everyone if she had."

Tom agreed wholeheartedly but didn't say so.

The two men chatted for a few more minutes. Not so much as a flicker of response seemed off. If Tom had been more trusting by nature, he'd have crossed Bowen off his list. He'd also made note of how much of what the deputy chief said fitted in perfectly with the scenario Tom had come up with.

Not needing GPS to find anyplace in a town this size, he drove to Mama Dunn's place next. She was a cook and waitress at a truck stop just outside town, and he hadn't checked on her work schedule, but he found her home. She even asked him in and offered a cup of coffee, which he declined.

Surprisingly, Nancy Dunn didn't give any sign she knew a thing about Tom beyond his introduction. Certainly not that he'd been in town for a few months now, playing a role. She was a lot more careful in her answers to Tom's questions than her son had been, but she expressed a significant amount of anger at Jordan, too.

The longer they talked, though, the more the anger dwindled into wrenching sadness.

"Steve was a good boy!" Her eyes strayed to the fireplace mantel, where Steve appeared to have received star billing, from a grinning toddler picture through his graduation photo. "Everyone always looked up to him."

"I understand he was a heck of an athlete," Tom remarked, to keep her going. Seeing that row of images, he found himself annoyed again at his private acknowledgment that her oldest son had been an exceptionally good-looking young man. Jordan had had good reason for her attraction.

The father, he noted, had been a big, burly guy, undoubtedly handsome in his day.

No surprise, Mrs. Dunn was a pretty woman for her age. He'd have wondered about why she hadn't remarried had it not been for his memory of Jordan's speculation. If her husband had been as abusive as his son, this woman must, on some level, be rejoicing in the ability to live without fear, without having to worry about pleasing anyone.

He chose to be blunt with her about Jordan's medical records. He started with the ones from the ER across the state border. "The fact that Steve recognized she needed medical care but didn't want her to receive it here in town where he and she were known is a real red flag."

She stared at him, then faltered, "I... I didn't know about that."

Truth or lie?

He laid out what he knew about Jordan's injuries in that final confrontation before saying, "I understand you loved your son, but you must have been aware of his temper."

Her cheeks flushed, a color especially unattractive when accented by the blush she'd applied, but he also saw her grief. "I...knew he could get real mad." More softly, she added, "Like his daddy did. I hoped, well, that he'd never hit a woman, especially one he loved." She looked down at the hands she'd woven together on her lap. "I guess I didn't want to know. Once or twice I didn't like the way he talked to Jordan, but, well, his daddy could be hard on me and the kids, too."

"You put up with it."

He hated to see the shame in the eyes she raised to meet his.

"I was raised to think that's what a woman does. I never could've done what she did." Her hands writhed. "I shouldn't have said what I did to her."

He pretended ignorance. "When was that?"

"Oh, a few times. Right after, and then when we came face-to-face not that long ago. She was doing the right thing, coming home because her mama needed her, and I was downright nasty."

"I suspect she understood," he said gently.

"If…if you talk to her, would you tell her I'm sorry?"

He thought, *Why don't you do that yourself?* but only nodded. "I will."

After giving her a moment to regain her composure, he said, "I get the feeling Kevin and your brother are still fixed on blaming Jordan."

"Steve was…well, you know. Special. The best-looking, the best athlete this high school has ever had. Kevin wanted to be just like his big brother. Ronnie and I never did get along that well, but I have to give him credit for making himself available to both boys, but especially Steve. When Steve didn't get the kind of football scholarship he wanted, I hoped Ron would talk him into going to the police academy. That would have been a good career for him."

Tom hid a wince. He hoped psychological testing would have eliminated Steve Dunn before he was ever issued a badge.

When he asked about her son's friends, she said, "Oh, there's some who might speak out if they came to run into her, but that's all. Not like they'd attack her or anything."

"You know there's a possibility that a couple of men have been murdered with the intention of making it look like Jordan committed the crimes."

"I heard, but who would do that?" she cried. "No one I know."

He didn't say, *Oh, I'm sure you know someone who has done exactly that.* Instead, he thanked her for her time and went home to make himself lunch.

Somehow, he wasn't at all surprised to hear a deep-throated vehicle approaching entirely too fast and braking hard enough to skid on the icy pavement of his driveway even before he had a chance to heat up the frying pan to grill the cheese sandwiches he put together.

What did surprise him after a prolonged burst of *bongs* from his doorbell was the identity of his visitor. Kevin wasn't the only hothead; Officer Cody "Buzz" Bussert had been shaped by the same cookie cutter.

TOM SHOWED UP substantially earlier that evening, although he had waited until full dark. Still, his knock on the back door scared Jordan. He'd no sooner stepped inside, closed and locked the door, than he pulled her into his arms.

"Damn. I sit watching your house from my living room window *knowing* you could be in trouble, and I wouldn't know." He pressed a kiss to the top of her head before he loosened his grip. "I bought some timers for the lights today if anybody is watching my place. Which I don't expect now that everyone knows I'm a cop."

No, *she* was the bait.

After a couple of shaky breaths, she recovered her poise. "Have you had dinner?"

"I did." Without discussion, they went to the living room, where Tom carefully lowered himself to sit at one end of the sofa.

Jordan hesitated, then chose the sofa, too, but with a cushion separating them. "Can you tell me about your day?"

"Normally, I wouldn't," he said bluntly. "There are things a cop can't disclose. And honestly, when you've seen terrible things, sometimes you don't want to talk about it. That... can lead to problems in a relationship."

She nodded her understanding. Being stonewalled by your husband would be frustrating when you knew he was open with his coworkers but not you.

He continued, "That said, everything I'm doing right now, everyone I talk to, has to do with you. You're entitled."

He didn't say, *I know I don't have a hope in hell of gaining your trust if I hold back*, but if what he'd said last night was true, he had to be thinking that.

Watching her, he moved his shoulders a little, and she saw a nerve twitch in his cheek. Because he hurt? Was he doing physical therapy for this new wound? If he wasn't finding enough time, that *would* be her fault, she thought.

"Did you see Buzz come roaring up to my house?"

"No. Really? I must have been with Mom."

"Oh, yeah. He was mad as hell to find out that his talk with Chief Guthrie—the one I recommended—wasn't a fatherly chat, it was really what Bussert called a grilling. He blamed you, of course. After all, he was embarrassed by getting cut out of any calls or investigations concerned with you. Now he knows it's my fault. That anybody could suggest he'd have murdered complete strangers to get revenge on you shocked him. He's a good cop, and nobody is going to say he isn't. Especially *you*."

She rolled her eyes. "Back to blaming me."

"Yeah, but he resents me, too." He grinned. "Apparently

Guthrie left Bussert with the impression that I'm next thing to a cripple, which is fine in case he plans to sneak into my house one of these nights."

"I guess he hasn't seen you running."

He smiled crookedly. "Or maybe he has."

She gave him a reproving look. "You were getting better until you got shot *again*."

"Bussert couldn't believe anyone would look at him for something like that. Yeah, he and Steve were good friends, but I could see some doubt when I laid out the facts for him. I got the impression no one had ever encouraged him to look at your medical records or the photographs from the scene."

His matter-of-fact comment made Jordan want to cringe, although she refused to do so. She was done being ashamed in any way about her brief marriage or its ending. Still, she didn't love the idea that Tom was stirring new talk about her. She could just imagine the whispers. *Do you know how long she was unconscious? I hear she had spiral fractures. Oh, and a broken collarbone, and...* She hated even worse to know police officers like Cody Bussert could look at photos of her, battered and pathetic.

"Has telling people about my medical records changed a single person's mind?" she asked.

"Yeah." His voice dropped to a deep, velvety note. "Steve's mother. She...asked me to tell you she's sorry for the things she said to you."

Jordan held herself very still. "You're serious."

"I am. I think she was sincere."

Having confirmation that "Buzz" Bussert still blamed her for everything up to and including climate change—assuming he believed in that—wasn't even a faint surprise. To know that her ex-mother-in-law had changed her attitude that drastically felt... Wow, Jordan didn't even know.

"Jordan?" Tom asked, in that same tone. One she could almost call tender.

"I think I feel even worse about what I said to her."

He held out a hand. "Any chance I can talk you into scooting over here?"

How could she resist? She wanted to cuddle with him, even if much more than that still scared her. Once she came in reach, he wrapped an arm around her, and she soaked in what she barely recognized as happiness.

Her happiness expanded as Tom talked more about where his investigation had taken him. Detectives Dutton and Shannon had been helping him canvass hotels and Airbnb and vacation rentals in search of any of the names on his list. No luck so far.

"Most of these men would have been fine camping out," he grumbled.

He even talked about his disappointment and anger at Chief Guthrie and Deputy Chief Bowen.

"Should you be telling me things like this?" she asked.

He tipped his head so she could see his smile and the expression in his vividly blue eyes. "Like I said, you're entitled. Besides…"

"You think you have to earn my trust."

"Don't I? But that isn't what I was thinking. I trust you. I'd like to see you less guarded, but no matter what, I know you won't open your mouth when you shouldn't."

The lump in her throat took her aback. Did she really still think he might betray her again—or was she just afraid of taking a risk?

He hadn't known her when he took this job. He was set up to suspect her, and she couldn't blame him for that. But unless the instinct she'd been listening to was completely wrong, he had since shifted to an intense focus on protecting

Black Widow

her and finding out the truth, just as he'd promised. Couldn't she forgive him for his initial lies and misdirection?

If what he was implying was true—that he might even be falling in love with her—how could she *not* take the chance?

For all the hurts she'd suffered, the times she'd lost confidence in herself, she felt an unexpected certainty that he was much the same. He'd said enough about his childhood and, more recently, losing his friend, she knew that was true for him, too. They *matched*...if she could erase her last doubts. Or were they fears?

"What are you thinking?" he asked, voice husky.

She couldn't say. Not yet. Her mouth opened, closed, then opened again. "I was conducting an internal debate."

His expression of satisfaction struck her as sexual because he might look like that after—

"So, okay, I was hoping you'd kiss me again."

There was that wicked grin. "Oh, yeah."

Chapter Seventeen

Jordan had never known how much she detested waiting. Funny, when that's what so much of her life had come down to since she raced home to sit, yes, waiting at her mother's side at the hospital. Would she live? Could she recover?

This was as bad. She'd spent the past three days wanting to scream, feeling like a rubber band stretched until it had to snap any minute. The bone-deep terror because somebody wanted to kill her would have been plenty on its own. But then there was Tom Moore.

Yes, she drove every day to visit Mom at the rehab facility. In theory, she could relax there. Tom discouraged any other activities, though, especially running.

"But shouldn't I be safe with you?" she'd asked. Or was that "whined"?

An expression she didn't like crossed his face.

"If he thinks the kind of attacks he's accomplished before are too high-risk, he has another option."

Jordan had instantly understood what he meant. Most of the men in town were hunters and were capable of shooting her with reasonable accuracy from a couple of blocks away, and then be on their way.

No wonder her skin crawled every time she stepped outside! Tom did believe nothing would happen daytimes—

too many potential witnesses were out and about—but why take a chance?

Sun shining outside the windows or not, Jordan hated being alone all day. She just sat waiting and listening. She lived for the moment she heard that light knock on the back door and let Tom slip in.

Depending on how late he came, they might keep a light on until a reasonable bedtime for her. After that, they'd sit together in the dark for a couple more hours. She was deeply reluctant to sleep. When she did lie down, it wasn't in her bed, but rather curled up with a mound of bedding in her closet. She'd gone upstairs, dug through the stuff she'd left here, and found her softball bat, which was now her constant companion.

Most often, in the hours she and Tom had together, they talked quietly. Favorite bands, movies, sports. Topics gradually became more personal. Tom's reminiscences weren't so much reluctant as rusty, she diagnosed, as if he had blocked a lot out for a long time. His childhood had been much tougher than hers, she quickly realized, but when she said so, he nuzzled her cheek and murmured, "Different. When I was young, I didn't expect anything else. It was tough when my foster dad died, but—"

"He died. He didn't leave you on purpose."

"Yeah," Tom said in a quiet, gravelly voice.

Jordan didn't know about him, but she'd never in her life talked to anyone as honestly. He'd reach out and take her hand; often they cuddled. Nothing in her life had ever felt as good as his solid, strong body, always warmer than hers.

He told her about the frustrations of working homicide in a large city, when separating good guys and bad guys from each other was rarely simple.

"Protecting you," he said one night, "feels clean in comparison with some of my investigations." He told her about the friend who'd been killed, how much he missed him, then about his wife and young daughter. Almost choking up, he said, "Emilia says he'd have chosen to save me and die himself. I think it should have been the other way around. He had more to lose."

Jordan understood, but...she would never have met him. She held him for a few minutes after that, although she knew he didn't do anything like cry.

They laughed, too, also quietly. Kept dipping into shared tastes from food to ideas for a bucket list. Sometimes she almost convinced herself they were just two people getting to know each other—but then she'd wish desperately she could see his face, and would remember why they sat in the dark.

And oh, she wanted him to make love with her. Every single night, when she gave up and whispered, "Good night," he kissed her. Those kisses grew more and more serious, deeper, hungrier, until breaking off was almost more than she could bear. She didn't even know if he backed off every night because of his promise to be patient—or because he really did fear he wouldn't hear a small tinkle of glass breaking or thump that wasn't a normal night noise.

So on the fourth day, when her doorbell rang at two in the afternoon not long after she'd gotten back from seeing her mother, she flinched. Would she dare open the door to *anyone*?

She did creep like a mouse to peek through the blinds.

There was Tom, holding a pizza box.

She flung open the door. "What are you *doing*?"

He grinned and stepped inside. "Visiting. Bringing you lunch." His smile faded. "I promised I wouldn't lie to you again. The truth is, I want to see you in daylight when we don't have to be so on edge. But I'm also hoping that seeing us openly socializing will make our target mad." He shrugged. "We haven't exactly been subtle about being friends and maybe more. It might have looked strange this past week, me not showing up during the day now and again."

She couldn't decide whether to laugh or cry. She'd been miserable, bored, lonely, scared, and now here he was. With pizza, no less!

"Especially now that he knows I'm a cop, he's got to be wondering what I'm doing nights," Tom told her, as they reheated the pizza in the microwave. "My best guess is that he'll believe I'm sitting at home waiting for him."

"So we want to convince him I'm also alone at night." Bait.

He didn't even try to deny that he'd set a trap with a goal of convincing this monster that Jordan was here at home, on her own and defenseless. He did give her a hard hug and say, "I'm sorry."

She smiled with difficulty. "How else can we end this?"

TOM HAD SPENT the morning doing what felt like never-ending research. His effort to find out where the killer had stayed during the week he'd potentially stalked Jordan in Walla Walla had hit a dead end. He'd searched for traffic tickets on either side of the state border. He'd prowled databases until his eyes were crossing after it occurred to him that someone who enjoyed murder might have committed the crime at other times and in places unrelated to Jordan. Nothing jumped out at him.

"That's because you're not seeing what's right in front of you," Guthrie had the nerve to say. He snorted. "That woman has you cross-tied."

Tom didn't know what his expression had given away, but the chief seemed to shrink a little and kept his mouth shut when Tom stalked out of the office. He'd been even more ticked when he'd passed Bowen lurking in the hall probably eavesdropping. The SOB had grinned.

Walking out to his vehicle, Tom decided there wasn't a reason in the world not to expose his relationship with Jordan to the world, as long as nobody had reason to think he was staying nights. It wouldn't be a bad thing if his friendliness to her served as a goad to someone angry at the idea of the police investigator potentially romancing the woman the killer hated so much.

Tom believed an attack was just a matter of time. He pictured somebody who wouldn't be able to resist, whatever the risk. Somebody driven by deep, hidden anger. Somebody who thought he was smarter than everyone else. Look how much he'd gotten away with so far. And for how long.

Because all that was true, Tom ground his teeth at the thought. Jordan had been through hell because cops had looked for the easiest answer. He wasn't letting himself off the hook.

Increasingly, he leaned toward believing the killer *wasn't* someone who vented to anyone who'd listen. Like steam, every time you let go of some of the anger, the pressure lessened. But if you let the rage eat at you, that made for an explosive buildup.

Today, eating across the table from Jordan in broad daylight, Tom stopped thinking about much of anything but how beautiful she was. How he loved seeing emotions flit across her face, the purse of her lips, the way the weight of her mass of hair emphasized the delicacy of her neck. He loved the range of her smiles, too, from impish to wistful to true happiness. He wanted to think he was responsible for that smile.

He let her talk about her mother, who was eager to come home and claimed those darned physical therapists were working her harder there than they ever had here, in her home. "She's not complaining, though. I think she's on pins and needles as much as I am."

Her mother couldn't possibly be feeling the tension Tom did, with sexual frustration twined with fear for Jordan.

He'd put the leftover pizza in the refrigerator and was leaning against the counter wondering whether he shouldn't get out of here before he did something he shouldn't, when Jordan looked at him.

"You really think we're safe right now? That he won't go for me during the day?"

"I really think," Tom agreed. Damn. Was his body betraying his thoughts?

"I...suppose you need to go?"

"I never want to go," he said, grit in his voice.

Her lips parted. "Then...would you kiss me?"

Every time she asked, it just about killed him.

"Is that all you want?" he had to ask, knowing how thin his self-restraint was.

But miracle of miracles, she shook her head. "I want you," she said softly.

He was on her so fast, she let out a startled squeak, but she also met him with open arms.

This kiss went deep and frantic within seconds. She tried to climb him, and he helped even as he tasted her, drove his tongue into her mouth, squeezed her butt and got her sweater halfway off.

Lifting his head for a breath, he took a look around. Blinds drawn and doors locked or not, the kitchen felt too open. Besides, he had to get a grip on himself. She deserved tenderness. One of his worries all along had been about what her sex life with Dunn had been like. Abusers weren't likely to be patient, gentle lovers.

But if the guy had turned her off men, it wasn't apparent now. As Tom hustled her down the short hall and into her bedroom, Jordan slid her slender hand up beneath his shirt, kneading muscles, trying to reach his belly and chest.

At her bedside, he set about stripping her with maximum speed, and her cooperation would have made it happen even faster if she hadn't also been wrestling with *his* clothes. It being winter, they were both wearing too much, in his opinion. He especially hated having to sit down to take off his boots.

But when he lifted his head, she'd just kicked off her jeans. He stared. "You're beautiful," he said hoarsely. "Perfect."

"Not compared to you." Pink-cheeked, she inspected him. He loved the way she nibbled on her lower lip.

He lunged, bore her back laughing onto the bed, and sucked her tender lip into his mouth. They kissed some more, until he couldn't wait and shifted his body lower so he could lick and suck on breasts even more gorgeous than he'd imagined. He slipped his fingers between her thighs, finding her slick and sensitive. Things sped up when she got her hand on him, squeezing and stroking until he had to roll away before this all came to an abrupt end.

His hands shook as he got the condom on. Tom didn't remember ever having that problem. He intended to slow down again as he lifted his weight over her, but her legs were splayed wide, and her arms wrapped tight around his torso. The temptation was too great. Any worry he was going too fast disappeared when she whispered, "Now," and arched her back in a spasm as he pushed inside her.

She was tight, welcoming, everything he'd ever needed. Her hips rose to meet him; she dug her fingernails into his back and came with what would have been shocking speed if he hadn't been teetering on the edge so that he fell with her. His shuddering release went on forever.

Stunned, struggling to pull air into his lungs, he could only think, *Yeah*. With Jordan, he could live gladly.

"I'VE UNDERESTIMATED THIS BASTARD," Tom growled two days later.

"You're the one who said he's not impulsive, that he's patient."

"Yeah, but—" He made a sound in his throat and pulled her close for a quick kiss. When he lifted his head, he said, "That last bit of slush melted today."

"I noticed."

Tom only nodded. The fact that it would have been next to impossible not to leave footprints was a good reason for this guy to hold off.

"I may have misjudged his intentions," he added. "He could still be zeroed in on me. If he's gotten his hands on something of yours he could plant in my house…"

With impressive calm, Jordan said, "Should we move to your house?"

"No. Then your fingerprints would be all over it." Tom sighed.

"You look awfully tired." Now she sounded tentative. He must really look haggard. "I could stay awake for a while now so you could get some sleep."

He studied her drawn face. "You're not getting much more sleep than I am."

"No, I… I suppose not."

Tom shook his head. "If he comes in shooting, you wouldn't have time to wake me up. I'll be okay." How many more nights would he be able to make that claim? If this nightmare dragged on much longer—

Quit worrying about tomorrow, he told himself. What he needed was to be sharp tonight.

Something told him when Jordan said good-night, she

wouldn't be heading off to slumberland any more than he would. When that moment came, he kept the kisses gentle but unhurried. Whether she got the message he was trying to convey, he didn't know.

He did know that once he was alone in the dark, his eyelids felt as if they had ten-pound weights on them, and he had to keep getting up to walk through the house just to stay awake. Tonight, he was conscious of a level of pain he usually blanked out. No, he really didn't want to get shot again. He already felt like a damn pincushion.

Sinking back on the sofa, he listened to the silence. Jordan was in her mother's bedroom tonight. Not in the bed, in case bullets were fired right through the window.

More silence.

If I wanted to break into this house, he asked himself for the hundredth time, *how would I do it?*

JORDAN JERKED OUT of a shallow sleep threaded with nightmares.

Glass breaking had to be at the back door. By the time she understood, a distinctive *snap* told her the lock had been unengaged, and an intruder was in the kitchen.

A cry of fear escaped her before she could stifle it. She shrank deeper into the closet, shoving shoes out of the way. Tom!

Pop, pop. Those were shots, she knew, but not usual ones. A silencer? Whatever it was called. Her thoughts flew feverishly. She'd seen Tom's gun, and it wasn't fitted with anything special.

Creak. He was already right outside her bedroom door. The next shots struck her bed, which bounced. Oh God. She tried to will herself to be part of the wall at the back of the closet. Invisible.

Except...

Pop, pop, pop. He was firing farther away now, probably into the living room. Or Mom's room. Who knew? *Please God let Tom have been awake but not have leaped out to make a target of himself.*

Then she heard his voice.

"Drop the gun!" Tom yelled. "You aren't getting away this time!"

A snarled "You're a dead man" came to her.

More shots, some louder that had to be return fire. Terrified, she knew there was nowhere in the living room for Tom to hide. What if he was gunned down? She couldn't bear it.

Jordan steeled herself to crawl out of the closet, grab her wooden bat with shaking hands, and creep toward the door.

It was like being in battle. More shots. Plaster flew, bits hitting her face. Did she dare venture into the hall? Would either man have time to change out a magazine? The killer was running out of time, Jordan realized in some remote part of her brain. Neighbors must have called 911 by now. It hadn't even occurred to her that she should have.

Bang, bang, bang. Pop, pop, pop. How could they *not* be running out of ammunition?

Suddenly there was a massive crash, and guttural, animalistic sounds. She tiptoed into the hall, wishing it wasn't so dark, but saw enough to know the two men grappled with each other, one slamming the other against the wall. One body crashed to the floor.

What if she turned on the hall light? Only...it would blind them both.

Closer, closer... Oh God, Tom was down. The man with a knee in his belly wore something black over his head. Tom was holding on to the other man's wrists, keeping a handgun from lowering to aim at him.

Another pistol lay on the floor where she might be able

to snatch it up. Only...what if Tom or this monster had discarded it because it was out of ammunition?

Whatever her vow, she'd have picked it up if she'd been sure it had bullets left. Instead, Jordan summoned rage at the man who'd used a tragedy to try to destroy her life.

She jogged the couple of steps. His head turned, but his eyes were only black holes. Now he started to wrench that gun toward her, but Tom twisted his arm, drawing it back toward himself. The killer bellowed with pain or fury, and the gun barked again. Tom's body jerked from the impact. Both brimming with adrenaline and weirdly calm, Jordan readied for her swing, just as if she stood at home plate, and took it with everything in her.

The impact was hideous, like shattering a pumpkin, but she didn't care. She let the bat drop with a clatter, turned on the light, and fell to her knees beside Tom...and the man who lay unmoving, sprawled half atop him.

TOM HEARD HIMSELF swearing as he shoved the SOB off, rolled, tried to sit up. "Jordan—"

"Did I kill him?" She sounded...he couldn't decide.

"I don't know." Damn, he hurt. Yeah, he'd been shot again despite believing he was prepared. Would he have won the battle for the gun in his assailant's hands if Jordan hadn't intervened? He couldn't be sure and could never regret taking a bullet meant for Jordan.

"Sweetheart," he managed to say. "Come here."

Sirens were so close, he didn't know how he'd missed hearing them approaching.

"I have to let them in." Her voice was high, but she was hanging in there.

"Yeah. Okay."

He'd recognized the voice and not been surprised. He'd just as soon Uncle Ronnie was dead, but for Jordan's sake, it might be better if the bastard survived to be convicted to a lifetime in the penitentiary—the sentence he'd wanted *her* to serve. He could think about her every day for the rest of his life.

Tom couldn't quite make himself try to stand up.

Within seconds, they were swarmed with cops and medics.

"Take some photos before you move either of us," he snapped. Damn, was that Bussert looking so shocked?

From then on, events passed like a series of slides. As they loaded him to take him to the hospital, he heard Jordan again asking if Bowen was dead. Saying, "I hit him. He was trying to kill us both."

Then she saw that they were hustling Tom out, and tried to follow. When she got close enough to grab his hand, he tried to squeeze hers but failed. "S'okay," he said. "They need to ask questions."

"I'm sorry! So sorry!" Tears ran down her face, now that it was over. That's the picture he carried until, damn, he was under a bright light and a woman with a mask covering her face threatened to knock him out again. His last thought was comforting: this time, he believed Jordan would be waiting for him when he woke up.

Epilogue

Jordan had never envisioned the fallout beyond her small circle.

At first, once Tom recovered consciousness, she was occupied squelching his determination to beat himself up. He hadn't been asleep when Bowen broke in, but had been a step too slow. He should have rebounded faster from his previous injuries. Were all men like that? Jordan wondered.

She'd silenced him by insisting he was her hero, although he was determined to deny that. *She'd* saved him.

"I wish you could have seen yourself," he said. "Warrior woman. Although I hope I never see that expression on your face again."

She'd been trying to convince him he didn't have to pretend he didn't hurt, but in truth, his surgeon had encouraged him to get up and move. So now she and he were walking the hospital corridor just as she'd done with her mother a few months ago. He wore a sling, the bullet having struck the same shoulder as the previous wound. The surgeon had an air of reserve talking about what he'd done that made Jordan wonder how much of a mess it was in there.

Now, pausing at a rare window to look outside, Tom told her that ballistics had already established that Ronald Bowen had used the same gun to shoot Elliott and kill Colin Par-

nell—as well as wound Tom *twice*. They had him cold…
if he lived. Bowen hadn't yet regained consciousness. Jordan didn't feel as squeamish about that as she would have
expected to.

Tom also told her that the mayor had stopped to speak
to him that morning while she'd been meeting a contractor
who would have to erase evidence of the gun battle in Mom's
house before Jordan could bring her home. She'd rather her
mother not see the torn plaster and wood, bullet holes in the
front window and blood staining the floors.

"Guthrie has resigned. I don't know if it was under pressure or not." Tom's voice hardened. "If he hadn't, I'd have
pushed for it."

"But…why?"

"He had to know about Bowen's relationship with Steve.
It was bad enough that he let Steve's uncle investigate you,
given his partiality, but he should have understood that
Bowen was a potential suspect in the murders. He either
didn't, which is inexcusable, or he did and was complicit in
two murders and several attempted murders." Tom shrugged
his good shoulder. "Either way, he had to go."

"So why you?" she asked, although she had a suspicion.

"He wants me to take over the department. No one else
is remotely qualified."

Since they had reached his hospital room again, which
fortunately he had to himself, she waited until he had laboriously stretched out in bed again, stifling only a few groans,
before asking, "What did you say?"

"I agreed on an interim basis." He watched her with familiar intentness. She basked in the rich blue of his eyes.

When he tugged, she sat on the bed. She didn't remove
her hand from his warm clasp.

"Do you *want* to be police chief?"

"Right now, yes. This department needs a major housecleaning. Officers are inadequately trained, haven't been reined in the way they should be." He grimaced. "After that… I don't know. I think it's realistic to guess I've been shot a few too many times to ever plan to go back to an active job."

She wished she could tell how he felt about that. He had to regret not being able to pack up and return to San Francisco, didn't he?

Was he trying to read her, too? She wished she had as much confidence as she'd like, but did feel as if she had bubbles in her bloodstream. That had to be hope, didn't it? After the way he'd touched her, held her, the driving urgency of his lovemaking, she wanted so much to believe he could be falling in love with her.

When she stayed silent, he continued haltingly, "This is really soon, but as far as I'm concerned, where I work has to do with you."

The beat of her heart quickened.

"As long as you're here for your mother, as long as you want me around, I'll stay. But once your mother doesn't need you on an everyday basis, if you decide to go back to school to finish your BA or to grad school, I can get a job wherever we go."

We. He couldn't have used a more powerful word. No, he hadn't said, *I love you.* Anyone with sense would say it was too soon. Except Jordan knew that as far as she was concerned, it wasn't.

He was holding himself very still, she realized. He wasn't sure of her.

She swallowed. "I would…really like that."

His breath came out ragged. "Do you remember what I told you about my friend Max's wife?"

Jordan nodded, feeling a painful swell of pity for a woman

who'd lost the man she loved in exactly the way Jordan had just almost lost Tom.

"She knew about my background. That I'd become used to being alone. She all but whacked me over the head and insisted that, thanks to Max, I'd been given a chance to have everything. A wife, children, happiness. I mostly put what she said out of my mind until I met you. It was like a door opening, except after all my lies, I could see you closing and locking it. I couldn't imagine you forgiving me."

His raw, emotional admission brought the sting of tears to her eyes. With a cry, she bent forward to press her cheek against his, prickly from lack of shaving. She didn't dare hug him. He had to hurt everywhere.

"You were wrong," she whispered. "Of course I forgave you. And…and I want children and happiness, too. With you."

Tom's one good arm closed around her tightly enough to suggest he didn't intend to ever let her go, and she smiled and cried both. How had events so terrible led to this kind of joy?

* * * * *

COLTON'S SECRET PAST

KACY CROSS

Chapter One

Hannah Colton had more brothers than she knew what to do with most days, but Wade had always been her favorite. That's the only reason she took his phone call despite juggling crepe batter, a hot griddle pan and a five-year-old who had moved to step three in her campaign to convince Hannah to get her a dog. Washington at Delaware hadn't been so determined to win as Lucy was when she wanted something.

This occasion was what God had invented speakerphones for, if there was ever a doubt.

"Someone better be dying," she called in the direction of the phone and winced at her poor choice of words, considering Wade had been the one to call when their father had passed.

Not that any of them had mourned Robert Colton overly much. Maybe the loss of what could have been, but their father had made his choices long ago.

"Not this time." Her brother's voice floated from the counter as Hannah expertly flipped the crepe to let it cook on the other side for a precise one minute.

Most people only cooked crepes on one side when they were meant to be filled, but Hannah preferred the golden griddle-cooked color to be visible on both sides. It was this attention to detail that infiltrated all her cooking techniques over the years as she'd made her mark catering bigger and bigger events.

"Uncle Wade," Lucy broke in. "Tell Mama about the puppy you saw at Aunt Ruby and Uncle Sebastian's place."

Great. So Wade had been discussing the Great Dog Campaign with her daughter again. "Wade. What is the one thing I asked you not to talk about with Lucy?"

"Hey, Goose," Wade called to Lucy, ignoring Hannah's question. "Did you draw me another picture at school?"

"Oh, I forgot! I have it," Lucy announced and dashed from the room to presumably scare up the artwork in question.

"That was an inspired way to get her out of the room," Hannah told her brother wryly. "I hope it wasn't so you could start in on me about getting Lucy a dog. How much did she pay you?"

Wade laughed, and it did her heart good to hear the sound from someone who hadn't done much laughing until recently. Harlow had done that for her brother, and it thrilled Hannah to know that they'd found love again after giving up on each other in high school.

"It wouldn't kill you to get a dog. Betty Jane is a godsend, and you see how much Lucy has taken to her."

"Betty Jane is *your* dog," she stressed. She left out the part about why Wade had needed a therapy dog in the first place, though her brother's PTSD didn't seem to be nearly as touchy a subject as it had once been. "I'm up to my elbows in crepes for the Women Entrepreneurs of Wake County brunch. Did you have a reason for calling or did you just want to hear my lovely voice?"

"Uh, you called me?" he prompted. "Last night?"

Oh, dang. How could she have forgotten that already? The Great Dog Campaign was about to be renamed the Distract Mom Crusade, and she did not need any more of dog campaigns *or* distractions. "I did. Call you. I was just… I've got all these crepes. Hang on."

As quickly as she could, she plated up the remaining fifteen so she could chill them in advance of adding the mascarpone and strawberries. She had a little bit of time before she had to leave for the brunch at the civic center in Conners, where two of her employees, Judy and Todd, would meet her to help serve. As catering jobs went, this one was on the small side, but Hannah treated them all as if each client was her only one, plus she always managed the entire affair herself, regardless of the magnitude. That's why she had lots of repeat business and a steady stream of new customers via solid word of mouth.

Bon Appetit Catering was hers, and she'd built it from nothing. She wasn't just serving food at the Women Entrepreneurs of Wake County meeting—she was a standing member. She'd earned it.

She slid onto one of the stools lined up at the kitchen island where she did much of the prep work for her catering business, taking the phone off speaker in case little ears wandered into the room unexpectedly. Though it seemed as if Lucy had abandoned the kitchen in favor of her room, likely having fallen into a game or elaborate Barbie soap opera that was far more important than the picture she'd gone in search of.

"Okay," she said. "Hear me out."

"I don't like the direction this is headed," Wade groused, his voice shifting as if he'd found a spot to perch as well.

"What? I am a paragon of virtue and good sense." *Now* she was. Six years ago, no. But she'd done everything she could since then to atone for the unfortunate screw-up named Owen Mackenzie. "I would never bring up something that warrants the suspicion in your voice."

"You'd have to actually spell it out for me to hear it, Hannah Banana," Wade told her with a long-suffering sigh.

Fine. Yes. She needed to come out with her idea, but this was a delicate subject requiring careful wording. Especially if she hoped to convince her family, which was why she'd started with Wade. If she could sell him on it, he'd run interference with everyone else.

"Okay, so here it goes. I'm going to investigate Markus Acker."

"No. You are not." Wade's voice had taken on a hard edge that she imagined had made many a marine sweat during his time in the service. "End of subject."

"Un-end of subject," she countered, rolling her hand to mime lifting the imaginary restriction he'd just placed on the topic. "I need to do my part. Aunt Jessie is mixed up in this church that's really nothing more than a cult—"

"That's why you're not investigating him. He's a criminal. We know that much, but the extent of his crimes… We are not finding out what he's capable of with you as bait. Not happening."

Hannah sighed. So Wade could talk about bringing down Markus Acker but she couldn't? "This is my turn to help. None of the rest of you are caterers. I can easily figure out a way to cater an event for the church and use that as my foot in the door to do some additional investigation into the hold he has over Aunt Jessie."

This was necessary. Critical. Not only did she have a no-brainer excuse to finagle her way onto the Ever After premises, she owed her family for disappointing them. First, she'd married Owen, then she'd failed by not figuring out how to keep him around, at least for Lucy's sake. Sure, it wasn't technically her fault that Owen had turned out to be a low-life scum—her brothers' term, not hers, though she did find it fitting a lot of days.

Okay, maybe sometimes she thought it was *partially* her fault and that was her business. After all, she'd picked him. If she didn't carry that blame, who did?

No one else blamed her. She knew that. Rationally, anyway. Still, it felt like she had some atoning to do, and this was her shot. Wade could step aside.

"I cannot repeat this enough, Hannah," Wade said sternly. "Stay away from the church, don't try to contact Jessie, and for crying out loud, please do not walk up and introduce yourself to Markus Acker. If not for yourself, consider Lucy. She only has you."

"I know that," she countered, her mouth flattening as she internalized his point.

Did she really have the luxury of taking risks? No. If she had someone to help carry the load, then maybe, but that was a daydream she had no business harboring. Single mother forever or at least until Lucy went to college. That was her vow, and she was sticking to it.

But how big of a risk was it to cater an event and keep her eyes open?

"Han, promise me," her brother insisted.

"I promise," she intoned and crossed her fingers. "I won't contact Jessie and I won't accost Markus Acker in the middle of the street next time he jogs by."

"Mean it," he said gruffly, and she made a face at him even though he couldn't see her. Thankfully, Wade didn't notice that she'd left out staying away from the church, and she wasn't about to bring it up.

"I'm getting another call," she lied and then nearly yelped when her phone beeped to signal another call.

Maybe she should buy a lottery ticket since she seemed to be able to predict the future.

"I'll talk to you later, then. Tell Lucy Goosey I said to come over and play with Betty Jane."

She hung up without honoring that subject with a reply and switched to the other call from an unrecognized number, answering automatically because she'd already committed to it after mentioning the call to Wade. Normally she'd let an unrecognized number go to voicemail since it was usually someone wanting a quote for a catering job, which required a dedicated chunk of time to get all the details. She'd just deal with it real time as her penance.

"Hello?"

"Is this Hannah Colton?" the unfamiliar female voice asked. "Formerly Hannah Mackenzie?"

Something flashed across the back of her neck, heating it. She hadn't gone by that name in over four years. Not since Owen had hightailed it out of Owl Creek and probably Idaho as a whole, not that he'd bothered to tell her a blessed thing about his plans or final destination.

"Can I help you?" she countered instead of confirming the answer to the woman's question, because after all, Mackenzie was still Lucy's last name and until she knew exactly what the nature of this inquiry was, she would wait to share any information.

"I'm looking for Hannah Colton who was married to Owen Mackenzie. He's been in a terrible accident."

HANNAH DROVE TOWARD Conners, but not wearing her caterer's uniform, the smart white coat with the entwined *B* and *A* of her logo embroidered on the left breast. Instead, she'd scrambled to get Marcia to cover for her at the last minute at the brunch, dropped Lucy at her mother's house—which fortunately had always been in the cards due to the impending job—and then wandered around in a daze trying to remember how to breathe, let alone the four hundred things she still needed to get done. Because thanks to Owen, she was still a single mom.

Owen Mackenzie. A name from the past that she wished a lot of days would stay there. But she saw him every time she looked at Lucy. Lucy's features favored her mother's, but she had light brown hair, halfway in between Hannah's blond and Owen's dark brown. And she definitely had her father's eyes with her mother's green irises.

What she couldn't figure out was why the hospital had called her.

She and Owen hadn't spoken in years. If he had her phone number, it was news to her because he'd certainly never hit the call button even one time. Had he asked the hospital to contact her?

Okay, there were two things she couldn't figure out— why they'd called her *and* why she'd agreed to go see him in the hospital. She should have hung up and not thought a moment more about him. That's what he'd done to them.

But the lady who'd called indicated that there were complications from the accident and that it would be very beneficial for Owen to see her in person. In Conners. A stone's throw from Owl Creek, where Hannah and Lucy had been living the whole time without one single iota of contact from her ex-husband.

Curiosity, maybe, could be the driving factor here. Was he sorry he'd left them? It would be sweet to hear that. In fact, she had a serious fantasy about that exact thing. The second he saw her standing there, he'd fall to his knees, apologies pouring from his mouth profusely.

Of course, he had apparently been hurt in the accident. There wouldn't be a lot of falling to his knees, unless he rolled out of the hospital bed inadvertently. Which she would take. She wasn't picky.

Hannah laughed at herself. Yes, she was picky. She wanted a full-bore apology, first to her, then to Lucy second. Then she wanted to spit in his face and turn on her heel to walk out the door so he could see what it felt like to have some-one he'd depended on show him their back.

She drove as slowly as possible, telling herself it was due to the heavy snowdrifts on the sides of the plowed highway, but it was really to give herself time to settle. It worked, to a degree.

But when she got to the hospital, nerves took over. It would be a miracle if she didn't throw up at his feet, assum-ing he was ambulatory. She didn't actually know what con-dition she'd find Owen in. The lady on the phone had been so vague, continually repeating that the doctor wanted to talk to her in person.

After parking and finding her way to the correct floor, she crept down the hall to the room the receptionist had in-dicated, feeling like she'd stumbled into another world. One with a hushed sense of doom and urgency. She didn't care for the atmosphere at all.

A plate with number 147 next to a whiteboard was affixed to the wall. Someone had scribbled Owen Mackenzie on the white part with a marker.

The door was open. She forced herself to walk through it, her gaze automatically drawn to the figure in the bed.

Owen. Her fingers flew to her mouth.

His eyes were closed and he had a square bandage near his temple. There was so much white—his gown, the sheet, the bed, the walls. And machines. With beeping. She scarcely recognized the way her heart was beating, this erratic thump that couldn't find a rhythm.

And then he opened his eyes and fixed them on her. She smiled automatically because *oh my God*, it was Owen. Ashen-faced and obviously in pain, but she had never for-gotten that particular shade of brown framed by his lashes, like an espresso with just the right amount of milk to turn it a molten chocolate color.

His hair was longer, spread along his neck, and he should have shaved two weeks ago, but the scruff along his jaw had just enough edge to it to be slightly sexy. No. Not sexy. She slammed her eyes shut and drew in a shaky breath.

"Hello?" he rasped.

"Hi, Owen," she murmured and that was it. The extent of her brain's ability to form words. Her throat's ability to make sounds.

After all this time, after all the scenarios she'd envisioned, the tongue-lashing she'd give him if they were ever in the same room together again—that was all she could come up with? Lame.

"Are you one of the nurses?" he asked, blinking slowly. "Why aren't you wearing scrubs?"

Raising a brow, she eyed him. "It's me, Owen. Hannah. I know I've put on a few pounds, but come on."

Only five! Maybe seven, tops. Plus her hair was the same, since she hadn't changed styles in… Good grief. Had it really been four years that she'd been getting this exact same cut?

"Are we related? The hospital said they were trying to track down my family."

Confused, she cocked her head. "You're kidding, right? We're not related, not anymore, though I don't know that being married is actually the same as being related, come to think of it."

And now he had her babbling, which felt like par for the course. She'd been knocked sideways since the phone call back at home, and being here in this room with Owen hadn't fixed that any.

She had to get it together. This was her chance to make her fondest wish come true—Owen on his knees, begging her forgiveness, blathering about how sorry he was he'd left her. How much he missed her. How big of a mistake he'd made.

Then and only then could she hold her head up high and

walk away. Forget this man and the way he'd made her question her judgment every hour of every day, which was not a great parenting skill, by the way.

She'd get that confession out of him or die trying. She opened her mouth.

"Ms. Colton, I presume?" Hannah glanced at the door where a white-coated older gentleman stood with an iPad. "I'm Doctor Farris. Mr. Mackenzie is unfortunately suffering from amnesia. We had hoped that seeing you might jog something loose, but based on what I just heard, that doesn't seem to have happened."

"Amnesia." The concept bounced around in Hannah's head, searching for a place to land, but she couldn't quite connect all the dots. "You mean he lost his memory? That's a real thing? I thought Hollywood made up that condition for dramatic purposes."

"Oh, no, it's very real." Dr. Farris smiled kindly. "It's also not very well understood or studied so a lot of times, we're a little unsure on how to treat it. Conventional wisdom says to give it time, and eventually everything will come back to him."

"Sorry… Hannah?" Owen called, his gaze searching hers as if desperately trying to recall even a sliver of a memory that included her. "I wish I remembered you, but I don't. I don't remember who I am either. Can you tell me?"

Oh, she could. Absolutely. She'd had four years and change to stew about how this man had treated her. He deserved to hear every last horrible thing he'd done to her. Every last tear she'd shed.

But instead, she sat down heavily in one of the bedside chairs and blurted out, "You're the only man I've ever loved."

Chapter Two

The woman in Archer's hospital room was the exact opposite of one he'd have paired with his brother, which was yet another puzzle to solve. But apparently his research had been correct. Owen had somehow hooked up with this hot blonde in a sizzling pink dress and then lost her, like an idiot.

Of course, everything Owen had done in his life had been stupid. Including getting himself killed for a yet-to-be-determined reason by an unknown assailant, though Archer's money was on Big Mike Rossi or someone in his criminal organization. Who would have thought a quiet investigation into the matter would have landed Archer in the hospital with everyone—including Hannah Colton, aka the woman he'd been looking for—mistaking him for his twin brother?

Not Archer. This kind of lucky break didn't often fall in his lap, but he'd jumped on it, instantly coming up with the idea to fake amnesia as a plausible explanation for why he couldn't remember basic things about Owen's life.

It was working out fantastically so far. Other than the stitches and bruised ribs of course.

"We were in love once?" he asked Hannah, infusing his voice with enough confusion to choke a horse, but he had a part to play here.

Looked like that summer at theater camp would be coming in handy after all.

"I can say yes, from my side at least," she said as the doctor's phone beeped and he rushed off with a muttered apology. "But I can't honestly tell you what you felt for me. I came here hoping you'd tell me."

Archer nearly rolled his eyes at that. Figured Owen would screw up even the simplest of relationship staples like telling his wife that he loved her. No wonder she'd left him.

"I'd like to remember being in love with you," he said, which came out a little huskier than he'd have liked given the circumstances.

He had no call to be attracted to his brother's ex-wife, but geez. He hadn't expected her to be so beautiful. Or so… invested.

That was enough for him to put the brakes on anything approaching flirtation. He had a murder to solve, and getting cozy with Hannah Colton, his prime source of information, didn't go down well, especially not when she thought he was Owen. Which was not his original plan, but when he'd woken up earlier, everyone addressed him as Owen, probably because he'd had all his brother's identification in his car, though he wasn't certain why no one had found his real ID. All he was doing was rolling with it.

Hannah peered at him curiously. "You really don't remember anything?"

Shaking his head, he furrowed a brow and adopted the vacant look that Owen used to get when they were kids and he had to think really hard about something. "I don't even know why I was driving around Idaho. They told me I live in Las Vegas."

How was that for irony? Owen had settled in the same city where Archer lived, but they'd never come across each other, even though his brother had obviously dipped his toe in even bigger criminal organizations than before. He hadn't been able to uncover too much before his superiors at LVMPD got wind that one of their back office guys was trying to solve a case on his own.

Then one of his buddies on beat patrol had tipped off Archer that he'd attracted the attention of some very unsavory people high up in Big Mike's organization with his poking around, so one leave of absence later, here he was in Owl Creek. As Owen. It might end up being a great cover for a few days.

"I don't know either," Hannah said and crossed her arms, framing the vee of her blouse, which revealed a lovely slice of cleavage. "We haven't spoken in over four years. Since you vanished."

Archer didn't have a lot of experience interrogating witnesses, but he did have an eye for details and for synthesizing large amounts of data into information. Hannah wasn't comfortable. She sat on the edge of her chair and one foot kept shifting restlessly, as if she couldn't quite figure out where to put it. Her gaze never left him, but she'd seemingly spent the entire time they'd been talking cataloguing things about his appearance, her eyes shifting to his bandage, to his shoulders slightly visible above the sheet.

Did that mean she was telling the truth and hadn't seen Owen recently? He honestly hadn't known what to expect after finding Hannah's address in Owen's desk drawer at his house, but he wouldn't have been surprised if she had been involved in whatever shady dealings Owen had gotten mixed up in. Archer's investigation thus far had turned up a handful of Owen's associations with women, all of whom had their own rap sheets.

Except this one. She was a data anomaly, and anomalies bothered him. Ironing out wrinkles in data—that he enjoyed.

"I'm sorry for vanishing," he told her as sincerely as possible, hoping if he took the high road, she'd be a little more open with him.

Instead, she stared at him, agape. "Did you just apologize? Now I know you hit your head."

Archer nearly sighed. Owen wasn't much of an apologizer, no, or at least he hadn't been ten years ago, the last time he'd actually spoken to his twin. Full speed ahead, take no prisoners, consequences—who cares? These were concepts that resonated with Owen Mackenzie, not apologizing.

"In addition to losing my memory of people and events, I seem to have forgotten who I am too," he explained carefully. "This is me stripped down, I guess. No telling what I might do next. Maybe actually strip."

The joke fell flat as Hannah eyed him, her beautiful face a mask of uncertainty and suspicion. Well, yeah. He wasn't sure that was a real symptom of amnesia either, but it stood to reason that someone who had memory loss might also forget why they'd acted a certain way. Or what their motivation had been for being a jerkwad to this woman.

So maybe he could right a few wrongs here on behalf of Owen. Archer cleaning up Owen's messes had been nearly a full-time job for a couple of decades, before he'd gotten sick of it and cut all ties. This was one last hurrah that Archer had only agreed to because their mother had wept all over his shoulder, begging him to find his brother's murderer.

He would have done a lot for his mother in the first place, but then he'd discovered that not only was Owen dead, millions of Big Mike's money was missing.

No one had said he couldn't nose around *and* make Hannah feel better about whatever had gone down between her and Owen. She seemed so...genuinely wounded. As if she'd really cared about him. It was a puzzle why she'd fallen for a slick con man like his brother, and maybe she was faking it, but he didn't think so.

"Tell me what happened between us," he insisted gently, catching her gaze to infuse the request with some warmth, so she would know he meant it.

"We got married and you bailed," she said flatly. "As soon as you could, pretty much. I always assumed you had another woman on the side that you ended up liking better than me, but since you never bothered to explain, I never knew for sure."

The number of land mines strewn throughout her statements multiplied as he registered the hurt buried in her green eyes. "I can't imagine that being the case. More likely, I was scared. How did we meet?"

"Through mutual friends. George Kennedy. He was dating my friend from high school, Tory Baker. You surely haven't forgotten George?" she prodded. "You guys were so tight. I think you spent more time at his place than you did at your own."

Probably because Owen didn't actually have a place of his own, but the time frame in question had come after Archer stopped answering his brother's calls. They'd always ended the same way, with a plea for money or for Archer to fix whatever jam Owen had gotten himself into. Since Archer had busted his butt to get a scholarship to UC Davis so he could move far away from the tiny Oregon town he'd grown up in, it was a great opportunity for a clean slate.

"I don't remember George," he said, sure this bit was going to get tired eventually.

"This is so strange," Hannah confessed, her brow furrowed as she studied him like a bug under a microscope. "You're not anything like you used to be."

"How did I used to be?"

She bit her lip. "I don't know. Larger than life. You were such a talker. Free with the compliments, that was for sure. You turned my head in an instant that night we met."

Yeah, that gelled. Owen had always been a fast talker, especially when in the middle of a grift. What had he been trying to scam Hannah out of? Her pants, most likely.

He kept that to himself and gave her a gentle smile, mostly because the situation seemed to call for it. "I am in a hospital bed. Maybe I can get some of my largeness back after I'm not so banged up."

"Oh, my goodness, I am so sorry!" Hannah's hand flew to her mouth, and she poured out of that chair faster than warm syrup on pancakes to hover at his side, her gaze tracking along his face with concern. "Where does it hurt? What can I do?"

She stopped just short of laying a hand along his jaw with what he imagined would be a great deal of tenderness. She had that look about her as if she'd be a fabulous Florence Nightingale for any guy who couldn't fend for himself.

Technically he fell in that category, unfortunately. The amnesia was fake, but the injuries were not, and he did feel a bit woozy due to banging his head in the crash. The doc had mentioned something about broken ribs too, which explained why he couldn't quite catch his breath.

But Hannah might have something to do with that too.

Man, up close and personal, she definitely squeezed a guy's lungs. The scent of vanilla and sunshine drifted over him with warmth more suited for another kind of activity entirely. "I'm pretty happy with you just being here."

Geez, what was wrong with him? Flirting with his brother's ex, who was a suspect besides? Maybe he'd hit his head harder than he'd thought.

She smiled then and he forgot how breathing actually worked as her green eyes lit up with some sort of inner glow that he suddenly couldn't look away from.

"I thought about not coming," she told him and opted to perch gingerly on the side of the bed, her hip not quite touching his, but close enough that he could feel her heat through the thin hospital sheet and even thinner gown. "But in the end, I couldn't stay away. I needed to see you again, if for nothing more than closure."

"That would be a shame," he murmured. He wasn't done with her at all. And not for the investigative reasons he should be worried about. "Tell me more about you. What are you doing with yourself now? With your life?"

"I run a catering company. I started small, but I've really grown and now have ten employees, four full-time," she stated proudly.

"Wow, that's impressive."

He meant it too. Most small businesses could count themselves lucky if they ever had the dough to hire even one or two full-time employees.

Unless, of course, they were helping Owen launder dirty money through their business. Just because Hannah hadn't physically laid eyes on his brother in several years—assuming she was telling the truth about that—didn't mean she wasn't involved in the shady dealings that had gotten her ex killed.

Money made a lot of people do things they normally wouldn't and there was a lot of Big Mike's missing. He had his suspicions that Owen had been the one to make it vanish, and at the moment, Hannah Colton sat right at the top of his list for the person most likely to know where the dirty money was.

Being laid-up in this hospital bed sucked, but it did provide some unique advantages. Such as a dedicated audience with the woman who might hold all the answers he needed to solve the puzzle of what had happened to Owen. And maybe unravel a few other mysteries as well, like what Hannah's touch would feel like on his face.

"I've done okay with the money you left behind," she said. "I didn't want to use it, but I didn't have anything else, and you'd been doing so well with your investment banking company, I figured I could consider it a loan. But then you never contacted me again, so I eventually reinvested the principal. If you'll give me your banking details, I can have the money wired to you by tomorrow."

Delivered with a steel spine and a defiant toss of her head. She hadn't mentioned the sum of money Owen had given her, but people didn't wire small amounts due to the fees. They just Zelled it or whatever. The fact that she could transfer several thousand dollars at the drop of a hat—and wanted him to know she could—meant something, but what, he couldn't tell yet.

"I own an investment banking company?" he prodded, figuring that might be the best place to start digging.

He bit his tongue on the outright lie Owen had fed her.

"Mackenzie Holdings," she reminded him. "The money you left—it showed up in our joint account, and when I asked you about it, you said you were liquidating some assets, so you might have sold the company. I'm not sure. You disappeared the next day, so I never had a chance to ask."

Owen must have been laundering money even back then. If his dealings with this criminal organization went back that far, it changed things. How, he wasn't sure yet. There would be traces. Patterns. Data. Once he started pulling on it, he'd unravel it fast. Just as soon as Hannah filled in a few more blanks.

But before he could press for details on this mysterious money that had appeared, a uniformed officer wearing a heavy overcoat in deference to the frigid February temperatures knocked on the doorframe.

"Mr. Mackenzie, do you have a moment?"

"Of course," he called, as Hannah shifted to view the newcomer.

Not just an officer. The Wake County Sheriff Archer realized when the man stepped forward to hold out his hand.

"Sheriff Clemmons, Mr. Mackenzie. I'm investigating your accident, and I'm afraid I have some news that might be difficult to hear. It appears someone tampered with your brake lines."

"What? What are you talking about?" Archer did his best to feign shock and dismay, while a grim certainty settled in his gut.

He'd felt the brakes growing squishy, but he'd talked himself out of the slight niggle of concern since he'd traveled almost the entire way from Las Vegas to Owl Creek without incident. Surely whatever was going on with the brakes had been a product of his overactive imagination, which he'd fed consistently on the drive, hashing through the evidence he'd gleaned thus far on the organization Owen had gotten tangled up with.

"Slow leak," the sheriff confirmed. "It's too clean of a cut in the line to be anything other than deliberate and done in such a way that you wouldn't notice the leak right away. A pro job in my opinion. Did you get any work done on the car before you drove up from Vegas?"

An oil change. In preparation for the trip. Man, if Big Mike Rossi had his fingers that deep into the cracks of Vegas… Not that it would take much to pay off the service technician to do the job.

Thankfully, Archer had the perfect excuse—amnesia—and could reasonably deny it. Besides, if he showed all his cards, the sheriff would start asking questions. Big Mike would hear about it and more bad things would happen.

Archer's skin grew a little clammy. If he hadn't left Vegas, would he have been the victim of another, more fatal accident? Had one of Big Mike's goons followed him to Owl Creek?

The sheriff needed to stand down, that much was for sure.

"No." He shook his head slowly as if thinking about it. "I

don't think so. But I don't actually remember. I bumped my head and lost a lot of what used to be up here."

He pointed to his temple, and the sheriff nodded understandingly. "I'll be in touch. Are you staying around for a while?"

"At least until they release me," he acknowledged with a smile that he extended to Hannah. "Maybe longer than that."

Pending how things turned out with his brother's ex-wife. If she wasn't involved in Owen's money-laundering scheme, he might be in the market for a little downtime with her. Just for a few days while he kept his cover in place. He could fix the mess Owen had made of her heart and break things off cleanly. Let her have her closure while tying up all these loose ends. Two birds, one stone.

That's when his blood iced over. It didn't matter if she was involved or not. Either way, he'd just painted a big target on her back by coming here. If Big Mike didn't know of her existence before, he would soon.

Archer might have put Hannah in grave danger over his obsessive need to solve the slew of problems dropped in his lap.

Chapter Three

The doctor returned shortly after the sheriff left, giving Hannah no time to ask Owen what in the world was going on. Someone had cut his brake line? Did that mean it wasn't an accident?

A slight throb started up behind her left eye, and if she was really lucky, it would be a full-blown migraine by dinnertime. Of course she'd left her prescription medication at home in her haste to leave for Conners. The fun of this day might never end.

"Oh, good, you're still here," the doctor said to her as he tapped his iPad. "Do you have a moment to speak in the hall?"

With a glance at Owen, who subtly nodded, she stood and followed the doctor from the room. He didn't actually pause right outside the door, opting to stroll to the nurse's desk where presumably they would have a bit more privacy.

From whom, she wasn't sure. Did he not want Owen to overhear their conversation?

"Mrs. Mackenzie, I app—"

"It's Colton," she interrupted, hating to be contrary, but she hadn't gone by that name in years and didn't plan to start. She didn't even know what she was doing here. "Sorry. Owen and I are divorced. I'm not sure why someone contacted me of all people. Did Owen have my number in his phone?"

The doctor's mouth pressed into a thin line as a couple of nurses zipped by at a steady clip. "No, it wasn't that simple. He didn't have an emergency contact on record. In cases like this, we take whatever measures we can to find someone. We asked a few of our insurance people to try to find anyone from Mr. Mackenzie's life to notify of his accident. I apologize for the intrusion. I got bad information that you were currently married to him. Nevertheless, it's critical that Owen have some familiar things or people around to help him regain his memory. Amnesia is a terribly misunderstood condition, and we don't have a lot of data on how to reverse it."

"It is reversible, though?"

The doctor rocked back on his heels as he contemplated her. "I do believe Mr. Mackenzie's amnesia is reversible, yes."

So he'd go back to the way he'd been before. That would be...*awful*. Immediately, guilt panged her chest.

What was wrong with her wishing Owen would stay this version of himself? He was a literal shell of the vibrant, colossally confident man she'd met once upon a time. Early-Twenties Hannah had loved his boldness. He'd marched right up to her and told her he was going to marry her the moment he laid eyes on her for the first time. She'd been so swept off her feet by him.

And then she'd spent the last four-plus years getting back on them.

Slick men with practiced lines didn't work for Late-Twenties Hannah. For Single Mom Hannah. For Business Owner Hannah.

That was a sobering reminder. *No* man worked for her far better than any specific kind of man, even this brand-new Owen who had the same handsome face but nothing else that even remotely resembled the man she'd married. No matter how intriguing it was to think about getting to know this version of Owen a little better.

But then the doctor continued. "Regaining his memories is going to take time, though. And it would be helpful if he's exposed to things that might jog his memories, like you. I realize it's a bit of a stretch to ask you to spend time with him, given that you're divorced. It's a lot more difficult of a situation than I'd anticipated."

"He doesn't have any other family?"

The doctor gave her a look that she interpreted as—*if anyone would know, wouldn't it be his ex-wife?* Maybe in a lot of marriages, but not hers. He'd never mentioned any family to her, and she'd always assumed he'd been raised by a single mother who had passed. Ashamed all at once that she'd never pressed him on it, she lifted a hand to her burning cheek.

What must Doctor Farris think of her for not knowing basic things about her ex-husband?

"The people we put on finding a contact are pretty thorough since they're usually trying to track down people who have outstanding balances. They couldn't find any trace of relations other than you," he confirmed.

Her heart kind of caved in a little at that. He didn't have anyone. Except her. And he really didn't even have her. How sad was that?

Granted, he'd probably brought his solitary state on himself. He'd alienated a woman who'd loved him and thought he'd hung the moon. Abandoned his own daughter, without so much as a phone call on her birthday, ever. If he could even cite her birthday, she'd stand on her head.

He had no one because he cared about no one.

Stay firm. No sympathy.

She'd come for an exorcism, not a reconciliation. How else could she verify that she was well and truly over him than to face him one final time? Only, she hadn't expected to find herself dropped into an upside-down world where Owen didn't even *remember* her.

Her stupid heart pinged again. If she could get him to remember her, he might regain his other memories. In time. But that would mean she'd have to come back. Probably more than once. She couldn't hop in her car and drive away forever, tossing the man in her rearview with her soul free as a bird.

"Maybe if I talk to him some more, I can help him remember other family," she suggested, knowing in her heart it wouldn't be likely. Insurance people wouldn't miss something like a whole family, but somehow manage to dig up the contact information for a woman he'd divorced over four years ago.

But she had to try. Then she'd be off the hook.

"That would be a good place to start," the doctor said with a kind smile that reached his eyes behind wire-rimmed glasses. "I hope you realize I just want what's best for my patient. That's all."

She nodded. At the moment, that was her. She was the best thing for Owen.

After a deep cleansing breath that did not work to calm the slosh of emotions spilling over her edges, she marched back to Owen's room, determined to make some progress.

When he caught sight of her coming through the door, his lips tipped up in a tentative smile that took out the backs of her knees unexpectedly.

No. Bad Hannah. No reacting to the vulnerable, hot-as-sin man in the bed.

"They said you don't remember any family," she said, infusing her tone with the same no-nonsense steel she used to make sure Lucy knew she wasn't playing around. "When we got married, you said you were on your own. I thought that meant your parents were both gone. Maybe you remember how they died?"

Owen cocked his head, watching her with an expression she couldn't read. "You never met my parents?"

"Does that mean you remember them?" she prodded hopefully, dragging the chair closer to the bed where she could talk to him without getting too close.

"No, it means I'm fascinated to learn about our relationship, and I guess I just always thought that married people hung out with each other's parents, like at Christmas and such."

That was a promising lead if she'd ever heard one. "You have memories of Christmas with a family?"

He frowned, his expression going slightly vague as if struggling to make his brain work. "It's more of a general idea that Christmas is about spending time with people who matter. I don't know if I've ever done that. What did we do at holidays?"

"You worked," she reminded him bluntly. "We were only together for two Christmases, and you spent the entire day on the phone the second one."

He'd complained about Lucy crying for most of it, but she'd been a baby. Babies cried. It had always been baffling to her how hostile Owen had seemed about his own daughter. That was probably at least half of the reason she hadn't mentioned Lucy yet.

What if his daughter brought back all his memories and he got that look of disgust on his face like in those days after she'd been born? Worse, what if he *didn't* remember her?

"I'm sorry," he said softly. "I have a feeling I have a lot to make up for when it comes to you."

He didn't know the half of it. "You don't remember our

marriage at all? Not the wedding at the courthouse? Not living in your swanky condo?"

Owen had insisted that she move into his place in Conners, away from her large family. They'd never gotten along well, which frankly should have been a sign.

"I wish I did remember."

His brown eyes bored into hers, probing, as if he could find all the answers he sought right there inside her and that would be enough for him. She would be enough.

For half a second, she wanted to let him. Invite him in and rekindle the fierceness between them. Things had been so good at first. She'd been so blinded by everything about him that she'd let him become her entire world. To her detriment.

She shook off the odd connection that had sprung up as she stood there in Owen's hospital room. She wasn't twenty any longer. A man would never be her entire world again. About the only thing she had to thank this one for was Lucy and the seed money she'd used to start her catering business, which she would gladly pay back, but had considered due compensation for not insisting on alimony or child support.

Lucy wasn't Owen's in any way except as a sperm donor.

What if Owen remembered her and wanted to be a part of her life? An ice pick stabbed at her eyes from the vicinity of her brain, a sure sign that she'd be spending the rest of the day in a dark room.

She wasn't the same woman any longer and Owen certainly wasn't the same man. He'd have zero shot at wooing her the way he had the first time around.

But *guh*, he'd developed a whole new slew of ways to get her attention, from the deepness in his gaze to the subtle differences in his hair and scrubby beard. Slick Owen had been super gorgeous, sure, but Quiet Owen pinged her in a place deep inside that she was having trouble getting to settle down.

"Try," she commanded him. "Think really hard about

your investment banking company. You had an office on State Street, in the Grant building. It was fancy, but kind of sterile if you want my honest opinion. I visited you there a couple of times. Once we had a picnic in the park across from your office. Surely you remember that day."

It was the day he'd asked her to marry him.

Owen shook his head, a tinge of sadness pulling at his expression. "I'm sorry. There's just nothing. I can remember things like I'm supposed to brush my teeth after I eat but there's just blackness where people should be."

What in the world would make her think that pushing him would shake loose a flood of locked-up memories? She'd have to google some information about how to help an amnesia victim recover.

"I'm sorry too," she told him honestly and moved to the bed after all, drawn by the sheer unhappiness she sensed from him.

Probably he deserved to be miserable, but she just didn't have it in her to be the source of it. Sure, it would be nice to hear him say that he'd regretted leaving her every minute of every day, but he'd have to remember her to figure that out, and the odds were slim that would happen today.

He watched her settle, the bandage on his temple a constant reminder that he'd been hurt. And she'd been interrogating him like he'd committed some kind of crime.

"How do you feel?" she asked softly.

"Like I've been hit by a bus," he confessed readily. "I bruised my ribs and I get a little woozy when I stand up, so I've been ordered to stay in bed for twenty-four hours. Then they'll do another evaluation."

He didn't seem too upset about that part of his situation, which was a touch frightening—that a vibrant man like Owen would consent to lying in a hospital bed like an invalid. It would be more in his character to be ripping out the IV needle and shoving aside the sheet with the proclamation that he was fine—everyone quit treating him like he was ninety.

"Hannah?" He blinked up at her. "I'm really glad you're here. It couldn't have been easy to get in the car, knowing you'd be seeing me again after the way I treated you."

Her eyes went wide and she had to blink a bunch to fix the sudden dryness. That was practically an apology and an expression of regret all in one. The ice pick behind her eyes vanished in an instant. "You really don't remember the way you used to act, do you?"

Old Owen didn't apologize. For anything. He certainly didn't acknowledge that there was anything to apologize for.

"I don't, no. But I have a feeling I was a piece of work. Maybe this is my chance to change that."

Then he did the worst thing he possibly could have. He reached out and covered her hand with his. It was the most innocuous kind of contact possible. Two people touching skin. No big deal.

It was a big deal. And it was far from harmless the way her entire body reacted, heating in an instant.

That was familiar. But also completely different because she recognized it as something separate from her feelings for him. That she *could* separate the two. Being attracted to someone didn't have to engage her heart—in fact, it was far better if it didn't. Twenty-year-old Hannah hadn't possessed that kind of insight. And she still hadn't forgiven Owen for teaching her the difference.

"I have to go," she choked out and nearly fell off the bed in her haste to remove herself from the source of her consternation.

She'd have to move to Mars at this point to accomplish that.

His dark eyes tracked her with a solemnness she had to look away from. "Will you be back?"

Would she? "I don't know. This is just…a lot."

And then she fled before he could do something else to confuse her, intrigue her, light her up inside. All of the above, all at one time. It was overwhelming.

None of it dissipated with distance either. She could scarcely catch her breath, could barely feel the frigid steering wheel of her car beneath her gloveless hands after she threw herself into the front seat of the Honda she'd bought within a year of being in the black with her catering company.

This wasn't over. Far from it. But whether she'd make the journey back to the hospital remained to be seen. She had a business. A daughter. People other than herself who counted on her.

But at the end of the day, Owen needed her too, and she was having a very hard time figuring out why that felt so good. And how to stop it.

Chapter Four

Hannah pulled up to the front of the dark gray clapboard on the lake, a wide swath of property spread out on each side that sloped down toward the water. There was plenty of room for multiple vehicles in the crushed stone half-circle driveway that often hosted at least one guest's car, as it did today.

It was Ruby's. Hannah's sister had recently given birth to her first child, a son named Sawyer, who'd just turned four months old. With the baby's arrival came a new SUV, the kind that could hold the additional kids likely in her future. It was no surprise to find Ruby here since she often dropped by with Jenny's first grandchild.

Lucy was still at that enthralled stage with the first baby she'd been around for any appreciable length of time. Honestly, it was a blessing she'd been after Hannah for a dog instead of a baby sister or brother.

For who knew what reason, that made her think about Owen. Again. Okay, she'd never stopped. It wasn't a crime, and no one had to know that she'd finally admitted to herself that she couldn't hate him like she'd hoped.

"Mama!"

Lucy dashed out of the open front door to throw herself at Hannah. Little girl essence engulfed her and she breathed deep, already missing the baby scent that had faded far too quickly.

She lifted Lucy into her arms, grateful that today wasn't the day she'd realize she couldn't pick her up any longer. "Hey, there. How's my girl?"

"Lu Lu, you can't unlock the door and run out," Jenny called, wiping her hands on a towel as she charged out after her granddaughter, stopping short when she saw that Hannah had Lucy in her arms. "Hi, hon. Did you get your business taken care of?"

"Yeah, I guess so," she mumbled, both glad she hadn't told her mother what she'd needed to drive to Conners for and sorry she didn't have a sounding board.

Jenny's opinion mattered to her, even after Hannah had grown into adulthood. A lot of her friends considered their parents old-fashioned and out of touch, but she'd never thought that way about Jenny, and besides, her mother had been dealt a pretty tough row to hoe when she'd learned—after he passed away—of her husband's secret affair with Aunt Jessie.

Hannah followed her mother inside the house, setting Lucy down in the foyer so she could greet Ruby, then steal the baby from her. There was no human on earth who could resist a sweet face that happily blew bubbles while being held. His Aunt Hannah cooed at him.

"You are the bestest boy ever, aren't you, my darling?" Hannah told the baby and rubbed noses with him. "Any time you want to come visit me and let your mama go out on the town with her handsome husband, you tell her."

Ruby raised a brow. "Sure about that? Because I would totally take you up on it."

"Name the day," Hannah shot back, meaning it. "I would be thrilled to have the baby all to myself. Grandma always horns in when we're over here."

Laughing, Jenny did exactly that, scooping the baby out of Hannah's arms. "Get one of your own."

"One is all I need," Hannah joked back, her throat inexplicably tight as she swung Lucy up into her empty arms, rocking her daughter back and forth, somehow staying on her feet despite the weight difference between her kid and Ruby's.

"Mama, I'm not a baby," Lucy insisted and squirmed free to run over to the TV, plopping down in the swivel chair in front of an episode of *Peppa Pig*, the one with Grampy Rabbit's hovercraft, which was her favorite.

The exchange wasn't out of the norm. Hannah had just been messing around, but the reminder that Lucy wasn't a baby any longer hit her extra hard today of all days, especially after seeing Owen. She'd buried the wound deep, but it had been sitting there festering for four long years, and their marriage wasn't the only thing he'd torn from her.

She'd always dreamed of having a big family like her own mother had. That possibility didn't exist any longer. And it was hard. *So* hard.

"What's wrong?" Ruby demanded, her attention on Hannah since she didn't have a baby in her face to occupy her at the moment.

Thanks, Mom. Hannah swallowed. "Nothing."

"Liar." Her older sister eyed her as if she were twenty years her senior instead of two. "You might as well spill it. You know you can't keep a secret."

That was true. The second she'd agreed to marry Owen, Ruby had been the first person she'd told. A plus sign on the pregnancy test? Ruby. Owen was acting strange and not looking her in the eye? Her sister had been the one she called.

"Because it's not a secret." She let out a long breath that sounded as long-suffering as she felt. She waved them both over to the kitchen where little ears couldn't hear and low-ered her voice. "I saw Owen today."

"Owen!" Jenny and Ruby screeched at the same time.

"Shh," she hissed out and jerked her head at Lucy, who was still face first in the TV, laughing at something Peppa had done. "I mean it's not a secret from you guys."

"Start talking," Ruby said grimly as Jenny frowned and hugged the baby closer. "And you better not start out with *it's not what you think.*"

What, was Ruby practicing her mind reading? "It's *not* what you think. He was in an accident. He has amnesia."

Both Ruby and Jenny glanced at each other, but it was Jenny who spoke this time. "That's pretty convenient, don't you think? He vanishes and shows back up, trying to worm his way into your good graces again. What better way to avoid having to explain himself or even apologize than to fake being injured?"

Ruby nodded, and the ice pick started up again behind Hannah's eyes. Dang it. Why had she brought this up again? Sighing, she massaged her temples, leaning on the granite countertop of the bar that separated the kitchen from the informal dining area.

"It's not like that. He's in the hospital in Conners. I spoke to the doctor and everything."

"That's where you went earlier," Jenny said with a sage nod. "I wondered why you looked like you'd seen a ghost when you left."

Because that's how she'd expected to feel when she laid eyes on Owen again. Instead, she'd glimpsed something far more affecting. "If he's faking amnesia to get off the hook, he's a much better actor than anyone working in Hollywood today. He's really injured too. He has a gash on his head with a bandage and everything. They're keeping him overnight for observation and maybe longer if the amnesia persists."

How had she shifted into a position where she was *defending* him? Because it felt like her defense too. As if she had to make sure everyone understood that she wasn't about to let him waltz back into her life without some really extenuating circumstances.

Wait, no. She wasn't letting him do anything with her *or* her life. No waltzing. No falling for his slick talk again.

"Not to put too fine a point on it, but why did they call *you*?" Ruby wanted to know. "Did you tell them he's a low-life creep and to make sure he jumps in Blackbird Lake when he's released?"

"Of course not. He's hurt, Rube. Like really banged-up. Worse, someone did this to him deliberately!" she told them in a hushed voice. "The sheriff came and said someone cut the brake lines."

Jenny's hand flew to her mouth. "Oh, my Lord. You need to stay far away from him then if he did something to make someone angry enough to try to kill him. It sounds really dangerous."

Well, duh. Of course she'd thought of that. But he needed someone familiar to help break through whatever was blocking his memories.

The real question was why she cared.

"I'm fine, Mom. I know how to be careful."

"Do you know how to tell that man to get lost?" Ruby asked. "Because it sounds like you need to practice. A lot."

Boy, her mother and sister had a lot of opinions about what Hannah needed to do and not a lot of faith in her or her judgment, obviously. Her heart sank a little. Yeah, she'd screwed up in the good judgment department where Owen was concerned. But couldn't they give her a little credit for having learned a few things since then?

"Mama, come watch this with me," Lucy called from the living room, a pointed reminder that the adults might be two rooms away in the kitchen, but they weren't in a vacuum. Her daughter could clue in at any moment that they were talking about her father and start asking questions.

The ice pick stabbed at her eyes again. So what if she did? Owen was *Lucy's father*. Or at least he'd had a hand in creating her. Obviously, he'd opted out of his patriarchal duties years ago, which was why she'd gone to great lengths to make sure he couldn't hurt Lucy by never chasing him down to insist he visit or pay child support.

Everything was a mess. She had no idea what she was supposed to do half the time as it was. Playing the part of both parents was exhausting enough without tossing giant unanswered questions into the mix.

Hannah threw her mom and her sister an apologetic glance and dropped the conversation like a hot potato. Gladly.

Gliding into the living room, she stood behind the swivel chair and stroked Lucy's hair. "This is a funny part, for sure."

Lucy laughed and the sound reverberated in Hannah's chest.

Owen had missed out on every second of this kind of thing so far. As much as she'd been trying to get him to admit he missed Hannah and was sorry he'd left her, a part of her wondered how he felt about his daughter. Had he ever thought about the tiny baby he'd walked out on and mourned the loss of being a dad?

Her hand froze on Lucy's head. What if that's why he'd come back to Owl Creek? What if he'd been sorry about skipping out on being a father and had come back to rekindle his relationship with *Lucy*, not Hannah?

Chapter Five

Being in the hospital sucked worse the longer Archer remained stuck there. The bed could pass for concrete and no matter which way he shifted, something still hurt.

Big Mike would pay for this. Eventually. Archer spent a few glorious moments fantasizing about punching the crime boss in the ribs and seeing how he liked not being able to breathe without wincing.

As if pain was the biggest worry Archer had. Immobilization ranked pretty high on the list too, especially if some goons had made their way north. Passing for his brother might eventually climb a few notches on the list of concerns, but only if Hannah Colton returned to the hospital, and given the way she lit out of here yesterday, he wasn't holding out much hope that he'd ever see her again.

Except the next time he looked up, she stood in the doorway, her beautiful face composed and her hair in a simple ponytail. Her eyes told a different story though. Deep and troubled, they sought him out and nearly walloped him with the strength of her conflict.

She didn't want to be here. That much was clear, especially given the way she hadn't actually entered the room. Her crisply ironed dress hit below the knees, drawing attention to her curves beneath, but he had a feeling that was not the effect it would have on most people.

Archer wasn't most people. He had a very fine appreciation for Hannah Colton that transcended her no-nonsense dress and hairstyle. Maybe even because of it. He had a feeling she'd dressed that way on purpose, to give him the impression she was all business.

But he knew better. No woman who had caught the attention of Owen Mackenzie could possibly be as buttoned-up as this one appeared to be. She must have a whole different side to her, one he'd like to uncover—*after* he figured out whether she and his brother had been working together.

Dang, was it too easy to forget all of that. He and Hannah watched each other, and she finally broke the silence.

"I didn't want to come back," she told him needlessly.

Why she'd been so reticent was the important question. A woman in cahoots with Big Mike didn't have anything to worry about. In fact, she might have been sent to monitor him in a way goons never could.

His gut told him that wasn't what was going on. He'd been fooled before by women in the past, so it was all the more reason to keep her closer than a friend. Nice that cozying up to her fit his agenda too.

He smiled at her, letting it turn genuine because it was easy to do so with her. "But you did. I'm glad."

"I'm only staying long enough to help you work on regaining your memories. I'd still like to pay you back the money you left behind, but I guess I can't exactly wire funds to an account if you don't remember your banking information."

He shrugged and shook his head, squelching the pang of admiration that she'd continued to bring this up. "I have a banking app on my phone, but I guess I'm not the kind of guy to save passwords because I can't get into it."

She didn't have to know that Owen had configured his

banking app to allow log-on via fingerprint and his wasn't identical enough to his brother's to allow it to open. Ironic. Facial recognition worked fine but not fingerprints. The technological downside to trying to pass for his twin.

It also didn't matter because all of Owen's assets had been distributed to his next of kin and the bank account closed already, but the logistics of this whole charade fascinated him on an objective level.

"I brought some pictures. I thought they might help."

She strode into the room—finally—and gingerly perched on the edge of his bed, tapping on her phone, then turning it toward him so he could view the screen.

"This is our wedding day."

Oddly struck by her phrasing, he stared at the wide shot of a slightly younger, smiling Hannah standing outside the Wake County courthouse with her hand clutching the crook of Owen's elbow. Except he blinked and it morphed into a picture of himself, as if he'd stumbled over one of those 3D puzzles that flipped perspective if you refocused your eyes.

Just as quickly, it became Owen again, with his much shorter hair and clean-shaven jaw.

A strange ache traveled down his throat as he wondered what his own wedding day might look like. Whether his brother's last thoughts had been of this woman. What he'd lost. The promise shining in his bride's eyes, which he'd thrown in the garbage bin.

It shocked him how much a simple picture affected him.

"Were we happy?" he choked out hoarsely, cursing himself for asking because what did it matter?

Hannah met his gaze then, her eyes liquid and the moment heavy. Neither of them looked away as she got a little misty, and he realized that it did matter. To *her*. And he'd reacted to that at a visceral level.

"I was. So happy," she confirmed with a catch in her voice that thrummed through him. "I thought you were too."

There was so much unspoken in that, he scarcely knew what to do with it. Hannah could be the best actor west of the Rockies, but he'd bet his last dollar that she'd genuinely been in love with Owen.

Then her expression hardened. "That was a long time ago. You've done a lot since then to reverse that. I'm not here to reminisce. I'm trying to help you get your memory back so I can move on. Finally."

Man, his brother had really screwed things up. Hannah's hurt over the way he'd treated her couldn't be more evident.

He made a note to look into Hannah's finances and associations because it was impossible for him to tell fact from fiction when it came to her, especially when she was sitting here by his side, her light floral scent teasing him.

If only he'd met Hannah first, she might have a completely different outlook on how a Mackenzie man treated a woman. The *right* Mackenzie brother.

He shook off that completely unproductive thought.

But it wouldn't go away. All he could picture was his own face in that wedding photo. It wasn't fair that Owen had gotten all the devil-may-care genes, while Archer had been gifted a double dose of responsibility and caution.

Wouldn't it be something if he could settle into Owen's life for just a few days and find out what it sounded like to hear the whoosh of consequences fly by as he ignored them?

"I don't remember you," he murmured, his gaze lingering in places that it probably shouldn't, but his brother had knowledge of her body that he didn't, and he did want to play this part well. "But I want to. What does it feel like to kiss you?"

The question didn't seem to faze her in the slightest and neither did she look away. "I'm not going to demonstrate to see if that jogs anything loose, if that's where you were headed. It was kissing. Just like any other."

Well. That told him a heap right there. Owen was a lot of things, but generous wasn't one of them. Nor did he pay a lot of attention to other people's feelings. Wants. Needs. The lack of flowery, poetic praise of his brother's prowess didn't shock him, no, but his own primal response to hearing it did.

He wanted to give her an experience that would transcend whatever unsatisfying physical relationship his brother had foisted on Hannah. She deserved better.

"It just seems to me that we have a chance for something new and different now," he told her huskily. "I'm not the same man I used to be, Hannah. I don't know how we were before, but I know how we are right now, and if I kissed you, you'd have zero call to compare it to any other kiss."

Her cheeks flushed and he enjoyed that enough to brush off any residual guilt that niggled at him. This was his chance to be the reckless Mackenzie brother. To do what felt good, instead of following the letter of the law.

Besides, he was on leave from the force. This wasn't a crime scene, and he didn't have to analyze one piece of data. Or rather, he'd already examined a lot of the evidence. The more time he spent with Hannah, the more time he *wanted* to spend with Hannah. Plus, it was the best way to keep tabs on her if she did know where Big Mike's missing money was.

And if she didn't, fine. Either way, if he'd found her, so would Big Mike. That was reason enough to toss out his playbook and embrace the new one that had been handed to him.

"You shouldn't talk like that," she murmured, but a woman who was genuinely uninterested in being flirted with would move to the chair. Or the doorway.

"Because I'm in this hospital bed?" he asked with a glance at the thin sheet covering him, which honestly wouldn't provide much of a barrier at all if she had a mind to snuggle up next to him.

That thought made the bed decidedly more uncomfortable as his body reacted in wholly inappropriate ways that the sheet had no shot at hiding.

"Because of Lucy," she shot back and crossed her arms, staring him down. "I didn't get to the rest of the pictures."

"Who is Lucy?"

Not their dog, that was for sure. Fire sparked from her gaze as she tapped up another picture on her phone and swiveled it in his direction.

The little girl in the photo had her mother's face and her father's eyes. His eyes, with green irises. A blend of them both.

The room spun for an eternity and when it stopped, everything had changed.

Chapter Six

The look on Owen's face as he studied the picture of Lucy scored Hannah's insides with white hot knives.

It wasn't recognition she saw there. If he'd had one iota of an inkling that Lucy existed prior to this moment, she'd eat her very sensible Anne Klein ballet flats.

No, this was a portrait of a man being introduced to something rare and precious. His gaze traveled over the photo keenly as if memorizing every tiny nuance. No detail was too small for him to learn.

"I want to see more pictures," he commanded quietly.

How could she do anything other than comply? This was the whole reason she'd come, to test out whether she should mention Lucy at all. In the end, she had to. He deserved to know about his daughter, if he truly hadn't retained even one small memory of her.

More to the point, this was his chance to prove he was still the same Owen as before. The one who cared zero about his own flesh and blood. Somehow, she didn't think that's what was happening here.

Her hand steady and absolutely not a reflection of the earthquake happening inside, she thumbed through to Lucy's last birthday. Jenny had hosted, naturally, since the multitudes of Coltons wouldn't fit in Hannah's smaller house.

There were shots of Lucy blowing out the candles on the cake Hannah had made for her—Little Mermaid, and not the chintzy kind from the grocery store. Hannah had painstakingly cut out a mermaid shape and decorated it with eighteen colors of icing. Her daughter's fifth birthday only happened once, after all.

She had a feeling Owen hadn't even noticed the cake.

His gaze suspiciously shiny, he glanced up at her. "Does she have my last name?"

Hannah nodded. "I kept it for her. I went back to Colton, but she's officially Lucy Mackenzie."

"I want to know everything. Tell me."

Geez. The man had tears in his eyes and steel in his tone. It was overwhelming. Owen certainly hadn't cared one bit about Lucy before, as if she'd needed yet another clue that everything was different this time around.

But for how long?

This was not the way this was supposed to go. He was supposed to casually glance at the pictures and get that vague look on his face, the one that clued her in that his interest had waned. Instead, he watched her with the exact opposite of disinterest in his gaze.

"Everything is a lot to cover," she said with a half laugh. "Lucy is five going on twenty-five. She's around adults a lot and her vocabulary shows it. She spends a lot of time with my mom at her house when I have catering gigs at night."

"Because you don't have anyone else at home to babysit her?"

He was wondering if she'd moved on in the man department. It was a subtly asked question, but she didn't think she was wrong. It was also the first time he seemed to realize she could very well have a new husband at this point.

No reason not to be honest about it. "There's no one else at home. Everything Lucy is and ever will be is due to me and my influence. That's not going to change. Ever," she emphasized, in case he was getting ideas that he might like to poke his nose in Lucy's life.

But he shocked her once again by pursing his lips and shaking his head.

"I'm sorry, Hannah. You shouldn't have been left to your own devices. A man should take more responsibility than that. Should think about things a lot different. A little girl like that is a gift, not an albatross. It's a shame she's missed out on knowing what it's like to have a good father."

Since she couldn't very well say what she was thinking—that Lucy would *never* know what it was like to have a good father due to her mother's terrible choice of husbands—she flipped to another set of pictures. Lucy's first day of pre-school. Swim lessons at the public pool, a necessity since Hannah's house sat so near the lake. Random photos snapped when Lucy wasn't paying attention, of her doing mundane things like coloring or turning the pages of a book she was teaching herself to read.

"Is she smart?" Owen asked, his gaze glued to the photo of Lucy at four carrying books in both hands.

"As a whip and a Rhodes scholar combined," Hannah acknowledged with a proud smile. "I'm sure all mothers say things like that, but Lucy is special. She memorizes a story when I read it to her, usually the first time, and she knows if I skip pages."

Owen's gaze swung to hers, his brow furrowed. "Why would you skip pages?"

Spoken like someone who had never been asked to read *Don't Let the Pigeon Drive the Bus!* eighteen times in one night. "She's the master of 'just one more story, mama.' Some days I don't mind but some days, I'm just really tired."

That was literally the last thing she'd planned to confess to Owen, of all people, but he'd asked so earnestly to know about Lucy. Hannah's journey as a mother was so tied up in that question that it would be impossible to separate the two.

And it was hard being a single mom. Owen was 100 percent the reason she'd been forced to be one.

"I would love to read to her," Owen announced with a bit of wonder in his voice, as if it had never occurred to him that such an activity existed or that he'd be in a position to do it.

Not that she planned to give him an opportunity either way.

"Maybe one day," she said evasively, scrabbling to get a handle on this situation before it spiraled out of control.

If her aim had been to get Owen to admit he still cared nothing about his daughter, she'd failed miserably. Actually, she hadn't come close to figuring out what his goal was with his return to Owl Creek, not even a little bit.

"My family helps out with Lucy a lot," she said brightly, lest he get the idea that she might be tired because she had no help. He was the only deadbeat around here. "Do you remember my family? I have a lot of relatives. Oh, I mean, I guess I've lost a couple since we got divorced. My father died last year."

"I'm sorry, Hannah," he murmured. "About your dad and that I don't remember him."

"He wasn't much of a dad." She snorted. "Sometimes I wish I didn't remember him either. He was like one of those guys you see on the news, who had a whole second family that we didn't know about. Worse, he'd shacked up with my aunt Jessie and had a couple of kids. I guess the six he already had weren't enough."

She elaborated a bit about how all this had come out after her father had died and how she'd met her half siblings Nate and Sarah, but there was a lot of reservation on both sides about jumping into the middle of a relationship when there was still so much hurt to go around.

They were all trying though.

Owen's eyes had widened as she spun the sordid tale. Thankfully, he didn't seem to realize she'd neatly segued the conversation away from Lucy, and she'd gladly spill all these terrible secrets to keep her daughter off Owen's mind.

She and Lucy were a bit alike in that regard—neither of them knew what it was like to have a good dad.

Oh, goodness. What if Owen had new family that he didn't remember either? That was a reality she hadn't considered at all. Her throat tightened. He could be married and have two kids for all she knew!

No, surely not. The insurance people would have turned up marriage records or birth records if that was the case, wouldn't they? They'd called her because they literally couldn't find any other family to notify.

"So then it came out that Aunt Jessie has gotten mixed up in a cult," she continued with a flourish. "The Ever After Church. In Owl Creek of all places, if you can believe it. The head is this real piece of work named Markus Acker and he's cozied up to Aunt Jessie. She contested my father's will, insisting that her kids deserved some of the money, but I think Markus put her up to it. It's just been a mess."

All at once, she wondered how much Sarah Colton knew about her mother's involvement with Markus and the church. Maybe Hannah could have her cake and eat it too if she took a little more initiative to strike up a friendship with her half sister. She could nose around a little to see what she could dig up on behalf of her family at the same time, right? It wasn't a crime.

"The Ever After Church?" Owen repeated and Hannah nodded.

"It's not a real church, not as far as we can tell," she added. "There's a compound where the members live not far from here. It seems to be largely geared toward convincing the members to give the church lots of money."

Owen's brows knit as he seemed to absorb that, but then the nurse bustled in to take his blood pressure and other vitals. He endured it with good humor, another strange factor of his new, improved personality that Hannah would have had to see to believe. He'd always had a short temper and very little patience for people in service jobs, which should have been a much bigger red flag in the beginning than she'd realized.

Late-Twenties Hannah knew the value of people in service jobs since she had almost a dozen working for her now. Never again would she ignore that telling aspect of a man's personality.

Unless of course the man in question seemed to have done a 180-degree turnaround on his stance toward nurses. And Hannah.

As soon as the nurse left, Owen asked a few more pointed questions about the church, an oddity that Hannah chose not to examine too hard when his focus had shifted exactly as she'd intended.

But then during a pause, he hooked her with his warm brown eyes and covered the back of her hand with his. "Can I see some more pictures of Lucy?"

Ugh, she'd thought they were done with this subject. So much for the segue to Aunt Jessie.

With little call to tell him no, she grudgingly pulled out her phone again from her pocket and found some baby pictures. That would be the best test of his memory, to view photos of what Lucy had looked like as he'd last seen her.

But he shook his head and pushed the phone away, his expression crestfallen. "It's incredibly painful to see evidence of how much of Lucy's life I've missed. I want to meet her. Now. In person."

Dismayed, she stared at him, wrestling with the fact that this kind of stance was exactly what she'd hoped for when she'd mentioned Lucy. It was exactly what she'd have wished to hear. Once.

But wishing for it and hearing it spoken aloud—where she'd have to address it—were two different things. "This is not the time to be making those kinds of requests."

"It's not a request," he countered, his mouth set in a firm line. "I'm her father. I have rights."

Oh, goodness. Her soul hurt as the weight of his meaning crushed her. He could fight her for custody. Demand visitation. Insert himself into her life in all sorts of terrible ways. What had she done?

Lungs on fire with the effort to simply breathe, she shook her head. "Not at the moment you don't. You're in the hospital. They haven't released you yet. Maybe once you regain your memories, we can discuss—"

"Bring her here."

Geez, Owen had never been this stubborn before, especially not when it came to relations with another person. "I think they have rules," she suggested calmly, grasping desperately at straws.

He could *not* start up a relationship with Lucy, only to remember in a day, a week, that he despised children, even his own. Especially his own.

As crushed as she felt right now, how would a precious five-year-old feel after opening her heart to the one person in the world she could rightly call Daddy, only to have him callously reject her later?

No. No way. It was a mistake to have even brought it up. Hannah had made the cardinal error of thinking with her heart, not her head—the curse of wanting to do the right thing.

"The doctor said it was critical that I be surrounded by

things from my life," Owen insisted. "That's the whole reason they called you. Why wouldn't seeing Lucy be just as valuable?"

"Because you've never seen her as a child," Hannah snapped back, thrilled to have this incredibly important fact to cling to. "The last time you saw her, she was a baby."

"All the more reason to let me get to know her. Hannah," he said, his tone softening. "I've lost so much already."

Good grief. It was as if he'd reached right through her chest and grabbed her heart, squeezing with exactly the right pressure to wring out the maximum amount of emotion. Whether it was empathy, grim determination to get him off this path or panic, she couldn't say.

"I'll think about it," she promised and fled for the second time.

She had a feeling she'd do nothing but think about it for the foreseeable future.

Chapter Seven

It was only a matter of time before someone realized that Archer wasn't Owen and that he didn't really have amnesia. Probably due to a monumental slipup, like cussing out his brother in Hannah's presence.

Owen had a daughter.

A bright, beautiful little bundle of joy who had no relationship with her father or her father's side of the family. It was heartbreaking.

Archer's research into his brother's ex-wife hadn't mentioned a kid. That was a pretty big thing to overlook. Of course, the blame for his shock lay squarely in the lap of the deceased and it was a good thing Owen was already dead or Archer would kill him.

It was bad enough that Owen had never bothered to mention that he'd gotten married in the first place, but failing to tell their mother she had a granddaughter—that was unforgivable. Amelia Mackenzie had her faults, and refusing to see Owen's was a big one, but she was still their mother, and she deserved to know her grandchild.

Archer had a little mad left over for himself. Not that he had any clue what an uncle was supposed to do, but finding out he was one meant something to him. Finding out he'd been deprived of this information meant something too—his brother was a jackass of the highest order.

Since the hospital hadn't found a trace of Owen's relatives, Archer could only assume his brother had doctored his records to remove all references to his family—both his birth family and his ex-wife. That was fine. Archer had cut ties with his brother too, but really it wasn't fine, not with Lucy in the mix. He stewed about it for a good long while after Hannah had left.

Of course, the real issue here wasn't what an uncle would do in this situation. He'd somehow managed to become a father in the same stroke that he'd claimed to be Owen. The complications from that one split-second decision had just spiraled out of control.

He could not maintain this charade. He couldn't end it either.

So much for being the devil-may-care Mackenzie brother. That's why he'd never embraced his brother's life philosophy—his conscience wasn't geared to ignore things like responsibility and consequences. And Lucy was one obligation Owen had left behind that Archer would not be able to properly rectify. Not the way he'd like.

Actually, he didn't know how he'd fix this if he could. It was the first time Archer had ever encountered a situation he didn't know how to handle. You couldn't analyze a little girl and put the pieces back together into a whole that suddenly made sense, then move on.

This was a lifetime commitment, no two ways about it. And Archer had zero intention of walking away from it. He just didn't know what his relationship with Lucy—and Hannah—would look like at the end.

The doctor came by and chatted with him for a bit. Archer knew the routine, answered all the questions by rote.

Yes, he felt okay other than the banged-up ribs and the gash on his head.

No, he still didn't remember anything, not even bits and pieces or floaty memories. The doctor had told him that's how it usually happened, that the brain would start releasing blurry, disjointed images first, eventually followed by a flood of stored-up information. It would likely be overwhelming, so the doctor wanted to keep tabs on him here at the hospital.

That was a lucky break, which soon might not be the case. Eventually they'd release him and then he'd have to come up with an excuse to stay close to Hannah, especially after the alarming story she'd told him about the Ever After Church.

As soon as the doctor left, Archer grabbed his phone—a burner his assistant had couriered to him on the sly, along with a credit card, bless him—and did a search for Markus Acker. It was better than being ticked off at Owen and far more productive.

The face of the man who popped up did not give him any warm and fuzzy feelings. He was good-looking of course, as Archer expected from someone who was likely running a solid grift with a lot of moving parts. Acker would be charming in person. Likable and approachable. You'd never suspect a guy like that of lifting your wallet, if you even noticed it was gone, as he dazzled you.

There was only a tiny bit of official information on the Ever After Church, which told Archer a lot more than if they had posted gobs and gobs of propaganda.

This was an organization that liked to keep a low profile.

If only he had access to his workstation at the lab on South Jones, which was nothing like the CSI lab on television shows. He worked in a drab office where dedicated men and women analyzed what was often trace evidence left at

crime scenes. There was little glamour, but they put criminals behind bars with hardcore scientific evidence.

And he was good at what he did. Which meant he could
cut a wide swath through the layers of Ever After Church
ownership and finances in a matter of hours, if he had the
right tools. Instead, he had to make do with a phone and
busted ribs.

Fortunately, a couple of reporters seemed to have latched
on to the church's activities. Archer recognized their bylines
popping up over and over as they linked a lot of shady stuff
to Markus Acker and some of his cronies.

One story had multiple hits about Acker's alleged right-
hand man, Winston Kraft, though it was clear from the con-
text that the guy's position in the church was "unknown."
That was code for "uncorroborated," which meant the reporter was not wrong, just covering his bases.

Dude was a piece of work and a half. He'd been arrested
for kidnapping his own grandchildren, supposedly to gain
control of the insurance money left to them after the deaths
of their parents. Once the children had been recovered, it
came out that their grandfather might have been responsible
for the car wreck that had killed their parents, one of whom
was Kraft's own son.

Archer shook his head. Nice people this church attracted.

And then there were the bodies.

Authorities had found a remarkable number of them buried near the Ever After Church compound, but the investigation had only uncovered a tenuous link to Acker thus far. The
link was there, he was fairly certain. Someone would find it.

The name *Colton* scrolled onto his screen. His gut went
icy. Lizzie Colton—no mention of whether she was a relation of Hannah's, but surely she was—had been kidnapped
and held in a cabin high in the mountains, then managed
to escape—good for her—only to wind up unconscious in

the woods. During a snowstorm. She was lucky she'd been found by search and rescue so she could finger her assailant, who'd been apprehended. So far, no one had tied the kidnapping to the church, but Archer didn't believe in coincidences.

Something tied these events together. Everything had a pattern: shells, Braille, quilts, seasons, iambic pentameter. He just had to find the telltale slime trail the Ever After Church had left behind as it wormed its way through Idaho. Pick up the breadcrumbs so to speak.

There was only one way to do that effectively. Follow the money.

Of course, he couldn't do it himself and that stung almost as much as his busted ribs.

The nurse wasn't due by for another fifteen minutes and it was a good bet Hannah wouldn't be dropping in so soon after she'd fled the scene. So he felt fairly safe dialing his assistant's number from memory.

"Hey," he said when Willis answered. "It's Mac. I need you to do me a favor."

Quickly, Archer rattled off the details, which Willis would not need repeated, and left his assistant to do some quiet sleuthing into the Ever After Church on his behalf. If this hunch was nothing, fine. There was no way it was nothing, though, and he didn't like the picture these pieces had started to form.

Especially when he was already following the money. Big Mike's missing money, specifically, and there'd already been slime trails heading in the direction of Owl Creek formed by Owen Mackenzie.

Thirty seconds before the nurse was due to stroll into his room, he wiped his internet search history and did a factory reset on the burner phone, then stashed it back under his mattress. Couldn't be too careful in a public hospital where anyone could come into his room disguised as an orderly or a janitor or even the guy who collected blood samples to take to the lab.

"How are we today, Mr. Owen?" the nurse called as she picked up the electronic tablet from its holder by the door and read over the notes in his medical chart the morning shift nurse had left.

He didn't have to glance at her name tag to know it read Mary Jane Meyer. She'd told him the first day that everyone called her MJ, so he did too. "Fine. I like what you've done with your hair."

She shot him a pleased smile. "You're the first person to notice."

"Ingrates. What, are they blind? You had to have cut off, what, six inches? And the bangs are doing great things for your cheekbones."

His return smile was genuine, mostly because he appreciated the care MJ took when seeing after him. But also because in his line of work, people like nurses always noticed more details than anyone else, so they gave him the best leads.

And you never knew when you would need those details or under what circumstances you might be asking for them. Scoring points ahead of time never hurt.

"Oh, go on," she told him, flapping her hand in his direction. "Flirting will get you everywhere."

If MJ was a day under sixty, Archer would hand in his badge. But if he'd made her feel good about herself even for a few minutes, it was worth his time.

"I hope it'll get me an extra pudding at dinnertime," he suggested with a wink and MJ laughed as she took his blood pressure.

"Consider it yours." She noted the numbers on her tablet and leaned over to change the bandages on his head wound, inspecting the stitches at the same time. "Your pretty girlfriend left already? She can stay as long as she likes. I won't tell anyone."

"Thanks, MJ," he said, not bothering to correct her since he couldn't honestly say what Hannah was to him at this stage. Or what he'd want her to be.

He slept fitfully after MJ left, constantly checking his burner phone for messages from Willis. Time crawled.

Near sunrise, Willis finally sent a few cryptic texts that meant he'd found some information that Archer would consider useful, but he'd have to be out of this hospital bed to hear it since he couldn't very well meet his assistant off premises until they released him. Neither could he take advantage of whatever Willis had found.

Being in the hospital sucked. And if he kept saying it, eventually it would help matters, right?

Bored and not a little stir-crazy, he rolled over for the umpteenth time as the sky outside lightened. The next time he looked up, Hannah stood in the doorway of his room, but this time, she wasn't alone.

Lucy was with her. *Lucy.* Her bright, curious gaze sought his and when she locked him in her sights, he felt his soul shift. It was as if he'd opened a vein and poured his own lifeblood into an empty space where nothing had been before and then watched as it became something—this little human who shared his DNA but had the exact same color eyes as her mother.

"Hi," he croaked out since she was still watching him with avid curiosity.

"Mama says you're my father," she told him without any warning and the short sentence tore into him with the force of a bullet fired at close range from a gun in the hand of someone who knew how to use it.

It was one thing to academically understand that the brother he'd decided to impersonate had a daughter. And that pretending to be the little girl's father would be part of the gig. It was another thing entirely to hear that harsh truth straight from her mouth.

She thought he was Owen. Of course she did. Because he'd spent the last few days telling everyone he was and playing the part of an amnesiac to sell it. He'd never regretted that decision more than he did in this moment.

But he couldn't be sorry either.

Lucy deserved a father and Owen would never have been one to her, even if he'd lived. He certainly couldn't change course and decide to be one now. But Archer could.

"Hi, Lucy." He greeted her solemnly and held out his hand. "It's very nice to meet you."

Lucy didn't hesitate in the slightest and stuck her tiny hand in his, her fingers so delicate that it made no sense how they could reach so far inside him, brushing the walls of his heart with such strength.

"Mama said you were hurt," Lucy recited, her gaze wide as she took everything in, sliding to the white rectangle on his temple. "Are you going to be okay?"

Her concern bled through him. She'd met him four seconds ago and her immediate concern was for his health? A testament to her mother no doubt, and he glanced up to see Hannah standing near the door, in the room, but not in the middle of this reunion that she'd opted to allow.

They shared a long glance laden with meaning, but he had no shot at interpreting what this woman was thinking. Why had she decided to bring Lucy after all? He'd been convinced she'd never go for it.

"I'll be fine," he assured her and before he could say yes or no or get his wits about him, Lucy hopped up on the bed to sit next to him, her mouth curved in a wide smile that revealed a missing front tooth.

She had a stuffed dog clutched at the crook of her elbow,

which she held out to show him. "This is Mr. Fluffers. He came in a box, but he wasn't scared of the dark."

"That's very brave of Mr. Fluffers," he said because it seemed she expected some type of response and that one had rolled off his tongue. "What kind of dog is he?"

"A golden retriever like Aunt Ruby's and Uncle Sebastian's dog. He's named Oscar though. Will you let me get a real dog if I come live with you?"

"Lucy," Hannah interjected from the doorway, strangling on her daughter's name. "We talked about this in the car. Your father wanted to meet you first and then we can talk about what happens next. I'm sorry," she said to Archer, her expression full of emotion he couldn't identify.

But wanted to. He wanted to be able to read her, to know they shared this parenting journey and would have each other's backs when it came to something like their daughter asking for a dog. And to presumably stay at his house... in Las Vegas.

Oh, man. He shut his eyes for a brief, fortifying moment that did not work to settle his stomach. This was not the kind of mess Archer normally cleaned up for Owen. Most of the time, Owen's screw-ups involved owing people money he couldn't pay back or having committed to something that he blew off, like picking up Mom from the airport.

How was he supposed to navigate stepping into the role of father when he didn't even live in this state? Then he had to laugh at himself. Like that was his biggest problem.

"Do you want a dog?" he asked Lucy, partially to give himself breathing room and also because he suddenly craved knowing things about her. All things. Favorite color. TV shows she liked. Did she walk to school?

An objectively fascinating development, this desire to not just meet Lucy, but *know* her. Would he have this same reaction as an uncle—only an uncle with no ability or reason to assume he'd ever be anything else? Or was this yet another step in the chain reaction that he'd unwittingly set off when he first answered to the name *Owen*?

Enthused by the subject of dogs, Lucy nodded yes a bajillion times and tucked Mr. Fluffers back into the crook of her elbow, where he seemed quite at home. "Uncle Wade has a dog too. Betty Jane. She's the best, but I can't play with her sometimes because she has a job. All the dogs have jobs, mostly to find people and sometimes to make sure they're not sad."

He glanced up at Hannah who lifted a shoulder. "K-9 search and rescue, and therapy. She is surrounded by working dogs. I never realized before."

"So you want a dog whose only job is to be yours and to sleep with you and be your friend," he told her with an affirming smile, and Lucy's eyes lit up as if she'd switched on a beacon inside. Oddly, it did the same thing to him.

"Yes, please," she chirped, obviously willing to reveal all her hopes and dreams to the father she'd never known with zero trepidation.

She was fearless and brave.

Owen frequently adopted this slightly hooded expression like he had 147 secrets and he intended to share none of them with you. As if you weren't worthy to be let in on his thoughts.

Right this minute, he hated Owen a little bit. As unproductive as that was. But he couldn't stop himself from wondering yet again what might have been if he'd met Hannah first.

Only he hadn't. He'd met both Hannah and Lucy while pretending to be Owen and now he was good and caught in the lie. Good and screwed too, thanks to his brother, on multiple fronts since he couldn't undo any of this. All he could do was keep plowing through this murder investigation, while ensuring the family Owen had rejected stayed out of Big Mike's sights.

If Archer secretly enjoyed sliding into his brother's life while keeping Hannah and Lucy safe, no one had to know.

Chapter Eight

Hannah debated whether to take Lucy to see Owen again the next morning. But really, she couldn't keep them apart. Not in good conscience.

She was flying blind here, going against better judgment, which was her Achilles' heel. On the drive to Conners, she spent a lot of time convincing herself the whole point was to help Owen regain his memories so he could name someone else in his life. Someone who could shoulder the weight of responsibility for his welfare, allowing Hannah to off-load it gladly.

Except that wasn't really the reason anymore.

She'd lost count of the ways her ex-husband was like a different person. One that appealed to her in ways she'd scarcely started to unpack. And she'd gained a reluctant curiosity about how long it would last. A slim hope that he might stay different even after he got better.

Frankly, he had to be. The die was cast, now that she'd introduced him to Lucy. He didn't get to screw up his relationship with his daughter a second time.

When she got to Owen's room, the doctor was there. Spontaneously, she asked if he would clear it for Hannah to take Owen to the courtyard in the center of the hospital. It would be his first foray out of the hospital since he'd come in on a gurney. She hoped he'd appreciate the change of scenery, but she hadn't anticipated the doctor expecting her to roll him out in a wheelchair.

Owen accepted the idea with grace, but he had some trouble transferring from the bed to the seat of the wheelchair. Automatically, she reached out to help him, her hand landing on the small of his back.

Oh my. He hadn't felt like that before, as if he'd hidden a slab of heated concrete under his gown. The long, slow flip in her tummy was not welcome. Worse, it was nearly impossible to ignore. As was his grimace when she snatched her hand back, causing him to land heavily in the seat.

"Are your ribs still bothering you?" she murmured and he glanced up, unfamiliar warmth radiating from his brown eyes.

Great. He'd noticed that she'd reacted to touching him.

"Not so much," he said, but she had the impression he wasn't being completely honest.

Trying to be macho, probably. For her benefit or Lucy's, she wasn't sure, but she could have saved him the trouble on both counts. Lucy had no idea how a father was supposed to act other than what little she might have discerned from her grandfather before he passed, Uncle Buck or her cousin Greg, who had recently gotten custody of his late best friend's kids.

Hannah wasn't swayed by anything Owen could or would do. She'd learned a long time ago to let whatever he said go in one ear and out the other.

They rode the elevator down to the first floor, Lucy jabbering a mile a minute about the two girls she liked best at preschool. To his credit, he listened intently and never interrupted or showed even a smidgen of impatience when Lucy told him the same knock-knock joke twice in a row. She'd figured out that she liked making people laugh and thus, in her five-year-old brain, assumed that everyone would find the same joke twice as funny the second time. Hannah hadn't had the heart to destroy that myth, yet.

Owen actually did laugh both times and it didn't even sound forced. Another point in his favor.

Hannah wheeled the chair into the courtyard, half convinced Owen was going to try to ditch the contraption or at least complain that he wasn't an invalid, but he shocked her into silence once again by asking Lucy if she wanted a ride.

She squealed and immediately jumped up into Owen's lap. He winced as her elbow caught him in the ribs, and Hannah braced for a string of profanities or something else Owen-like, but he just carefully rearranged his daughter and grasped the wheel with one hand to ferry her around the walking path. With the other, he held Lucy tight against him.

Mouth slightly ajar, Hannah watched as Owen stopped near one of the planters exploding with flowers. He snapped off the head of a columbine and handed it to Lucy, who grinned like she'd just been given the whole bouquet.

Well, that was…great. She swallowed. It was. Totally fabulous. They were getting along famously for two people who didn't know each other at all, and for all intents and purposes, hadn't known about the existence of the other a few days ago.

"Mama, look at me," Lucy called and threw up her palms. "No hands."

"I see you, baby."

Boy, did she. Her daughter sitting in her father's lap was a picture she'd never in a million years have conjured up, even in her wildest imagination. It put a misty smile on her face even as it socked her in the gut.

Lucy would never again be just hers. As long as Owen kept stepping up to the plate, of course, and being the dad he seemed poised to become. It was terrible to wish so fer-

vently for something she had a niggling suspicion wouldn't
happen and then it would be on her that she'd let him disappoint their daughter. Yet at the same time, she'd have Lucy
all to herself again in a catch-22 that made her head hurt.

"Guess what?" Lucy said the next time Owen wheeled her
past the place where Hannah had elected to stand out of the
way. "Daddy says I can get a dog and keep it at his house!"

Oh boy. Hannah's smile froze but she checked her knee-
jerk reaction. "We'll have to discuss that a little more before it's final, okay?"

Lucy crossed her arms and threw her mother a look.
"That's what you say when you aren't going to let me."

"It's fine, Hannah," Owen said, his lips curving up in an
expression Hannah knew well.

It was the same look her brother Wade got whenever Lucy
had conned him into something. *Men.* They were such push-
overs when a sweet, diabolical little girl put her evil scheme
in motion.

"It's only fine depending on what happens after you get
out of the hospital," she muttered, careful not to say too
much.

"If you say no, I'll never come out of my room again,"
Lucy announced with her mutinous face that she rarely trotted out because she knew it wouldn't get her very far.

It still hurt. "I'm not saying anything other than we have
to talk about it."

The face didn't change. At least until Lucy turned back
to Owen, and then it was all smiles for her dad who had
never told her no.

Hannah sighed. Wasn't this great? It was totally fine that
Lucy was freezing her out for being the responsible parent,
but cozying up to the father she'd known for all of five minutes. Hannah wasn't jealous at *all* that he got to be the fun
dad, the absentee dad who lived in Las Vegas and would

take her daughter for long weekends, leaving Hannah alone and wondering what her life had become.

Wasn't this just like Owen to swoop in and scoop up Lucy for all the sepia-toned moments he could stuff into a day, skipping over all the bad stuff. The real stuff. The 1 a.m. nightmares and upset tummies that were no match for three sets of clean sheets. He'd skipped out on the things that Hannah had been forced to endure alone.

But he'd also missed out on all the good stuff. The firsts. The onlys. He wasn't there to witness her first steps. The look on her face the first time she ate ice cream. Lucy would never again lose her first tooth and get her first visit from the tooth fairy. At least Hannah could rest assured none of those things would happen when Lucy was with Owen.

Finally, Owen called a halt to the wheelchair ride, his face a bit ashen. His breathing seemed labored, and she caught him wincing as Lucy pouted over being asked to get down.

"Come on, Lady Mackenzie," she called, figuring it was time to step in since Owen had no clue how to handle Obstinate Lucy of the One More Time Clan. "Your dad is in the hospital for a reason, and he's spent more than a reasonable amount of time entertaining you. Give him a break."

Lucy hopped down without further argument, her lips still pouty, but at least she wasn't presenting her case for why she should get an additional fifteen minutes next time. She'd be storing up details on the PowerPoint slides in her head though, for her future campaign.

Hannah wheeled Owen back toward the elevator, both of them quiet as Lucy had a one-sided conversation with Mr. Fluffers about the picture she was going to draw when they got home.

The elevator was plenty deep enough for her to stand behind Owen, but that felt too subservient so she stood next to him. A decision she instantly regretted when he grazed a finger down the back of her hand.

She glanced at him.

"Thank you for this," he murmured. "She's a miracle. I'm not sure if I'm more upset that I missed so much of her life or that even if I hadn't, I wouldn't remember any of it. I want to know everything about her faster than I can absorb it all."

And now she felt selfish and petty for being glad he didn't have any cherished moments with his daughter except for the ones from the last two days. "You're welcome."

She left it at that, because none of this was real. Owen would regain his memories and suddenly, he'd realize he hated kids, as he'd told her umpteen times in the weeks after she'd announced the pregnancy she'd thought they'd both celebrate.

Somewhere underneath all of this was a scam. There had to be. She refused to get caught out again by this man.

Only it was too late. The dad was out of the bag. Lucy had met her father and she'd never let Hannah hear the end of it about the dog she'd been promised.

She could only hope that when Owen pulled the carpet out from under them, she'd have the skills to help Lucy get over her disappointment.

Somehow, she got Owen and Lucy extracted from each other and hustled her daughter to the car, already glancing at her watch and doing mental gymnastics to rearrange her baking schedule for the rest of the day. Bon Appetit had three events coming up, a wedding and two bar mitzvahs.

Just as she was about to put the car in gear and pull out of the lot, her phone rang. The caller ID on her navigation panel announced that it was Wade, so she answered it with her thumb.

"You're on speaker," she warned Wade before he could say a word. "And Lucy is in the car."

"Hi, Uncle Wade," she called from the back seat. "Mr. Fluffers says hi."

"Hi, Goose." Wade's deep voice reverberated from the speaker. "I can call back later."

"I have a superbusy afternoon."

Thanks to taking the morning off to visit Owen, which she refused to feel guilty about. But neither did she want to explain why she was behind. No one in her family agreed with her decision to introduce Lucy to Owen, which was too bad. It would have been nice to have someone on her side. Someone who would tell her it was fine, that she hadn't made a horrible mistake. That she did owe it to everyone to see if things could be different.

"I'll make it quick then," Wade said. "We need to have an emergency family meeting. Soon."

Hannah sighed and it almost came out without the extra drama. "I'm full up on family meetings, Wade."

So far, she'd attended an emergency meeting to find out she had siblings she'd never known about. Then the one where they found out Aunt Jessie had joined a cult. Plus the one where it came out that Aunt Jessie was contesting Hannah's father's will.

What could possibly be left to discover?

"You can't miss it," he insisted. "We've got some important news to share."

"Text me the details," she said without committing to anything she'd regret later.

But honestly, if her brothers had left her out, she'd have words with them. Nor could she stand the idea of ditching the meeting on principle, only to have to wheedle the news out of someone later, when she'd be alone trying to manage whatever bombshell was about to be dropped.

What if it was something about Markus Acker? What if someone else in her family had stepped up to the plate and done the work she'd vowed to do—*and* had discovered something about his church while she'd been waffling around about Owen?

As her phone pinged with the meeting time and place, she had a moment of panic that the meeting would be about someone else picking up her slack on the Ever After research front. Yes, taking Lucy to meet her father had ranked as an important enough task to leapfrog Markus Acker. But now she regretted that she'd made that task into such a priority in the first place, let alone that it had hampered her promise to investigate the church.

When she got home, she picked up her phone and called Sarah before she could think better of it. Voicemail. No worries. She left a message telling Sarah she'd like to connect, squelching the slight guilt that she'd done so under slightly false pretenses.

But not really! She *did* want to get to know her new sister. Half sister. And technically their relationship wasn't *new-new*, like Sarah had just been born. They'd just only learned about each other. Though Hannah knew that Sarah and Nate had known a bit about their father's other family over the years, but had chosen not to reach out until recently. It was a weird situation, and she didn't blame them for preferring to stay in the shadows.

After her aforementioned busy afternoon wound to a close, Hannah threw herself into the nighttime routine of bath and then helping Lucy pick out clothes to wear to preschool tomorrow, a task that always went better if they did it the night before. Lucy never stuck with her first choice—or second or third—and before Hannah had hit on the idea of letting Lucy pick when they had plenty of time, the wardrobe changes often made them late.

"I want to wear my pink sundress," Lucy announced as

she pulled on her pajamas without help, a big girl staple that still managed to puncture a hole in Hannah's heart.

Yes, she academically knew that Lucy would eventually do everything for herself, but as tasks slipped from her grasp, she felt the keen sense of loss. The reminders that the little girl who needed her would eventually grow into a young woman who would move away and leave her mother to chart a life by herself. Thinking about it sliced deeply.

"You can't wear a sundress in February," Hannah told her automatically, falling right into Lucy's trap. That's what she got for letting her attention wander.

"I can if I wear a shirt underneath and leggings," Lucy pointed out.

Since this was still the first round of clothes selection, Hannah didn't see much value in arguing. "Fine. You'll be uncomfortable with a whole second outfit on under a dress that isn't made for layers, but you're the one who will have to wear it all day."

"I want to wear it to go see Daddy," she informed her mother as she pulled the dress, hanger and all, from her closet, draping it over the chair at her desk that would eventually be used for homework when Lucy hit elementary school, but worked fine as a wardrobe stager.

"I'm not sure if we're going to see your father tomorrow," she hedged.

Hannah had thought they would take a break from the hospital. They'd been two days in a row already. It probably wasn't good for Lucy to see Owen every day. They might form an attachment faster if she did that.

Plus, Hannah really wanted the break too. Seeing Owen on a consistent basis was starting to do a number on her. Making her think about things she shouldn't be thinking, letting phrases like *second chances* and *reunion romance* clog up her brain when she should be focusing on things like braising and basting and baking.

"I want to see my daddy," Lucy insisted as she pull out her purple leggings and laid them by the dress, then frowned at the combo. "He said I could come anytime I wanted. Where are my black leggings?"

And focusing on parenting, Hannah added silently. "Your black leggings are in the drawer where you found the purple ones."

"No, they're not." Lucy pulled open the drawer and proceeded to dump the contents onto the floor to demonstrate that she'd gone through the entire stack.

Hannah stifled a sigh. "Lucy, pick up your clothes and put them back in the drawer. Neatly. I'll check the dryer."

The missing leggings weren't in the dryer or folded into Hannah's own laundry, which was still piled on top of her dresser. Maybe she'd put them into one of her own drawers by mistake. But when she opened the first drawer, the entire thing was in a disarray, as if someone had pawed through it recently. All her drawers looked like that actually.

Returning to her daughter's room, she counted to ten before she let her exhaustion get the better of her. "I've asked you not to go into my room and get into my things without asking."

"I didn't, Mama," Lucy said. "I don't go into your room unless you tell me I can. Did you find my black leggings?"

"You didn't go through my drawers?" she prompted, hoping Lucy would come clean.

Her daughter just shook her head, still distracted by the missing leggings. "I need the black ones in case I get dirty snow on me. The purple ones will show because my boots aren't tall enough."

Hannah bit her lip and forced back the comment on the

tip of her tongue about leggings being inappropriate for winter in the first place.

"Can we go see Daddy on Saturday?" Lucy asked right when Hannah had lulled herself into a false sense of security that they'd moved on from that subject.

"Maybe," she allowed, wondering how in the world she'd balance everything when she had an event on Saturday that she absolutely couldn't pass off to one of her employees since it was for a hundred people. The serving logistics alone required a military grade campaign to execute and that was her job.

No wonder she'd misplaced laundry. She'd probably messed up her drawers herself looking for something and forgot, thanks to all the major distractions.

"Wear the purple leggings and pay attention to where you walk. Then you won't get snow on them."

Finally, Lucy moved on to the teeth-brushing portion of their evening routine and then settled into bed for her prayers. The first five sentences were all about Owen in a sweet plea to the heavens to watch over her daddy and help him get better.

Hannah swallowed against the knot in her throat. The barn door was open and the horse was out. There wasn't much use in closing the door on her daughter's relationship with her father.

And who knew? Maybe Owen would regain his memories and realize he had been missing out on being a father to Lucy. Maybe everything would be fine.

But she had a niggling sensation that she was fooling herself.

Chapter Nine

Hannah managed to stay away from the hospital until Sunday, but guilt and curiosity got the better of her by noon. Plus, Lucy had promised to eat all her vegetables for a week if she could visit her dad, and that was too good of an offer to refuse in Hannah's book.

Since she hadn't originally planned to leave the house, a shower was in order. Hannah plopped Lucy in front of an episode of *Peppa Pig* in the living room.

"What's the rule?" she asked as she paused the show, holding the remote out of Lucy's reach.

"Don't move from this chair unless the house catches on fire," Lucy recited with a little bop of her head. "And then I should come tell you so you can call 911."

"Exactly." Hannah unpaused the show and set the remote on the dais next to the TV.

The timer in her head counted down along with the math she knew like the back of her hand. A shower took eleven minutes including time for the water to warm up, a necessity when it was 30 degrees outside. Five minutes for hair and five minutes for makeup, two to slide into clothes and boots. Five episodes of *Peppa Pig* would give her an extra two minutes with conditioner, a luxury she rarely indulged in, but she did have an acute awareness that she'd be seeing Owen later.

When she stepped into the shower, she found herself humming. Until she grabbed the shampoo and dumped some in her hand, only to find that it was body wash instead.

Frowning, she glanced at the row of bottles lined up along the ledge formed by the high window. They were out of order. She always put them back in the same sequence because she used them in a certain order. Plus, they weren't all right at the edge like she'd left them.

Odd. The ledge was too high for Lucy to reach unless she'd somehow dragged a stool into the shower and stood on it without Hannah hearing her. Unlikely, since she'd have to drag it from the kitchen.

The drawers left in disarray plucked at her consciousness. If she'd done that without remembering, she could have easily rearranged the bottles on the ledge without realizing. Probably just an accident due to her extreme level of distraction lately.

Hannah dismissed it from her mind, already having burned through one of her extra minutes by grabbing the wrong bottle. She flew through the rest of her shower and emerged, hurrying through toweling off and drawing her hair up into a simple ponytail. Makeup she took a little bit of extra care to get right, telling herself there wasn't anything wrong with wanting to look nice in public. She could run into anyone in Conners.

But she knew she would be seeing Owen and on the drive over, her nerves let her know about it.

Lucy chattered the entire time from the back seat, repeating, "Blah, blah, blah, that's how daddies talk!" from one of the episodes of *Peppa Pig*, then asking Hannah how come her daddy didn't say *blah, blah, blah*.

By the time they got to the hospital, Hannah was already looking for her sanity. And her migraine medication.

Then they walked to Owen's room, Hannah pausing at the door to knock. Owen glanced over, his brown eyes lighting up with warmth the moment he caught sight of her. Then he smiled, his gaze traveling down to take in Lucy by her side.

All of the air whooshed out of her lungs as she registered his genuine pleasure that they'd come. When was the last time anyone had been that happy to see her? Maybe Betty Jane had occasionally woofed a greeting when she'd dropped by Wade's house. Possibly Lucy's eyes danced occasionally when she spied Hannah in the pickup line at preschool, but she was just as often miffed that it was time to go, announcing that she wasn't done playing yet. Usually she gave her mother a hug, though.

This was different. Owen's joy at seeing them took over his whole face and she had to take a moment to appreciate the fact that he seemed just as happy to see Lucy as he was to see Hannah.

"Hey," he called softly as if afraid to scare them away by talking too loudly. "You're here. I've missed you both."

Unprompted, Lucy scampered up onto the bed and threw her arms around her father. "I wanted to come yesterday, but Mama had an *event*."

"I catered an event," Hannah corrected with a smile as the sight of her daughter entwined in Owen's arms squeezed her heart. "You make it sound like I was invited to the White House for dinner."

"I have something for you, my darling," he said to Lucy and pulled a package from the other side of the bed, handing it to her.

Oh, man. Hannah sucked in a breath, dreading all the ways a gift he hadn't cleared with her could go sideways. The package was almost bigger than Lucy, wrapped in pink paper with giant letter *L*s formed with raised silver sparkles that would likely rain all over her daughter's clothes and then end up in the carpet of Hannah's Honda.

Judging by Lucy's squeal, the package was already a hit and she hadn't even opened it yet. When she tore into the pink paper and raised the lid of the box, both mother and daughter gasped. Lucy pulled the pink raincoat from the box reverently, her eyes shining.

"Mama, it has unicorns," she breathed.

Hannah nodded, unable to speak coherently because what was she supposed to say about Owen buying his daughter a Stella McCartney raincoat that she knew for a fact cost over two hundred and fifty dollars? *Thank you? We can't accept? I've been drooling over this coat for three months and couldn't rationalize spending that much money on something Lucy would outgrow?*

"It's too much," she finally murmured.

Owen just smiled indulgently. "Blasphemy. Nothing is too much. Besides, you haven't seen what I got you yet."

Hannah's brows nearly hit her hairline. Owen had gotten her a present too? "That really is too much."

"Except it's not," he corrected and pulled another box from beside his bed, handing it to her as Lucy hopped off the bed to try on her coat, twisting this way and that in an attempt to see all the unicorns at once.

Automatically, Hannah took the package, noting the heavy metallic rose-colored wrapping paper was almost the exact shade of the dress she'd worn to the courthouse to marry Owen. Because he'd remembered the ceremony or because he'd seen the dress in the photograph she'd showed him?

More to the point, was there some significance to him picking that shade? What was she supposed to take from this?

"Open it," he instructed with barely concealed glee.

"What is this all about, Owen?" she muttered, her gaze on him, not the package. There was an angle here and she refused to miss it while ogling a pretty box.

"It's about me being grateful that you're taking time out of your busy schedule to spend a day with me in the most boring place on the universe," he said, his gaze solemn and deep and full of things she didn't understand but wanted to. "It's about me realizing that I have a lot to make up for. It's me saying thank you for letting me know Lucy."

Hannah glanced at her daughter—and his too—but she was thankfully dialed into the beautiful, impractical raincoat and ignoring them both.

"Open your gift, Hannah," he instructed quietly. "It might be the wrong size and then I'll have to figure out how to send it back when it was an enormous pain to get the hospital to allow deliveries here in the first place."

"Did I get a unicorn raincoat too?" she asked wryly, secretly hoping the answer was yes, because what woman didn't need a beautiful, impractical coat that cost more than her water bill?

"Only one way to find out," Owen told her mischievously as he nudged the box closer.

Rolling her eyes, she fingered the tape loose, hoping to save the paper. It was really nice paper, the kind she could reuse for a myriad of crafts later. When she lifted the lid of the box, she forgot about the wrapping, her suspicions about Owen's motives and possibly her own name.

"This is not a raincoat," she whispered as she gingerly lifted out one of three bottles of twenty-five-year-old Aceto balsamic vinegar from Modena packed in crinkle paper shavings. "Owen, what in the world…"

She could barely stand to hold it in her hand for fear of breaking it. Neither could she fathom ever putting it down again. The glass cooled her palm, thick and dark to protect the contents from harsh light. The bottle's design alone marked it as something special, never mind what it held.

"This is definitely too much," she insisted as she met Owen's gaze, very much afraid that the slosh of emotions inside had somehow surfaced on her face. "Even one of these bottles runs in the hundreds of dollars. Where did you even find something like this?"

"So you like it?"

"That's akin to asking Santa Claus if he likes Christmas. Of course I like it. Any chef on the planet would kill for access to balsamic vinegar of this quality."

And she'd just been given three bottles. By a man who had no reason to have come up with such a thoughtful gift. She hadn't even been a caterer when they'd been married. She'd developed her love of cooking after that, when she'd been desperate to figure out how to support herself and her daughter, not just on her own financially but mentally and emotionally too.

But this gift wasn't going to go on a shelf in her industrial kitchen. This was a private, personal gift for her as a woman, not a caterer. There was a subtle line between the two and Owen had found it. How had he clued in that she would appreciate this far more than flowers or jewelry?

Before Owen never would have.

The fact that Current Owen paid this kind of attention to both her and Lucy knocked her for a loop.

Before she'd had any time to get her feet under her, the doctor strolled into the room. "Oh, good to see you, Ms. Colton. If you have a moment, I'd like to speak with you in the hall."

That did not sound good. Owen caught her gaze and tilted his head toward the door, then called out to Lucy in a clear ploy to keep her busy. As if they'd often conspired together to allow Hannah to slip from the room while he occupied their daughter.

It was dizzying how quickly Owen had picked up on the dynamics required to keep a five-year-old busy. And the reasons one needed to.

"Yes, hello, Dr. Farris," Hannah said as she joined the doctor at the nurse's station a couple of rooms down from Owen's.

It was busier than the last time she'd spoken to him. Nurses rushed by in both directions, and the phone next to the empty workstation rang and rang with no one to pick it up.

The doctor regarded her for a brief moment, and she had the impression he was gearing up for something. Bad news? She firmed her mouth, mentally preparing for the worst. Though what that could be when Owen clearly had all his faculties and some extra ones that he'd developed out of nowhere, she had no idea.

"I'll cut right to the chase, Ms. Colton. We're at a point where we can't keep Mr. Mackenzie in the hospital any longer. We're releasing him today, but I have reservations about his ability to function without help."

"What?" Her brain spun in an effort to keep up with what the doctor was telling her. "How can you release him? He doesn't remember anything about his life."

"That's the reason we're having this discussion," he said flatly, his eyes still kind behind his glasses. "Physically, he's fine. His ribs are healing and the stitches in his head will dissolve over time. He needs some basic wound care, and it wouldn't hurt for him to stay on bed rest for a few more days until he's feeling up to more movement. But from a trauma perspective, a hospital is overkill. And he doesn't have any insurance."

Hannah's eyes went wide. "How can he not have insurance? Who has been paying for his stay thus far?"

"We're not monsters, Ms. Colton," the doctor said with an unamused laugh. "We don't just take patients based on their ability to pay. That's the reason the folks in that department started looking for next of kin, actually, and found you. I'm sure they'll work with him to develop a payment plan for the balance owed. We've kept him this long because I had a personal interest in his recovery, but we've done everything we can do for his memory issues. Now it's just going to take time."

"But what is he supposed to do?" she asked as the enormity of Owen's situation worked its way into the cracks of her very foundation. With no insurance, the bill he'd be receiving would likely be backbreaking. "He can't work if he doesn't remember his job or how to do it or even where it is."

The doctor's gaze bored into her, willing her to read between the lines. Well, she didn't like those lines. Or what was between them. And shutting her eyes didn't erase the reality of what he was telling her.

"You want me to take care of him," she stated with zero inflection.

"He needs someone, yes. It would be difficult for him to navigate in a world he doesn't remember, especially while also trying to finish healing. Of course, he can relearn job skills and things of that nature, but he's not back to a hundred percent physically yet. I would recommend he not be left alone. And he needs to follow up with a primary care doctor in a few days."

Which meant the only option was for Owen to stay with her. At her house. So she could be the one to dress his head wound and make sure he didn't overexert himself while his ribs healed. She could cook for him. Fold him into her life.

Get used to having someone else around who could sit with Lucy while Hannah took a shower.

It sounded…not horrible.

But how long would that last? How long would she want it to last?

"This is a lot to consider," she said faintly. "What if he doesn't ever regain his memories?"

"That is unfortunately a possibility," the doctor warned her.

But she was busy reveling in how so very wonderful that sounded, to keep this version of Owen around for a good long while, the one that seemed thrilled with the idea of being a father. Who bought them lavish gifts selected with exquisite care.

They could be a family. For real this time.

If that was her reward for taking him in, she'd do it in a heartbeat. But of course, there was no guarantee. And how selfish was she, hoping that Owen never remembered who he was?

None of that mattered in the grand scheme of things. He needed her, not the other way around. What choice did she have but to take him in? Her conscience wouldn't allow her to do anything but that. He had no one else in the world to take care of him other than Hannah. If that wasn't true, they'd have found someone by now.

Even if he one day woke up and remembered he was Old Owen and tore everything to pieces once again, she couldn't walk away from him.

Chapter Ten

When Hannah got back to the room, Owen and Lucy were playing tic-tac-toe on a thick pad with the hospital logo in the lower right-hand corner.

She couldn't help but smile. "Who's winning?"

"Me, Mama," Lucy announced and put another *X* in a box, then drew a line. "Daddy sucks at this game."

"We don't say the word *sucks*," she reminded her daughter for the nine millionth time, which was a lost cause because Wade said it, and Lucy refused to accept Hannah's explanation that Uncle Wade was an adult and bound by different rules.

"I'm learning though," Owen said with a wink at Lucy, shooting Hannah a wide smile. "Mostly that my daughter is a shark when it comes to games."

"You didn't bet any money, did you?" Hannah asked dryly, and Owen shook his head. "Highly suggest you don't start. Lucy, why don't you let me talk to your father for a few minutes? If you sit in the chair outside until I come get you, I'll let you play Candy Crush on my phone."

The best treat in her arsenal. Lucy perked up and slid from the bed instantly, a testament to how rarely Hannah used it. Dutifully, Lucy followed her out to the chair in question, taking the precious phone as if she'd been handed the key to Fort Knox.

"What's the rule?" Hannah asked as she covered the screen with her hand before Lucy could start the game.

"No going to other apps. No in-app purchases unless I ask first. No laying down the phone for any reason," Lucy recited, and Hannah smiled in approval.

Calculating that she had about five minutes, Hannah scooted back into Owen's room. It was the first time they'd been alone together in what felt like forever. She had a fine awareness of the way he watched her, so carefully, as if afraid to miss even a single hair.

"What's going on, Hannah?" he asked quietly. "The doctor spoke to you about me being released, didn't he?"

"Yeah, he did." She let out the breath she'd been holding and with it, her reservations. "I'm going to bring you home with me."

It was the right thing to do. But Owen didn't fist pump or grin salaciously. He just let his warm brown eyes focus on her for an eternity until he finally asked, "Why?"

"You're just starting a relationship with Lucy," she said. "She would be devastated not to see you any longer. Besides, where would you go?"

"I'll figure something out," he insisted. "I wasn't planning to leave Conners, if that was your concern."

"No, my concern is that you don't have anyone else who cares what happens to you, Owen."

And by default, that meant she did. He caught the point too, judging by the way the warmth in his gaze spilled over to encompass them both like a blanket.

"Are you sure this is a good idea?" he murmured. "I was a pretty crappy husband. I can't imagine that you have many fond feelings for me."

"Let me worry about that." Especially since she'd already

gotten a jump start on that, wondering what in the world she was doing inviting her ex-husband to stay with her in the home she'd made with her daughter after losing everything by his hand the first time. "It's only temporary. Until you get on your feet again. Over the next few days, we'll have plenty of time to talk about what happens next. Whether you want to continue to have a relationship with Lucy going forward. How we facilitate that."

Owen caught her hand in his, lacing their fingers together in a surprise move that felt completely foreign—and she'd held hands with this man before. Lots of times. Granted, it had been years ago, and some days she felt like she couldn't remember being Early-Twenties Hannah at all.

She stared at their entwined fingers as the warmth he'd enveloped her in expanded and grew, becoming quite a bit more heated.

"Thank you," he said quietly. "For trusting me enough to say something like that."

Okay, now she was staring at him, trying to convince herself she hadn't misheard him. Before Owen would have never even realized she'd expressed a great deal of trust in him. That the very act of marrying him had been a gift of trust. And he'd trampled it.

"Everyone deserves a second chance," she said.

CHECKOUT TOOK FAR less time than Hannah was expecting, and before she could fully acclimate to this new reality, Owen had allowed himself to be tucked into the passenger seat of her Honda, seat belt arranged carefully across his healing ribs.

Lucy was thrilled to pieces that her daddy was coming home with them. Hannah had explained that he was still sick, so she'd offered to help take care of him so he could be closer to Lucy whenever she wanted to see him. With her freakishly keen insight, Lucy had added that this way, she wouldn't have to work around her school schedule to see him either. Which Hannah wished she'd thought of. It did make things easier all the way around.

Except for the weird things it was doing to her heart rate to be seated this close to Owen. Their elbows were practically touching over the center console. The flush of awareness spread across her skin, and she was afraid he might realize she was blushing.

It was stupid. She wasn't a blusher.

Shrugging it off, she put the car in gear and drove, painfully aware that Owen didn't even have a coat to his name. The few belongings they'd handed him at the hospital hurt her heart. "I can take you shopping sometime if you like."

Owen nodded. "I would appreciate that. I don't seem to have packed for a long trip."

Another reason this was a very bad idea. That telltale sign probably meant that he hadn't intended to stay in this area. The accident had forced him into a much longer stretch than he'd been planning. If—when—he regained his memories, he'd probably confess that he was just driving through. The fact that Hannah and Lucy lived near Conners may have never crossed his mind.

If he regained his memories. It was still a big *if.*

Nerves loosened her tongue, and she babbled about the sights the entire drive home to Owl Creek, pointing out Blackbird Lake as it came into view, Wade's house as she passed the drive, the new barbecue place that had opened not too long ago.

"This is your house?" Owen asked, surprise tinging his voice as she pulled into the driveway of the bungalow she'd bought from her brother, Chase, for a discount that she'd argued about until their mother had intervened, insisting that Hannah buy the dang house and let Chase help her afford it.

But she didn't go into those details. Her family had closed ranks around her after Owen had left, and she loved them for it. Regardless, the actions of Old Owen had no place here, at least not at the moment, and she'd like to forget about all of that. Start fresh. Like she'd told him—and she wholeheartedly believed it—everyone deserved a second chance, and she intended to give him one.

"Home sweet home," she confirmed lightly. "And yours for at least a few days. I hope it's okay."

"I just didn't picture you as a living in a house by the lake," he said. "It's better than okay. This is charming. It's a house I would have picked out for myself."

Looking at it with fresh eyes, she did have to admit the place was stunning, with the views of the lake and modern touches that set it apart from the rental properties closer to town. Wade's cabin lay just a quarter of a mile away, visible through the trees now that winter had stripped them of their leaves. Her place had come with a storage shed down by the water where she kept Lucy's floaties and some of the bigger equipment for her catering business.

"It's more than a home," she admitted. "It's a refuge. I hope you come to think of it as one, as well."

He caught her gaze, an emotion she didn't recognize spilling into the space between them as Lucy took Hannah's key and ran inside, leaving the adults standing on the driveway. She should be chilled given the temperature, but it turned out that the heat from sitting next to him in the car had seeped into her bones. Liquefying them. Her knees nearly buckled but she locked them and somehow managed to keep herself off the crushed shells beneath her feet.

"You're a very generous woman, Hannah," he told her sincerely. "I've never met anyone like you."

She laughed without meaning to. But this was all so absurd. "You mean you don't remember meeting someone like me. I'm still the same person you used to be married to, Owen."

"Somehow I doubt that. Maybe you have amnesia too," he teased. "But I see how you are with Lucy, and I have a feeling she's at least partially made you into the person you are now."

That was true and not an insignificant point. Everything that had happened to her since Owen abandoned her had worked to transform her into someone new. Someone she liked. She'd worked hard to provide for Lucy and be a good single mom, which she should honor instead of sweeping under the rug.

It was so odd for Owen to be the one to point that out.

"You're right," she admitted. "I have changed. I'm not who I was when we were married."

The way he was looking at her made her feel blushy again.

"I'm happy to meet you, Hannah Colton," he murmured and held out his hand. "Do me a favor and call me Mac. Maybe that will help us both feel like we really are meeting for the first time."

Mac. Short for Mackenzie. It was fitting somehow, and she did not want to examine how thrilling it was to think of him this way. As someone new, someone she'd never met. Someone she was astonishingly attracted to.

Without thinking through the consequences, she reached for him, allowing his fingers to wrap around hers. The jolt that traveled through her felt as foreign as it did electrifying. Why had she taken off her gloves?

Quickly, she pulled free, immediately missing his warmth. "It's chilly. We should go inside."

Owen—Mac—nodded as if nothing significant had happened.

Nothing significant *had* happened. She was being silly, thinking that it was so momentous for Owen… Mac…to have recognized that they were essentially strangers at this point, as if they had never met.

But she couldn't get it out of her mind that on Mac's side, that was his reality. He didn't think of himself as Owen, didn't remember Owen. But Mac? That was the man he was now.

What if because of that they could have a brand-new start in the very best way? As if they had no history? No bad stuff between them. It was a do-over on steroids that only she could facilitate.

Mac followed her into the house, commenting on everything from her large, well-appointed kitchen, to the floor-to-ceiling glass in her living room that overlooked the lake. Lucy popped up to show Mac her room, a reprieve Hannah took with every fiber of her being.

Blowing out a breath, she hung up her coat in the mudroom and slipped off her waterproof boots in favor of her house shoes that she'd never thought twice about.

But she'd never had a man in her house who would be looking at her feet. The serviceable brown slippers were a little worn-out but more to the point, might have graced the cover of Octogenarian Magazine. She might have to rethink her wardrobe choices in addition to how to feed another adult when she was so used to cooking for one adult and one very picky eater who turned her nose up at vegetables.

Mac returned from the back of the house, Lucy's hand in his, as she towed him around showing him the entire place, apparently.

"And this is where I watch cartoons," she explained as she pointed to the couch. "You can watch with me."

"Your father is probably not a *Peppa Pig* fan," Hannah called. Poor guy was probably overwhelmed by Lucy's excited chatter.

"How would he know if he hasn't watched it yet?" Lucy

returned with her typical eerie five-year-old logic. "Plus, you said he was sick. Cartoons are for when you're sick. They'll make him feel better."

"Can't argue with that," Mac said cheerfully and allowed his daughter to haul him over to the couch, settling in with remarkable grace as Lucy expertly cued up an episode of the show using her kids' profile on the streaming service Hannah preferred.

He looked quite at home, laughing as Lucy pointed out all her favorite characters. Oh, goodness. Hannah put a hand to her fluttering tummy, willing it to stop acting like *that*.

She had no call to be reacting to the sight of her ex-husband spending time with their daughter. Lots of people co-parented without dissolving into puddles of goo when they spied a father and daughter watching a TV show together. What was her problem?

The problem was that he didn't resemble her ex in any way, shape or form. He was Mac. She desperately wanted to grasp that fact. It was a lifeline at the moment. A way to balance her feelings for him that didn't interfere with the past.

It was a *good* thing that he was here. Good for Lucy. Good for Mac.

Her problem was that it was a bad thing for her state of mind. Not for the reasons she'd thought, though. But because she couldn't stop thinking about how different things could be this second time around.

At the end of the day, she couldn't call herself altruistic if she had an ulterior motive, could she? Inviting him here was about exploring this new Mac, bottom line. What could be. What this unexpected blessing of amnesia had done for them all.

Her problem was that it could have always been like this. If he hadn't left. If he hadn't been the type of guy who couldn't stick. They'd lost *years*.

And she had a slim sliver of hope that they could reclaim some of that time lost, that it could be like this all the time. Forever. As long as he didn't recover his memories.

Chapter Eleven

This charade had gone on *far* too long.

Seriously, how had Archer ended up at Hannah's house, still answering to the name Owen? So he'd fixed that by switching to Mac. Everyone at work called him that. It wouldn't be difficult to answer to.

Except it was ridiculous that he'd let it get to this point whether she called him Mac, Owen or Howdy Doody. He had to tell her the truth. Immediately.

Okay, granted, he'd thought maybe it would be excusable to give himself one day. *One day* to play Lucy's father, to try to make up for a whole lifetime of her being disappointed by Owen Mackenzie. Lucy deserved to have good memories of the man who had sired her, and only Archer could give her that.

But then he'd walked into this home and felt the love that had built it. Seen how Hannah parented her daughter, how bright and special Lucy was. Something had physically scored him inside, and he couldn't stand to keep lying to this wonderful woman and amazing little girl his brother had screwed over.

Except he'd never gotten even a second alone with Hannah from the instant they'd crossed the threshold. Until now.

"Hannah," Archer called the moment Lucy disappeared

into her room to fetch the stuffed dog she called Mr. Fluffers. "I need to talk to you. It's important."

Hannah paused, midchop, peering at him from behind the long island/bar combo that separated the living area from the kitchen. "I can listen and julienne bell pepper for this catering job at the same time."

"I mean *privately*," he stressed.

He couldn't in good conscience blurt out the truth where Lucy might hear him. Part of this confession would entail asking Hannah the best way to handle his exit, which needed to come sooner rather than later.

Hannah laughed. "We have a five-year-old daughter. There is no privacy unless she's at school, which won't happen for another fourteen hours."

"What about after she goes to bed?" he asked, ignoring the pang that accompanied phrases like *we have a daughter*.

He didn't have a daughter. He didn't have anything other than an overinflated sense of responsibly to fix the stuff Owen broke.

But he wanted to be the other half of the "we" in Hannah's statement.

Man, was it ever hard not to insert himself in the middle of this cozy scene and run with it, claiming Lucy as his own. He'd never thought about being a dad before, never wondered what it was like to shop for presents and watch with barely concealed glee as the little human he'd helped create discovered what was in the box.

Now he knew. It was like nothing else on the planet, and he wanted more.

But this was not his life, and he had no right to steal his brother's. Or let his brother's former wife keep thinking Archer was Owen.

Hannah laughed again, a sound he should not like so much. Particularly since he had a feeling it was at his expense.

"You have clearly never put a five-year-old to bed. There's always a fifty-fifty chance we'll be graced with her presence six times between the last story and when we finally pass out from exhaustion after fetching her a glass of water, fixing the curtains so they don't look weird, tucking in Mr. Fluffers again because he's cold—" this she accompanied with exaggerated air quotes "—and who knows what all she'll dream up as an excuse to get out of bed one last time. Especially with you here. I fully expect to be told there's a leprechaun under the bed and only Daddy can make it go away."

Mouth ajar, he blinked. "That's all going to happen in one night?"

"More than once," she promised, still chopping away while talking, as advertised. "If it can't wait, I can send her to Wade's down the shore. She loves to hang out with Betty Jane. That's a dog," she supplied helpfully. "But it will have to be after dinner because he's not home right now."

"That's...who's Wade?" he thought to ask, even though he knew Wade Colton was her brother from the research he'd done on her family. It seemed like a thing Owen would have forgotten, though.

"I thought I mentioned him. He's my brother," Hannah called from the depths of the pantry. "I have two others and two sisters. Six of us total. Oh, and Sarah and Nate. I really didn't mean to leave them out. It's just—you know, new. I have to keep reframing my family to include them."

"It's fine," he said. "If you think Wade wouldn't mind, that would be great."

"Sure. We do need to talk about...things," Hannah said as she came back into the kitchen from the pantry, empty-handed, her expression perplexed. "Lucy? Where are you? Have you been in my kitchen?"

"What's wrong?" Archer asked.

"Some things in the pantry have been rearranged and

a bottle of oil is missing. I need it to sauté these peppers." Hannah frowned and opened one of the cabinet doors, then another one. "Some of the dishes in these cabinets have been moved too. It's like my dresser drawers all over again. This is so weird."

Archer's gut pinged and his senses sharpened to full-alert mode. "What do you mean, like your dresser drawers? Some things were rearranged in your dresser too? The one in your bedroom?"

Hannah nodded, biting her lip. "I thought it was Lucy, but I just remembered that my shampoo bottles were out of order. I probably did that, though. I'm just so distracted lately..."

She trailed off, but he knew she meant because of him, which did not ease his guilt any.

"Can you show me your shampoo bottles? And the dresser? I'd like to see everything that you've noticed is different, no matter how small of a change you think it is."

"What? Why?" Now Hannah's expression veered toward alarmed and she scrubbed at her neck as if agitated. "Do you think something is wrong?"

Yeah, something was wrong. Someone had been searching her house, pretty methodically too and on more than one occasion, by the sounds of it, but not carefully enough to avoid detection. His blood chilled as he thought about the implications. Big Mike had fingers in a lot of pies. There was absolutely no reason to believe Hannah had skated under his radar—and a lot of reasons to believe that he'd already known about her because she'd been working with Owen.

No. He couldn't picture Hannah in that role any longer. There was no way she'd been Owen's accomplice. Or was that his emotional response instead of the analytical one?

Archer nearly sighed out loud. When he couldn't remove his own prejudice from the equation, how could he rightly call his conclusions unbiased?

Hannah might be involved. He didn't know for certain.

But even if she wasn't, that didn't mean she hadn't popped up on Big Mike's People of Interest list. Five million dollars was a lot of money to be missing in the first place, but if it could be traced to a crime organization, Big Mike had more than a vested interest in recovering it, regardless of whether there was an innocent little girl in the mix.

"Nothing's wrong," he assured Hannah, or at least he hoped he'd used his most reassuring voice.

Archer was an analyst, not a comforter. But he'd dang well better learn how to smooth over his tendency to be business first since he clearly wasn't going anywhere.

His plan to tell Hannah the truth evaporated as his mind instantly chopped through the data with the same efficiency she'd applied to make short work of the peppers. The sooner she knew he wasn't Owen, the sooner it would get out to someone in Big Mike's organization. And it was far better for everyone to think that the hitman assigned to take out Owen had failed.

For now. At least until Archer could get some more facts.

"Nothing's wrong," he repeated. "I'm just curious. I like to figure things out and if I can help ease your mind about what's going on around here, I'd like to."

That much at least was true.

Seemingly mollified, Hannah asked him to wait while she put Lucy to bed, a mysterious ritual he wanted to know more about. In time, he hoped he'd get to be involved.

A solid thirty minutes later, Hannah led him to the back of the house via the hallway to Lucy's room. The guest room Hannah had shown him to earlier lay in the opposite direction, off the kitchen. He didn't assume it was an accident that the rooms were so completely separate, and he appreciated the reason.

But if it came down to it, he couldn't protect Hannah or

Lucy if he was so far away. Archer suspected he might eventually be sleeping on the floor outside Lucy's door pending what he discovered regarding the not-so-invisible fingers who had searched the house.

The moment he crossed the threshold to Hannah's bedroom, he realized his mistake. It smelled like vanilla and sunshine, exploding with colors and light. Exactly like the woman. He could scarcely look away from the bed where he could easily imagine Hannah sleeping in something scanty and...way off-limits. A guy like him shouldn't even be fantasizing about her clothed, let alone anything else.

She didn't even know his real name.

Archer swallowed. "You said something about shampoo bottles?"

Hannah nodded and let him into the bathroom that was even smaller than the bedroom. He could reach out and pull her into his arms with no effort whatsoever from this distance. Which was an idea he quite liked. And also needed to stop thinking about.

"I line up all my bottles on that window ledge." Hannah pointed at the long rectangle that sat about six feet off the shower floor. "I don't like them on the floor, and shower caddies always slip off the showerhead, so I stopped buying them."

Too high for Lucy to be the one who moved them around. Kudos to whoever did rearrange them though—checking for hidden keys and other important things inside random bottles was exactly what he'd have thought of too.

"Makes sense," he said, curious why she thought she had to justify her own personal organization system.

"You always got so mad when the shower caddy wouldn't stay put," she told him, biting her lip in the way he'd started to think of as her Owen face. Anytime she recounted something he'd done in the past, she always looked like she wasn't sure if she should be talking about this stuff.

"I was a jerk, Hannah," he told her bluntly. "You don't have to sugarcoat anything for me. I can take whatever you want to dish out about how I used to act. I need to hear it. I don't ever want to be that guy again."

That was literally impossible, but he also appreciated the lessons on how not to be like Owen if he ever had a doubt about whether he was his twin's polar opposite.

"When you say things like that…" Hannah hesitated, her gaze flitting between him and the floor.

Unable to help himself, he reached out and tilted her head up with his thumb, fanning out his fingers to cup her face. "What? When I say things like what, Hannah?"

Her skin warmed his hand as she stared at him. "Things that make me think you're serious about being different. Serious about being a father. It's overwhelming."

"I mean every word," he said gruffly, and it was the truth. At least as much as he had the ability to make things better for her. To fix the things Owen had broken.

Of course, Archer was in the process of creating a whole new set of difficulties the longer he stood here with his hand skating along Hannah's jaw. Because he couldn't seem to pull away. Or make himself stop staring into her eyes, willing her to see *him*. Not Owen.

"I don't know what to think half the time," she murmured. "It's like you're two different people."

Archer's heart stuttered. "What do you mean?"

She let her lips drift upward. "In my head, I refer to you as Before Owen and Current Owen. It's like Before Owen vanished, and Current Owen is who showed up in his place."

That, he could work with. It was better than her realizing he wasn't Owen—he could be a hybrid version of himself. "We can thank amnesia for that, I guess. Since I don't remember who I was, I'm doing whatever feels natural. Maybe this me was always trapped inside and I just needed a swift punch to the head to uncover it. It would be nice if you could forget Before Owen, too, and I'm sorry I can't figure out a way to help with that."

Was he a horrible person for reveling in Hannah's focused attention? His brother had messed up his relationship with this woman and all Archer wanted was a redo. A way to set things right and maybe slide into something that seemed like it would be amazing at the same time.

There was no way the universe would be so cruel as to ensure Owen had screwed it up for Archer too. Who better to give Hannah this second chance than someone who knew exactly what it felt like to be betrayed and disappointed by Owen Mackenzie?

Besides, Hannah had a steel core that Owen would never have recognized. A sense of humor Owen would never have understood. A warm personality that his brother would not have appreciated.

But Archer did. On all three counts.

"What are you doing, Mama?" Lucy called as she strolled into the bathroom rubbing her eyes. "I heard a noise."

Archer dropped his hand before Lucy could clue in that he'd been about half a second away from reeling in her mother for a very long overdue kiss.

Thank goodness for interruptions. Kissing Hannah would have been a very bad idea for a multitude of reasons, none of which he could think of at the moment.

"Hey, Lu Lu," Hannah called brightly and stooped down to engulf her daughter in a hug, despite the fact that the little scamp should be in bed. "Sorry we woke you."

Witnessing the two of them entwined put a lump in Archer's throat. Hannah and Lucy loved each other so openly and easily. His relationship with his own mother was complicated by her inability to see Owen for the scammer he was. She loved her sons equally and thought it was a virtue, failing to see that not holding Owen accountable for his sins devalued her love for Archer.

Yet Archer still did as she asked, chasing after Owen's killer, desperate to win a little more of that love over to his side. Where it should be.

"If I had a dog, I wouldn't be worried when I hear voices," Lucy announced slyly, her gaze full of wide innocence as she slid it over in his direction, likely because she'd already figured out he was the easy mark.

Archer had to laugh. "Is that so?"

"Or," Hannah interjected lightly, "you could think to yourself, oh, that's right, my daddy is here now and there's nothing to worry about because he's going to take care of me."

That sentiment put a whole lot more than a lump in his throat.

"I will definitely do that as long as I am physically able to, Lucy Mackenzie," he said, the catch in his voice wider than the Grand Canyon.

"You don't have to say my whole name at home, Daddy," she told him with a lofty toss of her head.

"Well, the thing is, I've never said it," he told her truthfully. "And I like saying it because it's my name too."

Lucy grinned. "We can be twins."

Well, that was a sobering—and telling—reminder if he'd ever heard one. As cozy as this stolen family time was, he had no right to be wishing he'd been the one here with Lucy this whole time, tucking her into bed every night for the last four years. His brother had really missed out on something great.

"Back to bed, Ms. Thing," Hannah said and scooped up her daughter to carry her out of the bathroom.

Leaving Archer behind. Because he wasn't part of their routine. Not yet. Probably not ever. He was living on borrowed time in the first place. If Big Mike did figure out there was a man living in Hannah's house who looked like Owen Mackenzie and answered to that name, Archer's life would be in jeopardy.

He took himself off to bed, settling into the guest room that he imagined Hannah had decorated herself with earth tones and shades of peach that were a perfect balance between masculine and feminine. It was ironic. This place felt more like a home than the one he lived in every day, and he'd only been here less than six hours.

Chapter Twelve

In the morning, Archer taught himself how the coffee maker functioned and had a pot brewed before Hannah emerged from her wing of the house. She came into the kitchen wearing a long quilted robe that would have been dowdy on anyone else.

On Hannah, it made his mouth go dry.

"Good morning," he choked out hoarsely and cleared his throat.

Moron. The long talk he'd given himself about letting his slight crush on Hannah get out of hand clearly had not worked. It was just so hard not to think about how his brother had basically done whatever he'd wanted his entire life with no regard to consequences, and his reward had been Hannah and Lucy. Who he'd promptly abandoned.

And Archer's reward for doing the right thing his entire life was the opportunity to lie to this woman about his identity and pretend to be Lucy's father. All so he could figure out a way to repair the damage Owen had done, plus investigate who had killed him. Oh, and look for the millions of dollars of missing money in his spare time, while keeping his eyes open about a potential threat to this precious family he'd stumbled over.

No problem.

Was it too much to ask that he get a little bit of something good out of this whole deal? A very brief shot at feeling like this family belonged to him, even if only for a couple of days?

Completely oblivious to his internal angst, Hannah crossed to the coffee pot and inhaled the rich aroma. "There is no better scent in the world than freshly brewed coffee. Thank you. I used to preprogram the machine to brew it before I got out of bed, but when Lucy was a baby, she had a lot of digestive issues. More often than not, the coffee would sit on the burner for an hour, sometime two, before I could actually take the time to drink it, so I quit doing that. It was just easier to make the coffee fresh in the morning when I was ready for it. It's nice to have someone else make it for once."

Fascinated in spite of himself, he took his own mug and slid into one of the barstools at the long kitchen island. "Tell me about Lucy as a baby. Start at the beginning. Don't leave anything out."

Hannah laughed and it was as nice of a sound in the dim morning light as it had been last night. Maybe better because Lucy was still in bed asleep. As far as he knew anyway. He'd never appreciated Hannah's warning that they'd have zero privacy more than he did at the moment, because he'd like nothing more than to back her up against the counter and see what it felt like for her to laugh against his mouth.

Right. Because *Lucy* was the biggest obstacle to that fantasy.

"That's a tall order," she countered lightly, sipping her coffee. Then she moaned and let her eyelids flutter shut. "This is amazing. What did you do to this?"

He was too busy stuffing away his inappropriate reaction to her coffee-drinking that he couldn't answer for a beat. "I put grounds in the filter and turned it on."

"Liar," she accused with a smile. "I do that, and it comes out okay. This is a whole other level."

"I'm heavy handed with the scoop, I guess." He shrugged, ridiculously pleased that she liked something he'd done for her enough to comment on it. Moving on. His reactions to Hannah's reactions were a dangerous subject. "Back to Lucy. If you can't tell me everything, at least some highlights. Anything. I'm not picky."

Hannah joined him at the breakfast bar on the backside of the island, but she didn't sit in a chair. Instead, she leaned a hip on the counter, facing him, and he tried not to think about how easy it would be to swivel his chair with the sole intent of pulling her into his lap. Or between his legs for an embrace that would feel far too intimate for a kitchen.

Though this island did have a very large, very solid white marble top that could be put to a lot of uses that had nothing to do with chopping vegetables.

"Since you deserve a medal for this coffee, and Lucy stories are my favorite, I guess I can come up with a couple." She warmed to her subject, riffling through the file folders in her brain for whatever she might deem worthy of sharing. "You see how good she is at tic-tac-toe. It's not just that one. She learned to play card games at three. Slap Jack is still her favorite, but she picked up Uno this past Christmas from Wade, along with three or four others, all of which she will kick the pants off you if you play with her. She's so competitive. I have no idea where she gets that from."

Owen. No question.

His twin made everything a competition, from who could finish eating first to who could pick up a girl the quickest at a bar. That one had gotten old fast, especially when Owen had been a champion at identifying the one Archer had noticed first, and then swooping in to pluck the girl away with his charm.

That had been one of many reasons Archer had cut off contact with his brother ten years ago. It was just too much.

Still was. The pattern had obviously continued, with Owen beating Archer to the punch once again with Hannah. Only this time, Owen wouldn't be coming back around for a second try. This shot was all Archer's. If only he could figure out whether there was actually a shot to be taken here.

"I'd love to play with her," he told her honestly. "I am a very good loser."

Hannah laughed like he was kidding, but Archer was the opposite of competitive. He'd had to be growing up with Owen. Someone had to be second and it was never his brother, so that left Archer to learn how to be okay with never winning. It was how he'd gotten good at analyzing a situation.

When you weren't focused on beating everyone else, you could take a step back and notice details. See the lay of the land, so to speak. Take time to put pieces together and take a top-down view to what the whole looked like.

"It's your funeral," Hannah said, her mouth lifting at the corners in a tiny smile that was somehow better than her normal one. As if they were sharing a secret. "Like I said, don't bet any money you don't want to lose. She is a shark when she scents candy money coming her way. My brother, Fletcher, walked away ten dollars poorer last week, and I'm fairly certain he thought he was going to let her win as a courtesy, only she beat him fair and square. Four games of Uno in a row."

"I'm not sure if that should make me proud or terrified," he admitted.

"Exactly," Hannah said with another of the tiny smiles that were quickly becoming his favorite. "That's one of the things they don't tell you about parenting. It veers between making you gooey inside over your little person's accomplishments and worried you're not going to be able to guide them toward using their powers for good instead of evil."

The underlying stress and uncertainty beneath her joke came through loud and clear. Would he ever not insert judgment on his brother's stupid decisions? How could he avoid it when Owen had skipped out on standing side by side with this amazing woman to help her raise the human being they'd made together? It was unconscionable.

"I'm sorry, Hannah," he said sincerely, also wondering how many times he'd have to apologize for Owen's bone-headedness before he felt like it was enough. "I should have been here, helping you figure out how to keep Lucy from turning into a pool hustler before the age of twelve."

Hannah didn't laugh that time. Okay, so he wasn't as good with the jokes yet, or it was too soon. He wasn't sure.

But then she shocked him by covering his hand with hers. "You're here now, Mac. That's what matters. The past is the past. Let's move forward."

The grace radiating from this woman... It humbled him. And pricked at his eyelids enough that he had to blink a bunch to avoid a show of unmanly tears.

"I can get on board with that," he agreed readily, since leaving the past in the past was the only way he could move forward. "And before we go too much more forward, I do want to say thank you again, for inviting me to stay here. For being so willing and open to give me a second chance with Lucy. It means a lot to me."

She went dead silent for a beat and then nodded once. "I'm choosing to trust you. Because it means a lot to me that you want to be here. That you want to have a relationship with Lucy. Don't disappoint me on this. Or her. She deserves to know you."

"I completely agree," he interjected fiercely. This was the one thing that was nonnegotiable, no matter what happened.

"I'm not going anywhere this time. When I say I want to be her father, I mean it."

This part at least crystallized for him.

He'd figure out what his promise looked like once everyone knew the truth later. He'd...adopt Lucy. Or something. Whatever made it legal for him to be her daddy from now on, he'd do it.

But first, he needed to get square with Big Mike's agenda, whatever it was. Get the trigger finger who had offed Owen behind bars. Find the money. At this point, he'd take finding a flipping clue in lieu of the money. As long as he could call it progress toward the end of this charade.

On that note, now that he wasn't hampered by being in the hospital, he could do a lot more low-key nosing around. "If it's okay with you, I'd like take a tour of the town. I didn't get to see too much of it as we drove through. It's called Owl Creek, right?"

Hannah nodded. "Do you want me to play tour guide or explore on your own? We lived in Conners before, when we were married, but my family is from here. I've got a few roots, to say the least."

Once again, he was struck by the fact that she'd uprooted herself to move to a new city with her new husband. Had Owen even realized how difficult that must have been for her to be a newlywed with a baby in a city an hour's drive from everything familiar?

"If you have time, I'd love for you to show me around," he said, immediately scrapping his plan to do some investigating.

He'd rather spend time with Hannah, given how fleeting those opportunities were. And how quickly the possibility would dry up as soon as he confessed his crimes, of which there were many.

She certainly wouldn't look at him the same way as she was right this minute once she found out he wasn't Owen.

Hannah's phone buzzed and she rolled her eyes at the text message. "I forgot my mom is having a get-together this afternoon. You're invited, of course. Can we do the town tour another day?"

"Why do I get the sense this invitation has an ulterior motive?" It did, of course, and he didn't even need the giant neon sign of her expression to explain that as her gaze flicked over the text message that had just come in.

"My family is understandably concerned about your reappearance in my life," she said delicately.

No punches being pulled here, obviously. "So this is a chance for everyone to check out what's happening."

"Pretty much. Is that going to bother you?"

Normally, yes. Archer wasn't much for being on display, and he liked being examined like a bug under a microscope even less. But he got the point. Owen had hurt Hannah once. He'd abandoned his daughter. Anyone who loved them would stand between them and the man who had wreaked the destruction. He respected the notion, if not the reality.

But this was his reality and he'd signed up to be Owen for the foreseeable future, however short that may be.

"It's your family's right to be sure you're safe and happy," he told her sincerely. "Besides, I would like to meet them, especially the famous Uncle Wade. Lucy talks about him so much that I feel like I already know him."

Hannah was looking at him strangely. "It's a little shocking to hear you say something like that, even after everything that's happened. You and Wade never got along."

"My fault," he returned, because it was a sure bet that Owen was to blame. "I'm doubly eager to set things between us on the right note, then."

More like Archer would be spending an hour or two convincing Hannah's brother that he wasn't on the take. The man was a vet, former marine—Special Forces to boot—from what his quick research had revealed. Odds were high that Wade had scented Owen's less than savory nature from the first. If so, Archer would start out their rekindled acquaintance already highly appreciative of Wade Colton's opinion of his brother.

Hannah shook her head. "I cannot get over how different things are with you this time around. I might have accidentally on purpose forgotten the get-together, which I swear my mom was already planning before I decided to bring you home from the hospital. But I will admit, I was a tiny bit worried about bringing it up. I thought for sure you'd refuse to go. Or worse, agree to go, and then throw some kind of tantrum once we got there so I'd be the one who insisted on leaving early."

"Did I do that a lot before?"

Dumb question. Of course Owen had been a real class act when it came to spending time with Hannah's family. It didn't surprise Archer a bit that his brother had forced Hannah into the role of being the bad guy when it would have been so much more of the decent thing to do to have made an effort to get to know his extended family by marriage.

"Honestly, I need to stop talking about what you did before," Hannah said and dusted her hands off as if to say she'd already moved on. "I literally just said the past should be in the past, and I'm the one who keeps dragging us back there. I'm sorry. It won't happen again."

"Hannah."

Before she could pick up her coffee mug again, he snagged her hands in his and did exactly what he'd been trying not to do for a million years, pulling her into his space. Because he wanted to be close to her. Because he had to make sure she understood this was all about Archer, not Owen and their complicated history.

She stared at him, caught in the same draw between them that he knew she felt. It was in the very molecules of the atmosphere around them, tiny electric sparks that made everything brighter, sharper.

"Hannah," he murmured again. "It's okay if you want to compare the me I am now with who I used to be. It's okay if you don't. There are no rules. This is a strange, unprecedented situation. Please do and say and be however you want with me. You've earned it."

She gave a watery laugh that did nice things to his insides even as it scored his heart to realize she was fighting back tears. Because he'd given her permission to do what felt natural? How had she felt like Owen expected her to act before?

Archer shook his head. He had to get out of that mindset. It wasn't like he could ask Owen exactly how much of a jerk he'd been. He knew. Now his job was to repair the cracks his brother had caused.

"Amnesia is a gift," he told her sincerely, and he believed it with every fiber of his being. "To us both. You deserve to have a partner in this life as much as Lucy deserves to have a father. You've had to do all of this alone for so long. I can't begin to make up for the time we've both lost, but please don't spend what time we have second-guessing a single thing. I'm just happy being here."

She nodded, shaking a tear loose, and he fought the urge to wipe it away for her. They didn't have that kind of relationship. Not yet. Maybe not ever, but here in this moment, he had everything his brother had thrown away and it felt like he'd found a much greater treasure than Big Mike's missing money.

Archer planned to enjoy it for as long as he could.

Chapter Thirteen

Fletcher, Chase and Wade stood side by side at the end of the crushed stone driveway. They were three formidable figures in any circumstances, but Hannah knew they were waiting to greet Mac properly. She just hoped it wasn't so they could dismember him and hide the parts in the lake.

"Ugh, I'm sorry about this," she murmured to Mac, who was holding Lucy's hand as they walked up the drive from the street where they'd found a place to park two houses over.

When the Coltons came together, they were not a small bunch. And they took care of their own. She loved that her brothers had cared enough to close ranks. But she was equally glad she wasn't the one on the other end of their glares.

Fletcher and Wade were cut from the same cloth, both wearing their Serve-and-Protect-and-Possibly-Rip-Your-Face-Off personas like jackets. Though Wade with his eye patch was the one she'd bet most people wouldn't want to meet in a dark alley. Chase had a whole other kind of in-timidation factor. You could take the man out of the suit, but he still looked like he could buy and sell a small country before breakfast, while discreetly instructing the many people at his beck and call to end you.

"It's fine, Hannah," Mac murmured to her quietly over

Lucy's head. "I would expect nothing less than the inquisition followed by boiling oil and the rack if I answer any questions wrong. It makes me feel better to know that you've had your brothers in your corner this whole time."

That put a little lump in her throat because yeah, she did have a great family, one that she'd grown a lot closer to since she'd become a single mom. They'd told her the first time that Mac—Owen as she'd called him then—was bad news and she hadn't listened. Maybe this time she should open her ears a little wider, because they certainly hadn't been quiet about their intense dislike of both her ex-husband and the fact that he was staying at her house.

"So," Fletcher called, "the weasel has come home to roost."

"Fletch, behave," she called with the same warning note that she used when Lucy tried to sneak an extra cookie. "We're just here to relax and have fun."

"*You're* here to relax and have fun." Chase's crossed arms didn't hide his clenched fists, but then she didn't think he was actually trying to keep them out of sight. "We're here to get a few answers from Lover Boy about where he's been for four years."

Mac threw up a hand to stop the flow of Hannah's protest, which he'd somehow guessed she was about to make. He didn't flinch at the glares aimed in his direction, which earned him points. With her at least.

He stood there taking the brunt of her brothers' hostility with grace and determination. As if he truly understood he'd hurt her and running this first gauntlet was not only warranted but necessary. Something he wanted to do to prove himself.

"Take Lucy inside, Hannah," he told her calmly. "Your brothers and I have some air to clear."

Biting her lip, she glanced between them, wondering if

she should get a fan to blow away all the testosterone waft-ing around out here. Probably that wouldn't help. Instead, she opted to at least throw down another warning. "Owen doesn't remember where he's been for any number of years, no matter how hard you press. So maybe keep it friendly. And he goes by Mac these days."

Wade, who managed to pile twice the condemnation into his expression despite the patch covering one eye, grinned. No one could possibly mistake it for amusement. "We're all friends here. Right, guys?"

On cue, Fletcher, Chase and even Mac chorused their agreement. Men. Ugh. She was so done here. "Fine, y'all have at it. Let me know if I need to call the paramedics."

Fletcher showed his teeth in a mirror image of Wade's. "I'm trained in basic triage. We're all good here."

Turning her back, she grabbed Lucy's hand and flounced into the house, leaving them to their Y-chromosome conven-tion. So much for the "family meeting" that Wade had texted her about. Obviously *she* was the subject of the meeting.

"Why does Uncle Wade look like he's about to pee in his pants, Mama?" Lucy piped up with her question as Hannah dragged her up the front steps and through the front door. "I didn't even get to say hi."

"He'll be inside in a minute, Lu Lu," she promised through gritted teeth, wondering if she could say the same about Mac. If her brothers scared him off, she'd personally punch every single one of them in the nose.

"Where's Rabbit Boy?" Ruby asked the moment Han-nah hit the foyer.

Her sister stood halfway between the kitchen and the liv-ing room, bouncing Sawyer on her hip. Hannah shot her a withering glare. First Lover Boy from her brother and now this. "Rabbit Boy?"

"Because he runs the second he gets spooked," Sebastian, her husband, filled in as he took the baby from Ruby, crooning to his son in a way that told everyone exactly how he felt about being a dad.

"This is *my* life, you guys," she called to the room at large, knowing full well that she was the only one here who thought that meant they should butt out.

But then, this was her family calling her judgment into question. As they'd been doing for over five years, since she'd first hooked up with Mac. She didn't blame them, honestly. She didn't always make the best decisions.

Still. There was no proof she'd made a bad one this time. Not yet.

"It's a little bit of a suspicious situation, sweetheart." Jenny bustled out of the kitchen, Frannie right behind her. "You have to admit."

Kiki, her brother Fletcher's fiancée, wisely stayed in the kitchen but called out a distracted greeting from the counter where she was mixing something. She and Fletcher had been keeping a low profile with their relationship, but had recently announced their engagement. Hannah liked the woman her brother had fallen for. But man, how was it fair for that much gorgeous skin to be given to one woman?

Hannah's sister, Frannie, gave her a quick hug. Apparently, she was solo today as her other half, Dante, didn't seem to be among the judgment crew already lining up to give her even more opinions about how to live her life. Chase's girlfriend, Sloane, also seemed to be absent today. Too bad. Hannah needed all the newcomers to the family on her side. Surely they would be a little more reasonable since they didn't have the history.

"It's not suspicious, Mom," Hannah told her, shooting Jenny a wide-eyed look and a subtle head jerk at Lucy.

Fortunately, Harlow Jones was one of the newcomers who seemed to be on the right wavelength, which might have more to do with how long they'd known each other—since before she and Wade got involved again. She appeared from the depths of the kitchen where she'd been helping Kiki and greeted Hannah with a hug before bending down to speak to Lucy at eye level. "Betty Jane is in the back. Want to come say hi with me?"

Lucy lit up at the mention of her favorite dog and willingly followed Harlow out of the living room toward the deck that comprised most of the backyard, which sloped toward the lake. Since Lucy had spent so much time at Wade's house, she'd developed a natural affinity to Wade's significant other. The fact that Harlow was a Dog Mom had a lot to do with that.

"Bye," Hannah called out with only a touch of sarcasm at her daughter's retreating back. At least Lucy stopped to wave over her shoulder instead of ignoring her completely.

With the half-pint out of the way, Hannah crossed her arms and stared at her family.

"So," Frannie said.

"What are you doing?" Ruby asked a little more pointedly. "Did you seriously let Owen *move in*?"

"His name is Mac now. And he's recovering," Hannah corrected, shooting her mother a look. "You must have left that part out when you told everyone."

"Recovering. Also known as gearing up to leave again?" Jenny put her hands in the pockets of her apron, rocking back on her heels. "We just don't want you to get hurt by the same man."

Or make another bad call. Yes. She got it. She'd disappointed her family in a very significant way by marrying Owen in the first place.

But this was a whole different ball game. That's why she'd agreed to bring him before the firing squad. She'd told Mac that the past was the past. It was time to start putting her money where her mouth was and see how he fit into her life this time around.

Otherwise, it was just paying lip service to her agreement that he could have a role in Lucy's life. *This* was Lucy's life. These were her relatives too.

The problem was that she couldn't force them to accept Mac. She was having a hard enough time figuring out which end was up herself, let alone asking someone else to do so, someone who hadn't seen the way Mac watched Lucy sometimes when he didn't know Hannah was paying attention.

The man had changed. There were no two ways about it. Sometimes she thought he even looked different, but people did age in unexpected ways. She didn't look the same as she had in her early twenties either. It was time to see what the present looked like without the burden of the past.

"I appreciate everyone's concern," Hannah began but was interrupted by the sound of voices as her brothers escorted Mac inside.

He was still in one piece, thankfully. And he hadn't hightailed it away from Owl Creek after the interrogation. Everyone got points for both.

"He can stay," Chase said gruffly and ruffled the hair on Hannah's head like she was the same age as Lucy.

She ducked away from him with a tiny smile of thanks that she only meant for him to see. Because he was still her big brother at the end of the day, and whatever the Colton boys had orchestrated to ensure Mac didn't leave a gaping hole in her heart, she appreciated.

"He's solid this time," Wade murmured to her as he passed through to the kitchen, clearly looking for Harlow.

Fletcher bumped her arm and gave her a quick nod. Just once, and no accompanying verbal approval, but the nonverbal one was reflected in his gaze.

Hannah swallowed the lump in her throat. Everything got

a lot more real in an instant. If Mac had passed whatever test her brothers had put him through, that meant she hadn't made a bad call this time. That they saw what she'd seen—a man who was sincere about his second chance.

What did that mean? For her? For Lucy?

Mac moved into the circle to stand by her side, quiet, but definitely sending her family a message that he intended to be present this time. He'd had no clue what he was walking into here—honestly, she hadn't realized it would be a series of tests either—but he'd passed with flying colors.

So far. He still had to get through her sisters and Jenny.

"Hello, again," Mac said to her mother. "You must be Hannah's mom. I apologize if we've met before. I don't re-member. But I wanted to thank you for having me in your home, despite what must be serious reservations on your part. I want you to know I'm not going to disappoint your daughter or your granddaughter this time."

Jenny nodded, her assessing gaze roving over Mac as she processed what he'd said to her. "See that you don't, and you'll always be welcome here."

And that was that. The welcoming committee broke up into smaller pieces as Hannah introduced him to the rest of her family, including the tiny addition named Sawyer, the most popular guest at the party by far. Finally, everyone's focus snapped away from Mac and back to various party tasks. He'd been accepted, pending future bad behavior.

Hannah let out the breath she didn't know she'd been holding. Mac immediately turned to her, his hand grazing her arm.

"You okay?" he murmured.

"I should be asking you that question." She stared at him, drinking in this man who had willingly faced down a wall of Coltons to gain access to the inner sanctum, then managed to disarm her mother with one impassioned speech. "What did you say to my brothers?"

"The truth. That I may not remember Lucy, but the moment I knew she existed, pieces of me physically shifted places to make room for her and now she's there permanently."

Hannah's heart did a slow swan dive as she internalized the way he'd simplified something so vast and far-reaching. "That's how I felt when I first found out I was pregnant. I'd always hoped we'd share that feeling."

"Now we do," he told her, his gaze warming as they stood there in a bubble where only the two of them existed. One that he'd created by focusing on her so intently that she felt like the only other person in the room. The world.

Oh, goodness. She put a hand to her flaming cheek. What was she doing here? Falling into a fantasy where she and Mac were in sync, partners in parenting. Perhaps even more than just parents.

It was dangerous ground. A place that she hadn't foreseen she'd find herself solely by bringing him to her mother's house for a low-key get-together.

Nerves clamped down on her lungs, turning her breath shaky. How did she navigate the rest of this day?

Mac didn't seem to have the same confusion. He smiled and took her hand, which did absolutely nothing to calm her nerves. The opposite. Her heart rate shot into the stratosphere.

Mac even *felt* different. She'd never have said they had *sparks*. But the fireworks going off along her skin said otherwise. Of course she'd been in love with Before Owen. Probably. Sometimes she wondered if it had been more like an infatuation.

Because she'd never felt like this when he'd touched her before.

Was this part of starting over? Learning about each other, but as the people they were now, not who they had been? What else would be different?

The blush that heated her cheeks this time didn't escape his notice. "What are you thinking about?"

Nope. Not going there. "How I have no idea what I'm doing right now."

"You're at a party," he reminded her gently. "You're the one who said it. We're supposed to be having fun."

"I may have forgotten how."

"Step one. Hold on to me and I'll be right here, reminding you that everyone here cares about you. Forget whatever is waiting for us outside these walls and enjoy yourself for now."

Shockingly, that seemed to do the trick. She got hold of herself and straightened her spine. She was Hannah Colton. She could handle whatever this was. "We're just going to call you the Hannah Whisperer from now on, okay?"

His smile ratcheted up the heat, dangerously so. Making her think about things she shouldn't be thinking about.

Oh no. *Nonononono*. That was not happening, not now, maybe not ever, not that easily, not without a lot of groveling on his part. Tossing her head, she smiled back with a lot of teeth.

He'd have to earn it this time around. And she would not be so easily swayed by his looks and his money. That's how she'd use her head, not her heart.

Okay. The drama was over for today. She could relax, have fun with her family now that it seemed they were going to accept Mac at face value, and see how things went. Simple.

There was a knock at the door, and everyone turned simultaneously, glancing at each other while doing their own mental head counts. Had Sloane decided to join them after all? Judging by the look on Chase's face, he wasn't expecting her.

"You all going to just stand there or answer the door?" Jenny dried her hands off on a towel and tromped toward the foyer. "Never mind, I'll get it."

When Jenny opened the door, a petite brown-haired woman stood there, her face a mask of nerves and trepidation as if she hadn't quite figured out whether she was going to be eaten alive by the owner of the house right there on the porch or invited inside so the crime could happen behind closed doors.

"Sarah," Jenny said warmly. "You came."

Sarah.

Hannah shared a long look with Ruby and Frannie. Their mother had invited their half sister to come to the house where Jenny had lived with Sarah's father?

The party's drama quotient had just escalated a billion notches.

Chapter Fourteen

Some family get-together. Archer wasn't sure who Sarah was, but her arrival seemed to have put a pin in the forehead of every one of Hannah's siblings. None of them was moving, talking, breathing. It was almost as if they'd been frozen in place by nothing more than the presence of this diminutive woman.

Obviously there was a story here.

Instinctively, he slipped a hand around Hannah's waist and pulled her closer, wincing as he stretched the area of his torso where he'd cracked a rib. She didn't protest and in fact, seemed to curl into his side, as if seeking protection. Something hot and bright bloomed in his chest as his instincts bellowed to take care of whatever was bothering her.

"Are you okay?" he murmured. "I take it whoever Sarah is, she was an unexpected addition to the guest list."

"You could say. Sarah is my half sister," she explained, a tiny sentence with about a half ton of explosives lining the underside. "Remember I mentioned it? My father had an affair with her mother. Who is also my aunt."

Archer whistled one long low note as he called up all the details Hannah had spilled at the hospital. "My short-term memory doesn't seem to be a problem. So that's her?"

"Yeah. My mother's own sister. I mean, it's not Sarah's

fault. But she is a big neon flashing reminder of what a dirtbag my father was. It's a little surprising my mother would be fine with having her around. And vice versa. Sarah's mother is not the person highest on our list of favorite people right now."

Filing all of this away alongside everything else he'd learned about Hannah's family, he hung back to watch whatever was about to unfold. The Ever After Church had sucked in Sarah's mother, no doubt, and there was a possibility that Sarah had likewise become a member. If so, it was a fortuitous bit of timing that he'd managed to score an invite to the same party with the woman.

Willis had turned up enough about the church to put Archer on higher alert than he'd like to be at a party. But he'd already been subjected to a lovely chat with the male half of the Colton clan and then been sized up and spit out by Hannah's mother. He'd been warned, in no uncertain terms, that screwing over Lucy or Hannah again would result in some very unpleasant consequences.

Yeah. He got it. Owen wouldn't have cared, but he did.

That was the irony. Archer would never have stacked up those dominoes in the first place. If he'd been the one to meet Hannah all those years ago, he'd be five, six years into his relationship with her, and her family would welcome him with open arms.

He'd be lucky to escape with his skin intact once they learned the truth.

Sure, he hoped he could keep being Lucy's father, but he was savvy enough to know that he wasn't the one who got to make that decision, regardless of his intentions.

No time to wallow in self-pity. Archer swallowed his angst over things he couldn't change and people he'd never have a chance to know at a deeper level, pasting a smile on his face as Hannah bit her lip.

"That's some messed-up history," he muttered, turning his head so his comment didn't drift toward the newcomer. "But Sarah must be seeking her own answers, or she wouldn't be here. Introduce me. She might need someone on her side who isn't a blood relation."

Hannah squeezed her eyes shut and when she opened them, the emotion he saw there nearly knocked his knees out from under him.

"Thank you for that," she whispered. "You can't begin to know what that means to me. She's my sister. But not, if you know what I mean. I want to love her, but it's...well, it's a mess."

Oh, he knew exactly what she meant. It was like wanting to resurrect your twin so you could murder him all over again. A love-hate relationship that could never be reconciled now. The best Archer could do was learn how to do some serious posthumous forgiveness and move on. Live his life and swallow the regret. Fix the mess. Be present for this woman and her daughter since Owen couldn't. Baby steps.

Hannah grasped his hand, a sweet, unexpected move that filled him to the brim with what he could only call joy. Then they were on the move, headed toward Sarah. The first of her siblings to step forward—he was proud of Hannah for taking the lead.

And not a little exhilarated to be at least partially responsible for the genuine smile on her lips as she greeted her sister.

Sarah, for her part, seemed at least open to Hannah's brief hug. She had Hannah's eyes, he noted, the same as Lucy's. They must have all three inherited that lily pad green from Hannah's father. It was a tenuous link that he hoped Hannah would take positively, as opposed to a reminder that her father had shared his genetic heritage in a selfish and hurtful way.

"I'm Mac," he said as Hannah turned to him, and left it at that since he had no idea how to qualify his presence here. Was he Lucy's father? Hannah's ex-husband? Hannah's current rehabilitation project? Something more?

Boy, he'd love to know what that might be.

Sarah met his gaze with a touch of warmth and shook his outstretched hand. "Nice to meet you."

"Likewise."

He sensed Hannah's siblings breaking free of their stupor behind him and took advantage of the opportunity to get a bit of his own agenda into the mix before they remembered their manners. "I'm the outsider here. If you need a friendly face, come find me later."

Sarah's smile had a hint of Hannah in it too. "I appreciate the offer. Please take it in the spirit that it's intended if I say I hope I won't need to."

"I do," he assured her. Having been on the receiving end of the welcoming committee already, he hoped for a good reception for her as well.

His brief bonding time with the daughter of the woman rumored to be Markus Acker's girlfriend ended abruptly as Hannah's sisters, Ruby and Frannie, muscled their way in to say hi to Sarah.

The party jumped into full swing then as the Colton boys fired up the grill outside on the deck. Archer found himself hustled out with them, holding a plate of hot dogs. Wade shoved a beer into his other hand, which he sipped slowly enough that he couldn't even taste it, but he'd never been a big drinker. Plus, he needed his wits about him.

Sarah, he noted, had gravitated to the area below the deck where Lucy was playing with Harlow and an enormous husky—Betty Jane, Harlow had called her. The main source of Lucy's dog wishes. She was a beautiful creature, clearly well trained not to knock over his daughter, which he appreciated.

Er, Owen's daughter. Sure, he had to be completely error-free at referring to her as his daughter out loud, but there was no reason to be thinking of her as *his* in his own head. Well, none other than the fact that he hadn't been overstating what he'd told all of Lucy's uncles. Lucy was wedged inside him so tightly that he couldn't imagine ever yanking her free. Or wanting to.

His brother had been a piece of work all right.

Archer managed to do the impossible and relax as he and Hannah sat on the deck and ate hot dogs with her family. It was an idyllic setting, one he'd have never pictured himself enjoying. And not just the view out over the lake, which was spectacular, but the company too. Hannah. Her siblings. Even her mother had a quick smile and kind eyes that she spread around to everyone in attendance, Sarah and Mac included, neither of whom would be welcome at many other matriarchs' homes.

It spoke to the kind of people Hannah came from. He could not fathom why Owen would ever have been interested in someone like this strong, capable woman by his side. She wasn't at all his type. Which got Archer's senses humming. He was a huge fan of the Occam's razor brand of investigative analysis—ten times out of ten, the simplest explanation was the right one.

In this case, that meant she must be involved in Owen's scams. Somehow. He just couldn't figure out the link.

After the mountain of hot dogs had dwindled, Betty Jane gladly wolfed down the last as a treat from Wade when he thought no one was watching. Archer wasn't the only one with his eyes on the dog, though. Lucy's face had rarely turned from the husky, and he recalled his throwaway statement to her from earlier that she could have a dog at his house in Las Vegas.

That had been a mistake to offer, clearly. How would that even work? Once Hannah found out he wasn't Owen, the odds of her agreeing to let him play the adoring uncle would be zero. And if she really was involved in Owen's illegal activities, he might be arresting her and taking her away from Lucy entirely. No one would let the little girl within five hundred miles of him then.

It put a bitter taste in the back of his throat. Sometimes doing the right thing sucked.

Sarah had been equally quiet during the Colton clan's raucous conversation. No doubt she still felt a little uncertain about her place in the family, which he totally understood. Neither was it a surprise when she asked Wade if she could walk Betty Jane down by the water. It wouldn't surprise him if she'd deliberately looked for a way to separate herself for a regroup session.

But shockingly, after Wade agreed, Sarah turned to Hannah and asked if Lucy could walk with her. There was no way Hannah would have been able to resist the "Please, please, please" from her daughter in a sweet, wheedling tone, and the beseeching puppy-dog eyes put the icing on the cake.

Hannah laughed and told them to go on ahead, but the glimpse of how hard it was to parent a cute little girl gave Archer hives. How did Lucy not get away with literally everything when she knew exactly how to pour on the charm? It was eye-opening and would likely get worse the older she got. She was half Owen's daughter, after all.

Wade watched Sarah double loop the leash around her wrist and take Lucy by the other hand, then pick her way down to the water. To say his sharp gaze rivaled a hawk's wouldn't be an understatement, and only having one good eye didn't seem to be a detriment.

"I'm keeping them in sight too," Archer murmured to Wade, though it was fifty-fifty on whether Hannah's brother would welcome the extra vigilance.

Wade didn't shift his glance even an iota. "I would expect no less from Lucy's father."

For some reason, the sentiment settled heavily in his heart. Owen would have taken it as criticism or worse, Wade trying to tell him what to do. Archer saw it as the double-edged sword it was meant as—a condemnation of the past and a pat on the back for the present.

And maybe a third edge. He wasn't actually Lucy's father. Continuing to pretend he was wouldn't end well.

He should tell Hannah the truth. It was as simple as that. The longer he kept this secret, the worse things between them were going to be. Tonight. He should tell her as soon as they left the party. Swear her to secrecy. Trust that she wasn't involved with Big Mike and continue with his investigation, except Hannah wouldn't be in the dark.

When Jenny picked up some plates and headed for the kitchen, Kiki and Harlow followed her, leaving Hannah's siblings and Ruby's husband Sebastian sitting on the deck. Just as Archer wondered if he should volunteer for dish duty, Chase cleared his throat.

"Now's a good time to have a very quick emergency family meeting," Hannah's oldest brother said, which had the effect of silencing every conversation in an instant.

"You should stay," Hannah said as she pulled her chair in closer to Archer's, settling his internal debate about whether they expected him to excuse himself.

Chase's gaze roved over his, assessing, but he didn't contradict his sister. "You should all know that we don't think Dad's death was due to natural causes."

Obviously, this was no ordinary family meeting. Or was this how they all went?

Hannah gasped, clutching Archer's hand automatically. He squeezed back in support, though it didn't seem she even realized she'd done it. That seemed to answer his question— no, they didn't generally drop such bombs when Jenny disappeared into the kitchen.

"What are you talking about?" she demanded. "You think someone killed him?"

"Not someone. Jessie," Wade confirmed grimly. "She had a lot to gain from it."

Fletcher, who was on the job with the Owl Creek PD, nodded, which lent the most credence to the statement in Archer's book. If the lawman thought it too, it was likely the truth. But Jessie was Sarah's mother, which meant she'd killed the man who had fathered her children. It was a bold claim.

And Archer hadn't put enough pieces together yet to understand why the Coltons had chosen to include him in this announcement. Earlier, he'd heard Chase talking about his real estate business, which seemed to be quite far-flung and lucrative. Every bit of this got the motor in his brain whirring.

"You're serious," Hannah said, her gaze flitting back and forth between her brothers as she absorbed what they were telling her. "But the coroner ruled his death as a stroke. You can't force someone to have a stroke. Can you?"

Her brothers exchanged glances, but it was Fletcher who spoke. "There are ways you can introduce certain factors that could cause a stroke, yes. Emotional upset for one. Stress. Asking someone to lift something heavy."

There were more sinister ways as well. Archer kept his mouth shut though, as it would be highly suspect for Owen to know a blessed thing about ways a person could induce a stroke in someone.

"We're not a hundred percent sure Jessie acted alone,"

Chase said, his expression grim as he warmed to the subject. "Or even orchestrated it. Markus Acker could just have likely done the deed with Jessie helping him. He had more to gain than she did if she'd managed to get the will changed."

"But she didn't," Hannah supplied, which was information Archer didn't have. "And we don't know for sure that she would have given Acker any of Dad's money if she'd gotten control of it."

"Yeah, we do," Wade countered. "She's already given him all her own money, and we suspect that she's coerced the members of the church to cough up a lot of cash. The woman is bad news, despite being family."

Archer's senses moved from tingling to full-on lightning strikes. Any time a lot of money was at stake, all bets were off. If Hannah's brothers thought their father had been murdered, odds were high they'd found at least a shred of truth buried in the middle of what most folks would call coincidence.

There were no coincidences. Not in a police investigation, not in life. Not ever. Especially not when he was already on the trail of a lot of money. The odds of there being two different sets of "a lot of money" was 12 percent. Give or take a half percent because he was doing the math in his head.

In other words, the odds were low. There was a link between the Ever After Church, Hannah's father's death, Sarah's mother and Owen Mackenzie. Archer would stake his life on it.

Though he had a pretty good feeling he already *had* staked his life on it.

And he had Owen to thank for putting Hannah and Lucy in the middle of it.

Chapter Fifteen

Mac had asked if he could help put Lucy to bed and Hannah couldn't see any reason not to let him read a story or two. It was a legit request and Lucy ate up her father's voices, which Hannah had no idea her ex-husband could even do.

But he proved to be a master at changing his timbre for each character in Lucy's current favorite book about narwhals. Plus, he didn't try to skip any of the pages, even though the story had a lot of tiny text and kind of dragged in the middle.

Rushing ahead was a trap. Lucy had the book memorized and she'd call you out if you so much as accidentally on purpose acted like two pages had stuck together.

Hannah hung out by the door, at loose ends since she hadn't had a second free for five years at bedtime. What would she even do with herself if she didn't spend all her time filling the gap that Mac—the Owen version of himself—had left? Playing the part of both parents had been so much a part of her life that she didn't even think about it most days.

Except for a day like this one. Mac had not only picked up his own slack, he'd rendered her redundant in the equation. Lucy hadn't glanced in her mother's direction one time thus far. And why would she? She had her father's undivided attention, and he'd probably honor each and every request for "read it again" or "one more story" or "tell me one you made up."

Honestly, Hannah's attention kept drifting to Mac. This was an unprecedented chance to study him without his knowledge. He made such a dear picture sitting on the edge of Lucy's big-girl bed holding the narwhal book in his gentle hands.

She'd always loved his hands. Some women might like a man's hands to be rough, and sure, that was fine for a romance novel where the heroine fell for a bad boy, but this was real life. She'd never wanted anything more than a man who treated her well.

Yeah, that had worked out.

Except she'd promised to put that behind them, and she really was trying to see Mac in a new light. In fact, the more she studied him, the more differences she could pick out. Maybe it was the car crash or the distance of time, but his face seemed slightly less refined. Before Owen had polish. A layer of shine that she'd swooned over.

Now she knew better than to fall for a pretty face, which was why she might be slightly fixated on the fact that Mac's appearance didn't have the polish it once had. Probably it was the scraggly beard that he'd been growing since the crash. She didn't want to bring it up since the bandage he still wore over his stitches might make it awkward to shave.

Before Owen wouldn't have left the bathroom without ensuring he'd done everything in his power to look his best. Mac had let his hair grow out. It practically brushed his shoulders and framed his face in a way that she had to admit gave him a bit of a dangerous edge that she didn't hate.

Maybe there was more to the bad boy fantasy than she'd given credence.

And man, when had it gotten so hot in here?

Hannah fanned her face and ducked out to wait in the living room before Mac saw her acting so weird over him. It was *Owen*. She'd been in love with him, sure, but he'd never…revved her engine like some of her friends talked about.

Since she had nothing but time, Hannah's brain got busy coming up with its own entertainment. Not Mac-related! Her inner vixen seemed determined to push the envelope though, so she focused on the revelations her brothers had dropped at the party.

Her father's death might not have been due to natural causes.

Hannah could not get over the strange turn of events that had embroiled the entire Colton family since one of the members of the Ever After Church had tried to run Sebastian Cross off his property. Ruby had been right there in the middle of it and almost killed by a crazed Markus Acker disciple. The couple had managed to escape with their lives and fallen in love in the process, then immediately started their own family with the birth of sweet Sawyer.

So it hadn't been all bad news.

Just not nearly enough good news.

She still wasn't quite sure where Nate and Sarah fell on the spectrum. It wasn't every day that you learned about half siblings you hadn't known existed. If Aunt Jessie had been responsible for Hannah's father's death, it certainly wasn't the first decision she'd made that had sent shock waves through the very foundation of the Coltons.

The next time Hannah looked up, Mac stood in the doorway of the living room, his gaze resting on her. The expression on his face raised goose bumps on her skin as if he'd actually touched her, when in fact, he hadn't moved from his casual lean against the doorframe.

"Lucy's asleep," he murmured softly.

Because that's how you spoke in a house with a sleeping five-year-old. There was no call to be imagining that he'd adopted that low, silky tone in deference to the atmosphere, maybe to deliberately heighten the underlying sense of anticipation.

That happened anyway, whether he'd meant to lace the space between them with tightly wound tension or not.

"Thank you for reading to her," Hannah responded, her own tone matching his out of habit. No one wanted a cranky five-year-old out of bed after a long day at Grandma Jenny's.

Mac rambled across the room to where she was sitting on the couch, and she thought of a lot of other reasons it would be highly beneficial for Lucy to pick tonight to sleep like the dead.

He perched on the couch next to her, his frame slightly taut as if he hadn't quite figured out if she welcomed his presence in her space.

She'd have told him if she'd rather have been left alone. Or she could have retreated to her bedroom, effectively cutting off the rapport that had grown between them almost overnight. Co-parenting, even for such a short period of time, had proven to be a much greater bonding experience than she'd have guessed.

But no mother on the planet could remain unaffected by the sight of a man reading to the child they'd created together. Not to mention the dozens of other scenes she had in her head of the two of them together. Lucy had zero reservations about her father—she had just thrown open the walls of her heart and sucked Mac in.

Hannah didn't have the same luxury. She had to think with her head.

"Are you doing okay?" he asked, his gaze gently probing hers as if he truly cared.

The fact that he'd even thought to ask spun her a bit. "I've been better."

Honesty. She hadn't seen that coming either. Normally she put on her big-girl panties and showed the world that it couldn't break Hannah Colton. But this was the other part of being a single mom that she'd missed. The personal support of her, as a woman. As a partner. Having someone to   .
unwind with at the end of the day who cared.

Mac cared. It was there in the lines of his expression and the way he'd turned his whole body toward her as if there was nothing else in the room he'd choose to focus on but her. It was going to her head.

"You've had a bit of a shock, I would imagine," he murmured and reached out to finger a stray lock of hair away from her cheek in a move that somehow weakened her knees even though she was sitting down.

Before Owen had never done anything like that. If she was being candid, he usually had been too concerned with his own appearance to even notice if she had hair in her face or behind one ear or on the floor because she'd cut it off.

Mac's attention was doing something to her lungs because she couldn't catch her breath.

"Apparently the shocking events are still on the agenda for the evening," she muttered, cursing herself when he dropped his hand.

It was for the best.

"Sorry. I sometimes forget that we're not still together," he said and then shook his head before she could form the question he'd likely guessed she would ask. "Not that I'm saying I remember before. It's just that I feel so comfortable with you. It's like I already know how to be with you deep down in my soul. If that makes any sense."

Oh yeah, she got it all right. It was the same for her, despite not having that frame of reference from the first time either. Sure, she *should*, but it was so not the same. There was a whole other vibe going on this time, as if they'd slid into a space where they made sense together instantly, clicking like a key in a lock.

"It's okay," she told him. "If I didn't want to be here, I wouldn't be."

"Talk to me about what your brothers said," he prompted, instead of launching into a practiced seduction routine. "About your dad. If you want to. I can tell it's bothering you."

It set her back for a moment, even as she appreciated his segue. She didn't know if she was ready for something to happen between them, not so soon. But he seemed totally in tune with that, expertly transitioning back to his original query. He really did want to know how she was and not so he could get her clothes off.

"You really have changed," she said flatly as she stared at him. "You're definitely not the same man anymore."

Mac shifted uncomfortably and she felt bad for saying such an insensitive thing when he didn't remember anything about his life, let alone who *he* was.

"It's a good thing," she murmured, thinking how great it would be if *she* had amnesia and couldn't remember Before Owen either. It would be so much easier to let herself indulge in the quiet, intimate atmosphere that had sprung up around them.

"I'm trying to change the subject and you're not letting me," he said with a wry smile. "So I'll blurt it out. Do you think Jessie killed your father?"

"I don't know. I mean, I knew her a little when I was growing up, but she left my uncle Buck and their children a long time ago." Hannah dug a little deeper into the couch in search of a more comfortable spot, turning in toward the middle to face Mac. "She got sucked into this church business and showed up ranting and raving about the will out of nowhere. The weird part is that the will was already being split seven ways. Why kill my dad over it? Nate and Sarah's part wouldn't have been *that* much money."

"Some people kill other people over a pair of hundred-dollar basketball shoes with the right logo on them," Mac countered grimly. "Have you ever heard that alcohol amplifies someone's personality? Money does too. The amount rarely matters. If you don't value human life in the first place, the line you won't cross gets further and further away. But that doesn't mean your aunt is guilty. Only the court can decide that."

While the sentiment didn't give her any warm fuzzy feelings about her aunt, she did appreciate Mac acting as a sounding board. Talking to her brothers would only get her riled up since they were already set in their minds that Jessie had been involved.

To what end? They didn't have any evidence that she knew about.

But they might if she could get a toe in the door with Sarah. Her investigation had fizzled, that was for sure. If by fizzled, she meant never started in the first place. The party would have been the perfect place to cement a new friendship with Sarah and instead, she'd stuck close to Mac's side in case her brothers had decided to pull any shenanigans.

That didn't mean she couldn't use the party as an excuse to talk to Sarah. And only the guilt she felt at not having come up with anything useful thus far could tear her away from Mac.

"I think I'm going to turn in," she told him. The less he knew about her plan to befriend Sarah in order to pump her for information, the better.

Mac looked pretty disappointed when she stood up, but he didn't say anything other than good-night, allowing her to escape with all of her faculties intact.

When she got to her room, she called up Sarah's name in her contacts. It still startled her a bit to see two new names under the *C*'s. Colton, Nate, and Colton, Sarah, interspersed between Max and Ruby, who would always be Colton Cross in Hannah's phone, whether her sister went by that name or not.

Hannah hit Call before she could change her mind, fully expecting Sarah to send the call to voicemail. But she answered on the first ring. Surprised, Hannah gaped for a second and then repeated her half sister's hello.

"I just wanted to say thank you for playing with Lucy today," Hannah finally blurted out. "At Mom's house. I mean Jenny's house. I know she's not your mom."

Smooth. Hannah rolled her eyes at herself.

"You have a great daughter," Sarah murmured, obviously in a forgiving mood. "You've done a fantastic job teaching her manners."

"Oh, well." Flustered, Hannah waved that off, but couldn't avoid being thrilled that someone had complimented her little girl. Who was brilliant and amazing, of course. "Thank you for saying that. She can be a handful, so it's nice to know she remembered to act civilized in polite company."

Sarah laughed graciously and for some reason, that hit Hannah wrong. Sisters shouldn't laugh graciously at each other's jokes.

"I'm really calling because I think it would be nice to get to know you," Hannah announced, as if Sarah had won a prize in a sweepstakes.

But Sarah didn't seem to notice Hannah's weird tone. "I'd like that. I've never had sisters before. I have this pie in the sky idea that they're meant to be like best friends who are also blood relations, so it's extraspecial. And now I can hear you backing slowly away—"

"No," Hannah cut in, thinking it was fate that they were

both kind of awkward. "That's exactly what it's like. I've had it my whole life with Ruby and Frannie, and I'm sorry you haven't. I can fix that for the future though, and I'd like to."

"That would be nice," Sarah said a touch wistfully. "It's a little difficult right now since I live in Boise, but maybe we can connect by phone occasionally?"

Disappointed that she'd forgotten that important factor, Hannah nodded. "You bet. But I insist that you come visit me some time."

Maybe after Mac left. Hannah's heart twinged at the thought, but he couldn't stay here forever. There was no scenario where he'd still be in the guest room in a few weeks. Sarah could come then.

Of course, the investigation couldn't wait. They needed answers about what Jessie had been getting up to with the church, and even more so, what Sarah knew about Markus Acker. He was the linchpin in all of this, she just knew it.

Jessie couldn't necessarily have been called a good mother before she'd joined the church, but Acker had corrupted her, no doubt. He needed to be stopped. Maybe if he was out of the picture, Jessie would realize the error of her ways and return to her family. Families? Goodness, what did that matter if she really had helped murder Hannah's father? How terrible all of this must be for Sarah and Nate.

"I'd like to see your home," Sarah said a touch more enthusiastically, having now come a little further out of her shell over the course of the call. "Thank you for reaching out. It means a lot to me."

Hannah swallowed against another way of guilt, this time because she'd basically struck up a friendship under false pretenses. But not really! She did want to get to know Sarah. This was multitasking. Using her head instead of her heart, which never worked out.

And who knew? Maybe she really would get a new sister out of the deal, one who wouldn't give her grief about Mac and would be nothing but supportive when—if—she decided to see what Mac and Late Twenties Hannah looked like together.

But first, she had to figure out what she was waiting for.

Chapter Sixteen

Archer's ribs hurt. It wasn't the bed's fault, but he didn't have a handy scapegoat otherwise, so he whacked the mattress a time or two to unleash a bit of his frustration that it was 4:00 a.m. and he couldn't sleep.

Okay, some of that had to do with Hannah and his inability to stop making excuses to get closer to her. Mentally and physically. His crush on his brother's ex-wife had blossomed into a full-bore attraction that he couldn't shake.

Yet despite having met the Coltons a few days ago, he still didn't know if Hannah—and possibly her family—had some connection with Big Mike and/or his missing money, which were two different factors that he hadn't considered enough. It was one thing to be in cahoots with a known money launderer and another thing entirely to have helped Owen steal and conceal five million dollars from one of the nastiest crime syndicates around.

And he needed to make some headway on whatever link might exist before he fell in any deeper with Hannah.

Despite the hour, he made a call to Willis, who wasn't too pleased to be woken up.

"It's an hour earlier in Vegas," his assistant complained in lieu of a greeting. "This better be good."

Archer didn't bother with hellos either. "What have you found out?"

"Acker has a long history of founding churches that front as scams. Buy-your-way-out-of-hell kind of vibes."

No big surprises there. The real story was how he'd evaded the law thus far. "No history of arrests? None of his previous congregation members has ever turned state's witness?"

"Not that I've turned up. He's slippery. One of the cleanest track records I've seen for a criminal of this caliber. His assets are pretty layered, but it wasn't too difficult to track a few of his accounts offshore. I got a couple of feelers during my searches, so I stopped digging, but simple math would dictate his net worth is somewhere north of fifteen million."

Archer bit back the whistle. That was a lot of bought-and-paid-for redemption. No wonder Willis had hit up against someone else's feelers. "It could be his people monitoring."

"Could be. Could be internal too."

It wasn't a throwaway comment. Archer's blood ran a little cold. But it wasn't out of the realm to be dealing with dirty cops who were working with Acker. "Stop researching. I can pick it up from here."

Willis's eye roll came through the line loud and clear. "Gee, thanks, buddy. You couldn't have told me that at, like ten o'clock?"

Chuckling, Archer ended the call. Well, he was good and awake now. No point in trying to find a comfortable spot on his mattress, so he got up and did a few half-hearted sit-ups that made everything worse, including his mood.

When he picked up his burner phone, he saw that someone had texted him a series of numbers along with the phrase "Whatchu talkin bout?"—Willis's call sign when they were trying to stay on the down-low. In a few minutes, Archer had worked through the cipher, which resulted in another series of numbers. The kind that could have been texted unencrypted.

Willis was such a comedian. Payback for waking him up.

The numbers were coordinates. When Archer punched them in on his offline map, the street view narrowed in on a warehouse here in Owl Creek, which public record cited as being owned by Colton Properties. Chase was the CEO, a fact Archer had learned somewhere along the way.

He frowned at the data. Why would Willis put this in front of him? Not solely to give him grief. They'd been working together long enough that his assistant knew exactly how far to push that envelope and encoding a set of numbers inside another set of numbers was the hard limit.

This meant something. Archer stared at the aerial photo of the warehouse until his eyes watered, examining it from as many angles as the satellite cameras would allow.

And then he realized.

The date of purchase coincided with the date of Owen's death. Given his view on coincidences, this was a bombshell. Surely this didn't mean that someone in the Colton family had been working with Owen and double-crossed him, taking the five million for themselves. Real estate purchases didn't execute that quickly—unless it had been originally orchestrated as a joint purchase put into motion well before someone decided to take Owen out of the picture.

Archer turned this over in his head, letting the camera in his brain do much the same type of examination from every angle as the satellite had done on the warehouse. It was so common to use real estate holdings to launder money that it was almost cliché, which was one of the reasons this information tripped him up.

Big Mike wouldn't have set this up. He was way too savvy to try to push money through a shell company to clean it. Some years ago, Big Mike's syndicate did a lot of fancy revaluations of property around Vegas, then took out loans against the equity, which they paid back with dirty money. Slick work, unless you had someone like Archer on the job who followed every paper trail there was until he put all the pieces together. In a series of mistakes too convenient to be legit, the DA had screwed up the evidence, so there was no conviction, and Big Mike had never tried that particular scam again.

But that didn't mean someone else hadn't thought of it.

More research needed, stat. The fact that Willis hadn't already done it meant something too. This was one of the money trails his assistant would have gladly followed, except someone had noticed him nosing around. It was much safer to pass the baton to Archer, as long as no one realized he wasn't Owen.

The dilemma this created put an itch across the back of his neck. How could he tell Hannah the truth now? There were too many unknowns that needed to become known asap.

He had to talk to Hannah. Feel her out. Without tipping her off.

He waited until dawn and wandered into the kitchen to put on a pot of coffee, which had become his norm over the last few days, a routine that soothed him and hopefully endeared him to Hannah. The warm smile she gave him as she padded into the kitchen in her so-unsexy-it-was-sexy robe said that she did appreciate the coffee. And him.

Man, he needed to tone down his reaction to her. The odds of her appreciating it if he acted on the thoughts running through his head were probably in the negative numbers at this point. Owen had behaved like a class A ass to her, probably for the entire length of their relationship. He didn't blame Hannah one bit for categorizing him firmly in the "ex" category. But the fact that she seemed to so enthusiastically embrace putting him in the "father of her child" category spoke to her character.

And that was as attractive as anything else about her. Which put him back to square one and the cycle continued.

"Morning," she murmured and breathed in the aroma of coffee emanating from the mug she clasped in both hands under her nose. "I could get used to having you around."

"Could you?"

She glanced at him, clearly not expecting him to jump on the offhand comment, but dang—you couldn't throw a starving man a piece of bread while holding the remainder of the loaf in your hand and not expect him to slaver after the rest of it.

"Well, I mean, yeah. Lucy is taking to you like a duck to water. If she didn't want anything to do with you or I had evidence that you were mistreating her in some way, things would change faster than a heartbeat. But it's going pretty well and I'm happy you're finally in her life, despite the circumstances."

He nodded, used to her defaulting to Lucy as the reason he was here in her home. It made sense that she would put Lucy first, and as her temporary/fake stand-in/whatever-his-title-was father, he approved. "I'm happy that you're enabling us to have a relationship. We should probably talk about what that might look like down the road."

Hannah sipped her coffee, her gaze downcast as she contemplated that. "I want to say that's premature, but it's not. I'm letting her build up expectations that will be disappointed if we're not fully clear on how to move forward."

He threw it down. "I'd like her to come for visits in Las Vegas. I have no interest in dragging it through court, and they'd probably deny me any motions for joint custody anyway, so this is all dependent on you and your good graces."

Which would likely change as soon as she found out the

truth, but he wouldn't budge from his stance that Lucy deserved a father. He'd like it if Lucy would think of him as hers, even once Hannah determined it was appropriate to tell her that Archer was really her uncle.

"I'm strongly considering it, Mac. Please know that," she implored him. "But it's a lot to take in, a lot to consider. She's never been on a plane, and I can't take unlimited time away from my catering business to drive her."

"I'd pay for any airfare costs incurred," he interjected, though he realized that wasn't Hannah's objection. In fact, she probably had more money than he did given what he'd discovered during his research of Colton Properties and the cost of housing in Owl Creek, especially on the lake.

She smiled. "I wasn't worried about that part. My catering business does okay. Speaking of which, I still would like to pay you back for the money I used to start it."

"Keep it."

He waved that off. Not only did he not want her money, what little money Owen had legally to his name had already gone through probate and had been distributed evenly between Archer and his mother. He'd make a call to reopen the case as soon as it was physically safe for him to do so, now that a legitimate heir had been located. It was his role as the executor of his brother's estate—a ridiculous word for a few thousand dollars and a handful of furnishings—to ensure that Lucy got everything of Owen's, including any new property that he came across. In short, Hannah would just be paying that money back straight into Lucy's account that, as her mother, she would have conservator control over.

Geez, this was a convoluted mess. One he needed to straighten out, pronto.

"Besides," he continued. "You said I had a lot of money before. I'm sure I still have a lot of money."

Hannah cocked her head. "You don't know?"

"Amnesia. Remember?" He lifted his lips in acknowledgment of the ironic joke.

"Oh, goodness. I never thought of that. You can't access your bank accounts, can you?"

He shook his head, stomach squelching at the outright lie, which he hadn't been forced to do too many times, thankfully. "If you can't remember your PIN or what you set as your security questions, banks aren't overly inclined to take your word for it that you have amnesia and should be given access anyway."

"But you could go to the bank with your driver's license and gain access to your account that way, couldn't you?"

Archer nearly gave it all away by rolling his eyes at himself for falling into that trap. Faking amnesia was harder than they made it look in the movies. "Sure, but it's a regional bank in Las Vegas. I'd have to travel there to do that."

Good. Believable.

In reality, Owen's bank account had been closed and the money distributed to his estate. It had been such a laughable amount that it was a safe bet Owen had money stashed other places, most notably the five million he'd assuredly lifted from Big Mike. That's what Archer needed to be concentrating on, not Hannah's laugh.

"I'll drive you there if you need me too."

"You literally just said you didn't have time to drive to Las Vegas to bring Lucy to see me," he pointed out and shook his head as she scowled. "No, it's fine. I, uh…had some cash in my wallet and I have a credit card that doesn't require a PIN. Plus, I'm keeping a tally of what you've done for me so far. I'm the one who will be paying you back."

Good grief, he sucked at interrogation. So far, he'd failed to mention the warehouse purchase, but somehow elicited an offer from Hannah to repay the money Owen had left her and then dodged an offer for her to drive him to get his own money.

"We can square up later," she said with an enigmatic smile that he shouldn't be interpreting in quite the way that his gut was trying to.

"Speaking of finances," he segued as casually as possible. "Did you end up with a stake in Colton Properties when your father died? There was all that talk about the will, but I didn't quite understand how the estate was divided."

Hannah sipped her coffee, watching him over the brim, her gaze a touch too alert for his liking.

"That's a strange question. Are you really trying to figure out how I get along with my family since you don't remember?"

Suddenly feeling like he'd stepped in quicksand, he shrugged it off. "Maybe. I don't even know if I have a family."

"You certainly never mentioned any relations to me," she offered, which she'd told him before, but it still irked him that Owen had acted like an orphan when he had a really great mom and a brother who'd bailed him out of trouble more than a few times.

"Tell me more about the business I owned," he said instead of going down his original path in the direction of Colton Properties, which probably wouldn't have gotten him very far anyway, even if she'd answered his question.

Owen's investment banking company—in huge air quotes—was a thread he should have pulled on long ago, but he'd gotten distracted by the Colton money floating around.

Hannah slid into a seat at the island breakfast bar, near where Archer was standing, and he liked the intimacy of it, which had been instantaneous from the first day.

"I don't know very much," she said in a tone that told him she felt guilty about it. "You didn't really talk about it much. You didn't have a very high opinion of my ability to understand it, so you gave up after a few times."

"Explain it to me the way you understood it."

Cautiously, she sipped her coffee again, likely as a stall tactic, which told him a lot about how badly Owen had made her feel about her comprehension of his "profession." Jerk.

"Well," she said. "It seemed like you used person A's money to give person B a loan, and then you charged a monthly fee, kind of like interest. I always thought it was strange that you didn't do anything with stocks or capital for investments, but when I asked about it, that's when you got frustrated and told me I didn't get it."

"Seems like you understand it just fine," he said flatly. Definitely a money-laundering operation. It wouldn't shock him to find out that Owen had been working with Big Mike way back then too. "And for the record, fee-based loans are not what typical investment banks do, so your question was legit."

Her gaze shone with the light praise, which hooked him in the gut. Did no one in her life tell her how smart and beautiful and amazing she was on a regular basis? Obviously not if she'd lit up like that over what amounted to a condemnation of Owen more than anything.

"That's the real reason I wanted to pay you back," she admitted. "Because I thought you'd appreciate that I really did get it. It was capital for my business and an investment. You should reap the rewards of that. I've more than quadrupled that money."

"Hannah."

He shook his head and bit back some of the more effusive, flowery phrases that sprang to his lips instantly, things that would accurately describe how blown away he was by her. But this wasn't the time and place to indulge in the fantasy running through his head of finding out what Hannah slept in that required such a heavy robe to conceal.

Instead, he opted to cover her hand with his, marveling at how easily hers was swallowed up. And that's what Owen had done to her, then spit her out. It was miraculous that this woman even chose to speak to him, let alone repaying him a dozen times over with kindness and grace.

She didn't move her hand, simply stared at him from under her lashes, as if she'd grown shy in the last couple of minutes, when he knew for a fact, she was not.

"I'm sorry," he murmured. "It's small and mean to make you feel inferior or unable to understand financial concepts. Especially given how you've created a thriving business. It's impressive. Don't ever let anyone tell you differently. I'm really proud of you."

"I have to confess a dirty secret," she said with a half smile that did things to his insides that might not even be legal in some states.

"Tell me," he urged her, moving in a little closer to where she was perched on a barstool at the kitchen island.

"It's so bad," she teased, her smile growing a tad wicked. "I've dreamed about the day when I could tell you that my business is worth double what you unknowingly invested in it. And then I started doing pretty well and realized I was past that mark. And I started dreaming about telling you I'd tripled it. Today I was able to say I quadrupled that money, and your expression is so much better than in my dreams. I thought I was going to be rubbing it in your face. I never in a million years expected you to tell me you were proud."

That put a catch in his throat that he couldn't swallow. Or speak around.

No, she hadn't come right out and said she wasn't working with Big Mike, though he wouldn't be the slightest bit surprised to learn she could outearn him with a legit business. But he'd stake his life on his assessment that she was clean.

Her character shone through with every word out of her mouth. She was a good mother. She came from a tight-knit family full of law enforcement—not that he automatically trusted cops and veterans, but if there was anything Archer excelled at, it was taking bits and pieces of seemingly random information and forming a whole out of it.

The Coltons were solid people. And there was no way Hannah had any idea that she'd married a two-bit criminal, nor that he'd expanded his illicit career horizons after he'd left her.

And if that was true, odds were high she had no idea where the money was.

Chapter Seventeen

Hannah had to work an event that night, so Archer made a move to leave the kitchen, but she stopped him on his way, inviting him to stay as long as he liked. Since there was no place he'd rather be, he slid onto the same barstool she'd just vacated.

It was still warm.

As Hannah chopped sweet potatoes for what she informed him would eventually become curried sweet potato soup, they talked. And talked. It was as if getting to live out her fantasy of telling Owen that she'd made something out of herself had uncorked her.

He liked the uncensored version of Hannah. A lot. She had a wry sense of humor he appreciated, and she could do her job with her eyes closed, clearly, since she'd scarcely glanced down at the sharp knife in her hand.

She was so different than his brother's usual type that it was baffling what qualities Owen would have ever been attracted to in this woman. Unless…he'd used their marriage as some kind of front for his operation without her knowledge. He made a mental note to do some checking into whether his brother had ever put any assets in Hannah's name. Or even Lucy's. It was an angle he hadn't considered until now, and it bothered him that he'd missed it.

Hannah ducked down to root around in the cabinet built into the island. She stood, hands on her hips, gaze darting around the kitchen as if searching for something. "Drat, I really thought my ceramic soup tureen was in the house. It must be in the shed. I'll be right back."

"Want me to get it?" he offered. "It sounds heavy."

"Nah, thank you." Her smile was the kind of shy one from earlier, which was quickly becoming his favorite. "That's the only exercise I get these days."

"Cold out there," he commented mildly, unsure if this was one of those times she'd prefer chivalry to letting her be an independent woman who didn't need a man to lift a ceramic pot.

"Hence the 'drat' in my statement. Also, you're not supposed to be lifting anything heavy. Sit there and drink your coffee like a good boy."

She pulled on her coat and boots in the mudroom and exited out the back door before he could insist otherwise. Not that he could have done it. She was right about his ribs and carrying a soup tureen a hundred yards back up a hill from the shed by the lake wouldn't be on his doctor-approved list of stuff he was allowed to do.

Still, it didn't sit well with him to leave her to do the heavy lifting. Maybe he could volunteer to clean the house for her as part of his compensation for her kind care and for basically letting him freeload in her home.

When she came back lugging the white ceramic tureen, she was out of breath and he felt like a heel and immediately jumped up to wrestle it from her grasp. "At least let me take it from here."

"Thanks, that hill gets steeper every year, I swear."

"What's wrong?" he demanded as he caught the flicker of something in her expression.

"Nothing. I just thought I locked the shed the last time I used something out of there. It was open."

Carefully, he set the tureen on the clear counter space near the stove and made a show out of arranging the lid so she didn't see the alarm that had likely just climbed all over his face. "Does anyone else use that shed? Like Lucy?"

"No, she's not allowed down by the lake without adult supervision. Wade does sometimes, but that's usually during the summer, when he needs a life vest or something."

"When was the last time you remember going down there?" he asked casually, but Hannah was having none of that.

"You think this is connected to all the other stuff going on around here. The misplaced items."

When he turned, she'd crossed her arms over her coat and leaned back against the island, but he wasn't fooled into thinking it was because she'd relaxed. She was holding herself in.

And he'd done that to her. Scared her.

But maybe it was time that he gave her a few clues about what was really going on around here. He couldn't be with her or Lucy all the time and whoever had fingered her as a person of interest had resorted to breaking into her shed to look for the money. But whether it was because he'd shown up here masquerading as Owen or because Big Mike had figured out the connection between Hannah and the man who had double-crossed him, he couldn't quite say yet.

"I think it would be a good idea to stay vigilant," he said evasively, desperately sorting through the data in his head to see what might be the safest thing to tell her. "It's possible it's just a homeless person looking for a warm place to sleep."

"There are no homeless people in Owl Creek," she countered flatly. "There's an excellent shelter in Conners that takes people in."

Great. Yeah, there was a reason they didn't let him out of the lab very often. "Fine, then I think we should talk about getting Lucy a dog."

"A dog!"

The little voice behind him lifted his heart right out of his chest and he'd just seen Lucy mere hours ago when he'd read her a story before bed.

The voice-owner herself popped around a corner holding Mr. Fluffers, wearing a robe that matched her mother's, which was adorable. He had a sudden urge to buy them a bunch more outfits that would signify them as a set, his part in the deal to shower them with compliments and wear a smug smile because they were his family.

Speaking of fantasies...

"You're getting me a dog?" Lucy repeated, her face glowing with expectation that he'd move a mountain not to erase.

"You bet," he said, letting the smile on his face match the one on the inside. "Seems like you mentioned that you had your eye on one from your aunt Ruby and uncle Sebastian's training place."

"Lu Lu, let's get you some breakfast," Hannah cut in brightly and shot Archer a look from behind Lucy's back as she hustled her daughter to the table, then produced a bowl from a shelf above the countertop. "Cheerios or oatmeal?"

"Cheerios," she announced decisively and fetched a big purple box from the walk-in pantry herself. "Can I name the dog myself? I already decided to call her Misty Princess Pants."

"Brilliant," Archer told her. "I love it."

"Mac," Hannah called through gritted teeth as she plunked a carton of unsweetened almond milk on the table next to Lucy's bowl. "May I have a word with you?"

Brooking no argument, she clamped a hand around his

wrist and hustled him from the room, apparently intending to allow Lucy to finish preparing her own breakfast.

"You can't do that," she whispered heatedly, keeping her voice low since they were just in the hall outside the kitchen, where they could still see Lucy. "Now she'll expect you to follow through."

"I plan to follow through." The fact that she didn't think he would spoke volumes. "I don't know what I have to say or do to get you to understand that I'm in this for the long haul, Hannah."

Or at least as much as this woman would let him keep his vows.

She scrubbed at her forehead as if the subject had given her a raging migraine. "That's not the point I'm trying to make here. This is all new. For both of us. I get it. But this is a classic case of not checking in with her other parent before you offer something that may not be okay with the other parent. Me. I'm the other parent here, and this is my house. I don't have the time or energy to handle a dog."

Archer started to get the feeling he'd screwed up. "I'm sorry, I didn't think about that."

"Why do you think I haven't gotten her one so far? News flash. It's not because I don't want her to have something she's asked for repeatedly with that desperate little girl wheedling that knifes right through me. And then you swoop in with promises to give her everything her heart desires, and I look like the bad guy."

The pain in that statement did its own number on his gut, pairing nicely with the squelchy sinking sensation that he'd blundered far more badly than he'd intended. "Geez, Hannah, I definitely didn't mean to do that. Please back up a second. Let's work through this. Breathe with me here."

He was supposed to be fixing Owen's mistakes, not making a bunch of his own! If she started crying, he'd be done.

But she didn't. Without an ounce of protest, she did exactly as instructed, matching his deep, even inhales and exhales. When the mottled red faded from her cheeks, he risked lifting a hand to one, brushing it gently in a nonverbal apology that definitely didn't fit the crime.

"I'm sorry," he murmured again and dropped his hand since he didn't have permission to touch her like he wanted to. "I should cut to the chase and print that on a T-shirt. This is so far out of my realm of experience that I might as well be on a different planet. Parent World, where the quicksand doesn't just trap you, but everyone else too."

"I know. I get it, I really do." She lifted her lips in a tiny smile. "I'm thrilled that we're having this conversation in the first place. It's been rough being the only one on Parent World who can reach the top shelf."

"We're doing this together now," he informed her, the emotion in his voice roughening it unrecognizably. "You keep telling me when I'm doing it wrong, and I'll fix it. I'll learn. I want to be Lucy's father, and it's worth it to me to get it right."

The more he said it out loud, the more he felt it in his bones. Owen was gone, but he'd never been meant to be Lucy's father in the first place. No coincidences. Archer *wanted* the job. Didn't that count for something? In his mind, it counted for everything.

"Okay." Hannah nodded. "I'm not sure I'm the best teacher, but I'm all you've got."

"It's enough," he murmured. "I like the idea of being partners with you in this."

"I'm glad." She tipped her head toward the kitchen. "Now about the dog. It's one thing to vaguely promise she can get one to keep at your place, but—"

"That's what I'm saying. I want to give her this, Hannah. Let me be the one to teach her to take care of the dog. It's something we can do together. No burden on you. I'll handle all of it. The dog can come home with me, and it'll be something familiar for her in a place you're not. Assuming you're open to visits and we can work that out somehow."

Oddly, his impassioned speech seemed to sway her. She nodded again, her expression softening. "Okay. I like that idea."

"Okay?" Speechless, he stared at her. "Did we just have a mature conversation where we listened to each other and settled a major issue without bloodshed?"

She laughed. "You say that like that doesn't happen very often."

"You were at the same party I attended where your brothers not so subtly helped me to understand all the ways my leg bones would be broken if I so much as breathed on you wrong, were you not?"

Her grin widened at his comical grimace. "Point taken. We'll just make it a thing between us. Clan Mackenzie rules. We'll be mature about everything."

His heart stuttered as he absorbed what she'd just called them. *Clan Mackenzie*. Man, did that do unexpected things to him to be included in something so…intimate. She must have clued in on the gravity of the moment because her smile slipped from her face, and everything got heavy in a heartbeat.

"Sorry, that was little too much," she murmured.

"No." He shook his head, clasping her hand in his in case she had a mind to flee. "It's perfect. I love the thought of being in Clan Mackenzie with you. It's exactly right, exactly how I feel too."

Everything he hadn't known he was looking for.

He couldn't have been more drawn to this woman if they'd both been made of magnets. As if it had become a foregone conclusion, she swayed into his space, her grip on his hand tight, as if she needed to hold on to him before she lost her footing and slipped to the floor. He knew the feeling.

"Mac," she murmured, and it sounded like a plea.

If he didn't kiss her, he feared he'd never be whole again.

"What are you guys talking about?" Lucy popped into the hall, Mr. Fluffers in hand and a curious gaze fastened on the adults.

Archer sprang away from Hannah faster than a teenager caught by his mother in his room. "Nothing."

He'd forgotten Hannah's warning from the other day about total lack of privacy until Lucy went to college. Dang. Parenting was not for the weak.

Hannah was a little quicker on her feet. "We were talking about getting you a dog. Which we decided would be fine."

Lucy's squeal should have busted out all the glass in Hannah's house, but the panes stayed miraculously intact. Not so much his eardrums. "I take it that means you're excited. We can go look tomorrow since you don't have preschool on Tuesdays."

"We can't go today? Aw, man." Lucy pouted, her arms crossed over Mr. Fluffers, who was getting squished into oblivion.

"Sorry, darling, you mom has to work tonight, and school comes first," he told her as he smoothed out her messy hair, which had come loose from her pigtails overnight. When he glanced up, the emotion in Hannah's gaze weakened his knees.

She wasn't giving him back-off vibes. Quite the opposite. Her body language had a whole lot of "we'll pick this up later" in it.

"Thank you," she mouthed, which set off a glow inside him that didn't fade for the rest of the day.

Chapter Eighteen

The catering gig went flawlessly, thanks to Hannah's employees. It certainly wasn't due to her own contributions, which consisted of "gah" and "whu?" when someone asked her a question.

She had too many brain cells with Mac's name carved all over them to concentrate on anything approaching speech, how the soup ladle worked, walking without tripping. Complex stuff like that.

Not for the first time, she appreciated the fact that he'd asked her to call him Mac. It had contributed to the ease with which Clan Mackenzie had rolled off her tongue earlier in the kitchen, sure. But it also separated him in her mind—her ex-husband was Owen.

This new guy in her life was Mac. They had no history. She liked him. He made her feel things she hadn't felt in… well, ever. All of this was new all right, and not just the co-parenting journey they'd agreed to embark on together.

This was *different*. In her head, Mac had an ocean of possibilities wrapped up inside him and she wanted to explore them all.

But first, she needed to get her head out of the clouds and drive home from the party location on the other side of the lake, one of the giant custom-built mansions that seemed to be so prevalent in the resort town of Owl Creek. She'd liked the town a lot better when it had been a quiet place for families, but if it had stayed off the map, she'd have no business. So it was a good thing that people had moved into this area who didn't sneeze at one seventy-five a head.

Could she charge less? Absolutely, and she did if it was a resident who had been around for a while. But everyone else got the Bon Appetit going rate, which was worth it because she delivered excellent food and service.

Most days. Today wasn't a good example of her giving a top-tier performance, but the client had paid the balance in full before she'd cleared the driveway, so she'd call that a win.

She navigated—carefully—through the layer of snow that had fallen while she'd been inside the client's house, trusting her winter tires not to send her straight into a ditch, but that only worked if she didn't drive like a maniac. It took twice as long as it might have at another time of the year, but she didn't mind. Price of doing business.

As she unlocked the front door of her little house by the lake—a stark contrast to the one she'd just left—it occurred to her that this was the first time she'd ever left Lucy with someone other than a family member when she worked a catering gig.

Only Mac was *Lucy's* family. Clan Mackenzie. It was even Lucy's last name.

Neither Lucy nor her father were in the living room, which boded well since it was way past Lucy's bedtime. But surely Mac wasn't still reading to her.

She followed her instincts to Lucy's bedroom. Mac sat on the floor outside her room, hands resting on his drawn-up knees, his head thrown back against the wall. He gave her a sheepish smile when he caught sight of her and held one finger up to his lips like she wasn't fully aware that talking right outside her daughter's bedroom when she was asleep would be a bad idea.

Mac climbed to his feet and led her out into the living room, still wearing a sheepish expression. "I was listening to her breathe."

Oh, man. That hit her right in the heart. "I do that sometimes too."

"I was just thinking about how I'm not going to get to do that when I go back home to Las Vegas."

Even in the low light of the living room, she could see the angst climbing through his expression, feel the inner torment in the set of his shoulders. He didn't want to leave his daughter.

"We can work it out," she murmured, determined to make it true. "Whatever it looks like. She needs her father, Mac. But more to the point, you need to heal. Until your ribs are better and you have more than the memory of a goldfish, you're not going anywhere."

The brief smile he shot her tingled her toes. "I was worried I'd started overstaying my welcome when the dog situation happened."

"No hard feelings on that. I mean it."

And she did. She'd resisted a dog for a variety of reasons, but first and foremost because she'd already dealt with enough loss in her life. What if the dog didn't work out? What if this was another example of Hannah thinking with her heart and not her head, when she could have avoided the fiasco by not giving in to Lucy's heartfelt pleas?

But with Mac here, everything felt different. As if she could handle anything a little bit better, smarter. Even a dog.

"Good night, Hannah."

She laughed at the unexpected end to their conversation. "Is that my cue that you're about to turn into a pumpkin?"

"It's your cue that you might not want to be here with me

in this room while you're laughing, and the lighting is set on romantic." The hoarse thread in his voice definitely didn't make her feel like laughing any longer. "So I'm giving you an out. If you want to stick around, nothing would make me happier, but that choice comes with a warning that I'm having a hard time keeping my hands off you."

So much for being able to handle anything life threw at her.

Especially the way the vibe had gone hot so very fast, as if the heater had blasted the room to ninety degrees instantly.

Her brain turned to mashed peas as they stared at each other, and she tried to sort out whether she wanted to stay or flee. Or rather, which one she wanted more, because both were true simultaneously, and wasn't that the exact issue?

"I think I should go," she murmured, and his expression mirrored the crushing sensation in her chest. "Mostly because I'm not sure and I want to be sure."

He nodded. "That works for me too. I am not a fan of kissing a woman who isn't sure she wants me to be kissing her."

He didn't stop her as she dashed from the room, her face flaming as she contemplated all the ways that scene had made her feel gauche and unsexy. Surely she'd just killed any romantic feelings Mac might have had about her by fleeing from him when the moment had gotten a little too steamy.

But this was a prime example of a time when she needed to use her head. And getting involved with Mac physically wasn't smart. It just might feel really, really good and that might be enough of a reason to do it, as long as she could keep her heart separate. Huge emphasis on *could*.

IN THE MORNING, she stayed in her room instead of joining Mac in the kitchen for coffee like she had the last few mornings. Yes, it was cowardly, but she didn't have her wits about her yet, and she didn't think the lighting in the living room made all that much difference as to whether she might take him up on the offer to let him put his hands on her.

And they had a dog to add to the family today.

When Hannah finally did emerge, Lucy and Mr. Fluffers sat at the table with a half-eaten bowl of cereal in front of them, Mac sitting in the next chair sipping coffee and nodding intently as his daughter told a story at warp speed.

Hannah had to pause for a moment, hand on the doorframe, until her knees stopped feeling like jelly. Lucy was Mac's daughter. Through and through. She had half of his DNA. It was so strange to think like that, to see evidence that he was taking his paternity so seriously, as if he hoped to make up for what he'd missed over the last few years.

She liked unexpectedly stumbling over them together. Much more than she'd have thought. It put dangerous ideas in her head, ideas about ways to resolve the issue of Mac not being able to listen to Lucy breathe in her sleep at some point in the future—and none of them involved him leaving.

Enough daydreaming.

"Good morning," she called brightly. "I see someone is so excited to get her day started that she's eating breakfast without me."

"It's Dog Day," Lucy announced. "Princess Misty is going to love it here."

"It's Princess Misty now?" Hannah asked wryly as she poured some coffee into a travel mug.

She'd texted Ruby yesterday to ensure that Crosswinds still had the dog that Lucy had latched on to a few weeks ago. Sometimes they had dogs slated to undergo therapy training, but they didn't quite have the temperament, so those dogs had to be rehomed. It would have been a bad scene if Princess Misty had already found another home, but that wasn't the case, so full steam ahead.

Whether Hannah was ready to be a Dog Mom or not.

"Misty Princess Pants is a dumb name," Lucy announced as Mac and Hannah glanced at each other.

If someone at Lucy's preschool had said one nasty word to her daughter about her choice of name...

But Lucy breezed past it as if she'd come up with the idea of changing the name, so Hannah didn't press her. They piled into the car and Mac sat in the passenger seat, enduring the chatter from the back seat with no visible grimaces, which won him lots of points.

When they got to Crosswinds, Sebastian personally greeted them at the door and led them to the area in the back where trainers worked with several dogs who seemed to be in varying stages of progress.

Sebastian paused at a row of large kennels and spoke to one of the volunteers. Lucy was about to come out of her skin, bouncing like a pogo stick from foot to foot as the volunteer led a black-and-white Border collie from the depths of the kennels, then held out the leash handle for Lucy to take.

"Look, Mama, Princess Misty is already so good," Lucy announced proudly as the dog sat at her feet, ears perked for the next command.

"She is a good dog," Hannah said with a smile and a nod at Sebastian. "What do we say?"

"Thank you, Uncle Sebastian," Lucy singsonged. "You're my favorite uncle ever in the whole wide world."

Sebastian laughed. "You be sure and tell your uncle Wade that next time you see him. Maybe mention it a couple of times."

Yeah, that would go over well, but Hannah just rolled her eyes since he was kidding. Probably. She pulled out her phone to send Crosswinds the money for the adoption fee, waving off Sebastian when he tried to tell her it was on the house. He did good and valuable work here that she was proud to support financially, especially when he'd already invested money in Princess Misty's care thus far.

That's when she noticed Mac bend down to the dog and pat her gently on the back, murmuring to Lucy. Lucy mimicked his movements, glancing between Mac and the dog, her excitement nearly palpable. Hannah had no doubt he'd already started the dog ownership education process.

But the vibe had a lot of something else in it. A father and daughter bonding. Mac's face bled tenderness and his small smile had a touch of wonder. As if he couldn't believe he got to witness this first meeting of a girl and her dog.

Well, he could join the club. Hannah was getting to watch Mac and Lucy interact with the dog, and it was seriously melting her heart.

How much more of this could she actually take? It was like waiting for the axe to fall when you knew it was up there, suspended. Just waiting on the right sequence of events to drop and sever everything in two.

Except she wasn't so sure that's what was going to happen.

"Hey," Ruby called as she strolled down one of the aisles from the back, where she'd been doing a wellness checkup on a few of the dogs.

Hannah grinned as Ruby joined her in viewing the scene unfolding before them. Her sister's role as a veterinarian had long made Hannah proud and baffled that she came from the same stock as someone who had the chops to get through the rigorous course work required to get a degree of that caliber.

"You sure this is a good idea?" Ruby murmured with a head tilt toward Princess Misty, father and daughter, so it wasn't entirely clear which part she'd questioned.

Hannah chose the less complicated of the two as the subject of her response. "I'm going to do my best to make it work. Lucy would be sorely disappointed if I didn't."

And that's when she realized she hadn't actually picked

one or the other because the sentiment applied to both. Lucy needed Hannah to make things work with Mac, probably even more so than she needed the dog to become a member of their family.

How either of those happened depended on Hannah.

"I know he's her father," Ruby began and held up a hand when Hannah started to protest—likely because they both knew what she was about to say. "Give me a sec to make this point. I don't like the way he treated you when you were married. I don't like how he's treated you since then. You can't erase six years of someone behaving like a complete and utter jackass."

"I'm not trying to erase it," Hannah countered hotly. "I'm trying to forgive and move on. I can't erase my daughter's genetics either. He's a part of her, period, whether he chooses to embrace what that entails or not. Get back to me when Sawyer is five and tell me whether you wouldn't move heaven and earth to ensure that Sebastian is in his life, even if your marriage doesn't work out."

"That's totally different," Ruby scoffed. "Sebastian is noble and good and kind. Plus, he didn't leave me."

"Didn't he?" What was good for the goose was good for the gander. "Seems like I recall a period of time when you were pregnant and alone, Ruby. It wasn't all hearts and flowers for you either, but you gave it a chance and it worked out. Give me that same chance."

The hard cross of Ruby's arms said she had more to say, but she shut her mouth, so Hannah did too, her spine relaxing a touch when Mac caught her gaze and they shared a long look full of emotion. Only some of it had to do with Lucy and her tangible delight with Princess Misty. The rest? Well, she wasn't sure, but she did know that the next time Mac caught her in the kitchen with that heavy intention weighing down the atmosphere, she wouldn't be so quick to leave.

As they bundled Princess Misty into the travel crate Sebastian had loaned them, she had a sudden flash forward of the three of them—make that four—doing things like this all the time. As a family. Clan Mackenzie. Maybe they'd add a few more members to the clan. More dogs. More children.

Her throat went tight and hot as she lived in that moment for a few seconds. It was a dream she never thought she'd let surface. How could she? She'd vowed to sacrifice her own personal life to be Lucy's mom, but deep inside, it was a fear of a repeat broken heart that had kept her away from the dating scene. Since there had been zero immaculate conceptions for over two thousand years, she'd assumed Lucy would be it.

Was this the start of a real second chance with Mac, who had yet to hurt her, yet to abandon her, yet to disprove his claim that he'd changed? There was only one way to find out.

Chapter Nineteen

Archer had never had a dog before. But to be fair, he'd also never had amnesia, a daughter or an ex-wife, so he was pretty much winging everything on a minute-by-minute basis. What was one more thing to add to the pile?

He helped Lucy get Princess Misty—the name that seemed to be sticking—get oriented in Hannah's house. They showed the dog how to politely ask to go outside by bringing the leash to Lucy, which Princess Misty mastered relatively fast, thanks to the training she'd already received at Crosswinds.

That was some high-class operation. The fact that Princess Misty hadn't made the cut felt highly suspect given how the dog never barked, never scratched at anything and seemed to be constantly waiting for the next command. Archer wondered if Lucy's aunt and uncle hadn't finagled their inventory of dogs a bit to create the illusion that this Border collie wasn't slated to become a therapy dog.

If so, he was doubly glad that he'd pushed as hard as he had to get Hannah to accept the idea. She might not have ever made the decision to adopt Princess Misty otherwise, and then Lucy would have missed out on a rite of passage no kid should go without. It was humbling and gratifying to be a part of giving his daughter something that he'd never gotten to experience.

Owen's daughter, rather, but it got harder and harder to qualify that in his own head, let alone in reality.

Lucy was amazing and brilliant and while Owen had a head for finance, his mind didn't work nearly the same way as Archer's did, and he caught glimpses of Lucy's brain making sharp calculations that far eclipsed any logic Owen had ever exhibited.

Was it terrible of him to imagine that she might take after him in some small ways?

The next day, Hannah had a catering job and Lucy had preschool, so Archer took a rare opportunity to do some recon in town at the library, where he used Hannah's account to research the death of her father.

Stroke. Or at least that was how the coroner had ruled it. As Hannah's brothers had mentioned, there were some ways to force someone into a stroke, but it might be really difficult to prove that. Reading through the news articles he could find yielded nothing new or interesting, and it was a gamble to do too much heavy lifting on a public computer with a tie to Hannah's name, so he quit.

Archer wandered around town for a bit, at loose ends. This was the first time since taking the job at the LVMPD that he didn't have access to his lab or his computers. Having to sort through data strictly in his head was causing him a great deal of discomfort, especially considering he still got headaches occasionally from the accident. It might help if he could write some things down, but he didn't want to risk Hannah finding his notes.

Or worse, someone else.

To say the investigation wasn't going well would be an understatement. Thus far, he'd ruled out Hannah's involvement in Owen's dealings, then and now, but he couldn't quite strike the rest of her family from the list. Particularly Chase.

The timing on that warehouse transaction still bothered him, as did the assertion made by her brothers in his presence that their father had been murdered. The situation with Jessie Colton factored in, plus he hadn't begun to make a dent in sorting out the misplaced items at Hannah's house— which surely meant someone had their eye on her and likely him too.

And then there was the fact that he'd made zero headway on the thing he'd come here to investigate. The missing money. Find that, find the trail to Owen's killer.

Something needed to break soon. Especially since he couldn't keep up the amnesia act much longer. In fact, he'd like to come clean with Hannah sooner rather than later, preferably before something irreversible happened, like his will to keep his hands off her shattering into a million pieces.

Archer finally gave up doing anything productive and drove Hannah's car back to her house instead of staying in town for another two hours until it was time to pick up Lucy from preschool. He'd planned to go straight from the library to the preschool near the fire station at the west end of town, then spend some time with Lucy until Hannah's event ended. This was a life he could get used to…except for the lack of purpose and meaningful work to do.

Not for the first time, he tested out in his head what things could look like going forward. How often he could come back to Owl Creek to visit Lucy. And Hannah. He could not deny that mother and daughter had started to feel a bit like a package deal. At least that was how he wanted to see them.

How Hannah felt about that remained to be seen.

Parking the car in the driveway, Archer got out and flipped the key fob ring around his index finger as he strolled toward the house, then froze as he registered the slight crack in the front door. The not-closed front door.

Archer slipped the key fob into his pocket and glanced around for a makeshift weapon of some sort, settling on one of the umbrellas sticking out of a colorful pot to the left of the door. If nothing else, he could stab an intruder with the metal tip, but discretion would definitely be the better part of valor in this situation.

Cautiously, he eased the door open, umbrella raised, which would have been slightly comical in any other situation. It wasn't like he normally carried a gun in the first place; he wasn't that kind of cop. Nor had he expected to run into trouble at Hannah's house, but in retrospect, that had been a rookie mistake. Hadn't he just run through that data point not fifteen minutes ago?

This was his break. The one he'd asked for. Archer was about to catch the intruder in the act. With an umbrella as his only defense against someone who very likely might be carrying.

As silently as possible, he slipped over the threshold and slowly swung the door back to its original cracked position. No point in alerting the intruder that someone else had entered the house. Archer still had the element of surprise on his side.

Nothing out of the ordinary stuck out in the living area, so Archer toed off his sneakers, stowing them behind a chair so he could traverse the hardwood floor in his sock feet. Hannah kept the house on the chilly side so the wood creaked a little as he walked, but blessedly, the heater kicked on and covered the noise.

Experienced at being stealthy he was not.

The kitchen was empty of sketchy intruders. Archer padded to the wing with his bedroom and ducked low to peer inside. Nothing. No one in the bathroom either. He remembered at the last second to check behind the shower curtain, umbrella poised in case the prowlers had watched a bunch of bad slasher movies in preparation for the shakedown of Hannah's house.

Empty. He huffed out a breath of relief.

That left Lucy and Hannah's bedrooms. As he passed back through the kitchen, he swapped the umbrella for one of Hannah's pricey knives, pulling the biggest one from the butcher block and rolling his eyes at himself for not thinking of that earlier.

Not that he thought he'd have a chance against a well-aimed bullet. But someone might think twice about jumping him if he had some hardware that could do a lot more damage than poke an eye out. Plus, he had righteous indignation on his side.

He hefted the knife higher as he headed to Lucy's room. Mr. Breaking and Entering better not have touched a single thing in his daughter's room or everyone would find out exactly how motivated Archer was to defend his own.

The intruder wasn't helping himself to Lucy's stuffed animals, though. That left Hannah's bedroom. The logical place for someone likely employed by Big Mike to spend the most time since she'd been married to the guy who'd stolen his money.

But it was also thankfully devoid of criminals with neck tattoos. Archer lowered the knife and took a moment to let his heart rate return to normal. Had he left the door cracked when he'd left to take Lucy to school and Hannah to her event, then? Could all of this have been a figment of his imagination? Surely not.

Now that the imminent threat had dissipated, Archer combed the house, looking for clues. There. The lamp in the living room sat a quarter of an inch to the right of where it had been this morning. Visually, he could see it was off-center against the lines of the end table. The sofa cushions had been lifted and returned to their former positions. The one on the end stuck up a little higher than the others, though, and it was the one he'd sat on earlier to tie his shoes.

Cataloging what was changed or moved in every room didn't take long. Unlike the first couple of times the house had been searched, this was a pro job, with few mistakes. Nearly undetectable if you didn't know what to look for since a lot of the examined items had been put back exactly as they'd been. You had to have an extreme eye for detail with above-average spatial perception to be this precise.

Someone had called in a higher caliber of talent. Expensive talent. The kind you didn't mind using when the payout promised to more than cover the outlay of cost.

Archer's stomach turned over as he considered the implications. This was no longer a bunch of random criminals doing a rush job to find a double-crosser. What it was, he didn't know.

But the thing at the base of his throat was slick, black fear, no question.

Archer's *family* was being threatened. Hannah and Lucy were in danger. What if they'd been home and the intruder had decided to add a felony or two to his repertoire?

His phone buzzed, shoving the slickness into his mouth. Swallowing, he glanced at the screen. Hannah. Text message. She'd finished her event early and was asking if she could go with him to pick up Lucy.

Yes, yes, she could. She wasn't going *anywhere* without him for the foreseeable future.

Thankfully, they'd elected to enroll Princess Misty with a doggie day care to give her other dogs to play with when no one would be at home. Otherwise, the scene he'd stumbled onto here at the house might have been a much different one.

Which begged the question in his mind—the five-million-dollar question, which he already knew the answer to. How had this professional talent known that no one would be home? Someone was watching them, obviously.

Archer strolled to the car as if nothing had changed. Because the worst thing he could do now would be to tip off his unknown adversary. It might already be too late, but hopefully whoever was watching wouldn't think anything of Archer taking an umbrella into the house. He slid behind the wheel of Hannah's car, adjusting the rearview mirror casually to cover himself as he checked out the woods across from the house for the glint of binoculars.

A flash. Bingo. There was someone in the woods and he'd make an assumption it was the less bone-chilling option—binoculars—and not the scope of a rifle.

He started the car and backed out of the driveway, white-knuckling the steering wheel as he braced for anything. A shot to ring out or a tire to blow.

Nothing happened. He might be letting his imagination run away with him. But he hadn't manufactured the evidence that at least two different individuals had systematically searched Hannah's house. For what? That was the question he *didn't* have the answer to.

What data did someone else have that Archer didn't?

Hannah waited for him outside the library where they'd agreed to meet. She slid into the car, her cheeks rosy from the cold and a smile on her face. "Thanks for picking me up."

"You could have waited inside." *Should* have waited inside, he corrected silently, but he couldn't tell her why it was necessary. "It's cold. I would have texted you when I got here."

"I didn't want to make you sit here and twiddle your thumbs. I wasn't out here that long and besides, I'm from Idaho. We have to build up our fat layer to survive here."

She laughed, and it had the odd effect of making Archer's spine relax. "It gets cold in Las Vegas too at night. Sometimes."

The undertones of the conversation—the reality that they lived in different cities—tugged at his heart again, the way it seemed to constantly do lately. He hated that they weren't having completely different conversations about the future, but he couldn't make one single decision about what would happen once he'd dumped Owen's murderer behind bars. Plus, she deserved to know the truth.

"Hannah—"

She shook her head. "I know what you're going to say. I don't want to worry about what's going to happen when you go back home yet. We'll work it out. Somehow."

"I believe you. But—"

"No buts." She reached over and mushed his mouth together with her thumb and forefinger. "New subject. Ask me how my catering event went."

"How did your event go?" he mouthed against her gloveless fingers, playing along as he reeled in his wholly inappropriate reaction to her touch.

She chattered for a solid three minutes about how well it went and how cheerfully her employees worked together, while he envisioned the words coming out of his mouth. *I have something to tell you. I'm not who you think I am, Hannah.*

Then he thought about how her expression would change. How she'd be upset. Disappointed. Maybe furious. Maybe she'd refuse to let him see Lucy and wasn't that a bucket of cold water? He had zero rights, morally or legally, to pursue a relationship with his niece. No matter how much he thought of her as his daughter already.

It didn't matter. Everyone needed to know the truth. The words burned his tongue, but he couldn't spit them out. Not yet.

This equation didn't have a lot of positive outcomes, not that he could calculate. But he could do the easier math, the story problem that went something like: once Archer tells Hannah the truth about his identity, what are the odds he'd be kicked to the curb, leaving her and Lucy in the house by themselves with nothing other than a Border collie named Princess Misty for protection?

He couldn't tell her anything. She could accidentally—or even on purpose—tip off the wrong people.

Worse, his days of keeping a low profile were over.

The best way to draw out the eyes in the woods—and the employer of that surveillance crew—was to use himself as bait. He had to make some noise. Get some attention on his presence here.

The thought of putting Lucy and Hannah in those cross-hairs squeezed his heart until he feared it might actually burst. But what choice did he have? Magically come up with the missing data he didn't have on why someone had targeted Hannah's house as the most likely place to contain fill-in-the-blank?

He also couldn't leave. It would be far preferable to stick that target on his back and walk out the door. Go back to Vegas and let the goons come after him. But it was a huge assumption that they'd lose interest in Hannah's house when he wasn't even positive they knew who Owen was. Or that whoever was calling the shots wouldn't send a second set of guys after Archer, leaving the first set here.

This was a chess game with far too many moving pieces.

And he'd leave Hannah and Lucy here to fend for themselves over his own dead body.

Chapter Twenty

Mac had been quiet since they'd picked up Lucy from pre-school, but Hannah more than made up for it with her own chatter. Nerves, mostly. Could he tell?

Oh, goodness. She put her cold hands to her flaming cheeks as Mac stowed Princess Misty's travel crate in the hatchback of Hannah's car, praying he hadn't noticed her telltale face.

It wasn't every day that a woman decided it was time to seduce her ex-husband. Okay, that was not exactly what she'd decided. Maybe it was more of a conscious decision to open her heart to letting something happen between them. A full-bore Lady in Red routine wasn't her wheelhouse. Nor did she think that would go over very well.

What did a woman even do if that was her goal? Buy some sexy lingerie and wear a trench coat to dinner?

Yeah. This was helping her cheeks calm down.

Mac drove them home with Lucy twisted backward the whole way as she told Princess Misty all about her day. Which was more than Hannah had gotten. Lucy had barely even said hello before she'd asked if she could take Princess Misty to Wade's house for a visit so she could introduce her new dog to Betty Jane.

Lucy's mile-a-minute conversation with the Border collie covered the fact that Hannah had run out of things to say. More to the point, she was imagining that trench coat and having a serious crisis of confidence about her decision. Maybe she *should* be thinking about ways to move things forward. A signal that she was ready. Not lingerie. But something.

Or maybe she should abandon the whole idea and pretend nothing had changed.

Hannah made dinner in a daze, scarcely recognizing the ingredients she'd thrown into the wok for the crispy stir fry on the menu. Mac helped her serve and then took his customary place next to Lucy, which meant he was across from Hannah. So she could look at him without it being weird.

Except it was weird, because she'd started thinking about what it would be like to kiss Mac. It wouldn't be like kissing the same man she'd been married to, or at least that's what she'd been telling herself. The whole point of putting a stake in the ground meant discovering how things worked between them as the people they were now. She'd changed. She had to believe he had too.

But her nerves wouldn't stop kicking her butt.

After dinner, she cleaned up and then stopped Mac with a hand to his arm as he started to follow Lucy down the hall for bath time, grimly determined to figure out which way she'd go. "If you don't mind, I'd like to read Lucy stories tonight. Just…you know. The two of us."

Mac's lips lifted a touch. "You haven't had much girl time lately, have you?"

Relieved that he actually understood, Hannah nodded. "That's it exactly."

"I'll get Mistress Mackenzie bathed and then you can take over, okay?"

She grinned at his nickname for Lucy. That had been far too easy. Why she'd been expecting resistance, she couldn't say. But she did get that Mac's time with Lucy might be limited and that he'd of course want to spend every second he could with his daughter. Only he hadn't made a peep about that, content with the part she'd allotted him.

They were really gelling with this parenting thing. Shockingly.

When it was time to read, she passed Mac in the hall, exchanging a relaxed glance as if they'd often tag-teamed bedtime. It spoke to his desire to make this work too.

As she breezed through the doorway to Lucy's room, she paused to take in the sight of Princess Misty snuggled in next to her daughter, who already had a book in her hand. She was reading to the dog. Who was intently listening.

It was precious.

"Which book is Princess Misty's favorite?" she called.

Lucy rolled her eyes. "Clifford. Duh."

Hannah made a face. "Do we speak to others sarcastically, Lucy Louise Mackenzie?"

Lucy lifted a brow, looking so much like Mac in that moment that Hannah's knees nearly gave out.

"Only when the question is dumb," Lucy announced. "Then it should be fine."

Instead of continuing the teachable moment, which clearly would fall on deaf ears, Hannah sat on the pink comforter, careful not to disturb Princess Misty's tail. "Can I ask you a serious question that isn't dumb even though it may feel that way to you? I need an honest answer."

Her daughter cocked her head, hopefully clueing in that her mother's tone meant business. "Is this one of those times I should pay attention to someone else's feelings besides my own?"

"Bingo." Hannah stroked Princess Misty a couple of times, which soothed her far more than she was expecting. Wasn't petting a dog supposed to make the *animal* feel good? "So the question is, what do you think about meeting your daddy?"

"He's the best!" Lucy exclaimed instantly. "He got me a dog and lets me play with the bubbles for as long as I want at bath time."

An indictment of her mother's strict bathroom schedule. Because if she let Lucy linger, it put Hannah behind, and she often had prep for a catering event after her daughter went to bed. That tracked. Mac was all about fun and games and new experiences. But she'd already assumed that would be the case and had chosen to let them bond instead of being a stickler about rules.

"What if he was around all the time? How would you feel about that?"

Her face lit up. "Does he want to be in our family?"

Clan Mackenzie. Hannah swallowed at the sudden ache in her throat. "I don't know. Maybe. The grown-ups need to talk about it, but I wanted to get your thoughts on it first."

"It's a big decision," Lucy said with eerie wisdom. "He might want two slices of Grandma Jenny's chocolate cake at my birthday party, and then someone else might not get any."

Hannah laughed. "If you're good with having your daddy around on a permanent basis, I'll gladly make a second cake. We will always have enough food for everyone who wants to be at our table."

As metaphors went, it wasn't a bad one to embrace. As long as Mac wanted a place, she should do her part to ensure she made room for him. Regardless of what happened between the two of them. That was how adults did things.

"I drew a picture at school today." Lucy jumped out of bed and grabbed her backpack without asking permission, but Hannah let it slide. "Do you think Daddy will like it?"

She took the picture Lucy handed her and absorbed the stick people with surprisingly detailed clothing and shoes.

The important thing was the number of people: three. Not two like Lucy had been drawing for quite some time.

She'd included her dad.

That was answer enough for Hannah, though it changed everything whether she was ready for it or not. "I think he'll love it."

"Give it to him," Lucy instructed, before settling back under the covers and handing Hannah a book. "Don't skip the part where the monkeys jump on the bed."

Hannah huffed out another laugh, though it broke against the emotion in her throat. She swallowed again and set the explosive stick-drawing picture aside in favor of story time. Much to Lucy's delight, she made a point of reading the monkey book twice, all the way through, no skipping. Small price to pay for getting her head on straight.

Once she had girl and dog all tucked in and had turned the light off, she tiptoed down the hall to the living area, praying Mac was still watching TV where she'd left him. It would be par for the course for her to have made a monumental decision to try some variation of whatever Lady in Red ambush Hannah could cobble together, only to find an empty room.

It wasn't empty.

Mac glanced up as she came into the room, a slow smile spreading across his face as if he'd somehow picked up on her vibe. Oh, goodness. Had he? Something fluttered in her midsection that she hadn't felt in a very long time, and it wasn't the stomach flu.

"Lucy asleep?" he murmured as she stood there frozen, four steps away from the island that separated the kitchen from the living room.

"That or plotting a coup to take over the pantry so she can eat an entire package of Oreos single-handedly." Mac laughed, a warm, buttery sound that brushed across her skin.

That felt so nice, she cast about for something else funny to say so he'd do it again, but then she remembered the picture. "She made this for you."

His expression instantly a heartbreaking blend of awe and surprise, Mac took the heavy construction paper from her outstretched hand, his gaze zeroing in on the figures. "Is this me?"

She nodded, not trusting her voice to actually work. He glanced up, his gaze meeting hers, so full of unvoiced emotion that she desperately wanted to understand. That was enough to get her mouth moving. "She wants a family. Not a dad who lives in another state."

The gauntlet had been thrown. Or something a little more sexy.

Mac stood, crossing the ocean of carpet between them that suddenly felt like mere inches the closer he got. He placed the picture on the island behind her, his presence wrapping around her in a way that shouldn't be so encompassing when he hadn't actually touched her yet. Wait. Was he going to touch her?

Then he did, his hand cupping her face as he guided it upward to gently force her to look at him. "What do you want, Hannah?"

"I want to know what's going to happen when you get your memories back," she blurted out. A statement also known as the number-one mood killer available on the market today.

But she needed to hear him say the words. Even if it meant he'd remove his hand from her face—and she quite liked the brush of his thumb over her cheek.

Except he did drop his hand. And his whole body. To his knees, capturing her hand in his on his way down. She stared down at him, prostrate at her feet.

"Hannah," he bit out hoarsely. "I'm so, so sorry about

what happened before. I can't erase it. I wish I could, but please know that I can't imagine hurting you again."

"That's not an answer."

He nodded, not the least bit cowed. Which went a long way.

"It's not an answer. Because I don't have one. I've never been in this situation before. That I know of," he amended with a slight eye roll that made her lips tip up in a half smile. "But I do know that I'm not going to lose my memories of what precious little time I've had together with you and Lucy, here in Owl Creek. You're my family. Forever. I want to be the one to take pictures of Lucy's first day of school and help you put candles on her birthday cake. If you let me, I'd like to do this parenting thing alongside you. Holding your hand."

"And sleeping in my bed?" she added bluntly. Maybe there was a course you were supposed to take on how to be a Lady in Red before you actually tried it.

But the look on Mac's face drove that thought right out of her head, along with all of the other ones.

"If that's part of the equation, yes," he murmured. "I would be blessed ten times over to be given a chance to prove that I mean what I say. I'm not going to disappoint you this time."

No, she didn't think disappointment would be anywhere in her future if she let Mac into her bed. But she did recognize that he was giving her the choice. Instead of sweeping her off her feet and snowing her senses with what she knew would be an amazing kiss if she gave into the heated vibes swirling between them, he was letting her take the lead.

And she wasn't sure she could make that choice. Not yet.

"I can't talk about that right now," she told him honestly. "But I do want to be clear that what happens between you and I is not in any way a factor in you being Lucy's father. Show up for her. No matter what."

He nodded, squeezing her hand. "I plan to. It's not an option for me to walk away from her. Not now. Not ever."

Despite the fact that he was saying all the right things, she couldn't let her guard down long enough to figure out how to let him in. To his credit, he allowed her to slip away and didn't try to follow her when she fled to her bedroom.

The next morning, she skipped Mac's coffee and left the house early for an appointment with a potential client in Conners who wanted to throw a huge wedding that bordered on a party. If she booked with Bon Appetit, the profit would equal Hannah's entire annual forecasted income in one gig.

The future bride and Hannah hit it off instantly and by the time she left the woman's home, she had a signed agreement in hand, with a hefty deposit already sitting in her bank account. Riding high on the success, she pulled out her phone to text Maria, one of the moms she'd befriended on the last preschool trip she'd chaperoned for Lucy's class, thinking it might be fun to meet for coffee.

She had several missed texts and calls from Owen. She'd never switched the name label to Mac in her phone, and it was a bucket of cold water to see his real name paraded across her screen so succinctly. Calling him something different had worked to a degree to get her to stop thinking about the past, to stop instantly assigning him to the old places of her heart.

But he was still Owen underneath. A new name didn't change that, or at least that's what her brain kept telling her.

Her heart wanted her brain to shut up. To believe. To feel him in the new places, the ones he'd created since that first moment when she'd seen him in that hospital bed and every moment since then. Especially the ones with Lucy. Whoever said that it was sexy watching a man be a good father had been onto something.

In case his messages were urgent or related to Lucy in

some way, she read them, relieved to see he was just asking her where she'd gone and when she'd be back. Well, she didn't answer to him. Though it was a little sweet in one of the messages where he mentioned that he'd missed having their early morning alone time together.

Honestly, she'd missed it too.

She couldn't think about all of this. It was too much. She edited his contact entry to Mac and saved it, then hit the text symbol for Maria, asking her if she had some time free to chat.

Maria responded instantly that she'd love to have Hannah drop by. Feeling free as a bird since Mac would take care of Lucy all day if Hannah asked him to, she accepted. Maybe some people might call it avoiding an explosive issue, but Hannah preferred to call it waiting to address the situation until she had her feet under her.

Besides, Mac—Owen in this particular case—owed her. She'd been a single parent for four years, five technically since he'd never lifted a finger to help out for the brief period after Lucy had been born. If she took a few hours for herself after a great client meeting, that was what fathers were for.

Maybe after coffee with Maria she'd feel more like putting down some ground rules for what things would be like going forward. Probably it would be a very bad idea to get involved with Mac again. They should take a giant step back and figure out how to co-parent as two single adults.

Maybe at some point in the future things would be able to gradually change.

When she got to Maria's house, another vehicle sat in the driveway, so she parked on the street and walked back, dodging some ice patches on the walkway to the front door. Just as she got to the front porch, the door swung open and Ana Sophia, Lucy's friend from preschool, came out holding the hand of a man who looked so much like her, he could only be her father. Ana Sophia waved at Hannah and her father nodded his head as he passed, guiding his daughter to the car in the driveway.

Maria appeared behind them, her gaze on Ana Sophia as she watched the girl's father buckle her into the car seat on the second row of the newer SUV. The mother's expression was heartbreaking.

"Hannah," she called, finding a smile, but it seemed to be a bit hard-won. "I'd hoped Ramon would be gone before you got here. He was running late, but when is he not? You'd think spending time with his daughter would be something he'd be early for, but no."

"I'm sorry if I'm intruding," Hannah began but Maria cut her off.

"No, not at all. Please, come in. It's great timing. It's Ramon's day to have Ana Sophia and I'm always at loose ends when she's gone. The company will be nice."

"I'm sorry," Hannah murmured. "I didn't realize you and Ramon had separated."

"It's somewhat new." Maria led her into a cheerful kitchen decorated with bright colors. "We're trying to figure out how to manage, but honestly, most days, I just wish we could be a family again. It's so hard on Ana Sophia to have her parents living in two separate places and arguing about parenting decisions that we should be making together."

"I could see how that would be difficult."

And she could. In real time, in her head, as she imagined how the next few years would go as she and Mac tried to co-parent Lucy through text messages and brief snippets of time at the front door as they transferred their daughter between them.

"If it's not intrusive," Hannah said as she accepted the coffee mug from Maria with a brief smile, "is there any chance you'll work it out? Be a family again?"

"I would love that," Maria said grimly, her eyes growing misty. "But Ramon doesn't want to. This is all his decision, and I had no say in it."

Hannah absorbed the sentiment as if Maria had flung it at her, beating her over the head with the words. Because it was her own story, in reverse. She was the one holding back. She was the one who was going to tell Mac there was no chance and that he had no say in the decision.

And honestly, that's not what she wanted.

She didn't want to tell Mac that he had to see Lucy on his designated days, when she'd have to watch them both walk away to be father and daughter some place she wasn't. She didn't want to tell him there was no chance for them.

Clan Mackenzie. That's what she wanted. It was what she'd always wanted. This might be her one and only chance to make it real.

Chapter Twenty-One

When Hannah finally texted Archer to let him know she'd been at a friend's house, but she'd be home soon, he took his first breath of the day. Since he'd awoken this morning to find Hannah's bedroom door wide open and the woman nowhere to be found, a pair of giant hands had grabbed his lungs and squeezed.

Sure, he'd checked the garage and found her car missing. Probably she was in it, driving some place. *Probably*. But she hadn't mentioned anything to him about an event today, so naturally he'd assumed the worst—Big Mike had kidnapped her and forced her to drive her car to a remote location in the mountains, where he'd finish her off. Or she'd dashed out for milk and had been run off the road by someone employed by whoever had pulled the same crap with him.

So his brain got busy recounting the other hundred bad scenarios that could have happened while he texted her and called for a clue as to her whereabouts, pulse pounding in his throat. No answer. Meanwhile, he'd worn out the carpet in front of Lucy's room, checking and rechecking on her to ensure she'd slept through the worst couple of hours of his life.

She had. Then she'd bounced out of bed to announce that she and Princess Misty required pancakes for breakfast, and since Hannah wasn't home and wasn't responding to his texts, he decided that pancakes sounded fantastic. So he'd pulled out all the ingredients and used Hannah's fancy cookware to make a dozen of the fluffiest pancakes in existence, awed at how much nicer it was to cook in a well-appointed kitchen.

After breakfast, they'd watched *Peppa Pig* for an hour and then Archer had declared they'd had enough brain rotting for the day, and moved Lucy on to coloring at the table.

When Hannah breezed through the door near lunchtime, he had to physically restrain himself from sweeping her into his arms to kiss her senseless and then personally check every inch of her body to ensure she was in fact still in one piece.

"There you are," he said gruffly instead, stuffing his hands into his pockets. Obviously she was fine. And not lying in a ditch.

Man, did she wear that windblown, rosy-cheeked-from-the-cold look well. She might be the most beautiful woman he'd ever met.

"Mama, see what I did," Lucy commanded, and Hannah crossed to the table to ooh and aah over the drawings in question.

"I have a surprise for you, Lu Lu," she said brightly and glanced at Archer. "What would you say to a sleepover at Grandma Jenny's? Princess Misty is invited too."

Lucy cheered and raced Princess Misty to her room as her mother called after her to remember to pack pajamas and her toothbrush.

"A sleepover?" Archer asked, trying to catch up. Was this a regular thing that Lucy and Hannah did together?

"I hope you don't mind," Hannah said once Lucy was out of earshot, a delightful splotch of color climbing into her cheeks. "I thought it would be nice to have a night to ourselves."

Dumbfounded, Archer stared at her, his brain sliding into

a place that it shouldn't be without a whole lot of clarifications. "Are you asking me on a date?"

"Um, yes?"

He clutched his heart in mock cardiac arrest to cover up the fact that she had in fact nearly knocked him over with the admission. "I'm crushed at how unsure you sound. Maybe try again without all the question marks."

"Mac, would you like to have dinner with me tonight?" she responded dutifully but whacked him on the arm playfully, which worked for him and then some, because it allowed him to grab her hand and pull her into his arms.

Progress. In more ways than one.

"I'm practicing," he informed her when she blinked up at him with one eyebrow askew. "For later. I was making sure my ribs would be up for it if your dinner ended up being so good that I needed to thank you with a hug."

"How's that working for you?" she asked, her tone wry. But she didn't pull away.

In a shocking turn of events, she slipped her arms around him in kind.

He squeezed her closer, as if testing, wobbling his head in indecision. "I'm not sure. I'm definitely going to have to do this again to figure it out. Maybe several times."

That was the only way he could ever get his fill of her. His heart thrummed as her scent filled his head. Whatever had turned her *I'm not sure* into *sure*, he was a fan of it.

"If you're expecting an argument, you won't get one here," she murmured. "Maybe let's pick this up later, though."

"Yes, ma'am," he said with far less enthusiasm than the words deserved. "How fast can we get Lucy to your mom's house?"

She laughed, making it very difficult to release her as he'd absolutely intended to do. But then Lucy came back in the room dragging a pink overstuffed suitcase with the Little

Mermaid printed on the flap, so it kind of became necessary to give Hannah her mobility back.

"Mama, I can't get it zipped," Lucy complained, apparently not the slightest bit concerned that her parents had been wrapped around each other in the kitchen mere moments ago.

Good. Hopefully that meant she would continue to be unconcerned about such events, because Archer planned to repeat the casual affection as often as possible. His arms had already cooled far too much, and Hannah had only been absent from them for about ninety seconds.

Hannah bent to help Lucy rearrange what looked like half of her room dumped haphazardly into the cavity of the suitcase. Together they pulled the zipper closed—barely. But in no time, Lucy allowed Archer to heft the suitcase into the hatchback of Hannah's car. Princess Misty's travel crate went in next to it, then Lucy dove into the back seat to get clicked into her car seat, jabbering to the dog about all the fun things Grandma Jenny would do with them.

Archer went with them to drop off the kid and dog combo, and the moment they got back into the car for the return trip, the silence was so deafening that he almost asked if they could get Lucy back.

Almost. This was the first time he and Hannah had been truly alone, and unless he'd somehow misread all her cues—unlikely—this was a momentous occasion to be marked with adult activities. This was his one and only chance to make it memorable for both of them since he had the worst feeling that time was running out.

Archer was not a slouch in the female department, but this was different. He wanted Hannah with a fierce sort of possessiveness that he didn't recognize, and he was worried that it would come across as creepy instead of flattering. She deserved to be romanced. What would Owen do?

"Do we need to stop at the store to get anything for dinner?" he asked. Smooth. That had romance stamped *all* over it.

Hannah didn't seem to notice his lack of skills. But she did smooth hair back from her face a bunch of times as she stopped at a traffic light, as if nerves might be getting to her too. "I do actually. Do you want to go with me?"

"You bet."

It was a homey sort of task that a married couple might do. So maybe he had channeled Owen a little bit better than he'd thought he had, though he doubted seriously that his brother had ever accompanied a woman to the grocery store.

It turned out to be fortuitous though, because it allowed him to select a bottle of nice red wine to go with the steaks Hannah added to their cart. Her eyes widened a bit at the price, but he shushed her and also managed to beat her to the credit card machine at checkout, so she wasn't the one footing the bill in the first place.

"Mac," she protested as soon as they cleared the sliding glass doors at the entrance to the store. "I invited you to dinner. I was supposed to pay."

"You're cooking," he countered firmly. "Everyone knows that means that it's my job to pay. Besides, you charge your catering clients for the food. This is no different."

"You're not a client."

No, he was not. The reminder somehow managed to cast another silencer spell over the car and he couldn't think of a blessed thing to break it. Maybe they'd built this up too much with all the back-and-forth.

Plus, he had a heightened sense of the unknown variables between them. Like the fact that he wasn't Owen. That was probably 90 percent of the problem on his side. But that didn't account for what was going on on her side. And he wanted to know.

As soon as he'd carried the groceries into the house, he

stopped Hannah from immediately spinning into a cooking dervish with a hand on her arm. "What is this all about, Hannah?"

She glanced up at him. "Dinner?"

"No, *dinner*. It suddenly seems to come with a lot of expectations or something that have gotten us wholly uncomfortable with each other. I like spending time with you. I like laughing with you. You have a wry humor that I appreciate. I'd rather go get hamburgers at Dairy Queen than drink expensive wine if it means we can get back to where we were before."

"You like my sense of humor?" She seemed dazed by this admission and more than a little pleased. "You never did before."

"I was an idiot before," he growled, suddenly not the slightest bit interested in playing the part of Owen, who was actually the one responsible for the vibe between them.

The real question was: What would Archer do?

"Hannah," he murmured. "Obviously I haven't told you nearly enough what I think about you. And I think about you often. Everything about you appeals to me. You're an accomplished business owner. An excellent mother to my daughter. As beautiful inside as you are outside."

"Really?" she whispered, and he couldn't take the distance any longer.

Pulling her into his space, he cupped her jaw with one hand, tracing the lines of her cheek as she met his gaze without flinching. Something had changed in her head that had led to tonight and he didn't want to stumble over it. "Really. But I think you already know how I feel about you. The real question is how you feel about me. About this. About what it feels like is happening between us."

Without warning, Hannah's mouth fused to his. The moment the kiss registered, he scooped her closer and breathed her in, reveling in the sensations of her taking control of this. Whatever *this* was. He couldn't wait to find out.

She got a little bolder and he let her explore to her heart's content, jerking back his immediate response of pushing her up against the counter to take his own tour of her mouth. The little noises she was making drove him to the brink and he groaned in kind as everything got intense.

Her hands spread across his back, heating everything in their path. There was so much more of him she hadn't touched, so much of her he wanted to kiss. Her lips worked across his jaw, finding a hollow near his throat and the sensations threatened to overwhelm him.

This was not supposed to happen. Not like this. He needed to…think. Or something.

"Hannah," he growled and set her back a solid six inches. "You have to slow down or there will be no eating in our future."

"Oh, you're not hungry?" she asked, seemingly disappointed, her green eyes searching his.

"Yes, I am," he bit out succinctly. "And in about three seconds, you're going to find out what I'm hungry for. So I'm suggesting we take a breather. Have some wine. Before I lose my mind."

Her lips tipped up in a smile that had a bit of wonder in it. "You're…um, that attracted to me?"

His brain malfunctioned. There was no other word for it. It simply couldn't compute an answer to a question that ludicrous. He thought about all the graphic ways he could demonstrate that with a little show and tell but forced himself to breathe. At least until he could be reasonably sure he wasn't about to spontaneously combust.

She needed to know a few things before this went any further.

"You're the most intoxicating woman I've ever met," he

ground out. "I can't think when you're touching me. When you're not touching me, all I can think about is the next time you're going to touch me. And then I think about me touching you and the cycle starts all over again. I'm not the kind of guy who reads a lot of poetry or spends time coming up with flowery phrases, so I can't exactly say what's going on inside me other than it's big and bright and strong and beautiful and it has your name all over it."

Okay, those were not the things he'd meant to tell her. They'd just spilled out. And judging by the look on her face, he'd scored some points in his clumsy attempt to communicate.

"That was pretty good," she murmured. "For someone who didn't come up with that ahead of time."

"Hannah," he growled again as she lifted her hands to his chest, spreading her fingers wide to nip in, as if holding on.

"Shh. No talking. Not right now. The future can take care of itself. Just kiss me like you think I'm intoxicating again. That's the first time you've ever said anything like that. I'm having trouble accepting that you're talking about *me*. Before—"

"There's no before," he cut in roughly and caught her up in his arms, dragging her into his embrace with fierceness that she couldn't mistake. "Only now. You make me feel lost and found all at once. Nothing exists except you."

And then he proved it to her with a searing kiss that drove all rational thought out of his head. She didn't know how he felt about her. That was a *travesty*. So he poured every ounce of his raging attraction to her into the mating of their mouths. It was an onslaught and she more than met him halfway.

This was no tentative exploration. It was a volcanic eruption, the kind that only happened once every thousand years, the kind that decimated everything in its path with a river of heat.

He lifted her effortlessly to slide her onto the counter so he could access even more of her. She went willingly, wrapping her legs around him in an embrace so intimate that his eyes crossed.

Yes. This. Now.

The future could take care of itself. That was a concept he could get on board with.

Nothing else mattered but making this woman his. Not Owen, not Archer's investigation or his need to protect Hannah and Lucy. The only problem he wanted to fix in this moment was the one where Hannah was too far away, and she hadn't heard nearly enough about the way she made him feel. The way she made him believe in good things. The things she did to him inside, where no person should be able to reach, but she'd burrowed beneath his skin to take up residence.

So he told her. For hours. As they christened the countertop, her bed. As they ate the dinner she finally cooked. As they drifted off to sleep, well sated with each other.

Chapter Twenty-Two

What had started as a simple dinner with Mac to tentatively push things forward, move them in the right direction so to speak, had turned into something far more explosive. A stake in the ground. A demarcation to end all mile markers.

The man had slayed her.

Not that Hannah had a lot of experience to draw from, but she'd never felt like that. Ever. She'd be hard pressed to find evidence that she'd even *believed* a woman could feel like she had with Mac.

It certainly eclipsed any experiences she'd had with him before. In fact, if she didn't know better, she'd swear up and down that before last night, she'd never so much as kissed the man she'd spent the night with last night. Everything felt different. New. Better.

So much better.

The morning unfolded much like the night before had. Languid. No agenda. Just two people enjoying each other. At some point, she'd thought this dinner idea might be a precursor to seeing how Mac fit into her life. A test.

He'd passed. He fit into her bed so well that she'd woken up seriously contemplating ways to keep him there permanently. A lover suited her to the ground, but also made her giggle because she'd never thought of herself as the kind of woman who could have a man so intently devoted to her.

Mac lifted sleepy eyes in her direction, his dark hair spread over the pillow in a wholly appealing way that had her thinking the opposite might be true—he could snap his fingers and she'd become devoted to his every need.

"I like your laugh," he told her huskily.

"I like that you make me feel so bubbly inside," she informed him truthfully. "I guess I should be coy and act like I'm worldly and unimpressed. But if I'm being honest, those games irritate me, so I'll lay it out instead. I'm not the kind of woman who flits from bed to bed. This is it for me. And you're Lucy's father. I'm sure I don't have to tell you that one false move can set a child into a tailspin. No tailspins. Promise me."

He lifted her hand to his mouth, grazing her fingers. "I love Lucy. I would hope you already realized that. If I have it in my power to keep her from ever being hurt or disappointed by anything in her life, I will do it. Whatever it is. I promise you."

Good grief. And she'd thought he couldn't possibly say anything more perfect than the lovely words he'd whispered to her last night. "Okay."

"Okay." He smiled and pulled her close to lay a sweet kiss on her temple.

Could it really be that easy? Her heart stretched a little then, like a flower seeking the sun's warmth, only the sun looked an awful lot like Mac. She'd kept her tender organ packed away, or at least she'd thought she had. This man had somehow lifted away the foam peanuts where she'd buried her heart and revealed things she'd thought she'd never feel again.

Of course, they were still walking a line called amnesia. Though somewhere along the way, she'd stopped worrying about what would happen when he got his memories back. If anything, the gentle, appreciative man he was today would probably work doubly hard to make it up to her, when he realized how much he'd hurt her back then. She could handle a dozen roses every day for a month if he had a mind for it.

Not for the first time, she blessed the accident that had given her something so unexpected and precious. It was a terrible by-product that he'd been hurt, absolutely, and she hated that part. But she couldn't change it, so she was choosing to focus on the positives—and there were many.

Looping her arms around Mac's neck, she snuggled into his warmth and then looked at the clock. "Ugh, is that time for real?"

"Yeah." He nuzzled her ear. "You have a date?"

"I'm supposed to get Lucy before noon. And I have a brunch tomorrow that is going to take a serious amount of pre-prep. Ramona was supposed to do it, but she broke her arm skiing. So the boss gets to pick up the slack," she explained with a half laugh, half grimace.

"I'll help you. Let me pick up Lucy so you can start doing your dazzling chef-things," he suggested. "Then you can stay right where you are for another forty-five minutes."

The wicked thread running through his voice left no question as to what he planned to do during that time. But she didn't lean in immediately to get started on the implied premise. Instead, she pulled back to meet his gaze.

"What's going to happen after that?"

He didn't pretend to misunderstand. He let his embrace loosen but didn't drop it entirely, which had a lot of undertones she wasn't sure how to interpret. "This is the part where we talk about the future, isn't it?"

It sounded so awful the way he said it. That axe still hung over their happiness, waiting to sever everything good and new and exciting between them. While she may not be as

The whole conversation made her head hurt.

Wade didn't immediately answer the question and in the pause, she got a pretty good idea who one of the someones was. "It was Fletch. Wasn't it? He's got some fancy police equipment that detected it?"

"Don't be ridiculous. Owl Creek PD doesn't have that kind of money." Another pause. "He still has some contacts in Salt Lake City. They're quietly investigating Acker for some shenanigans he pulled when he joined the Church of Latter-day Saints some years back."

"So that's a legit thing? You can tell if someone is looking into a suspect's finances who isn't you?"

Wade's grunt confirmed it. Fascinating.

"You're not answering the question," he insisted. "Are you still trying to investigate him?"

Hannah stood in front of the mirror dripping, guilt gnawing at her insides. Her face had a well-loved glow that she didn't recognize, and her body bore a couple of marks that secretly made her quite proud when she recalled about how she'd gotten them. Of course, that made her think about Mac and anything else pretty much drained from her mind.

He'd been a distraction since day one. Even more so now. She'd almost completely abandoned her quest to find out more about Markus Acker, even after finding out it was possible he and Jessie had killed Hannah's father. That should have been motivation enough to make it her top priority once she'd found out her brothers suspected it.

Instead, she'd volunteered to help Mac get back on his feet and then jumped into bed with him.

She put her phone on speaker and dried off, then pulled on clothes as she answered.

"Yeah, I am," she told him. Intent counted. "I don't know how to look into his finances, but if I figure it out, I will be. Thanks for that tip, Waderkins."

"That wasn't meant to be a how-to, Hannah Banana," he said, defaulting to her nickname in retaliation for her using his. "Stay away from Acker."

"No argument here. I have zero plans to get anywhere near him."

Sarah, on the other hand, was a different story. She had every reason in the world to spend as much time with her half sister as she wanted to.

And should. It was a great reminder that she needed to get her mind off Mac and back on her real life. Whatever was going on with her ex-husband, she couldn't afford to fall for him again. That's how she'd messed up the first time—letting her heart lead instead of her brain.

Brain first this time. It made sense to cultivate a relationship with Mac for Lucy's sake. It made sense to let him do all kinds of delicious things to her after hours because it felt good. There was nothing wrong with reveling in an attentive man who deserved a gold medal for figuring out her feminine buttons with zero memories to guide him.

For once, she was grabbing something nice for herself. It was a lovely coincidence that what was good for Lucy worked out for Hannah too.

This was every bit using her head. She wasn't Heart-First Hannah any longer. And if in her heart she wanted Clan Mackenzie, no one had to know. Wanting something didn't have to be the thing that forced her decisions.

"Speaking of people you shouldn't be getting anywhere near," Wade threw in casually and she knew instantly where this was going, "how's Lover Boy?"

"Don't start, Wade. My relationship with Mac is my own business."

"Calling him a different name this go-round doesn't make him less of a heel."

"Also none of your business. And you have no clue what you're talking about."

It did make a difference. A huge one. He was starting over, and she believed him when he said he was not the same man. Why not commemorate that with a new name? It was a time-honored tradition. A form of rebirth. Muhammad Ali had done the same, along with a slew of other celebrities who were definitely more well-known by their new names than their old ones.

Besides, it helped her reframe their relationship and right now, she and Lucy needed that. Head talking. Not heart. Wade could shut his mouth.

"I just don't want him to hurt you and Lucy again," Wade said gruffly, and she gave him a break.

"I get it. Thank you. I know you're looking out for me, and I appreciate it. But please hear me. He's Lucy's father. When you have kids, we can talk about this again because then you'll understand that sometimes we have to make choices that hurt because it's best for them. Right now, I'm focused on her and what's best for her relationship with her father."

Mostly.

She wandered into the living room just as Mac strolled through the front door with Lucy in tow and when he smiled at her, her tongue went numb. Everything else woke up and danced the Macarena, especially the parts that were still pleasantly raw from his beard sliding across her skin, a sensation that was wholly unique to this version of the man.

"Wade, I have to go," she told him, her gaze fastened on Mac as they shared a glance full of things no one else could possibly understand.

She didn't even fully understand it.

When she set her phone down, Lucy rushed over for a hug, babbling about all the things she'd done with Grandma Jenny.

"Do you have a mom, Daddy?" she asked out of the blue.

Mac visibly recoiled, and she rushed to fill the gap. "Daddy has some problems with his head since he hit it, and he doesn't remember his mom. So he needs you to love him extra hard to make up for that."

Lucy's gaze swept her father, as if seeking assurance that no other strange phenomenon existed that she'd been previously unaware of. They hadn't told her anything about his medical conditions and probably Hannah should have checked with Mac first before spitting out something like that, but he relaxed, so she figured it had been the right move.

"Do you remember me?" Lucy asked with her typical five-going-on-twenty-five shrewdness.

This was one he'd have to take himself. And he didn't hesitate to kneel down next to her.

"I remember that you like pancakes in the morning and that *Don't Let the Pigeon Drive the Bus!* is your favorite book," he said and straightened the cuff of her jeans where they'd gotten caught on the Velcro straps of her pink glittery *Peppa Pig* high-tops. "I remember that your friend at preschool is Ana Sophia, and that Jack Harper pulls your hair on the playground. I remember that I gave you permission to deck him if he does it again."

Hannah smacked a hand to her lips before the protest slipped out. Permission to hit another child was definitely something they'd be discussing behind closed doors. Assuming she could get a word out edgewise when she had a feeling he'd be claiming her mouth for other activities the moment they shut the door.

Lucy nodded as if all of this made perfect sense to her. "And you gave me dogs."

Mac cocked his head with a vague smile. "Princess Misty is definitely sprightly enough to count as two dogs, that's for sure."

"I meant Mr. Fluffers too. He came in a box, but he wasn't scared."

Something clanked with a distinct metallic edge and re-verberated through the kitchen. Hannah and Mac jumped at the same time, both dashing toward the mudroom. Mac twisted her behind him in an impressive move that simultaneously made her swoony and also put a knot in her throat.

Did he think someone was in the house? Like the intruder who had moved stuff around?

Mac stopped her from entering the mudroom with a hand to her chest, presumably so he could check out the room first, then dropped his arm.

"It's the water dish," Mac announced, his relief evident. "Princess Misty turned it over by accident."

The dog in question hung her head, clearly ashamed.

Hannah stepped over the threshold and reached above the long wooden bench seat to the cabinet where she kept old towels. "It's okay. That's why we set up her food and water dishes in here where there's lots of tile meant for muddy snow boots."

While she mopped up the water, Mac stroked Princess Misty's fur, which seemed to help her realize she wasn't in trouble. Lucy called for her, and the dog perked up, dashing from the room to meet her mistress in the living room.

"Crisis averted," Mac said as he took the wet towel from her, then helped her to her feet.

When she rose, he caught her up in his free arm, careful to keep the other away from her so the towel in his hand didn't transfer water to her clothes. It was a nice detail that made her a little weak in the knees.

"I missed you," he murmured and laid a fiery kiss on her upturned lips.

"You were only gone for thirty minutes," she protested with a pleased laugh, but it died in her throat when she met his heated, intense gaze.

"I've been gone a lot longer than that," he told her with

quiet fierceness. "And I have a lot of making up for lost time to do. Starting with kissing you in the mudroom because I cannot physically stand to be apart from you right this moment."

Oh my. That was definitely not her head squeezing so tight it felt like it might burst.

Chapter Twenty-Three

The high wire Archer had started walking across when he'd woken up in the hospital with everyone calling him Owen had just reached impossible heights. And he was afraid to look down to see just how far away the ground was.

The splat was coming, though.

The Dinner Date, cemented in his mind in capital letters, had been over a week ago. He and Hannah had never picked up their conversation about the future. His fault. He'd only wanted to put off reality for a bit longer, and she'd pounced on the opportunity. Every time he started to bring it up, he thought about Big Mike and how vulnerable Hannah and Lucy would be without him here.

They needed his protection. He needed to keep being Owen for just a little while longer, until someone took the bait. He'd turned up so little to connect the Ever After Church with Big Mike and Hannah, but he knew the three were somehow linked. He could feel it.

Eventually the pieces would click into place, and he'd be able to see the whole picture. Until then, he had to sit tight.

But the voice inside laughed at all his justifications. He was still here with Hannah because he wanted to be.

She turned over and caught him watching her from his side of the bed. The one he'd claimed a week ago and hadn't given up yet. She hadn't asked him to go back to his room on the other side of the house either, and he wasn't about to bring it up.

"Is the door locked?" she murmured.

He answered her with a slow smile. "I never unlocked it earlier."

Hannah smacked him on the arm without any heat. "That's one of the unbendable rules. What if Lucy wanted one of us?"

Man, he'd never get used to the idea that a little girl might possibly seek him out in the middle of the night for comfort and cuddles. That she'd choose him, maybe even over her mother. It was almost enough for him to slide out from under the covers and flick the lock open. Almost.

Instead, he slid Hannah closer, wrapping his arms around her. "If she comes to the door, I'll put on my pants and open it. She's old enough to understand that she doesn't get free rein over all the rooms in the house. The double-edged sword of having a brilliant child, my darling."

Hannah stuck her tongue out, laughing. "That's half your fault. I like it when you call me things like that, by the way."

"What, darling?" he murmured, enjoying the feel of it leaving his mouth.

It seemed like something his brother would say, and he'd gotten in the habit of trying to please Hannah through that lens. After all, she'd been in love with Owen once. It didn't take a rocket scientist to assume she'd liked aspects of his personality, and frankly, Archer didn't figure there was a lot about a numbers guy like him that she'd appreciate anyway, so it was easier to adopt a bit of Owen's persona.

Especially since that's who she thought he was.

Misery coated the back of his throat as he took another step along that swaying high wire.

If someone had ever told him he'd fall for his brother's

ex-wife, he'd have signed them up for psychiatric evaluation. If they'd told him he'd fall for her while posing as his brother, he'd have signed himself up.

"Yeah," she whispered. "It makes me feel shivery."

That made two of them. It was going to be hard to give her up when the time came, but that's where this was headed. Especially when she found out the truth.

Not only would she be furious—she wasn't even in this for the long haul. Look how carefully she'd qualified that he wasn't allowed to walk out on Lucy. It hadn't escaped his notice that she'd never elicited a similar promise from him about their own relationship. Obviously, she didn't have nearly the same attachment to him that he did to her.

It was fine. He didn't get nice things for himself. That was the unwritten rule about being the good Mackenzie. His job was to clean up Owen's messes, not collect must-haves for his own life. Besides, he lived in Las Vegas, not Idaho. He had a job, a team. A condo that Willis had been going by every few days to collect the mail.

The more he contemplated what the future actually looked like, the bleaker it seemed. Was it so horrible to sink down into this place he'd unwittingly landed? To spend a few precious moments living a life he'd had no clue would fit him, let alone become something he desperately wanted?

It was working. For now.

He'd deal with the consequences later. It was the most Owen thing he'd ever done in his life.

IN THE MORNING, he almost started whistling as he padded down the hall to wake up Lucy for preschool today, as had become his habit over the last few days. He'd fought Hannah for the privilege of driving their daughter to school, which served an excellent double purpose of ensuring mom got some alone time. He also intensely disliked Hannah and

Lucy being in the car without him when he couldn't shield them from the dangers of the world that he knew lurked out there.

Sometimes he had a bad moment when he thought about Hannah being alone in the house by herself, but he couldn't be in two places at once. So far, whoever had their eyes on them hadn't made their presence known. It was highly likely the goons were under orders to observe and not approach. That's what he kept telling himself anyway.

At the doorway to Lucy's room, he had to pause for a moment as she came into view, her gorgeous light brown hair a stark contrast to the pale pink pillow case. Brown, not blond like Hannah, thus likely from Mackenzie blood. His blood. By a circuitous route, no doubt, but it still counted.

He'd make it count. There had to be a way to keep Lucy in his life, even after Hannah found out the truth. He didn't have a lot of hope she'd have any interest in keeping the intimate portion of their relationship intact, but surely he'd proven he meant to stick with Lucy.

Princess Misty sensed him and lifted her head from her preferred spot at the end of Lucy's bed. He liked the dog there. Just in case.

Sebastian had trained Princess Misty to bark if Lucy needed anything but otherwise, the dog never made a sound, a trick Archer appreciated. The more he got to know the individual members of Hannah's family, the more he liked them. Especially since Sebastian had kept quiet about the fact that he'd earmarked the Border collie for Lucy from the first, something Archer had learned when he'd had a side conversation with the Colton brothers while Hannah had been distracted.

He had Wade to thank for voicing that tip, which Hannah's brother had grudgingly shared at Jenny's get-together. All of Hannah's brothers were good people who cared about their sister and their niece. It made him feel a lot better that so many Coltons would be between Hannah and Lucy and danger if—when—the time came that Archer couldn't be around to make sure they were safe.

All in all, he could count his foray here in Owl Creek as a success if for no other reason than the family he'd come to think of as his was happy and safe. Clan Mackenzie. It would be the first time he'd fixed a mess Owen had made and come out better for it himself too.

His stomach hurt when he thought about what it was going to be like not to see Lucy every day. To watch her learn. Grow. To see her as a six-year-old, a seven-year-old. Hitting double digits, Princess Misty by her side. Cobbling together time with her as he and Hannah split parenting duties across state lines, if she'd let him continue to be Lucy's father even though she wasn't his birth daughter.

Today, he didn't have to worry about any of that, and they'd be late if he kept standing here watching Lucy breathe. He touched her shoulder, and when her green eyes blinked up at him, so much like her mother's, he couldn't stop the slick, hot emotion that poured down his throat, tightening it.

"Hey, Lu Lu, time to get up," he murmured hoarsely, shocked his voice had worked at all.

"Hold Mr. Fluffers," she commanded as she sprang out of bed, a bundle of energy despite having been deep asleep mere moments ago.

Wryly, he took the stuffed dog from her hand as she bounced over to the pink plastic table and chairs in the corner of her room where she set her backpack each night before bed.

"I'm wearing pajamas today," she announced as he tucked the dog into the crook of his arm, amused at the picture he probably made.

Not that he could even contemplate who he'd share a photo

with. His mother? He hadn't mentioned to her yet that he'd found Hannah and Lucy during his investigation of Owen's murder. She'd want to meet them and that wouldn't be helpful in this scenario. Maybe after everything shook out, Hannah might be willing to introduce Lucy to her paternal grandmother.

But the explanation for why Hannah didn't know Owen's mother existed would come tangled up with the additional surprise existence of Owen's twin brother. A subject better left for another time, when it would be less dangerous—and complicated—to untangle.

"I think you have to wear normal clothes to school, Lu," he commented mildly, far too used to her announcements to worry too much about handling the potential showdown.

The sly look she shot him didn't faze him either. "Sometimes we get pajama day."

"Is that today?"

She pouted for about five seconds. "No."

Smart girl. "I'll buy you new pajamas for next pajama day. How about that as a deal for why you're going to get dressed in regular clothes without any arguments?"

Her sunny smile back in place, she dashed to do as he suggested, wisely realizing it wasn't optional. These were some of his favorite times with Lucy, when it was just the two of them and he wasn't as worried about doing or saying the wrong thing. Not that Hannah's presence felt judgmental, but she'd been doing this a lot longer than he had, and she made it seem so easy. She never questioned herself or made mistakes, whereas he constantly had to think about how a parent should respond to situations, instead of his first inclination, which was—why not wear pajamas to school?

With a minute to spare, he got Lucy bundled into the car. March weather would nip some of the cold back, but not by much. That was one thing Las Vegas had going for it. Better weather. At least until summer when it got hotter than Hades.

Archer parked at Lucy's school and unbuckled her from her car seat, then helped her hop down out of the back seat of Hannah's hatchback. Lucy slipped her hand in his as they waited at the edge of the crosswalk for the monitor to stop the traffic, his throat getting tight again at the casual way this little girl had incorporated him into her heart with no questions asked.

It was a testament to Hannah, no question. Owen would have probably never even considered driving Lucy to school, let alone actually doing it. His loss. In more ways than one. Owen would never know this family, know what it meant to belong to them. Never know what he'd walked away from.

Archer knew exactly what he was giving up and it was killing him.

Lucy dashed off at the door of her classroom and her teacher waved at him as he paused for one last look, never sure if today was the last time he'd see her. On a razor's edge emotionally, an unfamiliar place he didn't like to be, he didn't notice the car following him at first.

But when he turned toward the lake to head to Hannah's house, the grey sedan turned too, not even trying to stay hidden. It was quite clear the car meant to keep pace with him and also to ensure that Archer became aware of his tail.

Just like the watcher in the woods hadn't bothered to hide the glint of his binoculars. The goons were either sloppy— not likely—or employing a subtle intimidation game.

Archer wasn't the average law-abiding citizen though. He had extensive training in recognizing patterns and putting pieces together that ordinary people might overlook. Yet he still didn't know who was behind all of this. It was bother- ing him at a cellular level, as if someone had figured out how to get beneath his skin and writhe around, making him wish he could peel it off.

The sun glinted off the windshield, preventing Archer from getting a good look at the driver. It took all of thirty seconds to memorize the license plate, make and model of the car, though, and would take Willis about that long to find out the registration information, once Archer texted it to his assistant.

But he couldn't do that and drive *and* keep an eye on his tail. Plus, it might be prudent to lure the sedan away from Hannah. Sure, odds were high these goons and their employer already knew he was living at Hannah's house, but there was a huge difference between being academically aware of a fact and leading someone who likely had a loaded weapon strapped to his waist right to a person Archer cared about.

He turned left instead of right at the road to Hannah's house. The sedan kept pace. Good. Archer glanced in the rearview mirror every few seconds, hoping to get a glimpse of the driver, but the sun was too bright this morning in a cloudless sky.

This was ridiculous. The car never sped up or slowed down, just kept following him. As a scare tactic, it didn't work. All it did was make Archer increasingly agitated. Another emotional response to something that he should be approaching with coolheaded logic. That's why he'd gone into forensic analysis instead of putting on a uniform and chasing down criminals in the street—he didn't have the juice for this kind of cat-and-mouse game.

Nor did he have a weapon, an oversight he needed to correct pronto.

Archer led his tail halfway around the lake, past the turnoff for Jenny's house, well past the marina. He thought about heading into the mountains toward Crosswinds, but the odds of being able to lose his shadow on the narrow roads turned his blood cold. So he kept on this same track, his brain turning over a hundred scenarios so he could plan his next steps, just in case the driver decided to finish off what someone else had started during Archer's drive out to Owl Creek all those weeks ago.

But instead of ramming him from behind as Archer had braced for, the gray sedan suddenly peeled off and vanished down a side street.

Regrouping? Trying to cut him off at some indeterminate point ahead?

Archer pulled over to the shoulder and did a quick U-turn, praying he'd shoot past the side road the sedan had taken before the driver got his car flipped around. If that had even been the goon's goal. At this point, nothing would surprise him.

No gray car appeared. Archer's heart rate didn't slow until he'd doubled back to Main Street, inserting himself into the middle of the normal Owl Creek traffic. That had been close. And not close enough to make any kind of progress on his to-do list.

All of this was coming to a head faster than he'd like. He had to tell Hannah the truth eventually, but would she be safer if she knew now? Or safer if she had no clue until he could unravel the truth?

He was still waffling on his mental flower-petal pulling—*I tell her, I don't tell her, I tell her*, et cetera, et cetera, for an hour—when he got back to Hannah's house. When he turned from stomping his boots off in the mudroom, she was waiting for him, her face ashen.

His blood froze as he realized the gray sedan might have been trying to lure *him* away from Hannah's house.

"Hannah? What's wrong?"

He reached for her automatically, yanking her into his

arms as he held on to her, trying to get his galloping heart under control, at least until he figured out what had her so concerned since it was so very clear something had.

"You were gone so long," she croaked out, likewise clinging to him as if she couldn't fathom letting go. "I was worried."

Archer cursed. *That's* what he should have taken the time to do—text Hannah. "I'm so sorry, darling. I didn't mean to scare you."

"I thought something had happened to you and Lucy."

"No," he said gruffly, which wasn't a lie, but neither was the truth as innocuous as his simple denial made it sound. "Nothing happened. But I thought… Well, it's probably my imagination. But I thought someone was following me."

She made a noise in her throat. "The same people who searched the house?"

"I don't know," he admitted, which sliced at something inside—he was far more used to being proficient at his job.

Except he wasn't doing his job. He was pretending to be Owen because it seemed like a good cover to do some snooping around, only he'd done precious little of that and had instead done the one thing he shouldn't have—fallen in love with Hannah and Lucy.

"You left your phone," she said into his shoulder and lifted her face to his. "That's what got me so worried. I couldn't even text you to see where you were."

"I didn't forget my—" *Phone.*

He swallowed the word because he hadn't forgotten *his* phone. He had, however, left *Owen's* phone in his room. And hadn't thought about it one time in weeks. Because it was useless to him once he'd combed through the contacts.

Curious that she'd picked up on the fact that he wasn't carrying it, though. Had she gone through his things? Why? Not that he was trying to hide anything—well, except everything—but it sat on his shoulders crossways.

He released her and stepped back, missing her warmth immediately.

"How did you…did you find my phone somewhere?" he asked cautiously, feeling as if he'd just walked out on ice that had started to crack.

"It was ringing," she said and held it out to him like it was nothing, just a phone, and not a ticking time bomb. "Over and over. There's like 35 missed calls."

There were only two reasons someone would call the phone of a dead man—they knew Archer had Owen's phone or they thought he was Owen. Who wasn't supposed to be alive.

A big gaping hole appeared in the ice, and he plunged into the frigid depths.

Chapter Twenty-Four

Why did it seem like Hannah had stepped out on a ledge and looked down to see she'd somehow ended up outside a window on the seventieth floor of a high-rise in a bustling downtown area?

Not that she'd ever been on the seventieth floor of anything, but the sense of one wrong step signaling a very big fall wouldn't abate, and the look on Mac's face wasn't helping.

"Mac?" she whispered. "Should I be asking you what's wrong? Who called all those times? Do you recognize the number?"

Mac stared at the phone still clutched in her fingers as if he'd never seen it before, nor did he make a single move as if he meant to take it from her.

"I don't recognize the number," he murmured in a voice that sounded far away. "Because it's not my phone."

She cocked her head, taking in his beautiful face and the shadows that had sprung up in his eyes. "What? Of course it is. I picked it up from your bedside table myself. I heard it ringing from the kitchen and I was going to ignore it. But they kept calling, and well, I'm sorry, but it was annoying."

Was that the problem? He was upset she'd gone into his room to retrieve the phone? Obviously he'd left the ringer on, which she personally found a little unusual, but some people did that because they were expecting a call and didn't want to miss it. If that wasn't the case, why leave the ringer on? And forget to take the phone with you?

"You don't understand, Hannah." Mac sucked in a deep breath, still not looking at her, his gaze locked on the phone screen. "It's not my phone. It's Owen's. I didn't want to tell you this way, but honestly, there was never going to be a good time to come clean."

"Come clean?" she whispered as something clutched at her lungs until she couldn't breathe—and she didn't even know what these words were that Mac was saying to her. Only that oxygen didn't exist in this place. "What are you talking about? How can it be Owen's phone but not be your phone?"

"Because I'm not Owen, Hannah," he said. "He's my brother. My twin brother."

A taut thread wrapped around her heart and yanked, slicing into the tender parts as she registered the truth of his statement in one irrevocable flash. Her soul knew it instantly. Of *course* he wasn't Owen. That explained everything.

Even so, in the next moment, inexplicably, denial rose to her lips. "No. That's not possible."

"It's not probable. But it's absolutely possible." His lips didn't lift at what might have been a joke in another life where this wasn't happening.

The man in front of her wasn't Owen. How could the man in front of her not be Owen?

Twin, he'd said. Her ex-husband had a brother he'd never mentioned. A keening sound hummed in her throat, and she choked it back because Coltons didn't fall apart when someone ripped the very fabric of their existence in two.

"I don't understand." *Good*. Firm. Her voice didn't really even crack. Too much, anyway. "Who are you if you aren't Owen?"

Like that was the most important question she could be asking here.

Oh, dear Lord. She'd slept with this man, and she didn't know his name. Actually, names constituted critical information all at once. She wasn't that woman, who fell into bed with a man she didn't know...except she had done exactly that.

Because he'd lied to her.

"I'm Mac, Hannah," he said softly, as if he'd sensed that she'd gone to a very dark place. "That part was always true."

"No," she said with a half laugh. A very unamused one at that. "No, you are not Mac. Mac is the name of the man who came into my life and clicked all the pieces into place. Mac is the guy I trust and who trusts me too. Mac is Lucy's father."

Her eyelid slammed close as she internalized that. Let it roll around inside and cut her and make her bleed a bit more. She'd let a stranger into her house and into her bed and into her *daughter's life*.

"Yes," he countered with quiet fierceness. "That is who I am. I'm Mac, short for Mackenzie. It's what they call me at the precinct."

"The...the *precinct*? Is that what you just said? You're a *cop*?" Why that struck her so hard the wrong way in the midst of everything else, she couldn't say. But this whole conversation bordered on ridiculous anyway, so she rolled her fingers, steeling herself. "Come on. Start talking. I need to hear everything else right now, whoever you are. Where is Owen, by the way? Does he know you're here? Was it his idea?"

Owen's twin. That much was obvious. One she hadn't even known existed. Didn't twins love to tell people they had a clone walking around? No, not the one she'd married and definitely not the one standing in her kitchen.

The Mackenzie brothers liked to switch places and dupe a stupid, stupid woman into falling for them. Not once, but twice.

What was left of her heart rolled over and then fell into ash somewhere near her ballet flats.

"Hannah, Owen is dead," Mac told her, his mouth hardening into a line. "He was murdered. I came to Owl Creek to investigate."

It hit her then. The million-dollar question. "You never forgot a blessed thing. You don't actually have amnesia, do you?"

She'd tacked a question mark on the end, but she knew already, even before he shook his head.

Oh, for the love of Pete. No wonder he'd kissed her like it was the first time. No wonder she had the sense she'd never touched this man, as if she'd been gifted something rare and precious, like a real second chance that actually felt very much like a first chance with a man who had been reborn. That's how stupid she was.

Only Hannah Colton could fall for a trick like this. She'd left her brain in her other coat and never bothered to retrieve it, obviously.

"Why?" she whispered. "Why would you do this to me? To Lucy? Was this all a game?"

He didn't reach for her and the distance between them spoke volumes. It was a testament to how hard and fast she'd fallen for him that the absence of his touch felt like a layer of skin had been ripped off.

"It was never a game." He shook his head. "It was an accident. Or rather *the* accident. I woke up in the hospital and found out the sheriff had unwittingly gifted me the perfect cover to gather hard evidence against whoever killed my brother. It was never my plan. I just went with it."

"Is that supposed to make it better? You're a liar *and* an opportunist. I see." She folded her hands over her stomach, right where it hurt the worst. "You should have told me the truth a long time ago."

At least then she would have had a chance to stop the train before it left the station. Now it was too late. She knew what it felt like to be loved by this man. And it was *painful* to find out the nirvana she'd found with Mac was all a flimsy house of cards.

"I still don't know your name," she whispered, terrified the keening sound was going to start up again.

"Archer," he murmured. "Archer Declan Mackenzie. I... you can still call me Mac."

"No, I'm fairly certain I cannot," she said with more wryness than she would have expected to be possible. The name Mac was so wrapped up in other indescribable things that she just didn't think she could force her tongue to make the word.

Archer. That didn't feel right either. It was even more foreign and now she regretted asking.

Deep breath. There was so much more conversation that needed to happen, but her energy level had started to flag. How much more of this was she going to have to take?

"Just for fun—keeping in mind that none of this is actually fun and also that I don't know how much I'll believe— but why are you telling me all of this now? You didn't have to. You could have jetted back to wherever you came from and never breathed a word about any of this."

He nodded as if he approved of the segue. "I could have. I could have made a decision to tell you sooner, but I thought I was protecting you. The less you knew, the better."

The snort came out automatically as she processed that. "Protecting me from what? Knowing the truth?"

"Hannah."

His voice came out a touch flat, but it was enough for her to realize he was struggling with his emotions. Because she'd started picking up on his subtle cues over the last few weeks. It was something she'd rather have not become an expert in, but wishing she hadn't jumped in with Mac—Archer, rather…and no, that would never stop being weird—didn't make it go away.

Owen had never been like that. He wore his emotions right out in front where everyone could see them and be forced to deal with them. Overly dramatic to the core. Everything had always been about Owen.

He and his brother were nothing alike. Stupid. The theme of the day. Of course this man wasn't Owen, and the fact that he'd had to *tell her* was sobering.

She'd seen what she'd wanted to see. A man who had changed. One who had fit the narrative in her head, who had finally figured out what he'd missed by leaving, who had made a conscious choice to be involved in her life and Lucy's.

Except he wasn't Owen. Owen hadn't made those choices.

And one tiny little corner of her heart had room to be utterly grateful that she at least hadn't been monumentally stupid enough to fall for Owen again.

No, she'd made a whole new set of mistakes with the wrong Mackenzie twin.

"I know it doesn't make a bit of difference, but I'm sorry it happened this way, Hannah," he said. "But the things going on outside of this house are real and dangerous. Someone killed Owen, and it wasn't an accident. Neither was the car crash that put me in the hospital."

It hit her then. Owen was dead. The steel in his brother's voice convinced her, even as she had a few brain cells left to question whether he was actually telling the truth. Head-First Hannah needed to be in the driver's seat for a good long while.

"If I google it, will I find evidence to support your claim that Owen is dead? I mean, as far as I knew, he had no family. Maybe you're one of those people who finds their doppelgänger online and poses as him to scam people out of money."

Oh my, was she in danger *inside* this house? Her heart rate shot through the roof. She had no assurance that Archer—Mac—wasn't the one who had searched through her things.

Dang it. He was still Mac in her heart and she couldn't seem to make herself transition to calling him Archer.

"There's an obituary online if you search for the *Las Vegas Sun*. Also, you can look up death records for Clark County and order a copy for yourself if you would like. I would recommend it as Lucy will be entitled to his effects, but I'll take care of transferring everything the department is aware of over to her as soon as I'm able to get back home."

Home. In Las Vegas. Where he'd return to, but not as Lucy's father—as her uncle. It was baffling to her that he'd played his part as a devoted father so well and easily when Lucy wasn't even his biological child.

But then, Owen was her biological father and he'd never cared one whit about reading her stories. A migraine threatened, the likes of which she hadn't had in some time. Not since Mac had stormed into her life.

Head aching, she ignored it in favor of verifying everything Mac had said. Her internet searches came up exactly as he said they would, and while a really savvy criminal could probably do some kind of fake website thing, it would have to be a pretty elaborate setup for no reason she could think of.

But that was the problem, right? She wasn't a criminal

and therefore had no expertise in all the reasons why someone would have posed as their own twin brother in order to gain access to a family. To charm his way into her heart without even trying. To fight with her over who got to put Lucy to bed.

"I still don't understand why you did this," she whispered. "What possible reason could have been good enough in your mind to scam us into believing you were Owen?"

Mac lifted his hands. "The people Owen was involved with are dangerous, Hannah. They ran me off the road on my way here. I do think they meant to leave me for dead, but I'm a little bit better of a driver than they'd counted on. I didn't know about Lucy, either, for the record. We'll circle back to that huge investigative miss on my part later. I couldn't undo the fact that everyone was calling me Owen when I woke up. It seemed like a gift that I shouldn't pass up, especially when I realized there were links between the criminal organization I know in my gut ordered the hit on Owen and the Ever After Church."

Oh, so this *could* get worse. Hannah's vision tunneled and went black. For her next trick, she'd hit the floor. But Mac's strong hands caught her by the forearms, holding her up. That was not okay. But neither did she think she could wrench away without her knees buckling, and if she fainted, he'd probably just catch her.

What was wrong with her that her heart soared at the thought?

"Hannah?" Mac murmured. "Are you okay?"

She blinked, and it turned out she was in his arms after all. Something was definitely wrong with her because it still felt like she fit there. "Not even a little bit."

Mac didn't release her either, choosing to tighten his grip. "I'm sorry. It's my fault. I should have trusted you with the truth a long time ago, but I wasn't sure... I am now, no question. But you have to understand that I didn't know why Owen never told you about his family. He was fully aware I'm a forensic analyst for the Vegas PD. I couldn't be sure you weren't working with him. At first. I know now."

Hannah sucked in a breath and then another until her vision cleared enough to steady her knees. There was an odd ring of truth in the idea that Mac had suspected her of something nefarious, solely because of her association with Owen.

With one last cleansing breath, she regained her feet and stepped out of the odd paradox that had engulfed her inside of Mac's embrace—a weird mix of being so angry with him but still having the immediate reaction of relief, of *thank goodness he's here.*

"Owen was involved with big-time criminals, wasn't he?" she asked.

But it wasn't really a question when it was obvious that's where all his money had come from—now that she thought about it. Current-Day Hannah had a bit more wisdom and a lot more practice at reading between the lines. Lucy was Owen's daughter after all, with his wicked sharp intellect and a keen sense of how to use it to get what she wanted.

Mac nodded, his expression serious but still devoid of anything approaching the tenderness she'd become so accustomed to seeing there, especially when he looked at Lucy. Could he have faked all of that? Sure. But she didn't think he'd been acting.

Not that she'd call herself a great judge of character or anything. *Ugh.* This whole situation reeked of a Hannah Special, one her brothers would have a heyday with.

"He was, yes. Money launderers," Mac confirmed. "The same ones I'm pretty sure the Ever After Church is using. It wouldn't surprise me to learn Owen was the go-between."

And there it was. All roads had led to this. And here she'd been berating herself for letting Mac distract her from her own investigation into the church. It was almost laughable. They should have been working together the whole time.

"That's who you think has been searching the house," she said with a grim nod. "The money launderers. Because if you wondered whether Owen had involved me in his schemes, someone else would too."

Mac's lips lifted into a brief smile. "I definitely should have been talking to you about this sooner."

A noise near the door distracted them both. A man stood there. A stranger she'd never seen before. And he held a gun.

"This is all so sweet," he snarled. "But I don't think I can stand to listen to another word of this gibberish. I need the key to Owen Mackenzie's safety deposit box now, and you're going to get it for me."

That's when he leveled the gun at Hannah's head and cocked it.

Chapter Twenty-Five

Everything slowed in that moment. Hannah's throat froze as Mac stepped in front of her, his hands raised. Talking. Mac was talking to the man.

But more importantly, he was standing *in front of her*. Shielding her from the potential bullet that the man might fire at any second. What was he doing? He wasn't bulletproof.

Her heart squeezed as he backed up a few tiny steps. Closer to her. To provide even more of a cover. This was Mac being heroic. And stupid.

"Let's just calm down," Mac said, his voice even, but it was also a tone she'd never heard before. "You don't want to do this."

"Oh, you're right, Mac," the man with the gun said in a singsong voice. "I forgot. I *don't* want to do this. Why didn't I think of that before I came in here? Shut up. I'm talking to the girl."

Girl? He meant *her*? She almost couldn't swallow the hysterical giggle that threatened to bubble to the surface, but her tight throat wouldn't have let it go anyway.

"She's not talking to you," Mac shot back before Hannah could figure out what she was supposed to say in response when none of this made any sense. "Whatever you want to discuss, I'm the guy."

"Sure, whatever. Fine. You get the key then, and we'll call it a day."

The stranger motioned with his gun toward the back of the house. Hannah and Lucy's wing. Because he knew that's the direction they should go to get this mysterious key he kept referencing. Or was it merely a throwaway gesture?

"What key?" Mac asked, reading her mind. That was her question too.

"Don't play innocent," the man said with a smirk. "You've been here all this time getting cozy with the lady of the house. You know where it is."

"I don't," he countered immediately.

Hannah one hundred percent believed he didn't know where this key was, since it wasn't something she had any knowledge of either. But on the heels of everything else, it wasn't a stretch to assume he had been playing her to get close so he could find it.

At least, that was the narrative her head kept repeating. Her heart stubbornly refused to get in on that action. After all, he'd stepped in front of her to face down a man with a gun. Willingly.

"What is this key you keep mentioning?" Hannah croaked out the question as she peeked around Mac's shoulder, the first time she'd spoken since she'd first noticed the gun in the stranger's hand. "We can't help you if we don't know what you're talking about."

She tried to gauge exactly who this guy was that they were dealing with. Midforties, probably. Average height and build. He had a nondescript look about him, as if he'd tried extra hard to blend into the background, but his gaze was sharp. Probably he didn't miss much.

The guy rolled his eyes. "Nice try. We both know you're in on it. Why do you think Mac showed up here in the first place? It's not because of the side benefits, though I'm sure he's enjoying those too."

"That's enough, Barnes." Mac's voice whipped out, low and lethal.

Wait—he knew the guy's name? Hannah stared at the back of Mac's head as it registered that the stranger had referenced him by name as well, but she'd assumed he'd heard it during their conversation. Now she wasn't so sure.

"You know each other?" she whispered, but didn't need his nod to put it together in that moment.

He'd told her the other people at his precinct called him Mac. The guy on the other side of the trigger must work with him. Was Barnes a cop too? Oh, man. That was bad for many reasons, but first and foremost because it meant he was probably a pretty good shot.

Mac's heroism suddenly felt a lot more like a suicidal move. He'd known all of this and still stepped in front of her.

"You want to know why I came to Owl Creek?" Mac asked in the sudden silence. "You're right. It was because of Hannah. I thought she might know something about Big Mike and his organization. Silly of me when I could have just strolled into the bullpen and chatted you up about it."

"Yeah, silly. This thing where you're trying to keep me talking in hopes of distracting me is not going to work." Barnes motioned with his gun again. "I've been waiting patiently for you to do your job and we see how that's turned out. Now we're going to do things differently. Starting with me shooting your girlfriend if that key is not in my hand in fifteen seconds."

Barnes started counting and Hannah's body went into fight or flight mode. Both at the same time, unfortunately, so her muscles had no idea what to do. And she was still behind Mac.

The kitchen island beckoned, where she had more than

one cooking implement that could be used as a weapon. It made her heart hurt to think about using her beautiful Mauviel copper pasta pot as a blunt instrument.

She would do it regardless. This was life or death.

The pot was behind her though. At least eighteen or twenty steps, which would mean she'd have to move away from her cover and dash out of the mudroom before Barnes could level his gun and pull the trigger.

She had to try. Using Mac as a human shield sat wrong with her anyway.

Mac raised his hands higher and took a step toward Barnes. "I can't produce a key I know nothing about. Stop counting and let's discuss this. Brainstorm. We can figure this out together since you clearly have information that I don't. What makes you think there's a safety deposit box, much less a key that Hannah would have?"

Barnes stopped counting, which did wonders for the pulse point hammering in Hannah's throat.

She edged toward the island. One tiny shuffle. Then another.

"I'm starting to think you're even less good at your job than I was expecting," Barnes snarled. "That, or you're a very good actor, which is more likely since you fooled Blondy here into thinking you were Owen. Nice touch, by the way. If it had worked. So let's pretend you're telling the truth and you have no clue that Mackenzie sent his ex-wife a package three days before he met an unfortunate end. Does it jog your memory for me to mention that fact? Maybe make you think twice about trusting her?"

The blood in Hannah's head rushed out, leaving her feeling woozy.

"That's not right," she managed to croak out. "Owen didn't send me anything. I haven't heard from him in years. I don't have any idea what you're talking about."

She'd have remembered something so explosive as that.

Especially since Barnes had just made Mac's point about why he wouldn't have immediately trusted her with the truth. Had he thought Owen sent her something too? Everything had flipped over on its head instantly and she needed to sit down. Or duck her face under the faucet and let a stream of water cool her burning cheeks.

"Or, you're lying because you were in on it and want the money for yourself," Barnes countered conversationally as if they were having a lovely chat about the weather. "This is why we're doing things my way now. Waiting around for Mac to do his job got old. Neither one of you Mackenzie brothers ended up being all that smart in the end."

"Is that why you killed Owen?" Mac asked in the same conversational tone. "Because he wasn't smart enough to see the double-cross coming?"

This man was Owen's murderer?

Hannah peeked out from behind Mac's shoulder, desperate all at once to see how Mac's accusation struck Barnes. Was it true? Would Barnes confess to them right here, right now?

Barnes just laughed, which told her more than he might have realized. Namely, that he was unhinged.

"Look at you trying to change my mind about how truly dumb you are," Barnes taunted. "He died because he tried to make off with Big Mike's money. No other reason."

"You mean he succeeded," Mac corrected evenly. "Or else you wouldn't be here. You think the money is in this safety deposit box?"

Obviously. Hannah didn't need to see Barnes to know that Mac had just pieced it all together. And done the impossible—put her firmly on his side. He'd been telling the truth earlier. Owen was dead. Killed by this dirty cop who must be working with the money launderers Mac mentioned.

Mac couldn't have created a better exhibit A for why he'd thought she might be in danger. She hadn't fully bought into his story before, but there was no way she could deny now that he'd acted according to the information he had in the moment.

The keening sound rose up in her throat again, but she couldn't figure out fast enough what part of this situation had cut her so deeply. The fact that Mac had so easily stepped between her and a gun—or that her daughter's father was indeed well and truly dead? Owen would never have a chance to change his mind and get to know the special little girl he'd helped create.

Maybe she should be most concerned about the gun still trained on them both. Right this second anyway.

One thing she did know for certain. She and Mac needed to have another very long conversation, this time with nothing between them but raw honesty. *After* they'd removed the threat of death and additional criminals darkening her doorstep, of course.

"You killed my daughter's father," Hannah screeched and took advantage of the stunned silence to grab an umbrella from the rack to her right, launching it at Barnes's face.

Mac sprang toward the threat, instantly taking advantage of Barnes's flinch. A shot rang out, shoving Hannah's heart into her throat.

Both men fought over the weapon. In an impressive show of strength, Mac wrenched the gun from the other guy's hand, pointing it at him. Just like that, Barnes sank to the ground, holding up his hands in a similar pose to Mac's a moment ago.

Hannah forced herself to breathe.

"This is not over," Barnes announced succinctly. "Big Mike's organization is vast and clever. Someone else will be along soon to pick up where I left off."

"Yeah, but it will give me a great deal of satisfaction to know that you'll be rotting in jail when that happens," Mac told him, and without taking his eyes off Barnes, he called over his shoulder. "Hannah, can you do me a favor and retrieve the bag from my room? It's the one by the door."

Dutifully, she dashed to his wing and found the bag in question, wondering if she should call 911 on the way back. But given the fact that there were already two cops in her house, she wasn't sure the addition of more would help. Better probably to let Mac handle it. And wasn't that a kicker to realize all of her anger from earlier had drained.

When she handed him his bag, he pulled two long black strips of something—plastic?—from its depths and then passed the gun to her. Wait, what was she supposed to do with this?

She nearly bobbled the weapon, but Mac's encouraging nod steadied her hand.

"Just keep it pointed at our friend here and everything will be fine," Mac advised her. "Pull the trigger if he moves the wrong way."

Efficiently, Mac yanked the guy's hands behind him and pulled the plastic tight around his wrists. Oh, it was a zip tie. That was ingenious. Mac levered Barnes to his feet and took possession of the gun again, thankfully, shoving it into his prisoner's ribs. Then, he marched him out of the house, calling over his shoulder that he'd be right back.

In a flash, Mac returned, gun still in his hand, but as soon as he cleared the mudroom door, he clicked a few things and then stuck it in the waistband of his pants at the small of his back, his expression grave as he crossed the mudroom floor in two long strides.

"Hannah, are you okay?" he asked, concern a physical force that nearly overwhelmed her.

"There's a bullet hole in my wall," she said and heaved a

shuddery breath. "But I'm physically fine if that's what you mean. What did you do with that guy?"

"He's cooling his heels in the storage shed." Mac's smile was fleeting but it felt like a flower blooming in her chest. "Forgive me for not asking first and for borrowing your key. I called Fletcher to come sort this out since it's a local matter of armed breaking and entering at the moment, but I'm sure we can add some other charges once my guys do their investigation into Barnes's ties to Big Mike's organization."

"Do I want to know who Big Mike is?"

"If you do, I'm happy to tell you anything you ask. No more secrets between us."

Mac held up his hands in much the same way he had earlier, when protecting her from Barnes. In fact, he'd been amazing under pressure. Calm. Authoritative. He'd literally saved her from a ruthless gunman in her own home.

This was a man she wanted to get to know better. What a strange paradox to already have such intimate ties to someone who was a virtual stranger. But then again, did he really feel like one? He was looking down at her through the same eyes as before. She'd pushed her fingers through that same hair falling down on his forehead.

Now that she knew he wasn't Owen, she could see subtle differences between him and his brother that she'd attributed to aging and maybe her own faulty memory. But that didn't change the fact that he *wasn't* Owen—and that actually awarded way more points in his favor than she'd have said earlier.

She hadn't been so colossally stupid as to fall for Owen twice. But who had she fallen for? *That* was the secret she wanted to unravel. Except that sounded a lot like Heart-First Hannah talking.

All of this was aggravating her migraine. "Maybe we should focus on this key that guy kept talking about."

Mac nodded. "It would be best to have that squared away. That must be what whoever searched the house was looking for. Are you sure you didn't get any packages? Maybe Owen didn't include a return address so you didn't know it came from him."

Shaking her head, she started to deny it again when something tickled at the back of her brain, coming into focus sharply. "When did Owen die? What was the date?"

"In August. The seventeenth. Why? What do you remember?"

She bit back an incredulous laugh. "He didn't send the package to me. He sent it to Lucy."

That's what this was all about? The mysterious package that had shown up here addressed to Lucy right before school had started for the year? Hannah had assumed Wade sent it via a third-party shipping company that had forgotten the card, but he denied it when she asked. At the time, she'd blown it off as her brother being cagey because she'd literally just spoken to him the day before about how much he spoiled Lucy.

"What was in it?" Mac asked.

"You're not going to believe this." She motioned him into Lucy's room and cast about until she spied the familiar brown fur, snagging it and holding it up for Mac to see. "Mr. Fluffers. That's what was in the package."

Dawning disbelief drifting over his face, Mac sank onto the bed and nodded to the stuffed dog. "Feel around inside him and see if you can tell if there's anything there. We can do a surgical extraction to preserve him as much as possible if you find something."

Good grief, could the man be any more earnest about saving Lucy's favorite stuffed animal from being destroyed? Her heart wasn't so lucky—he'd reached inside and squeezed it without moving a muscle.

Hannah perched next to him, carefully running the stuffing between her thumb and forefinger, her pulse thudding in her throat. Nothing, nothing, nothing…*something*. The barest prick against the pad of her finger.

"I think…this is it. It's here," she told Mac breathlessly as she worked the hard thing a little closer to where the dog's head attached to his body. "I have a seam ripper that will do the trick."

In seconds, she'd retrieved it from her sewing kit and sliced a few stitches until the silver tip appeared in the opening.

"Hannah, you found it," Mac murmured. "You know what this means, right?"

"No more secrets." She held up the key and then handed it to him. "And this means I trust you with it. I'm angry you lied to me, but it doesn't erase everything that happened between us."

"Hannah." Mac shut his eyes and when he opened them, she no longer thought he might sweep her into his arms. Instead, the iciest chill seeped into her bones as he stared at her. "I didn't tell you the truth because I thought there was a happily-ever-after in store for us. I told you because there's not."

Chapter Twenty-Six

Paperwork might very well be the death of Archer. And if it wasn't that, the huge hole inside where Hannah and Lucy used to be would probably do the trick eventually.

He hoped it would be sooner rather than later. Because being without them sucked.

The look on Hannah's face when he'd told her he was going back to Las Vegas had nearly ended him then. But he needed her to be safe and he was not the man to ensure that, not anymore.

The best way to draw every goon away from Owl Creek was to lie to Hannah and tell her that he didn't care anything about her. That they had no future—well, that part wasn't a lie. He didn't get nice things and he'd long ago accepted that.

Especially after Hannah told him he couldn't be Mac to her any longer. That she'd trusted him and he'd broken that irrevocably. He could still hear those words echoing in his head, neatly severing everything he'd held dear.

Of course that was what had happened. What would always be the result of his actions. Loss. He'd started out his relationship with Hannah and Lucy with a lie, so it seemed fitting to end it with one, especially since he'd had to shut down the conversation she'd started. The one that felt like she'd been about to insist they talk it out.

He didn't deserve to talk about anything.

Besides, he couldn't do forensics on the key from Hannah's house without any of the equipment in his lab. What would he do, bake its origins out of it?

Funny, Owl Creek still had snow on the ground, but in Vegas, it was early spring already with the days getting longer. Yet the place he'd called home for years felt like Antarctica. So cold he could hardly stand it. And his condo had zero warmth even with the heat set on seventy-eight degrees.

That's why he'd spent most of his time in the lab at his office, Willis sulking around as if afraid Archer might bite him given the opportunity. Yeah, okay. His mood hadn't been the best, but this was a forensic investigation, not a pool party. They needed to trace down what bank this key had come from. Owen clearly had expected to drop by Owl Creek and retrieve it himself, so he hadn't bothered to communicate this information to anyone.

Maureen, the department coordinator, knocked on the door of Archer's lab and jerked her head toward the front. "Visitor for you."

Hannah. Archer's heart did a slow dive before he could catch it. And then he had to get hold of himself. Hannah wouldn't have come to Las Vegas to see Elvis Presley back from the dead, let alone to see Archer.

The person waiting for him wasn't a woman anyway— it was a man in his midfifties who had *cop* written all over him, but the stilted kind who worked a desk and had for years.

"Bob Mitchell. Internal Affairs," he said and stuck out his hand for Archer to shake. "Wanted to catch you up on the charges against Jonathan Barnes since you're likely going to be tapped to testify."

Archer nodded. "Appreciate it."

"At the moment, we're looking at attempted kidnapping,

false imprisonment, assault with a deadly weapon and official misconduct. Would be nice to tie it up with a bow and add federal money-laundering charges or collusion."

"You haven't found a link yet between Barnes and Big Mike Rossi," Archer guessed, tempering his frown. That wasn't surprising. Barnes would have been smart enough to cover his tracks internally. "Will my testimony allow a judge to at least issue a warrant to look closer at Big Mike?"

"Unlikely." Bob tapped the tablet under his arm. "What you relayed in the affidavit is not a confession. Barnes never admitted to pulling the trigger on your brother, nor that he had any significant dealings with Big Mike. We need something else."

The money.

That was the link to end all links. He knew in his gut that Owl Creek lay at the heart of this. Owen had been headed for his former digs, no question, especially since he'd sent the key ahead. But only to keep on the down-low? Or was there more to it—like the presence of the Ever After Church and Markus Acker?

Somehow the money would tie all of this together. Finding it had just gotten a lot more critical.

Mitchell chatted at him for a few more minutes, but Archer didn't mistake this visit for what it was. Apparently, IA had bubkes on Barnes other than what amounted to a few years in prison for whatever they could get on him internally—misuse of police equipment and data, etc.—plus the assault charges from when he'd held Archer and Hannah at gunpoint. Mitchell was unofficially asking him to get more, which he technically couldn't do because Archer had already been told not to investigate.

For the first time, he started to wonder if Barnes wasn't the only one in the Las Vegas MPD with ties to Big Mike.

And if Archer might be in a little bit more of a precarious position than he'd assumed by coming back home.

Ironic that the biggest threat had come from an inside job. Barnes had been feeding Big Mike information the entire time. In fact, it wouldn't surprise him to learn that everyone had known he wasn't Owen the entire time.

This was far from over.

He closeted himself in the lab, kicking Willis out just in case someone came by looking for trouble, and locked the door behind his assistant. No point in taking chances this close to the end.

A few hours later, he had nothing. Only the serial number on the key, which didn't match any of the known records he had access to via the LVMPD's web of information. Granted, he'd limited the searches to the surrounding areas. Surely Owen hadn't carried five million dollars in cash to a bank across the country.

But then again, it was Owen. Who knew what his brother had been thinking?

He stared at the key, running a finger over the serial number, thinking it looked vaguely familiar, like he'd seen the number before. Likely just a function of having keyed it into searches so frequently over the last few hours.

It kept niggling at him though. And then he remembered. He'd seen it in Owen's phone once, fleetingly. Archer grabbed the phone, rolling his eyes at all the game apps and sheer disorganization of everything. Where had he seen this number? In a note app? No, nothing there, though how anyone would be able to find an iota of useful information in this mess was beyond him.

Contacts. It had been in the contacts section, a weird anomaly where the phone number had seemed too long but Archer had blown it off as possibly a foreign configuration that he wasn't readily familiar with. But he saw it for what it was now—the serial number of the key and a name. B.D. Starke. A quick Google Search had him nearly dancing out of his seat.

B.D. Starke wasn't a person. It was a bank. In Conners, right down the street from the hospital, no less. Because of course he'd been a stone's throw from the money the whole time, while he'd been busy faking amnesia and falling for his brother's ex-wife.

ARCHER ROLLED INTO Owl Creek near lunchtime, still questioning the wisdom of turning right instead of left to go to Conners. It was like he couldn't help himself. He was so close to Hannah. Was it so bad to want to cruise by her house and make sure she was okay? And maybe to see her for a second, just to assure himself the brief shining few moments she'd been his weren't a figment of his imagination.

He'd eventually like to call Lucy and tell her he was thinking about her. But his relationship with the little girl he wanted nothing more than to call his daughter might be a casualty of his bad decisions too. It was Hannah's choice, not his, and it was too soon. For a lot of reasons—first and foremost that he didn't know which direction the danger might come from.

He'd chosen this path and now he had to walk it.

What had Hannah told Lucy about Archer's absence? Had she caustically instructed the girl to never think of him again? Coldly told Lucy that Archer wasn't her father after all and that he'd lied about it for far longer than any decent person would have? Because all of that was true.

He only meant to swing by the house and just…make sure it was still standing. Maybe peer through the window and give his heart one good long last look.

Except Lucy was playing in the snow outside by the driveway, Princess Misty chasing snowballs as her mistress threw them. And Hannah stood next to them, laughing. Until she turned her head and caught his gaze through the windshield.

And then it was too late. It would be weird to drive off as if he hadn't seen her, his tail between his legs, wouldn't it? So he rolled to a stop and sat there for a minute, completely out of his element.

Hannah lifted her hand and waved, somehow conveying a bundle of nerves and unease in that one spare movement. Lucy had no such reservations. Her face split into a huge grin and she raced toward the car, calling, "Daddy, Daddy, Daddy!" at the top of her lungs.

The prick behind his eyelids nearly undid him, but he wasn't about to waste the positive energy, so he flung open the door and caught Lucy as she launched herself into his arms. Everything righted itself inside as he breathed in little girl scent mixed with snow.

"Mr. Fluffers had surgery and we baked cupcakes to make him feel better," she announced, settling into his embrace as if she'd done it a million times. "And Mama let me take Princess Misty to school for show-and-tell. She was so good, my teacher said I could bring her back. And—"

"Whoa," Hannah said with a laugh and pulled Lucy free, setting her on her feet with a tiny push toward the house. "Can you give me a minute to talk to your father before he goes deaf? Take Princess Misty inside and watch *Peppa Pig* until I come in to make lunch."

Dutifully, Lucy waved at Archer and darted off, leaving him standing there with his brain buzzing. He shouldn't be here. But something akin to hope exploded in his chest and he couldn't squelch it. No matter how much he knew he should.

"You didn't tell her," he said. It wasn't a question because obviously she hadn't. Why hadn't she told Lucy the truth?

"Tell her what?" Hannah's cheeks were rosy with the cold

but he barely felt the temperature as her face turned up towards his. "That you had to go away for a few days but that you'd be back? I did. And you did."

"You're sugarcoating it," he muttered and shook his head, trying to untangle what he *should* say with what he wanted to say. "You shouldn't call me her father in her presence like that."

"Why on earth not?" she said, clearly incredulous. "You've been more a father to her in the last few weeks than her biological one was in the whole of either of their lives."

"That doesn't make it true." It also didn't make his heart stop hurting any less to hear her praise. Because it didn't matter if he was good at it or wanted to be Lucy's father with a fierceness that eclipsed anything he'd ever yearned for before. Except Hannah.

She stared at him for a second. "You told me you were in this for the long haul. Did you mean that?"

"I said that when I thought… It doesn't matter," he told her brusquely, aching over the words he'd meant but couldn't honor. "I can't be Lucy's father."

Not now. Not when he'd made them a target by coming here. The whole time he'd been playing house, he'd shone a spotlight of attention on both of these people he loved. On all of Hannah's family. He'd fooled no one with his charade except himself.

"I'm trying to understand what's happening, Mac," Hannah said, wrapping her arms around herself. "Why did you come back if it's not because of Lucy? Spoiler alert. There is a wrong answer."

He started to respond with a comment about making sure they were okay and it got caught in his throat. She'd called him Mac. Casually. As if maybe she'd said some things she didn't mean in the heat of the moment and he shouldn't be so quick to dismiss the forces that had driven him here.

He didn't deserve her forgiveness. But he wanted it more than anything.

"I don't know," he choked out hoarsely. "I didn't mean to." That much at least was honest.

"You didn't mean to pose as Owen either, to hear you tell it," she said, her voice driving into him with staccato beats the equivalent power of a nail gun. "Maybe it's time to take some credit for your actions. Do what you mean to do."

Like sweep her into his arms and tell her he loved her? That would ruin things faster than anything else. He stood there, running a hand through his hair, unable to believe that there was any chance Hannah could love him back. Those scales wouldn't balance in his head no matter what he did because at the end of the day, she didn't really know him.

If she had any feelings for him whatsoever, she'd developed them when she'd thought he was Owen. He'd never been himself around Hannah.

"I came by because I couldn't stay away," he murmured, his throat aching with it. "I found the bank. The one that goes to the key. It's in Conners. That's where I should be but instead I'm here, wishing for things that I lost the chance to have before being given the chance to have them."

Her expression softened. "Who said that? Not me. You're the one who left, and I gave you that space because I can't force you to be here with me and Lucy. There's no magic to this, Mac. Just two people who have a lot of unsaid things between them because both of them are scared."

"I'm not—" *scared*. But that was the one lie that he couldn't seem to spit out, apparently. "What are you scared of?"

Better. Focus on her instead of the myriad of emotions rioting in his chest. Cold seeped into all the cracks of his body as he waited for her response.

"You," she murmured. "Us. That you're such a good and

decent human being that you won't take this chance that's been given to both of us, solely because your sense of propriety won't let you move past the way we met."

"I don't understand." His fingers rubbed at a raw place near his temples that had sprung up from the sheer friction of the repeat motion. "There is no us. You never—when you asked me to promise I wouldn't walk away from Lucy, that was the extent of what you wanted from me. A father for your daughter. And I was happy to take it."

"Were you?" she countered with raised eyebrows. "Okay. That's fair. I never asked you if you were interested in more. My mistake."

"Wait."

He grabbed her hand and drew her closer so he could see the things swimming in her green eyes for himself. The truth. Whatever that truth happened to be. There needed to be a lot more of it between them.

And yeah, it was terrifying. For more reasons than one.

"You don't even know who I am," he told her, and it came out a lot more like an accusation than he'd intended.

But she didn't seem overly bothered by it. Just shook her head and let her lips lift into a small smile. "Because you hid behind your amnesia. Behind Owen. He's gone now. Let's let him go and take some steps toward whatever this is."

"You could do that?" He stared at her skeptically. "Forgive everything and just…move forward? Get to know each other with nothing else between us?"

"I don't know," she admitted. More honesty. "Owen's ghost has been a part of my life longer than he was. I have some work to do too to banish him, same as you do."

"How do we… Is there a way?" he asked, genuinely perplexed that such a thing could be possible. That he'd be standing here in the snow with a woman struggling to deal with Owen's death the same as he was. "I've been living in

Owen's shadow for a long time. It doesn't feel like such an easy thing to pick up where he left off. Step into his place in this family."

Hannah's smile grew a lot warmer. "Owen never had a place in this family. The spot you filled was one you created."

Well, he wasn't quite sure how that was possible. Owen had far more right to this family than he did. But Owen was gone. Archer was not. And Hannah was saying she was open to seeing what it looked like if he didn't walk away after all. From either Lucy or her.

For the first time in his life, he didn't know how all the pieces fit together. And he wasn't going to have the luxury of stepping back to analyze before plunging in. It scared him. It scared him that Hannah had picked up on his fear. It scared him that none of that was enough to stop him from aching to take this shot.

"I don't know what to do next," he admitted as his heart threw open the doors to the possibility that his story with Hannah and Lucy might not be over.

"You said something about a bank in Conners?"

Chapter Twenty-Seven

Hannah kept trying to sneak glances at Mac as he drove toward Conners, but he kept catching her. How was she supposed to secretly study him if he wouldn't at least pretend not to notice her sweeping his expression for clues as to what was going on inside his stubborn head?

"What?" he murmured, shooting her a small smile.

It was the only kind of smile she could seem to muster too. It was like her heart could only let her be slightly joyful when so much hung in the balance. Undecided. But there was nothing that could stop her from getting tingles when her arm brushed Mac's against the center console.

"Nothing," she told him, and he let her get away with that for the second time since they'd climbed into his car after dropping Lucy at Wade's.

Her brother had given her the side-eye when he'd seen Mac standing silently behind her, but he hadn't said a blessed word, thank goodness. She'd told her family nothing, so as far as they knew, Mac was still Owen and still slightly suspect in their eyes.

Oh, the irony. When she told them the truth—and she would, pending how much she and Mac decided they needed to know—he'd probably shoot up in their estimation. And he'd been so lost in his own head about owning the blame for lying to her.

Granted, she'd had a full head of steam about it when he'd told her. But she'd had a lot of time to think after he'd gone back to Vegas, and she didn't see another way this whole thing could have unfolded. The problem wasn't whether she could forgive him. It was that he couldn't forgive himself.

And he was the one who had to figure that out.

At the moment, all she could do was come along for the ride.

"You're trying to catalogue the differences between me and Owen," Mac guessed with a lot more insight than she'd have credited.

"I've been doing that since day one," she admitted. "I just didn't know I was."

"Really?" He took his eyes off the road for a brief second as he glanced at her.

"Come on, Mac. You can't be serious."

Where would she even start with the list of things she'd subconsciously internalized that split the two brothers into completely different halves of what looked to be a whole to an uneducated outsider?

But it felt like an evolution of their relationship that she verbalized it for both of their sakes.

"Your face is totally different, for one." She ticked it off on her finger. "You have a kindness that softens the lines. It's in your eyes too. Your voice. Your mannerisms. Owen spent twenty-four seven focused on Owen. That's not something you could have ever hoped to emulate, even with months of practice because it's not who you are."

He pursed his lips. "So you're saying I'm a terrible act

She had to laugh at that. "Yeah, I'm afraid so. A'
when it comes to playing the part of your brother, wh

ably couldn't have told you his daughter's middle name at gunpoint."

It was a sobering reminder that she hadn't meant to introduce. They'd both been held at gunpoint, and she was painfully aware that the dangers hadn't been completely eliminated yet. If even slightly. Whatever they found at this bank in Conners would open the floodgates.

At least she hoped so. Everything hinged on the contents. It had to lead to the Owen exorcism that she and Mac desperately needed. The elimination of the feeling that she still had a target on her back. The fear that whoever Owen had been tangled up with would target her family. All of it could be solved with the key Mac had handed her for safekeeping while he drove his rental car toward Conners.

The place where everything had changed. If she'd known what would be in store for her when she'd walked into that hospital room to visit the man she'd thought was her ex-husband... It was mind-boggling.

"It's Louise," Mac murmured. "I pulled Lucy's birth certificate. Louise is my mother's name."

Speaking of mind-boggling. "Your mother is alive?"

Well, of course she was. Probably Owen's father too, and a host of uncles and other siblings maybe. How selfish of her not to even ask these questions about Lucy's paternal relatives, now that she had exhibit A on how Owen had hidden these parts of himself from her.

And then suggested his mother's name for Lucy's middle name. It was baffling why he'd do that.

"She is. Alive and well and living in Las Vegas. She's going to be thrilled to find out about Lucy."

"You haven't told her yet?" Good. She wasn't the only one still trying to figure all of this out.

Mac shook his head. "I'm investigating Owen's murder

at her request. I figured I should have that solved before I told her anything."

A heavy silence filled the car and Hannah picked at the thread on her seat belt, weighing what to say. "It's going to be tough to remove the specter of Owen, isn't it?"

He flashed her a brief smile as he signaled to go around a slower driver in a minivan. "Hard when you'll see him every time you look at me."

"But I don't, Archer." It was the first time she'd said his real name out loud. She let it settle into the cracks of her heart, filling them. "That's not something I can prevent *you* from thinking about, but I stopped seeing Owen a long time ago. In my head, you're Mac."

Oh. That's why he'd asked her to call him that. Because he knew at some point she'd find out the truth, and it would be very difficult to segue from Owen to something else. Which she appreciated on levels she hadn't fully examined yet. It spoke volumes about his intentions. And they weren't to vanish from her life.

Did he even realize he'd been two steps ahead even back then? He had to. Then why all the hesitation and stoic resolve to stay detached from what she'd so clearly offered—a second chance?

"You loved Owen though," he said simply, this time not looking at her. "That's a difficult thing to get past."

"Well, I can understand that," she said sinking down in her seat, but minimizing her profile didn't stop the barbs from flaying her insides. "I'm not too fond of my decisions on that front either, so I can see how it would be a problem for you—"

"No, Hannah, not a difficult thing for *me* to get past," he corrected gently. "For you. He's the one you married and had a baby with. It's totally understandable that he'd hold a special place in your heart and that I might not measure up."

"Uh, no, Mac, he doesn't." As if. Had she not told him enough times what a loser Owen was? How he'd left her and Lucy, *never* to return? "There's no measuring up you should ever worry about."

He went quiet for a beat. "Then why were you okay with it when I walked away?"

Her mouth fell open and practically cracked at the hinges as missing parts of the big picture came into focus. And the enormous mistake she'd made. "Are you being serious right now? You think I was okay with it? I cried for hours. But you needed that space to sort your head out. I needed that space. So we could both be sure this is real. I love you, Mac. You. Not Owen. *Because* you're not Owen, not in spite of it."

The whole paradox was almost laughable, but she didn't feel like laughing all at once as Mac pulled into the bank parking lot and rolled between the white lines, throwing the car into Park. He turned his whole body to face her, his gaze searching hers with intensity that she hadn't seen since the last time he'd kissed her.

It felt an awful lot like he might do it again and she was not planning to stop him.

"You're in love with me?" he murmured, his fingertips reaching for her cheek with a hesitation that felt almost reverent, as if he couldn't believe he had the latitude to make such a bold move.

She nodded, pushing her jaw into the palm of his hand. "If you sensed any hesitation on my part, it was because I was terrified you'd get your memory back and realize why you'd left in the first place. Finding out you're not the man I was married to is everything to me. And one day, it'll matter to Lucy too. You're the man he should have been but never could be."

Something lifted from her shoulders then—the weight of her eternal debate about whether she should lead with her head or her heart. And of course the answer was both. Intellectually, she knew there would be hiccups, but in her heart, she also knew this was worth it.

Archer Declan Mackenzie was worth it.

And then he did kiss her, unleashing so many unverbalized things between them that she forgot they were in a car, forgot there were ever any problems, forgot her own name. This was what love tasted like, what it felt like under her fingers. *Mac.* The answer to every question, the echo of every heartbeat.

He lifted his lips, and she squeaked in protest.

"We're overdue for some serious repeats of that kiss," he murmured a tad breathlessly and wasn't that glorious, to know she'd been responsible for it. "But first, I need to tell you that I love you too. And that we are in a parking lot, so while I am a huge fan of where your hands are, the locale is maybe not the best one for it."

Laughing, she held up both hands and then cupped his face with them. "We have a safety deposit box to check out and then yes to kissing some more while hashing out logistics, like whether you still want the same side of the bed or not."

His grin lit her up inside as she internalized that it was the first one he'd given her since he'd confessed he wasn't Owen. "Safety deposit box first, yes. And I don't care as long as you're saying you want me to have a place in your life. I meant everything I said when we were pretending I was my brother. I'm in this forever. I want to be Lucy's father, if you're okay with that."

"You already are," she told him softly. "It would be a lie to say differently."

"I'm still not clear on how we got to this point, though," he murmured as he nuzzled her cheek, then her mouth. "You're supposed to be furious. You're not supposed to love me when all I meant to do here was make up for the crappy way Owen treated you."

Was *that* what he'd been doing this whole time? Her heart melted and reknit itself into a whole that felt ten times better now that Mac had a permanent place in it. She drew back and smiled at him. "But that's *why* I love you. After all, you came back."

Somehow they made it out of the car and into the bank before it closed for the day. The clerk led them right back to the vault and pulled out an innocuous-looking safety deposit box, then left them alone for privacy. Sure, there'd been a moment it could have gone the other way when the bank employee had asked for ID, but Mac pulled out Owen's driver's license, and that was that. The last time, God willing, he'd have to pretend to be his brother.

So easy. Easier than she'd expected. It almost didn't seem real, as if she'd wake up and realize all of this had been a dream.

"That was too easy," Mac muttered, reading her mind. "This isn't going to be the answer, is it? It's going to be another dead end. You'll still be in danger, and I'll never be able to sleep until I know for sure that you and Lucy are safe."

"That's why you left," she said with dawning certainty. "You thought you could draw off the heat from Owl Creek if you went back to Vegas."

"The heat?" Mac shot her a grin. "We don't really talk like that. But yes. It was one of many reasons."

They could talk about that later. It didn't matter. Whatever was in this box had led Mac to her and to Lucy. It was a blessing, regardless.

"This is a big box. Right?" She glanced at Mac for verification, who nodded. "This whole time, I've been thinking—what in the world could Owen have put in a safety deposit box when they're so small. But this is an extra-large one. Maybe for a reason."

"Only one way to find out."

Together, they slid the key into the lock and it was moment-of-truth time. Mac lifted the lid. And there it was. Stacks and stacks of money. Hundred-dollar bills in neat piles. Her heart stuttered.

This was real. This was a lot of money. In a flash, any lingering doubt about any of the events that had transpired this far vanished. Mac had made every decision in the interest of keeping people safe. No other reason.

"How much money did he supposedly steal from the money launderers?" she croaked.

"Five million dollars," Mac said grimly and tapped each stack, mouthing numbers as he went. "And that's exactly how much is here if it's hundreds all the way through."

Agape, she stared at him. "You did that math in your head? That might be the sexiest thing I've ever seen in my life."

Mac chuckled, a pleased, but slightly embarrassed, smile gracing his lips. "Lots more where that came from."

Beneath the money, she spied something that wasn't the color of a hundred-dollar bill. Curious, she shifted some of the stacks out of the box and pulled the manila folder free, opening it. And then nearly dropped it when she read the name scattered throughout the paperwork.

"Mac," she whispered and held it out to him. "Is this what I think it is?"

He flipped open the cover and scanned through the files, his expression growing more and more astounded. "It is. It's a link between Owen, Markus Acker and the Ever After Church. This is explosive evidence, Hannah. I'm sure this is what got Owen murdered. I can use it to put the FBI on the case. He may have saved us all."

And with that, the ghost of Owen fizzled and faded away as Mac pulled Hannah into his arms.

Epilogue

Mac glanced over at Hannah as he rolled to a stop at the only red light between their house and Jenny's. And no, it never got old to think of it as "their" house, even though Mac's name hadn't officially been added to the paperwork yet.

She'd been a little busy making up for lost time. Lucy had gotten to spend the night at Ana Sophia's for her first big-girl sleepover as a result, which worked for everyone.

She caught his gaze. "What? Do I have something on my face?"

"You're the most beautiful woman I've ever seen," he murmured. "I can't believe you're mine."

Oh, well. *Now* she had something on her face—a lot of color and heat and some of it was leaching down into other parts at an alarming rate. "Stop that. We're on the way to my mom's house and I do not want to have to sit there thinking about what I'd rather be doing."

"Sorry not sorry," he teased and tore his gaze from hers in favor of watching the road, which she appreciated. "Did you figure out what you're going to say about us?"

"Mom, it's not going to work out with Owen. I met someone else."

Mac laughed and then did a double take at Hannah's expression. "That's not what you're really going to tell her, is it?"

Hannah stuck her tongue out at him and hummed happily. "It's the truth. And I have to tell everyone *something*. We can't call an emergency family meeting to explain everything that's happened and just leave out the part where you're going to be sticking around permanently."

Every day was the best day ever since Mac had resigned his position at the LVMPD. The badge in his wallet read Owl Creek as of yesterday and she owed Fletcher a huge hug for facilitating the transition so quickly. Mac's assistant, Willis, had happily relocated as well and Hannah had recently introduced him to Ana Sophia's mom, Maria. They seemed to be hitting it off, and Hannah appreciated that her friend smiled a lot more lately.

"What if we tell them I proposed to you on the way over and you said yes?" Mac suggested as he parked behind an SUV that might belong to Chase and Sloane but she had no idea because her vision had just gone gray.

"What? You're asking me to marry you? Now? Here?"

Mac turned to her and snagged her hand, bringing it to his lips in a shudder-inducing move that did nothing to increase her ability to breathe or think or figure out if this was really a dream she'd wake up from before the good stuff happened.

"I don't want to wait, my darling," he told her. "I want you to be an official member of Clan Mackenzie. As much as I like your family, there are already too many Coltons. Be a Mackenzie with me and Lucy. Forever."

"Oh, well, that's an offer I would be a fool to refuse," she said with a watery smile that matched his more closely than she would have credited.

She loved it when he got emotional and didn't hide it from her.

"Is that a yes?" he asked, his expression so hopeful that her heart soared.

"Well, hold on a minute," she said, one brow raised. "We haven't talked about kids outside of your adoption petition for Lucy. Is that it for you or are you—"

"Is that it?" His voice rose almost an octave. "Have you bothered to google the definition of the word 'clan' recently? You may need a refresher. We're having at least five more. Maybe six or seven, pending whether or not Chase can score us a much bigger house. Don't argue with your laird."

That got a genuine laugh out of her, the kind that mixed well with the misty tears his sweet proposal had already generated. "I wouldn't dream of it. Sounds like we're on the same page then. Very well, I'll marry you."

He matched her smile and produced a ring box from somewhere. Maybe by magic. When he flipped the lid, she practically melted out of her seat. The ring was nothing like she'd expected. Low profile. A simple band with channel set diamonds. "Mac, it's perfect. Exactly right. I can wear it when I'm baking or serving and it won't snag on anything."

He lifted a brow. "You say that like it was an accident or maybe I didn't already think about that when I picked it."

And then he slid the band onto her finger and of course it fit. Just like he did, in every way.

"I love you," she said.

"I love you too, but you have to stop crying or your brothers are going to jump me before I even get over the threshold."

"I can't help it when you're making all my dreams come true."

Sniffling, she tilted her hand to let the diamonds catch the low light. Was it terrible to be so happy when there was still so much unsettled? The Internal Affairs people had caught the other three dirty cops inside the Las Vegas Police Department, the ones who had been working with the money launderers, thanks to the testimony of that terrible man who had held them hostage.

The FBI had gotten involved once Mac turned over Owen's files, quickly tracing links between her ex-husband and the Ever After Church. It was enough to start investigating Markus Acker, and the federal presence in town had helped take attention off Hannah and Lucy, so Mac breathed a little easier.

From the files, Hannah had realized Owen hoped to cozy up to her and then use her brother's real estate business as a cover when he took over handling the money laundering from the church. Big Mike hadn't been too thrilled about the idea of losing that business, as best they figured, and likely had taken out Owen as a result. They couldn't prove it—yet—so Mac had put a bug in the FBI's ear. It was keeping the crime boss pretty busy, so Hannah and Mac ducked out of that mess, opting to focus on each other.

As a married couple apparently.

"Hannah," Mac said, caressing her name the way he always did, the way she liked best. "You're the one making my dreams come true. I came here to expecting to fix whatever Owen had screwed up and instead, you fixed me. I got all the rewards this time. You and Lucy."

He kissed her and she saw stars. Not the migraine kind— she didn't get those anymore—but the kind she'd never get tired of. This was *her* reward for finally figuring out she could use her head and her heart. Together. Finally whole.

* * * * *

COMING SOON!

We really hope you enjoyed reading this book.
If you're looking for more romance
be sure to head to the shops when
new books are available on

Thursday 21st November

To see which titles are coming soon, please visit

millsandboon.co.uk/nextmonth

MILLS & BOON

LET'S TALK

Romance

For exclusive extracts, competitions
and special offers, find us online:

 MillsandBoon

 @MillsandBoon

 @MillsandBoonUK

 @MillsandBoonUK

Get in touch on 01413 063 232